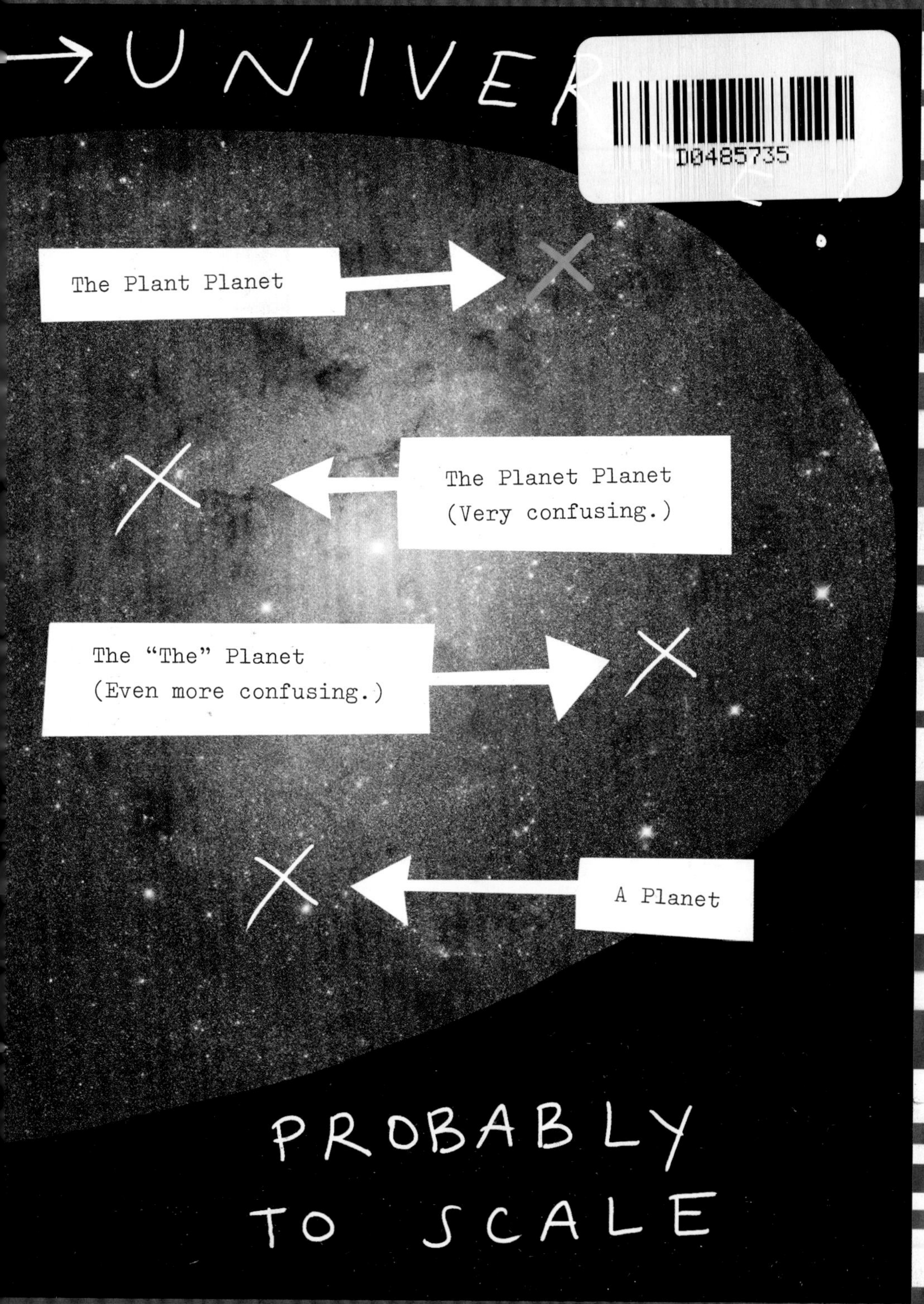
→UNIVER
The Plant Planet
The Planet Planet
(Very confusing.)
The "The" Planet
(Even more confusing.)
A Planet
PROBABLY
TO SCALE

ASTRO-NUTS

Mission Three: The Perfect Planet

By Jon Scieszka

Illustrated by Steven Weinberg

chronicle books · san francisco

MISSION THREE:
THE PIZZA PLANET

Many thanks to the Rijksmuseum, the Smithsonian, the
Biodiversity Heritage Library, NASA's Hubble site, the
Metropolitan Museum of Art, and so many others for adding
their collections to the public domain. All collaged elements
of this book come from these collections.
More information is available at www.AstroNuts.space.

For Famous Ray —JS and SW

Text copyright © 2021 by JRS Worldwide LLC.
Illustrations copyright © 2021 by Steven Weinberg.

Library of Congress Cataloging-in-Publication Data available.

ISBN 978-1-4521-7121-0

Manufactured in China.

If you are reading this, then you have been selected. Don't look around like that.
Act natural. Do not draw attention to yourself. Keep reading. The future of humans on Earth depends on you.
Here is your mission—read this book. It will give you all the information you need to know.

Design by Jay Marvel.
Typeset in Freight Micro, Typewriter, and Noyh.

10 9 8 7 6 5 4 3 2 1

Chronicle Books LLC
680 Second Street
San Francisco, California 94107

Chronicle Books—we see things differently.
Become part of our community at www.chroniclekids.com.

NNASA!

5

AstroNuts, YOUR ORDER IS READY.

Time to find the perfect Goldilocks/Goldilocks/Goldilocks Planet. Time to investigate THE PIZZA PLANET.

Mission Number THREE/THREE/THREE.

NNASA
CMD. esc.

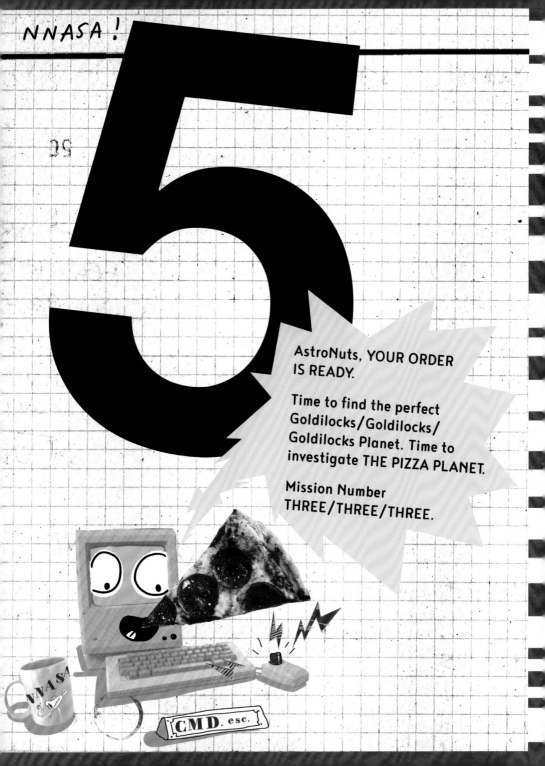

NNASA!
4
I'm gonna howl at the moon like a big pizza pie!
Owoooooooooo!!!!

NNASA!

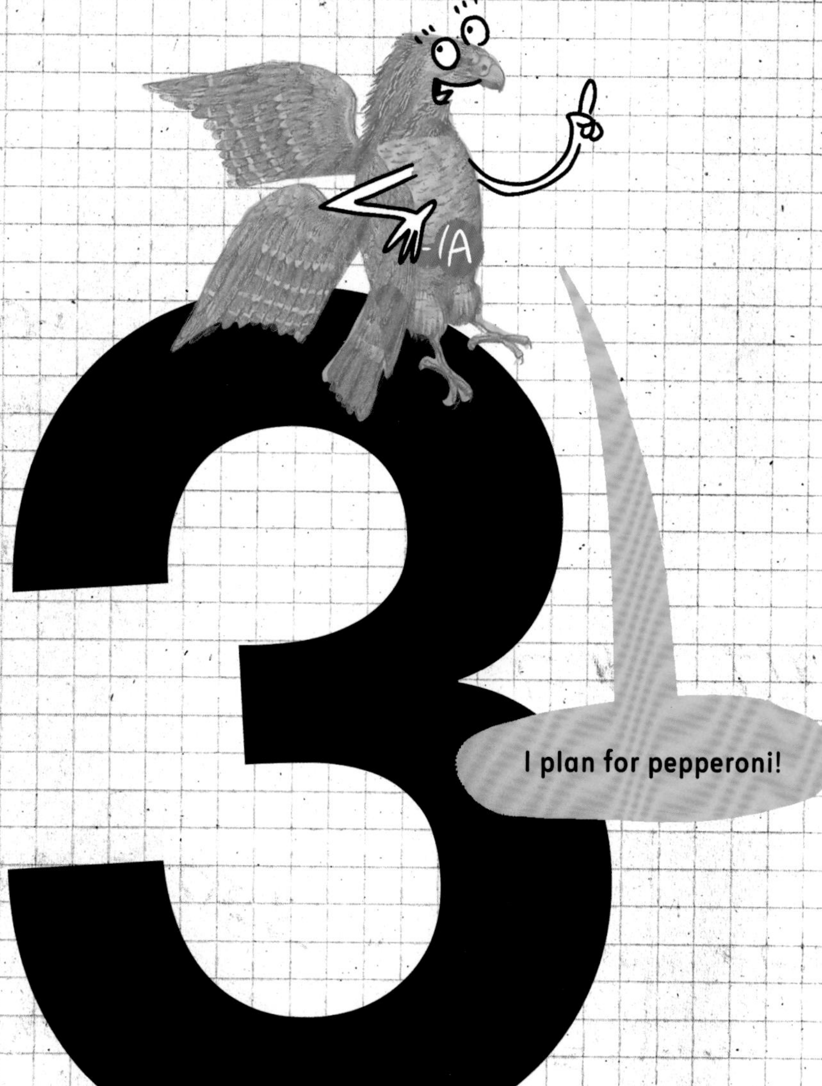
3
I plan for pepperoni!

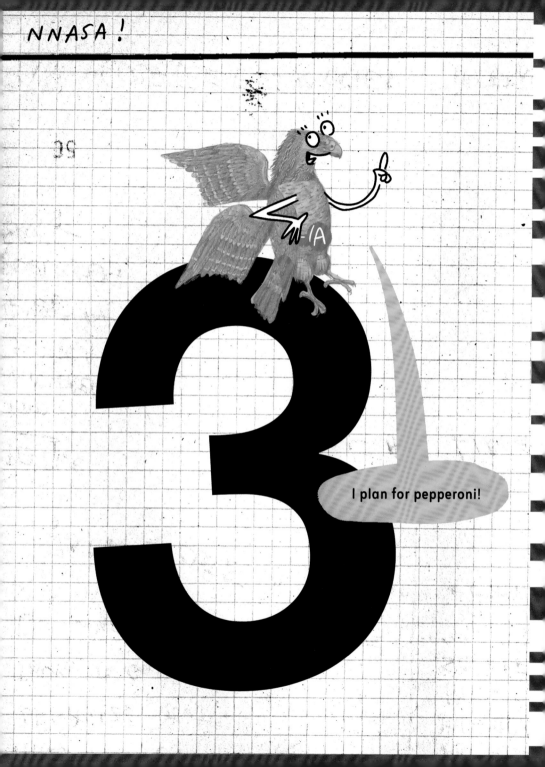

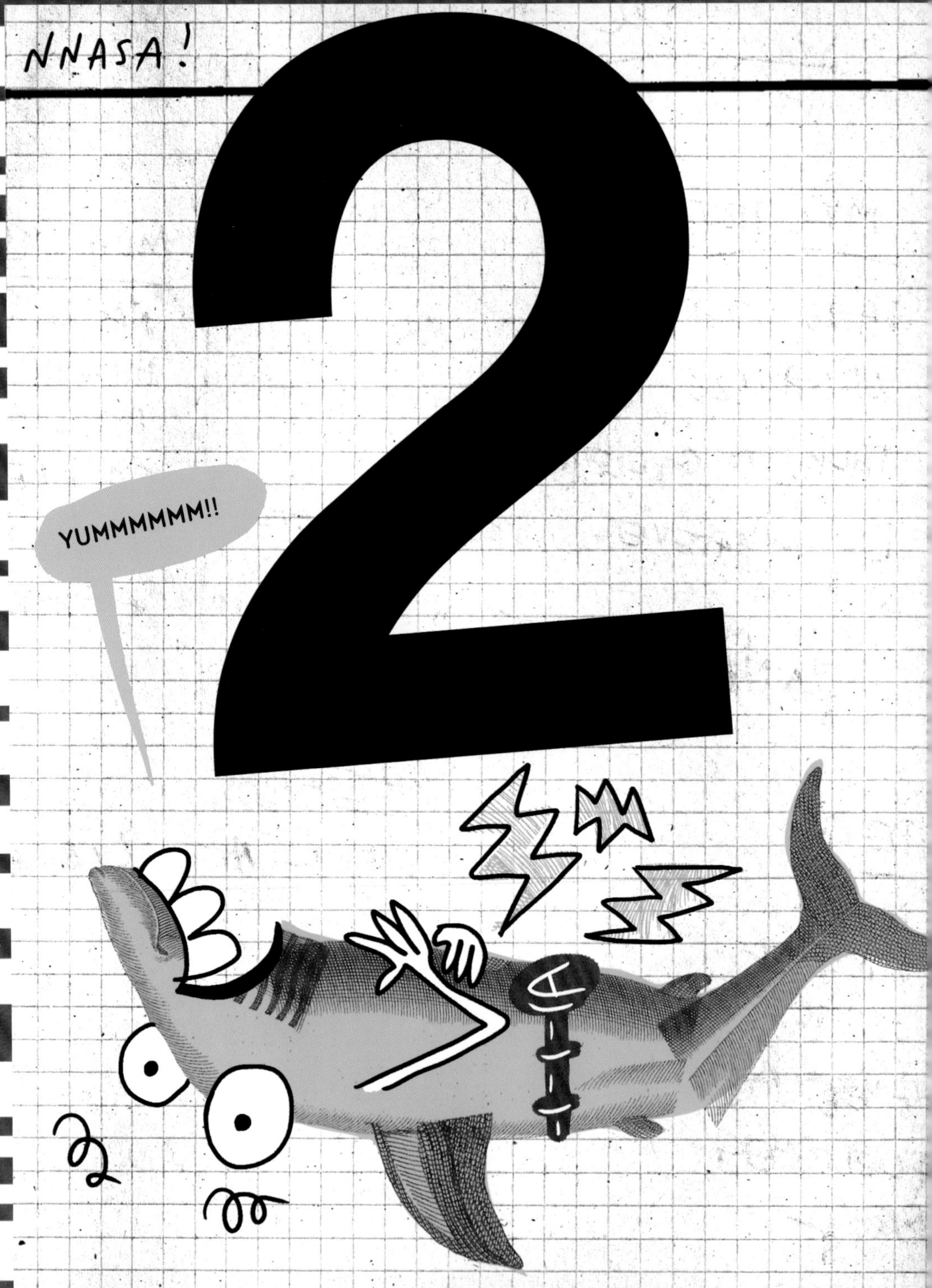
NNASA!
2
YUMMMMMM!!

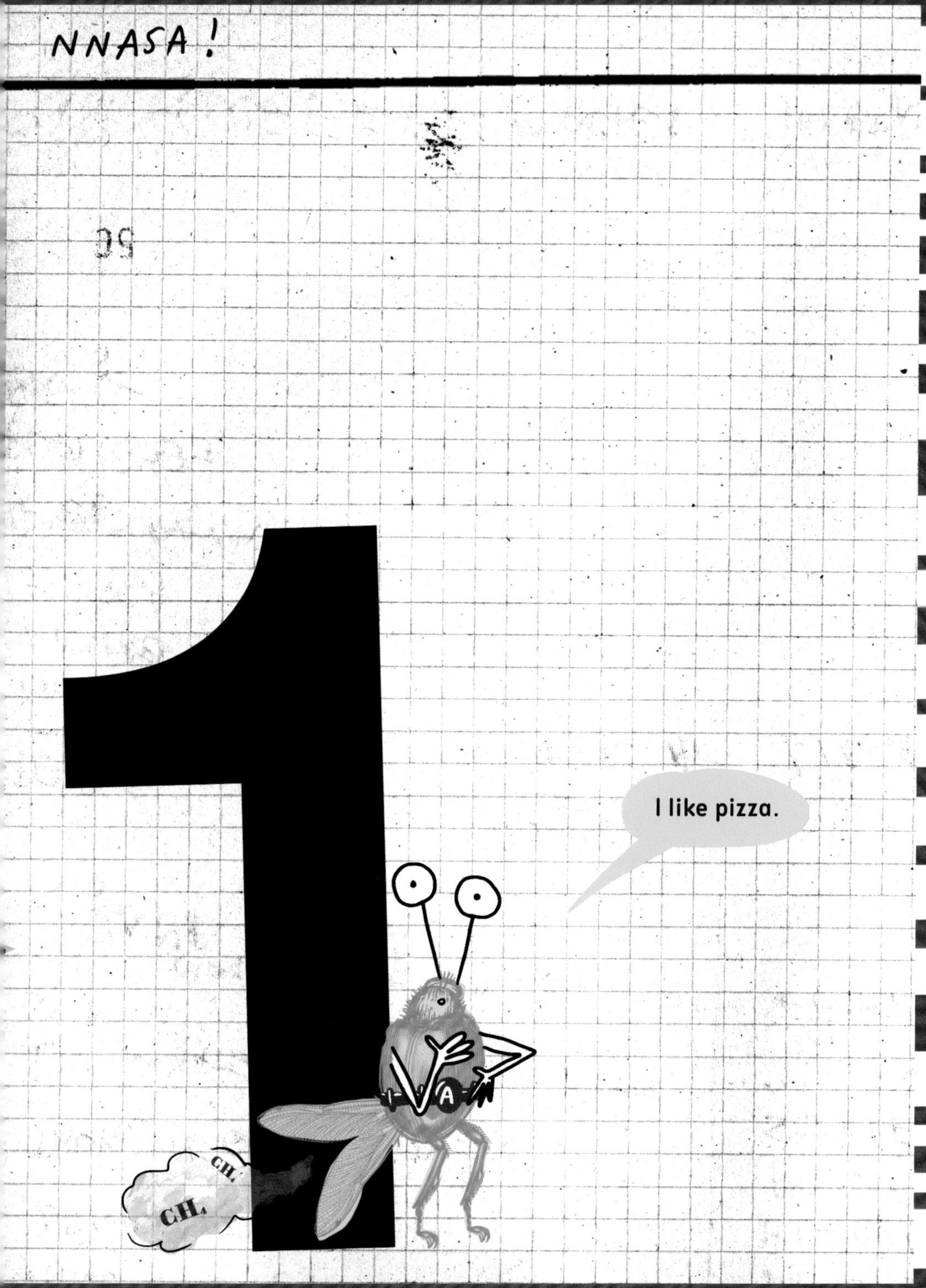
NNASA!
I like pizza.
CH_4
CH_4

AstroNuts—
STOP/STOP/STOP LAUNCH.
Change/Change/Change in Mission Plan.

NNASA has found the
PERFECT PLANET/PERFECT PLANET/
PERFECT PLANET.

Cancel Mission The Pizza Planet,
Mission The Robot Planet,
Mission The Cockroach Planet,
and Mission The Candy Planet.

AstroNuts, report to the
Abe Lincoln Beard Vehicle for New
Mission #3 The Perfect Planet.

Also—new mission assignments:
SmartHawk will be Mission Leader.
AlphaWolf, you will be Mission Helper.
That means you help. You listen to
SmartHawk, the Mission Leader./
SmartHawk, the Mission Leader./
SmartHawk, the Mission Leader./
SmartHawk, the Mission Leader./
SmartHawk, the Mission Leader.

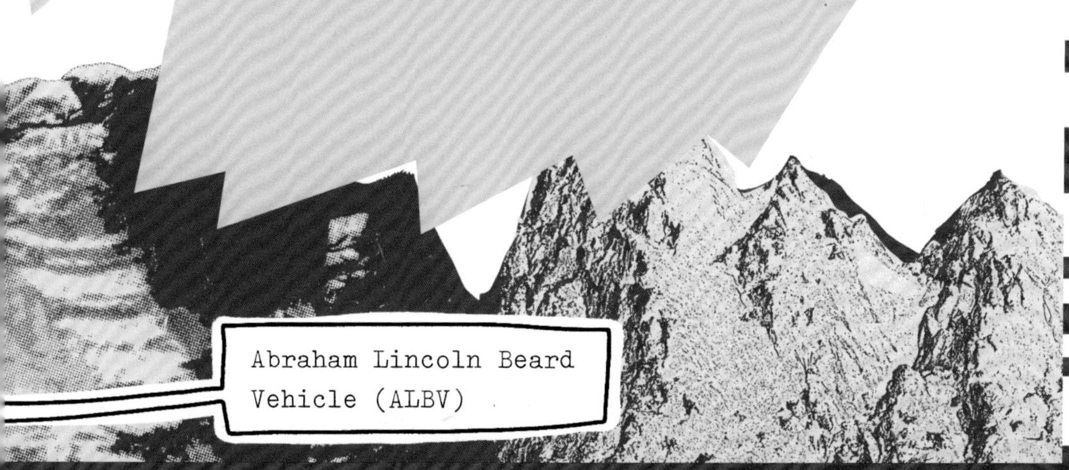
Abraham Lincoln Beard
Vehicle (ALBV)

The AstroNuts were seriously sad to be missing the Pizza Planet. And what was that about AlphaWolf? Did he get fired?

But they were NNASA professionals. So they got right to work preparing for the new mission in their brand-new Abraham Lincoln Beard Vehicle.

Ha! Ha! Ha! Very funny joke. I am always the Mission Leader. And we are going to THE PIZZA PLANET!

This is very unexpected. But we are AstroNuts. We always follow Command Escape's instructions.

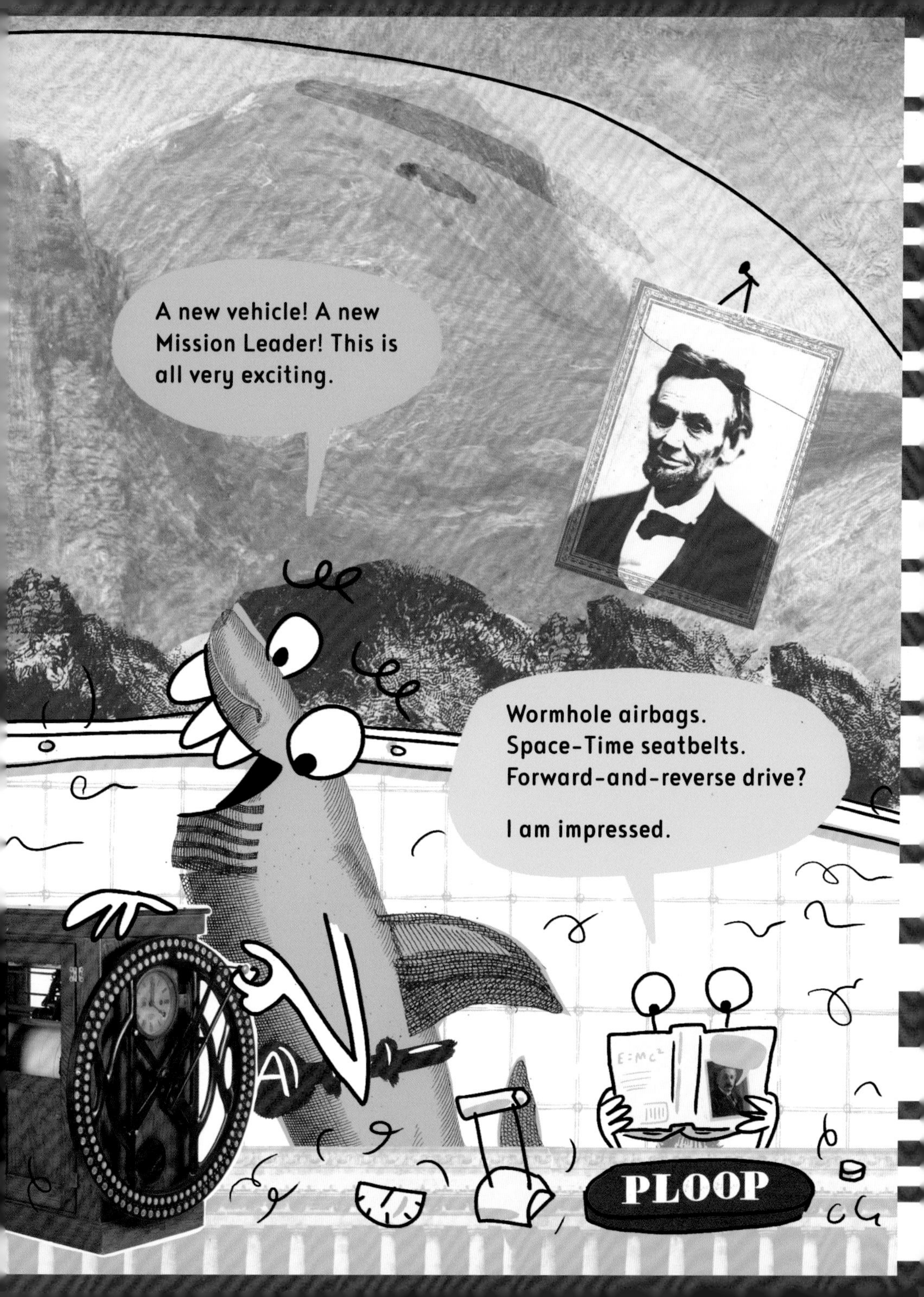
A new vehicle! A new Mission Leader! This is all very exciting.
Wormhole airbags. Space-Time seatbelts. Forward-and-reverse drive?
I am impressed.
PLOOP

NEW MISSION THREE:
THE PERFECT PLANET

Now even more thanks to the Rijksmuseum, the Smithsonian, the Biodiversity Heritage Library, NASA's Hubble site, the Metropolitan Museum of Art, and so many others for adding their collections to the public domain. All collaged elements in this book come from these collections. More information is available at www.AstroNuts.space.

For our Perfect Editor, Taylor Norman —JS and SW

5

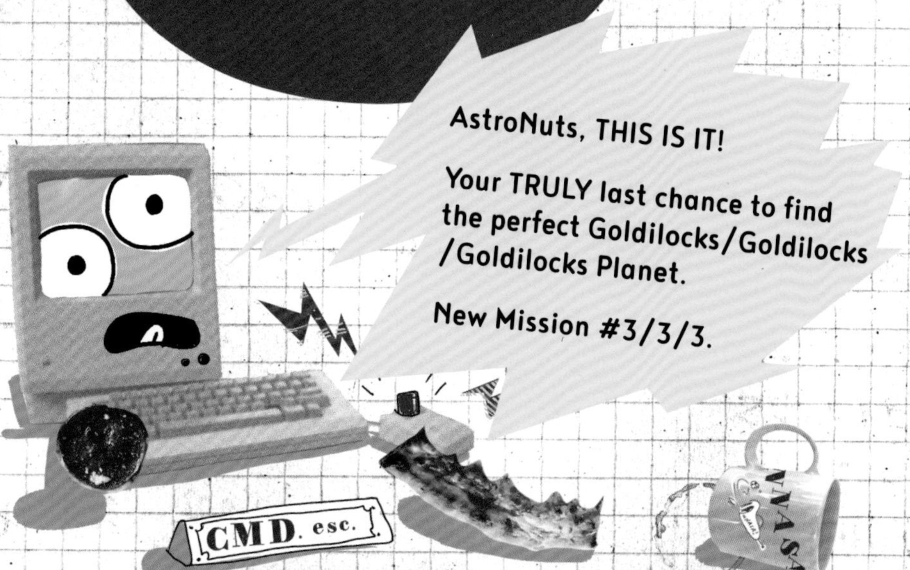
AstroNuts, THIS IS IT!
Your TRULY last chance to find the perfect Goldilocks/Goldilocks/Goldilocks Planet.
New Mission #3/3/3.
CMD. esc.
NNASA

4

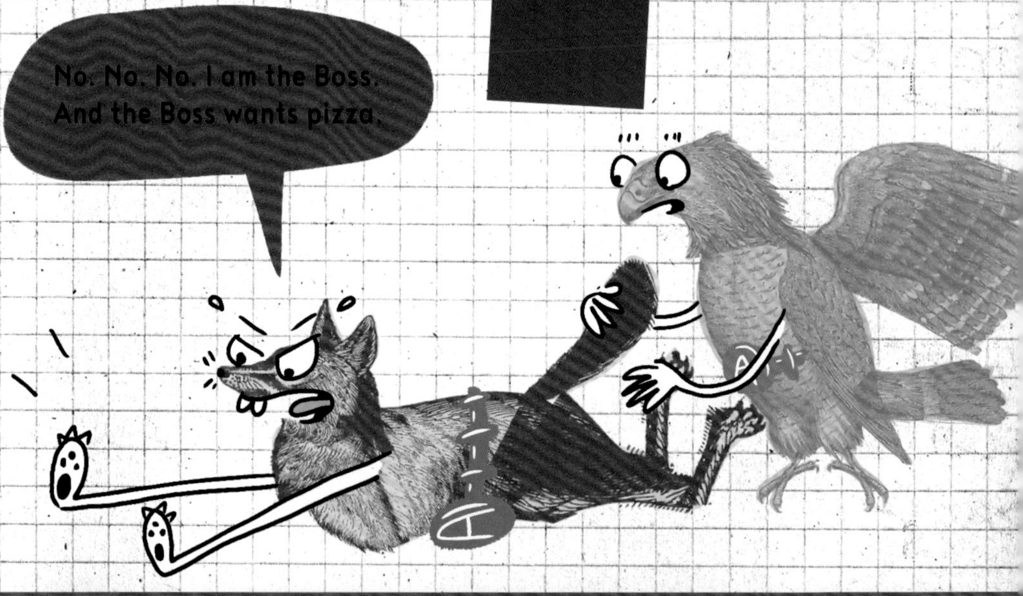

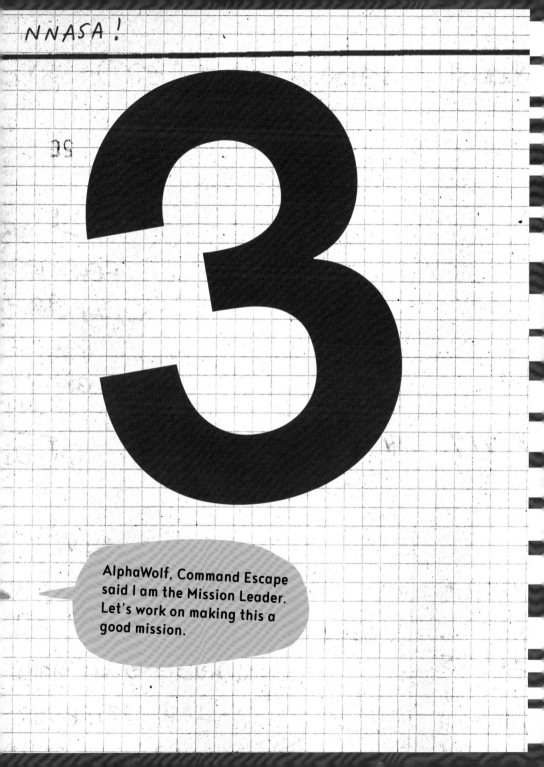

AlphaWolf, Command Escape said I am the Mission Leader. Let's work on making this a good mission.

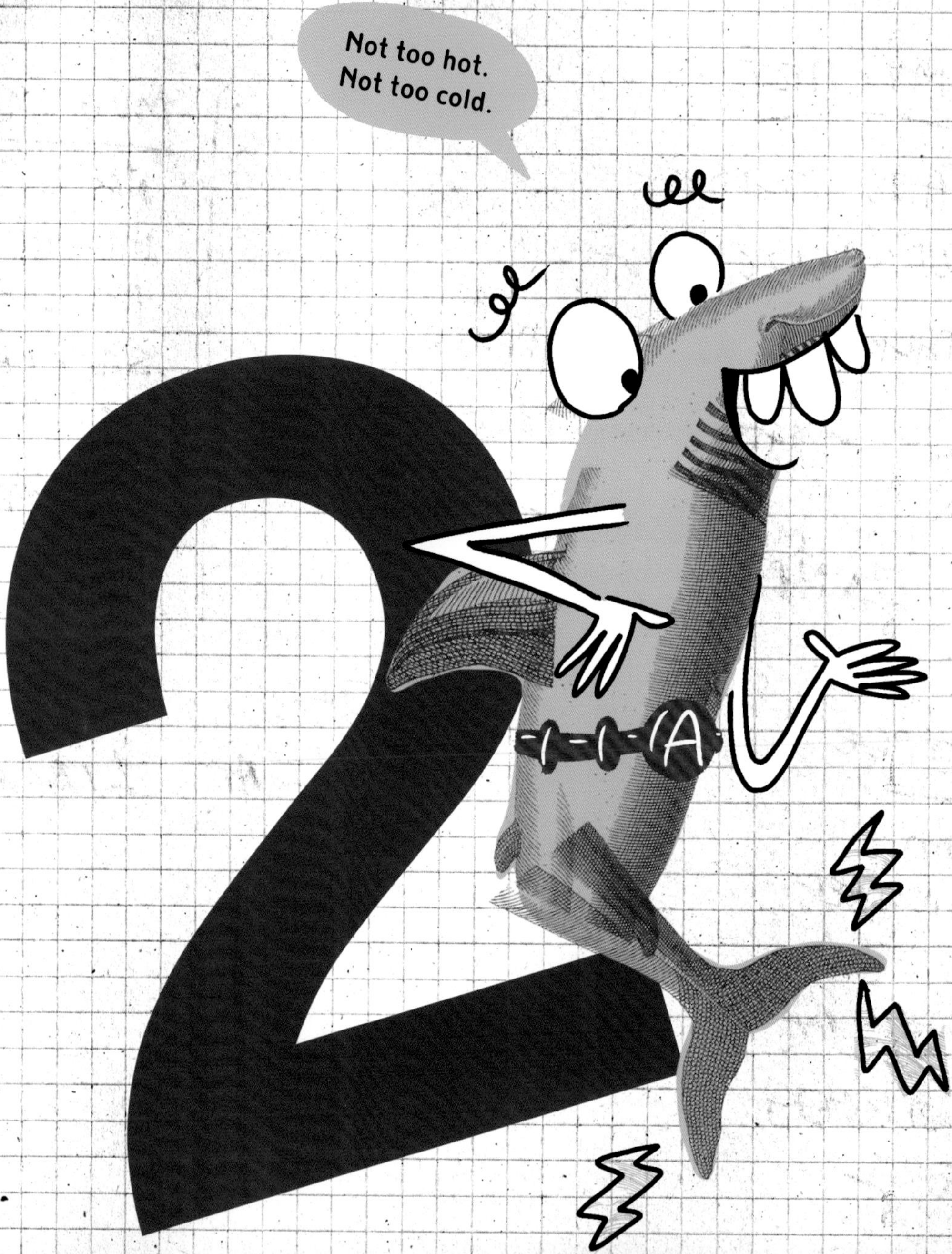
2
Not too hot.
Not too cold.

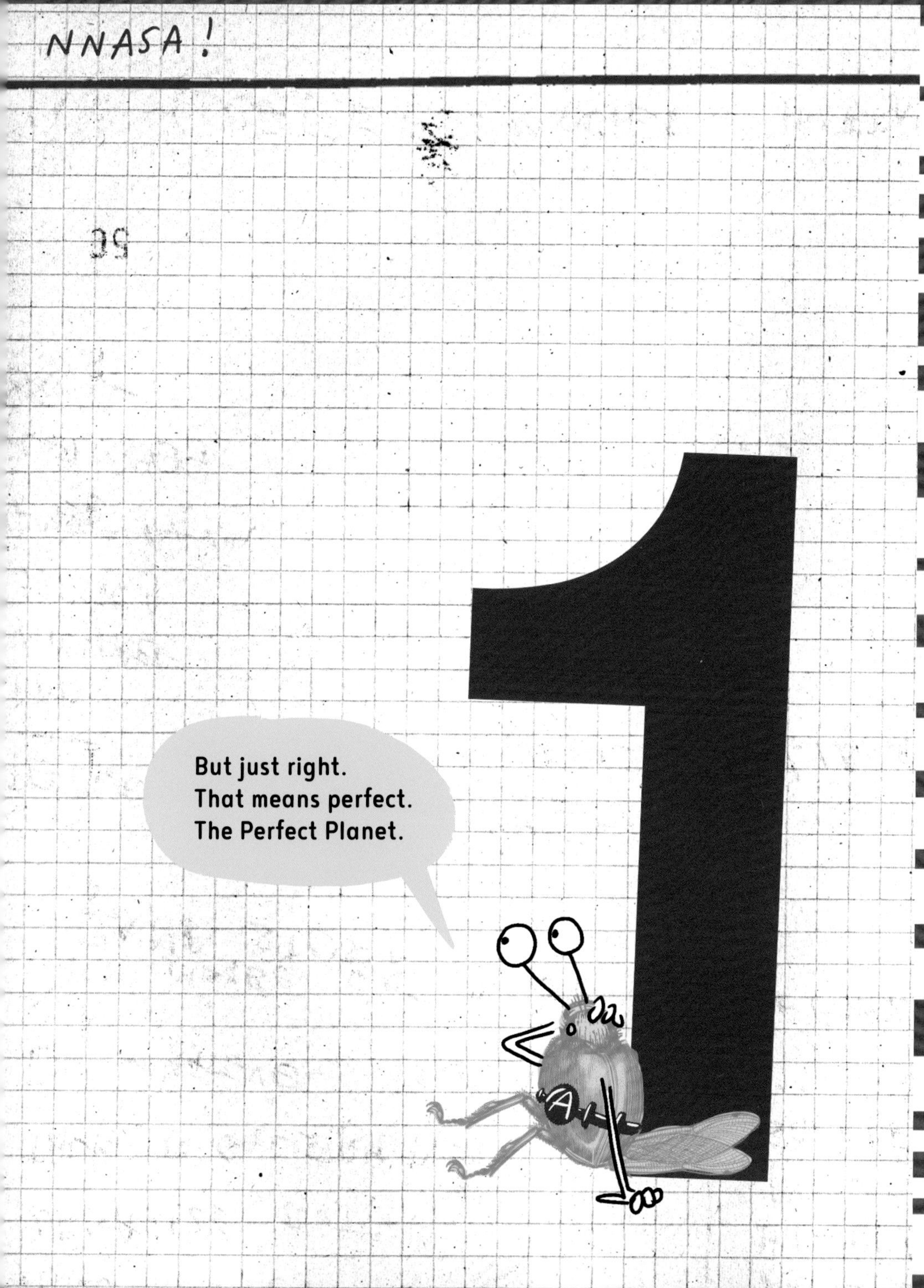
NNASA!
But just right.
That means perfect.
The Perfect Planet.

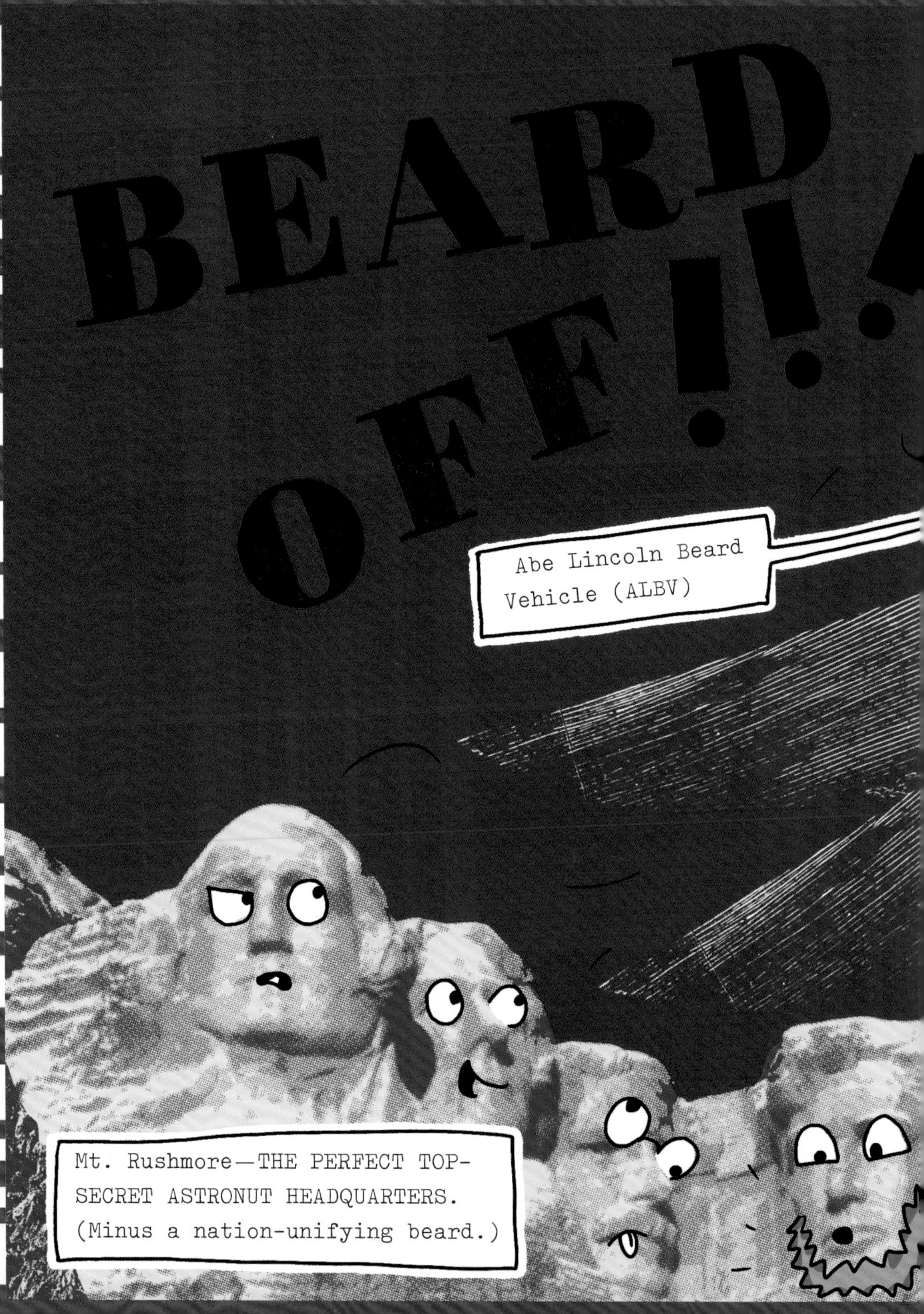

BEARD OFF!!
Abe Lincoln Beard Vehicle (ALBV)
Mt. Rushmore—THE PERFECT TOP-SECRET ASTRONUT HEADQUARTERS. (Minus a nation-unifying beard.)

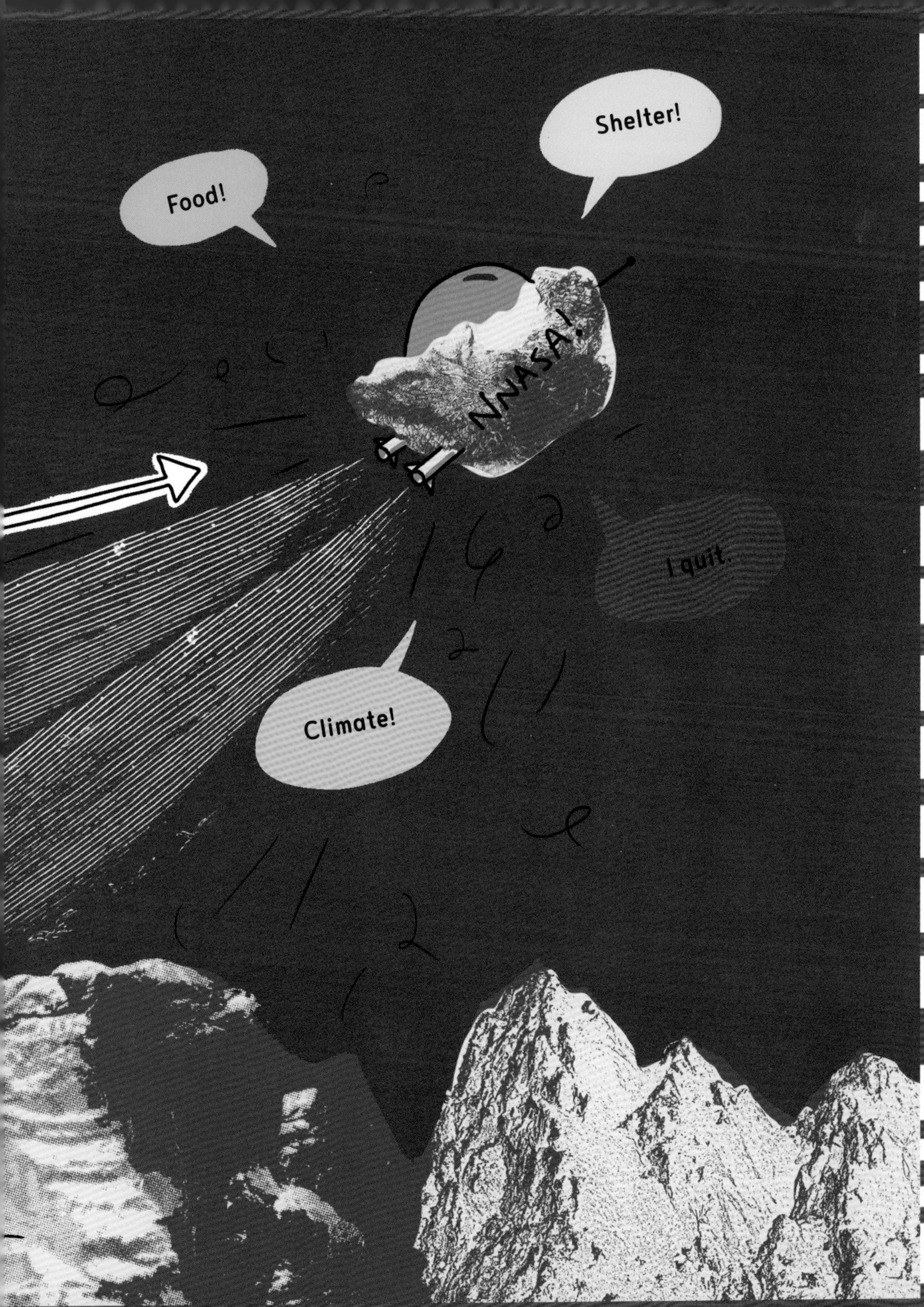
Food!
Shelter!
NNASA!
I quit.
Climate!

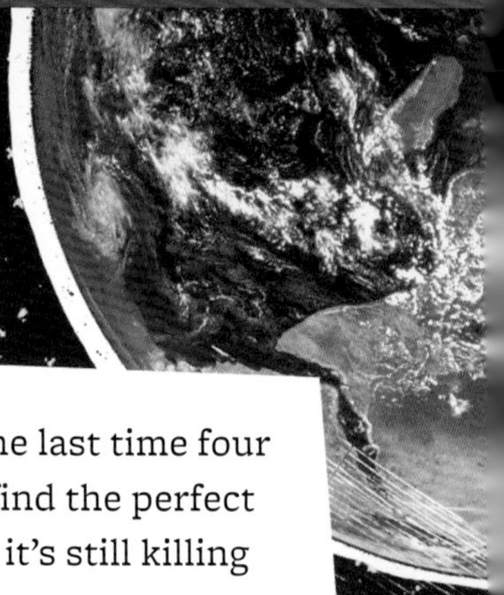

Oh, hello. It's me, your home planet Earth again. I've got good news . . . and bad news.

The bad news—not a whole lot has changed since the last time four superpowered animal astronauts blasted off me to find the perfect Goldilocks Planet. My climate is still killing me, and it's still killing you.

More bad news— Mission One: The Plant Planet didn't work out great for anyone.

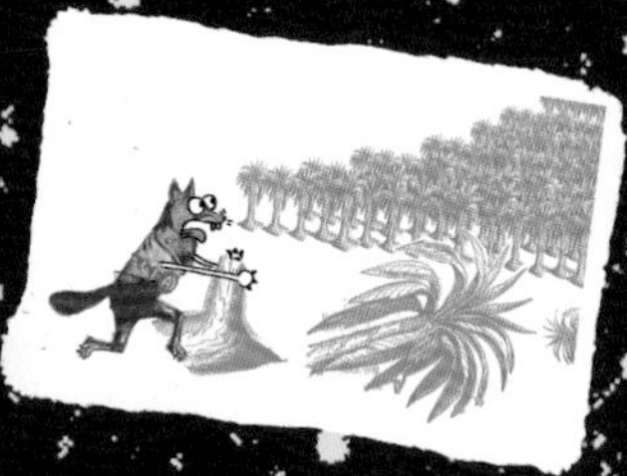

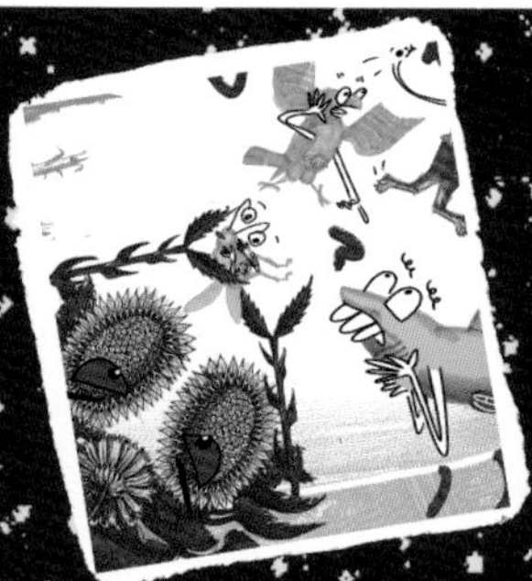

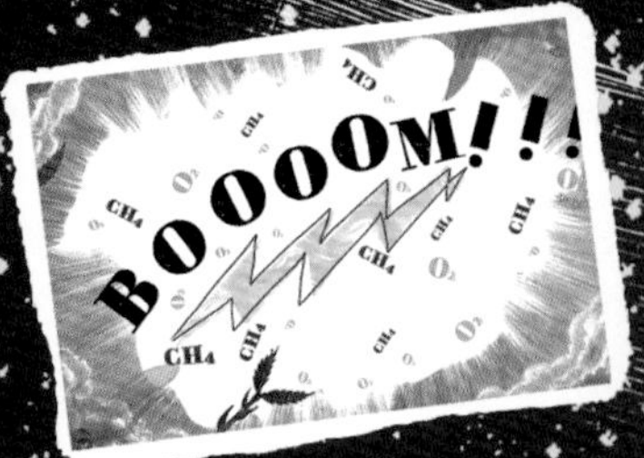
BOOOOM!!!
CH4
O2

Mission Two: The Water Planet did help some brave clams. But it didn't do anything for 7.8 billion humans looking for a new planet to escape to. (Even though AlphaWolf keeps saying both missions were "a great success.")

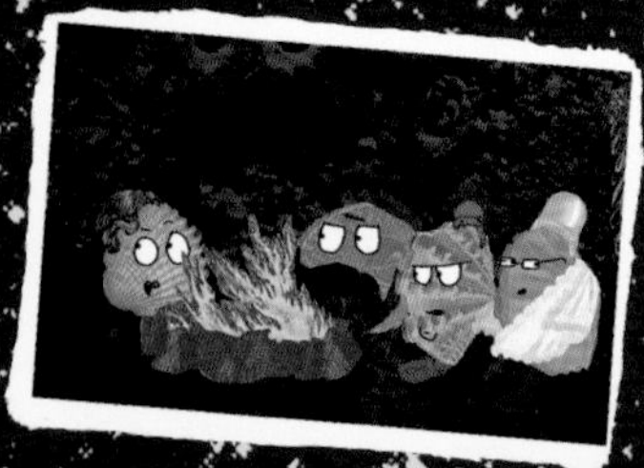

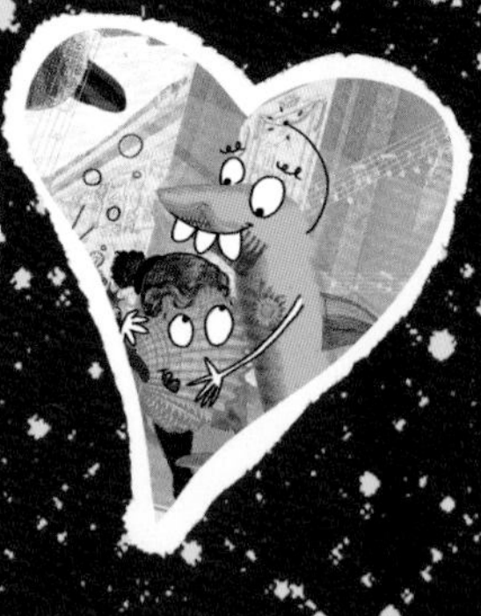

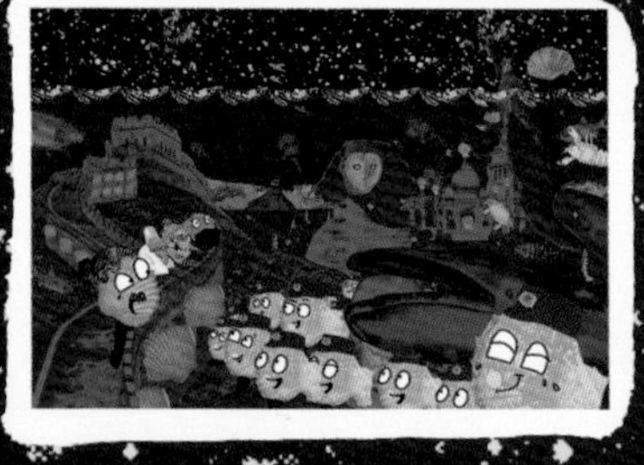

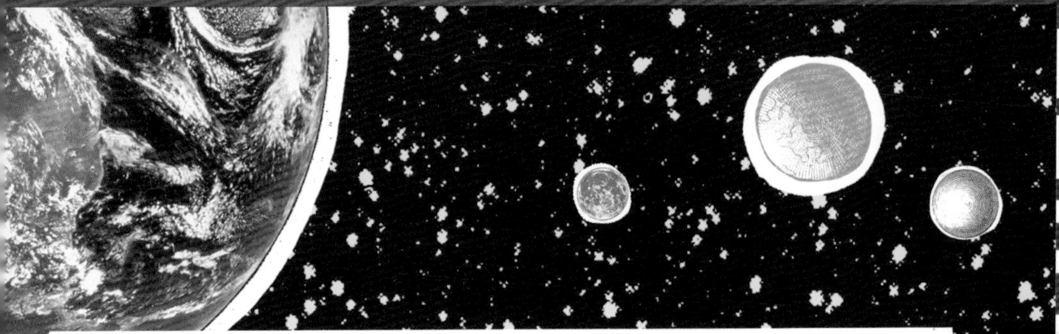

The good news—the secret NNASA (Not-NASA) program hidden inside Mt. Rushmore found what could be the most absolutely perfect planet ever for humans.

When I first heard about this idea, I was amazed. I was thrilled. Then I was worried. The planet was obviously perfect and fresh and beautiful in every way. But it seemed like an impossible trip.

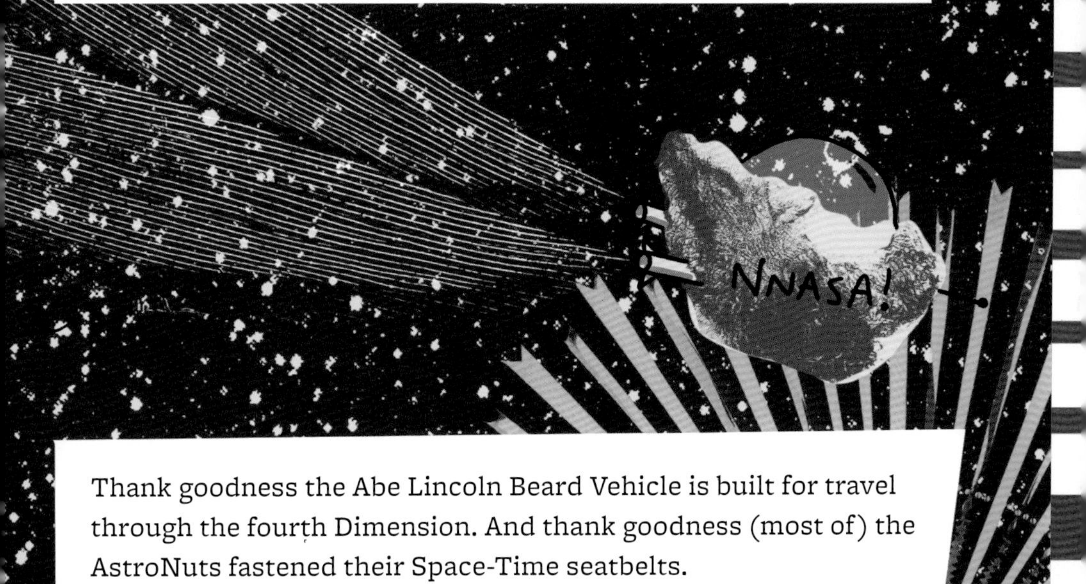
NNASA!

Thank goodness the Abe Lincoln Beard Vehicle is built for travel through the fourth Dimension. And thank goodness (most of) the AstroNuts fastened their Space-Time seatbelts.

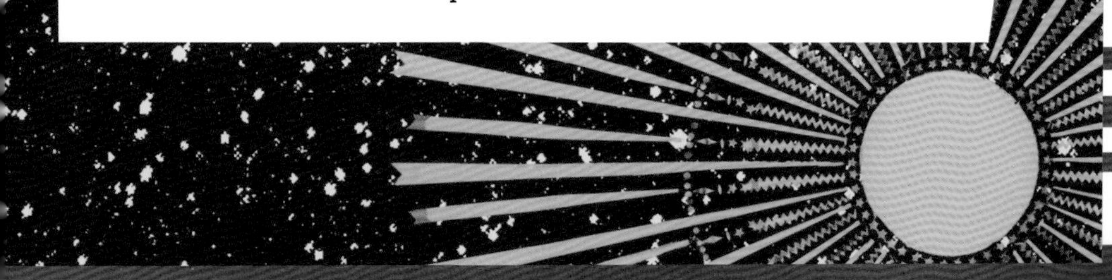

CHAPTER 1:

AHHHHHHHHHHHHHHHHH

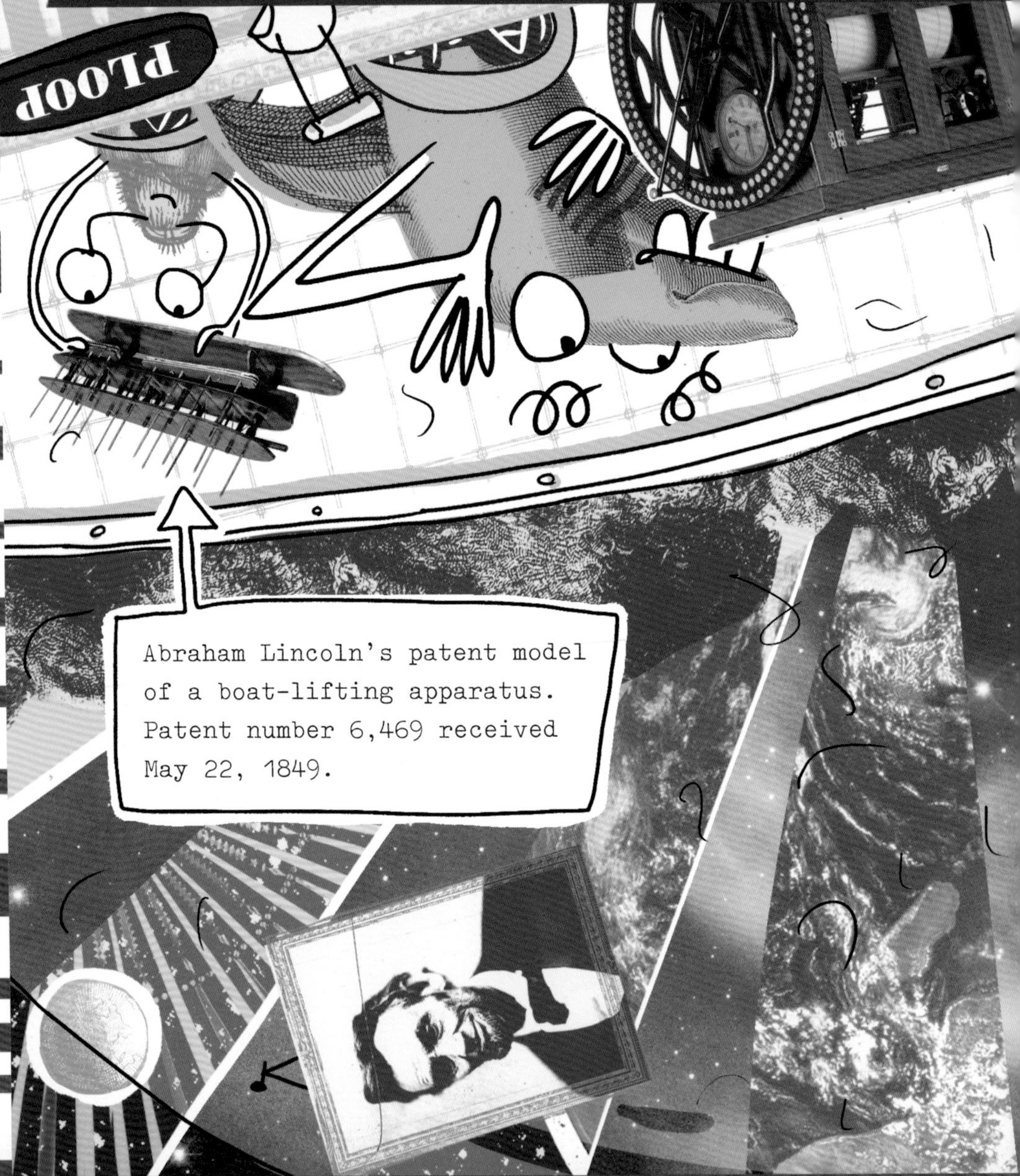
PLOOP

Abraham Lincoln's patent model of a boat-lifting apparatus. Patent number 6,469 received May 22, 1849.

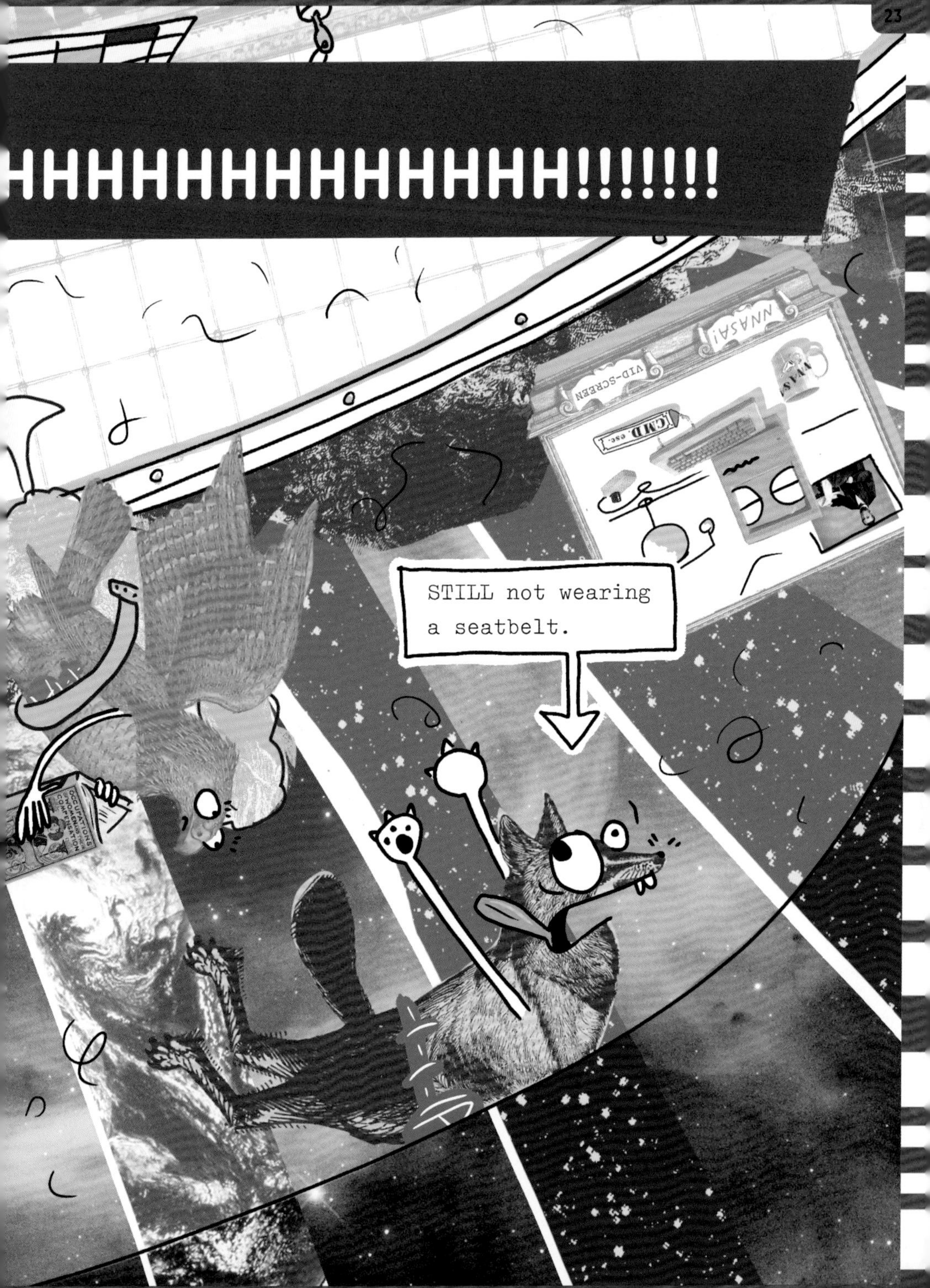
HHHHHHHHHHHHHHHH!!!!!!!
NNASA!
VID-SCREEN
CMD. esc.
STILL not wearing a seatbelt.
OCCUPATIONS COMPENSATION

Command Escape confirmed the AstroNut jobs of looking for human-friendly climate, food and water, and shelter. Then he dropped the real bomb.

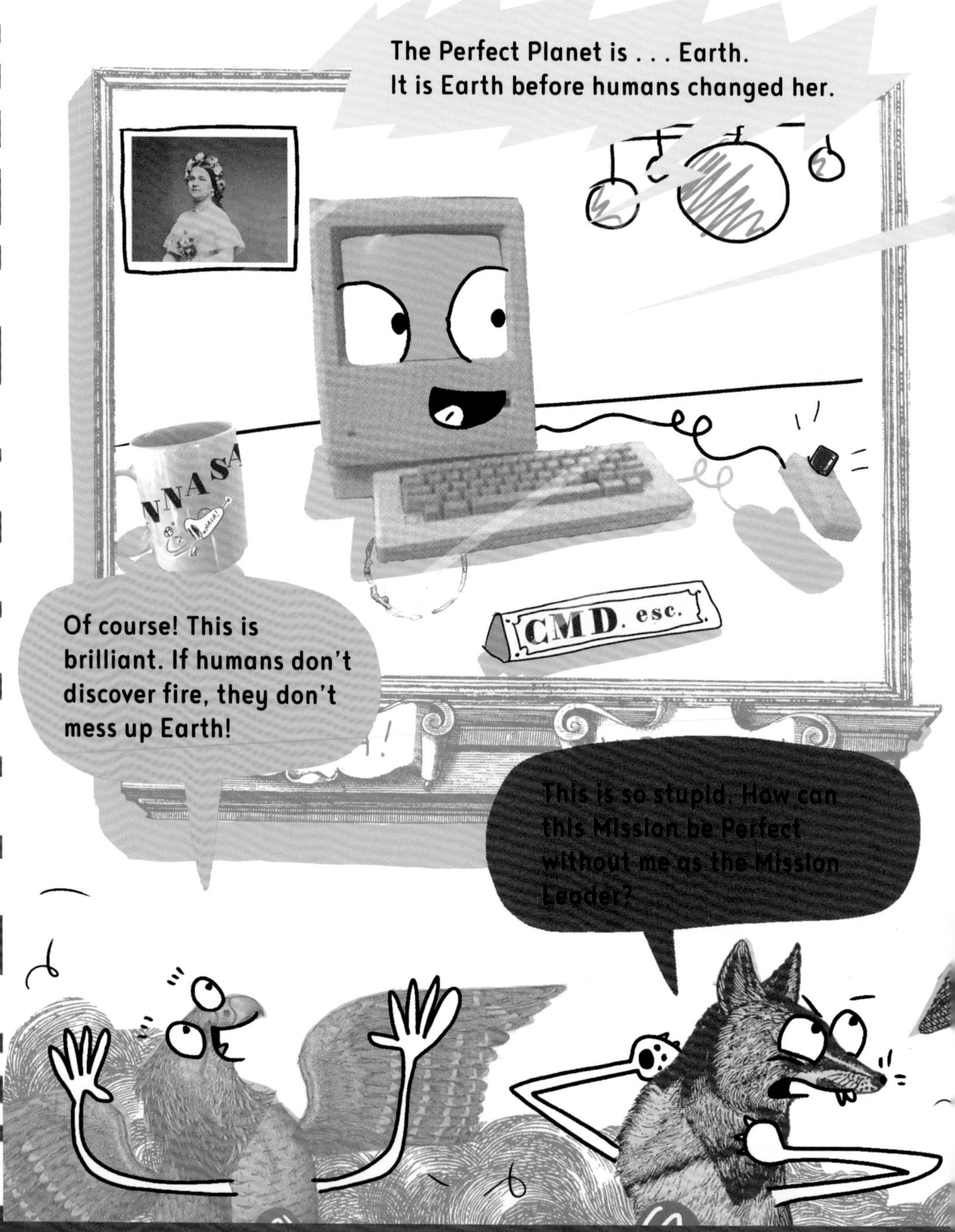
The Perfect Planet is . . . Earth.
It is Earth before humans changed her.
NNASA
CMD. esc.
Of course! This is brilliant. If humans don't discover fire, they don't mess up Earth!
This is so stupid. How can this Mission be Perfect without me as the Mission Leader?

On this mission, you must travel back in time. You must FIND/FIND/FIND the first intelligent humans and keep them from discovering fire.

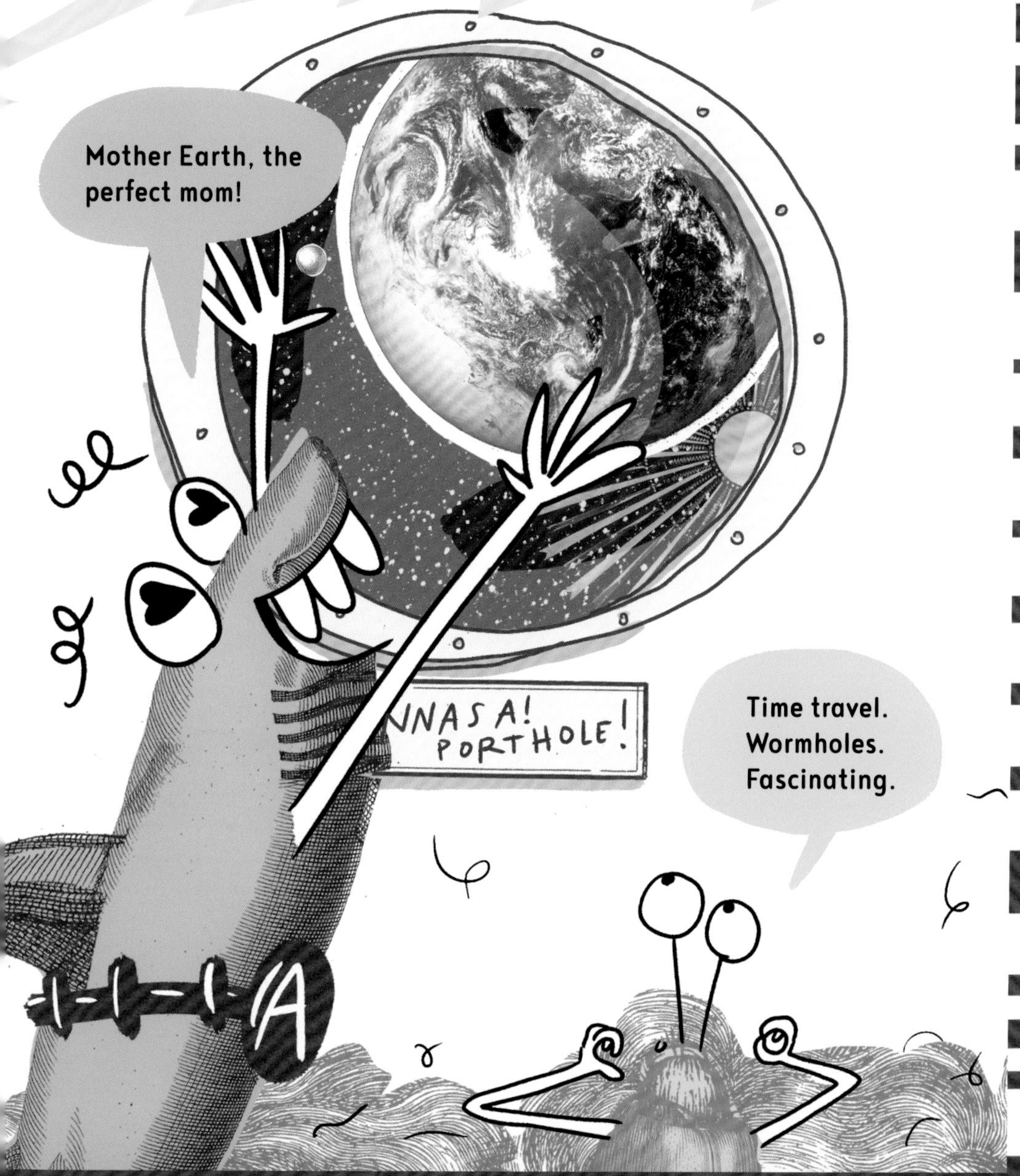
Mother Earth, the perfect mom!
NASA! PORTHOLE!
Time travel. Wormholes. Fascinating.

Crazy, right?

The Perfect Goldilocks Planet has been right under your feet the whole time. It's ME! EARTH!

If you think about it, for like, ohh . . . three seconds or so, it's kind of obvious.

Of course I am the Perfect Planet for humans. I have it all: perfect atmosphere, temperature, water, food, shelter . . . perfect everything for humans.

Who else did you think it could be? Venus, that overheated tart? Jupiter, that big old gasbag? Ice-cold Uranus? Don't make me laugh.

Space bass

Space capsule

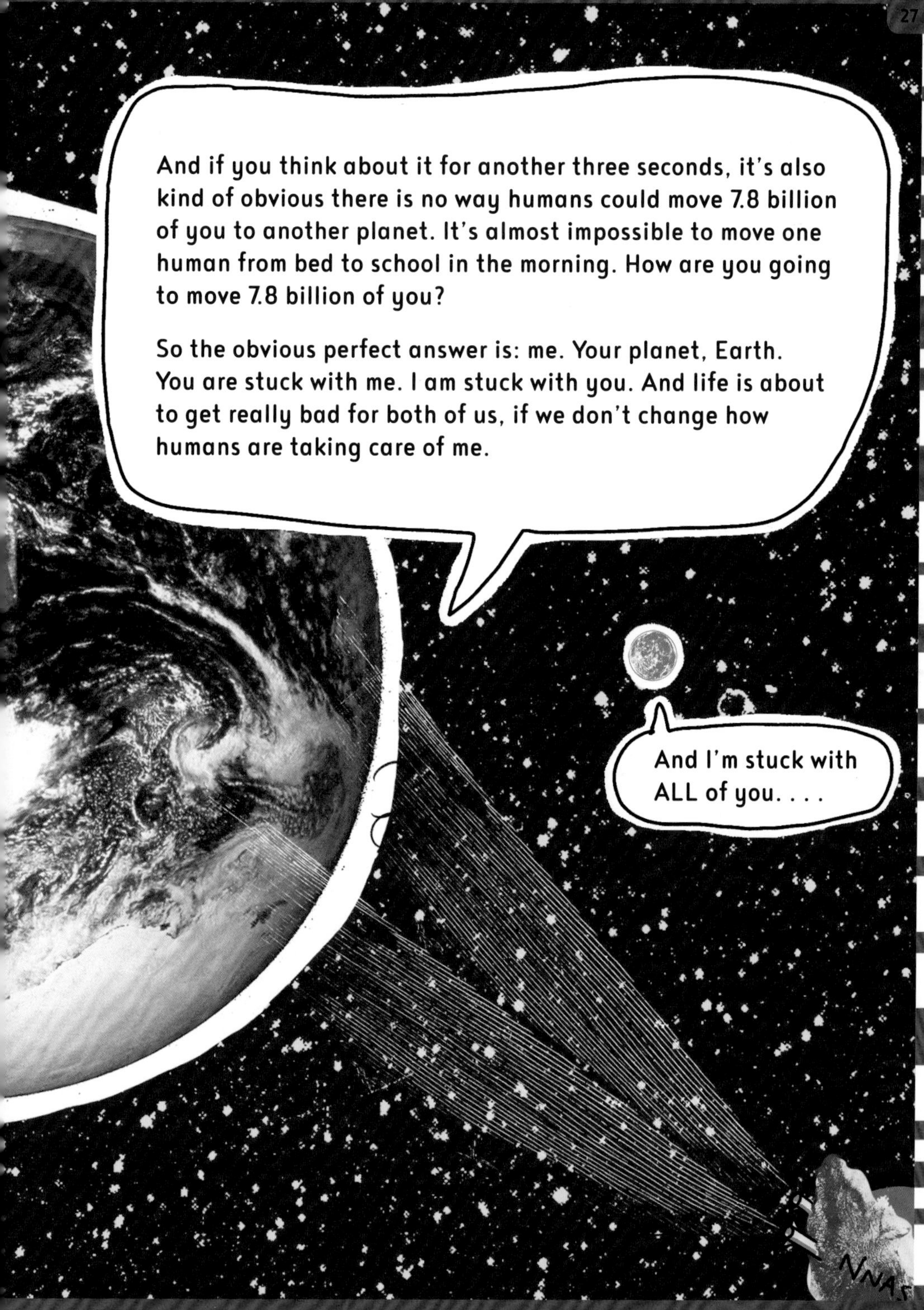
And if you think about it for another three seconds, it's also kind of obvious there is no way humans could move 7.8 billion of you to another planet. It's almost impossible to move one human from bed to school in the morning. How are you going to move 7.8 billion of you?
So the obvious perfect answer is: me. Your planet, Earth. You are stuck with me. I am stuck with you. And life is about to get really bad for both of us, if we don't change how humans are taking care of me.
And I'm stuck with ALL of you. . . .

Here's the brilliant plan the smart humans at NNASA came up with for Operation Carbon Reduction:

```
///// Official NNASA PLAN /////
//// OPERATION CARBON REDUCTION ////
```

PROBLEM — PROBLEM — PROBLEM — PROBLEM — PROBLEM — PROBLEM

- Humans burning fossil fuel have put too much carbon in Earth's atmosphere

- Too much carbon in Earth's atmosphere has overheated her

- Overheating has caused ecological damage of ice melt, sea rise, animal extinction . . .

- How can we change the last 200 years of humans' carelessness?

SOLUTION — SOLUTION — SOLUTION — SOLUTION — SOLUTION

- Stop humans from putting too much carbon in her atmosphere

- Teach humans different ways to create energy without burning fossil fuels

METHOD — METHOD — METHOD — METHOD — METHOD — METHOD

- Send our AstroNuts back in time to stop humans from discovering and using fire

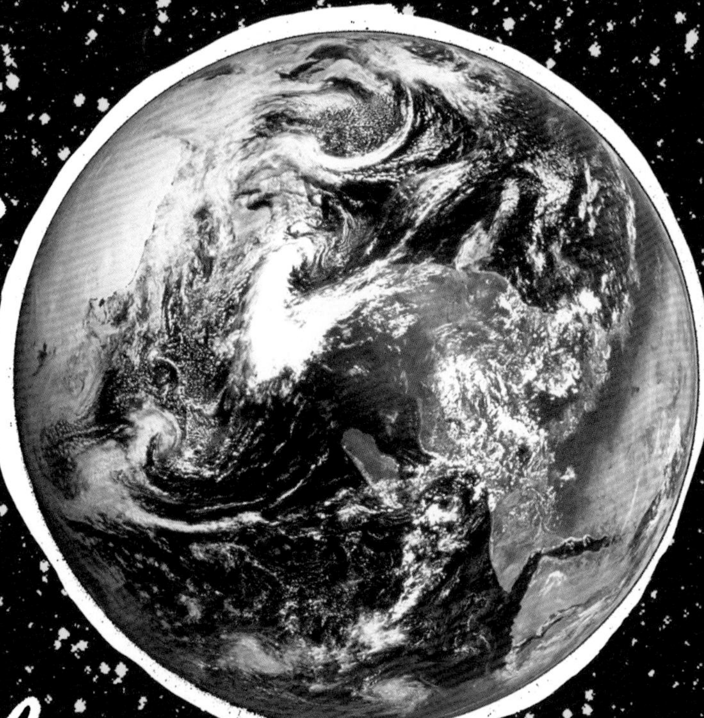

No burning, no carbon, perfect me, healthy humans, happy us.

Maybe.

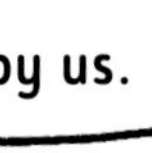

StinkBug read through the whole Abraham Lincoln Beard Vehicle manual in seven seconds. He learned how to pilot the ALBV back through time. Some people think this is not possible. StinkBug explained otherwise on his StinkCloud.

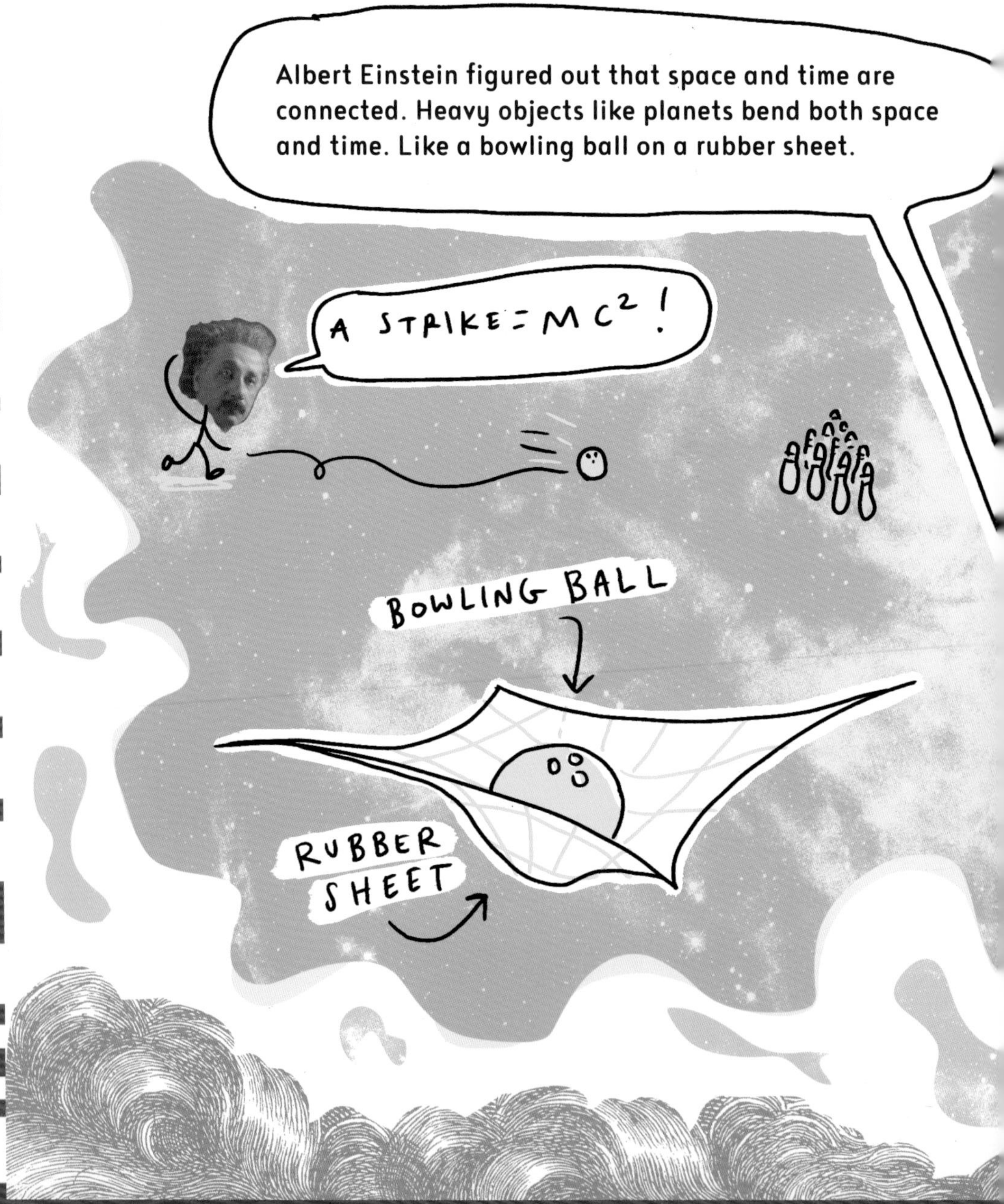
Albert Einstein figured out that space and time are connected. Heavy objects like planets bend both space and time. Like a bowling ball on a rubber sheet.
A STRIKE = MC²!
BOWLING BALL
RUBBER SHEET

Imagine space-time bent so much that it is folded over. Imagine two spots on this folded space-time connected by a wormhole tunnel. Driving through the wormhole lets us travel impossibly fast from one spot to another through space . . . and time . . . instead of driving the long way around.

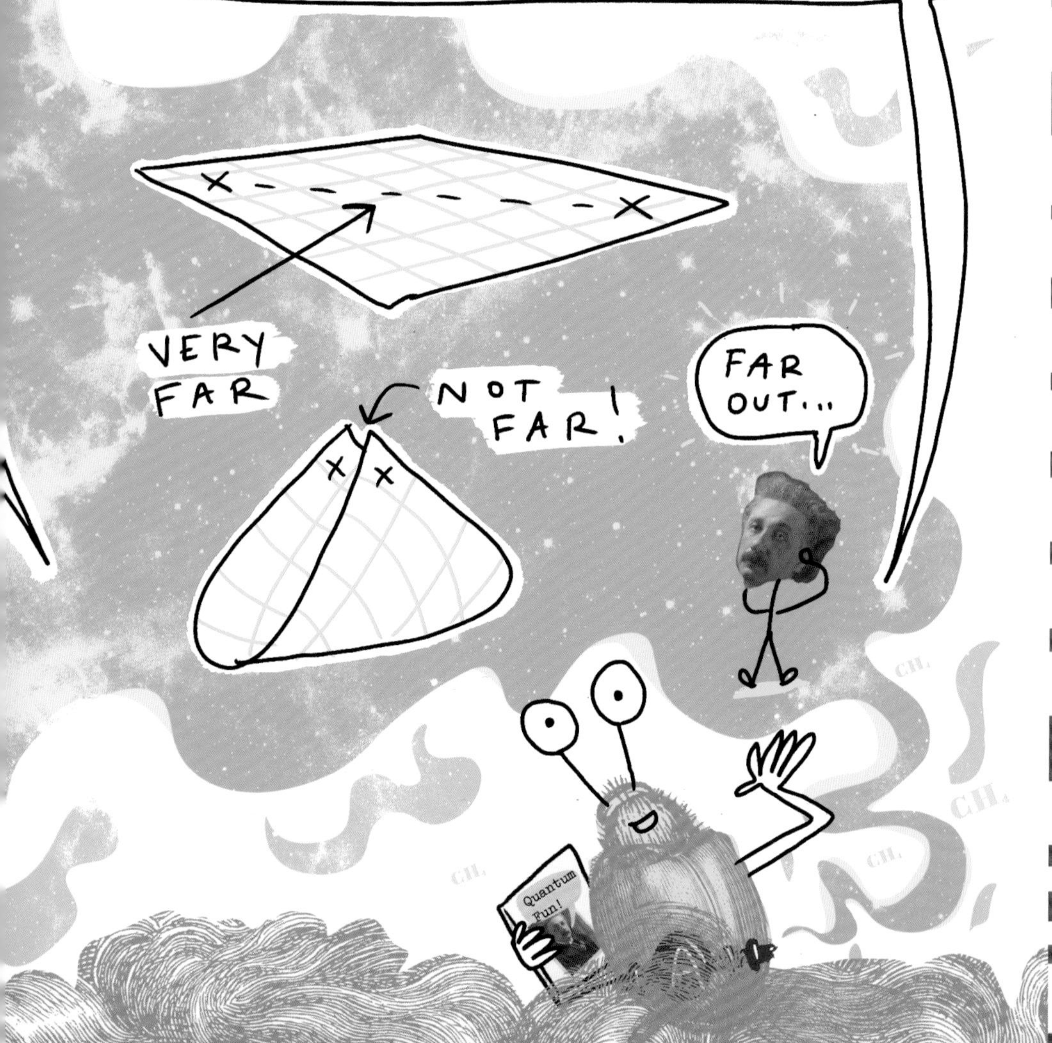
VERY FAR
NOT FAR!
FAR OUT...
Quantum Fun!

CHAPTER 2:
The Beardprint

Those of you who followed the adventures of the AstroNuts in Mission One: The Plant Planet will remember the blueprint of the Thomas Jefferson Nose Rocket. You will also remember being sworn to secrecy to not show this around to just anybody.

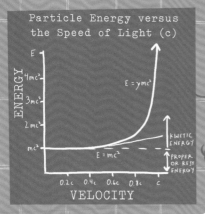

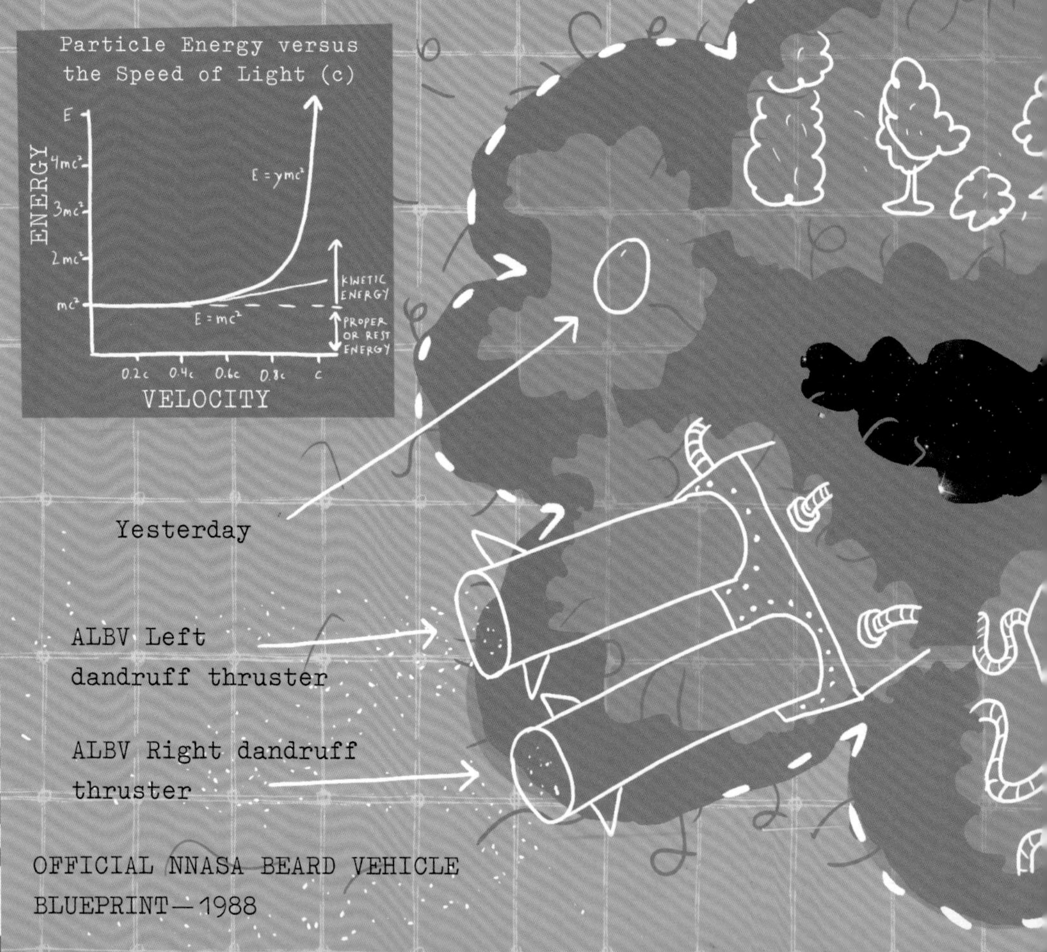

Particle Energy versus the Speed of Light (c)

$E = \gamma mc^2$

$E = mc^2$

KINETIC ENERGY

PROPER OR REST ENERGY

ENERGY

$4mc^2$
$3mc^2$
$2mc^2$
mc^2

0.2c 0.4c 0.6c 0.8c c

VELOCITY

Yesterday

ALBV Left
dandruff thruster

ALBV Right dandruff
thruster

OFFICIAL NNASA BEARD VEHICLE
BLUEPRINT—1988

New AstroNut followers and old, the same goes for this Top Secret blueprint. Keep it to yourself, OK?

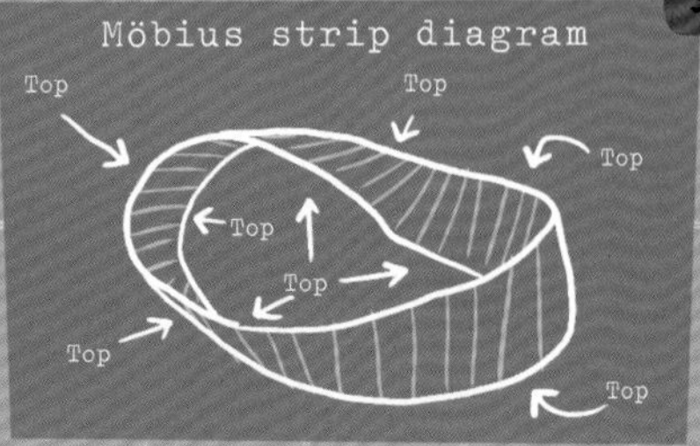
Möbius strip diagram
Top
Top
Top
Top
Top
Top
Top

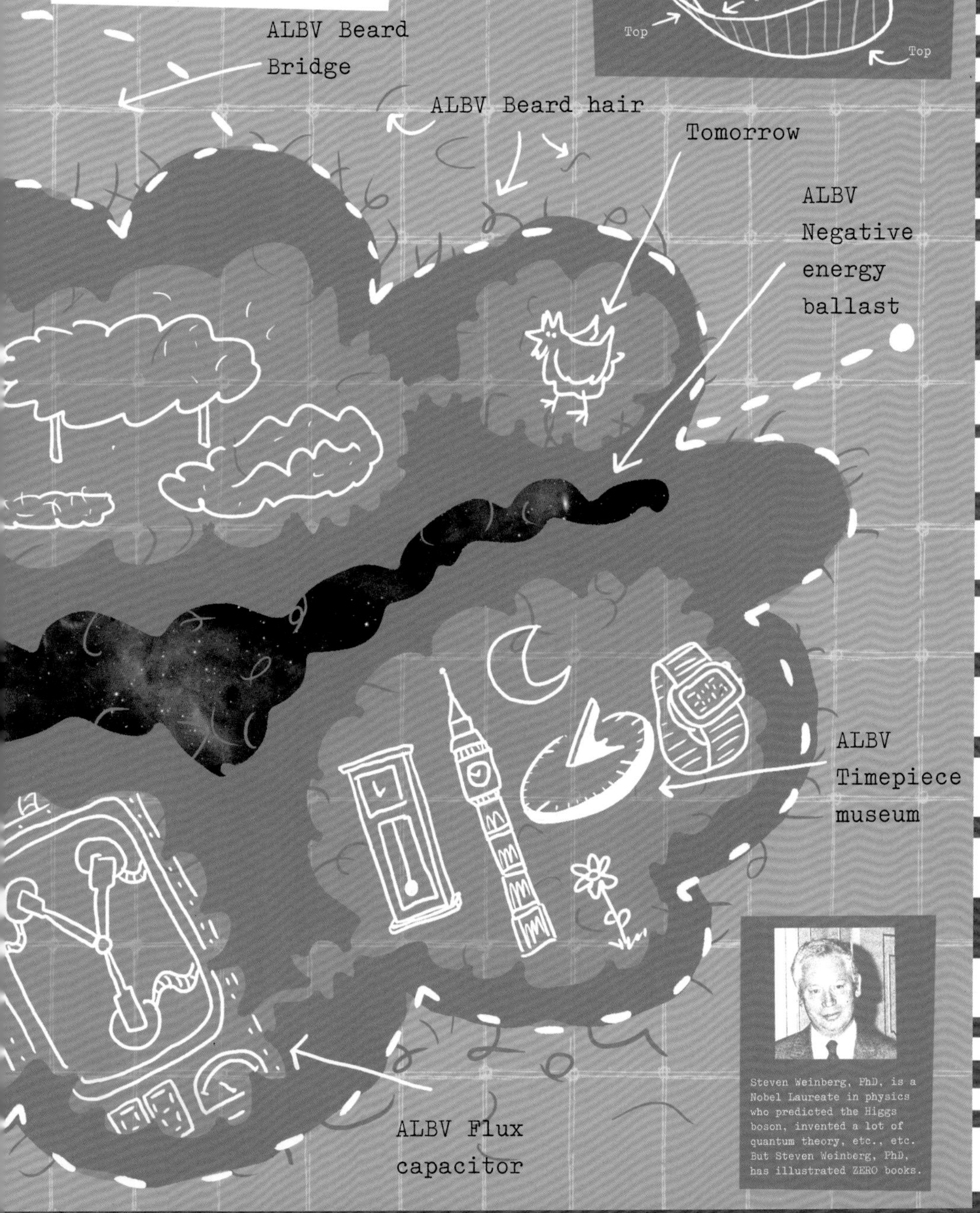
ALBV Beard Bridge
ALBV Beard hair
Tomorrow
ALBV Negative energy ballast
ALBV Timepiece museum
ALBV Flux capacitor

Steven Weinberg, PhD, is a Nobel Laureate in physics who predicted the Higgs boson, invented a lot of quantum theory, etc., etc. But Steven Weinberg, PhD, has illustrated ZERO books.

CHAPTER 3:

Mission Leader(s?)

///// Official NNASA transcript /////
//// of ASTRONUT NEW MISSION 3 ////

AlphaWolf: Okay, fine, I don't quit. I will be Mission Leader for just one more mission.
Command Escape: This is the very last chance/last chance/last chance for a Perfect Planet. We need a Mission Leader who can carefully plan/plan/plan and succeed.
StinkBug: That does make perfect number sense, AlphaWolf. You have not been successful as a leader. If this were baseball, you would be batting .00000. You are 0-2. You—
LaserShark: StinkBug! Don't be mean! AlphaWolf at least tried his best on the Plant Planet and the Water Planet.

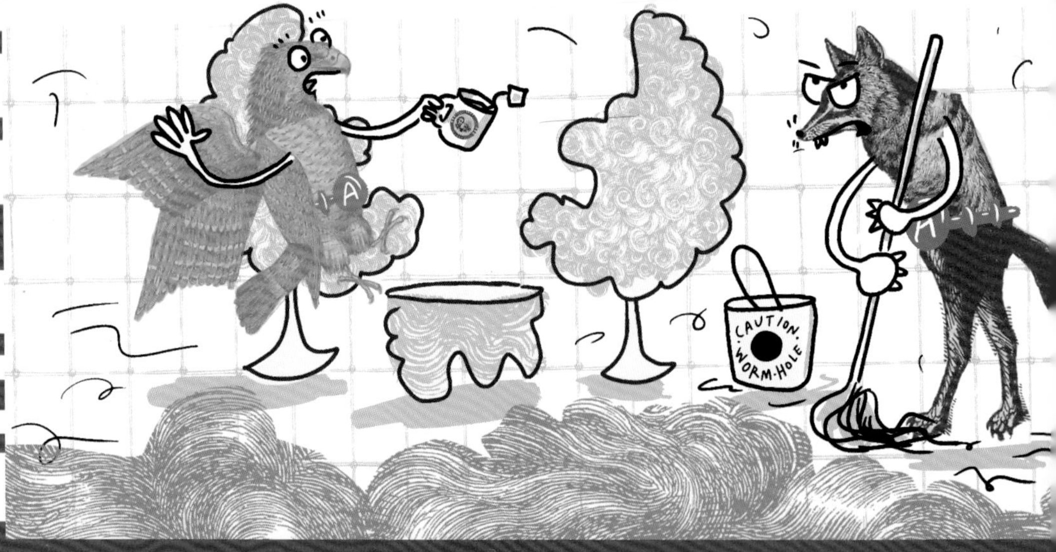
CAUTION. WORM-HOLE

SmartHawk: Guys, we don't have time for this. This is a very tricky mission. No one has ever traveled through time. We need plans. And we need to get started NOW.

AlphaWolf: OK, I get it. You are right, SmartHawk. I will be the Also Leader.

Command Escape: Incorrect/incorrect/incorrect—

AlphaWolf: Right. I am the Unofficial Leader.

Command Escape: No/no/no—

AlphaWolf: Fine. I will be the Secret Leader.

StinkBug: AlphaWolf, you know I do not play pretend. You are the Mission Helper.

LaserShark: Yoo-hoo, Alphie Helper! My Wormhole Muffins are ready. Can you please set out the Abe Lincoln doilies?

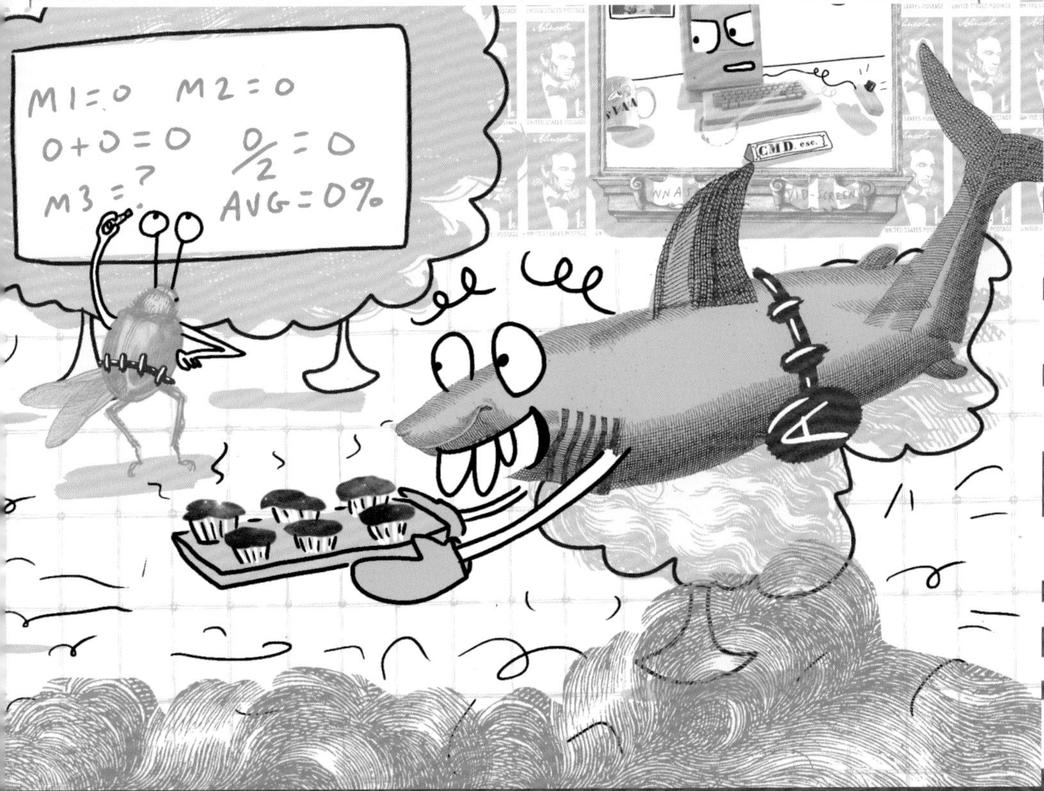
M1=0 M2=0
0+0=0 0/2=0
M3=? AVG=0%
CMD. esc.

This was really it. The AstroNuts' last chance. My last chance. YOUR last chance.

I was more than a little worried. Not just for the AstroNuts, or for the humans. Mostly for myself. Think about how you would feel if you were about to travel back in time and watch yourself as you were one million years ago.

Okay, that doesn't really work for humans. So imagine traveling back in time to watch yourself as you were five years ago. Imagine watching the beginning of something bad happening to you. Would you be able to change the past? Would you be able to make a better future? Or would it just be painfully sad all over again?

Like that time five years ago when you thought your bright-green pants looked so cool that you should wear them to school and show everybody and your mom tried to warn you that they were "a bit bright" and maybe best for just around the house but you were so sure you were right and didn't listen and wore them to school and the very first kid who saw you pointed and yelled "Green Bean!" and you had to spend the rest of the year trying to shake that stupid nickname even though you never wore those green pants again but you never really did until you changed schools.

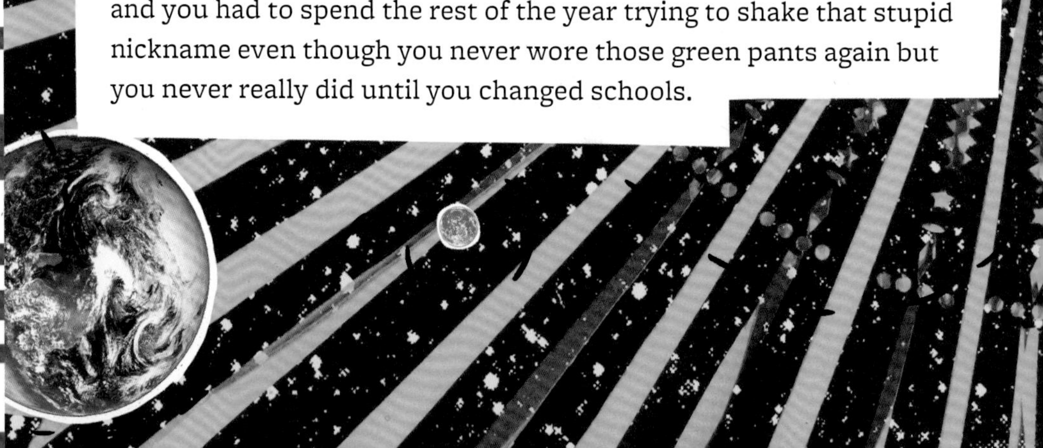

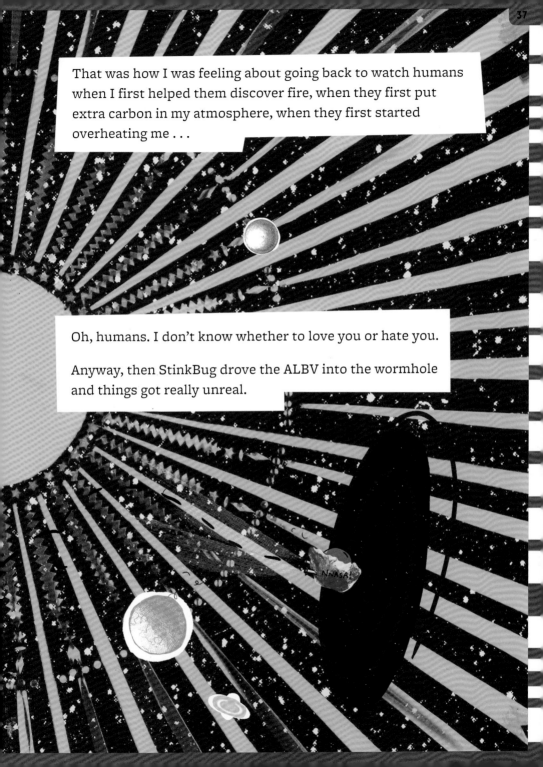

That was how I was feeling about going back to watch humans when I first helped them discover fire, when they first put extra carbon in my atmosphere, when they first started overheating me . . .

Oh, humans. I don't know whether to love you or hate you.

Anyway, then StinkBug drove the ALBV into the wormhole and things got really unreal.

CHAPTER 4:

The Wormhole

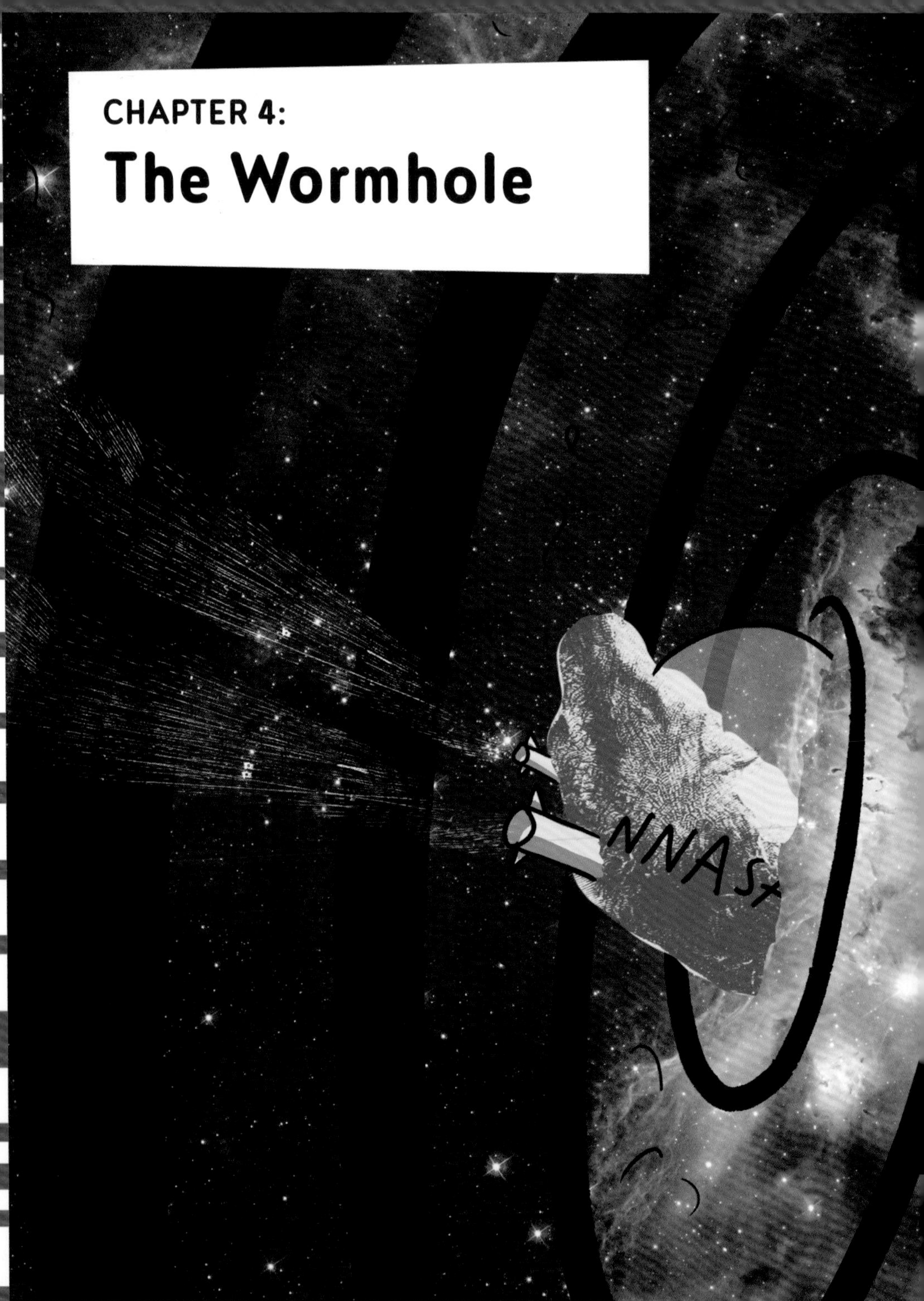
NNAS

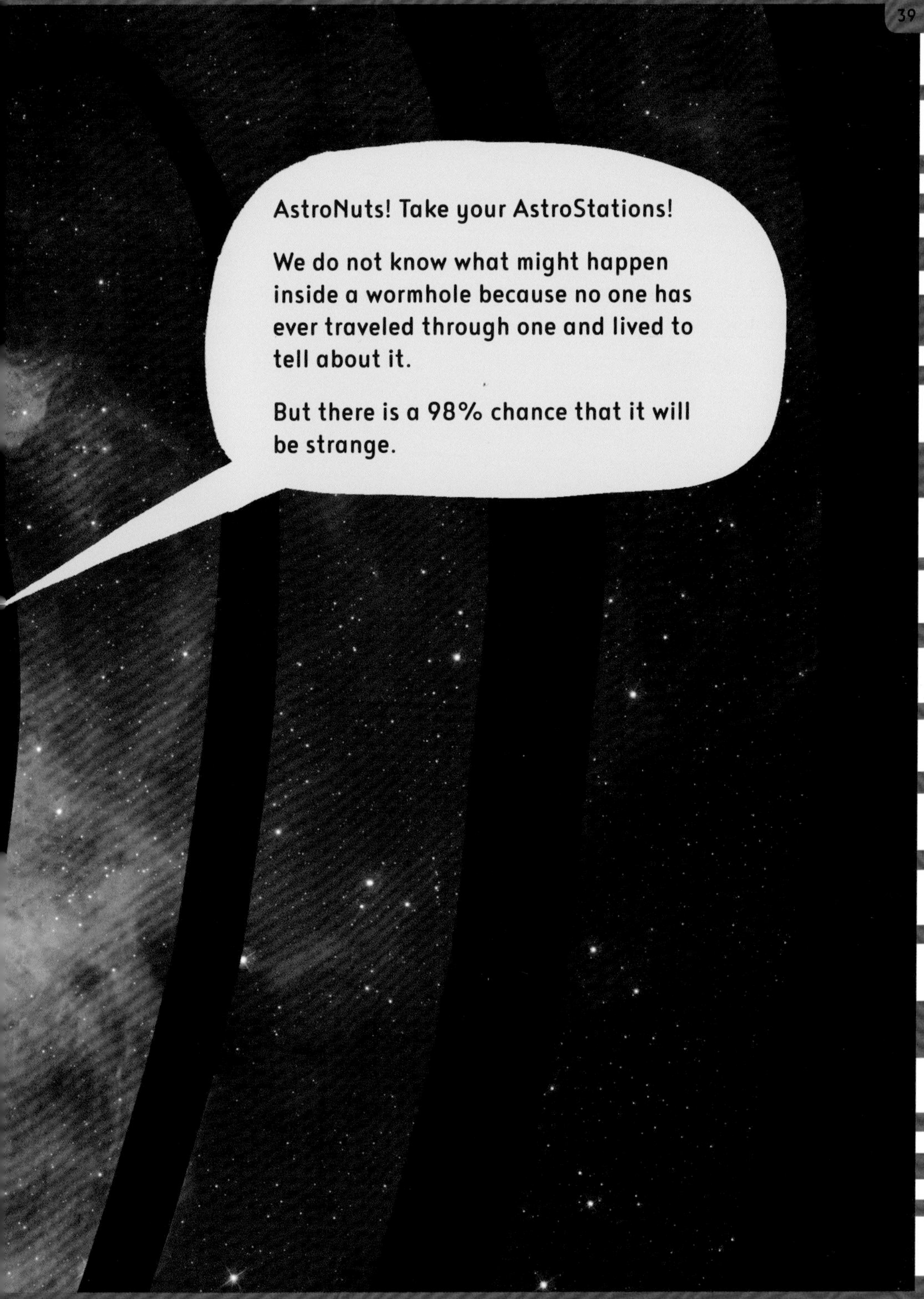
AstroNuts! Take your AstroStations!
We do not know what might happen inside a wormhole because no one has ever traveled through one and lived to tell about it.
But there is a 98% chance that it will be strange.

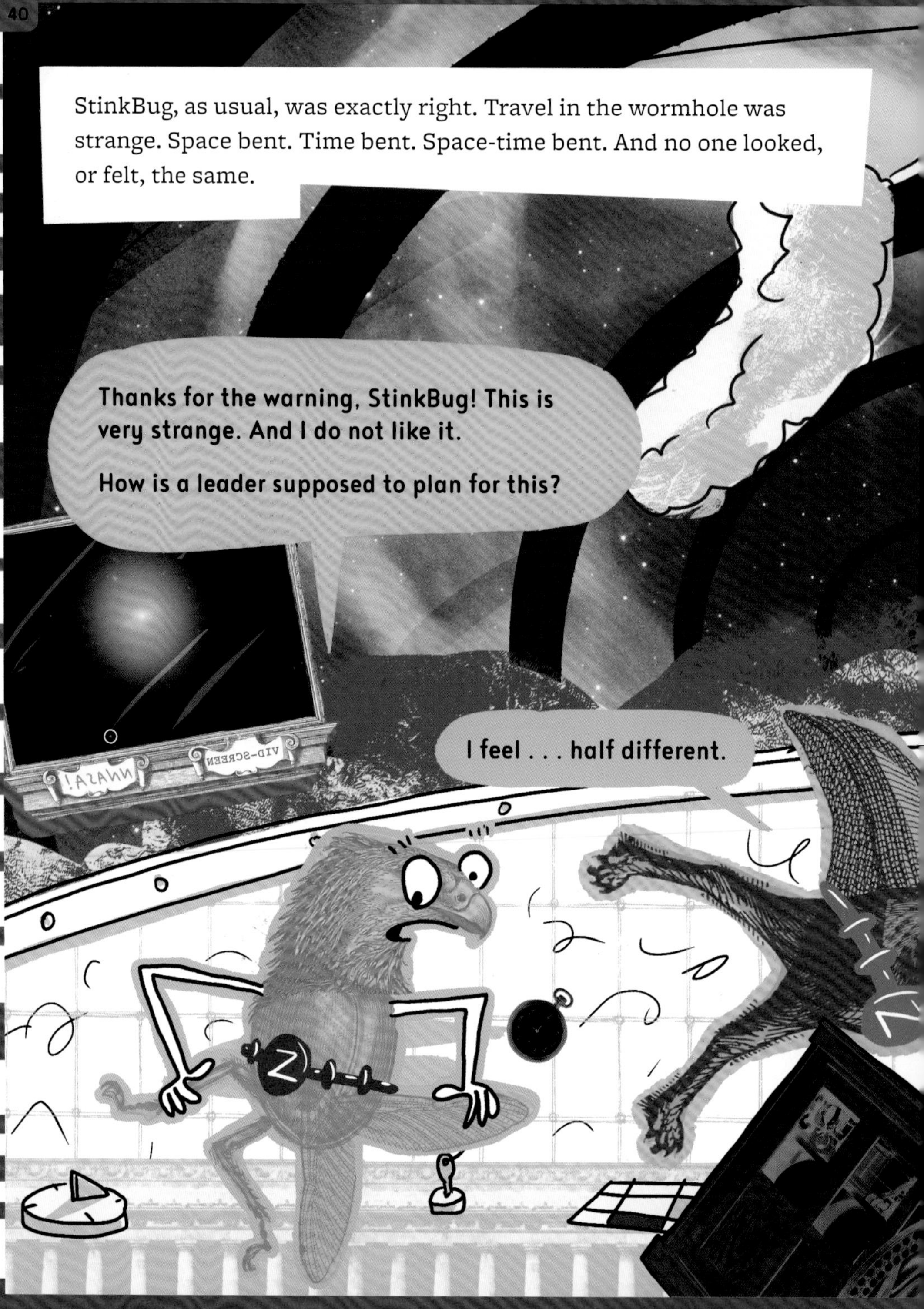
StinkBug, as usual, was exactly right. Travel in the wormhole was strange. Space bent. Time bent. Space-time bent. And no one looked, or felt, the same.
Thanks for the warning, StinkBug! This is very strange. And I do not like it.
How is a leader supposed to plan for this?
I feel . . . half different.

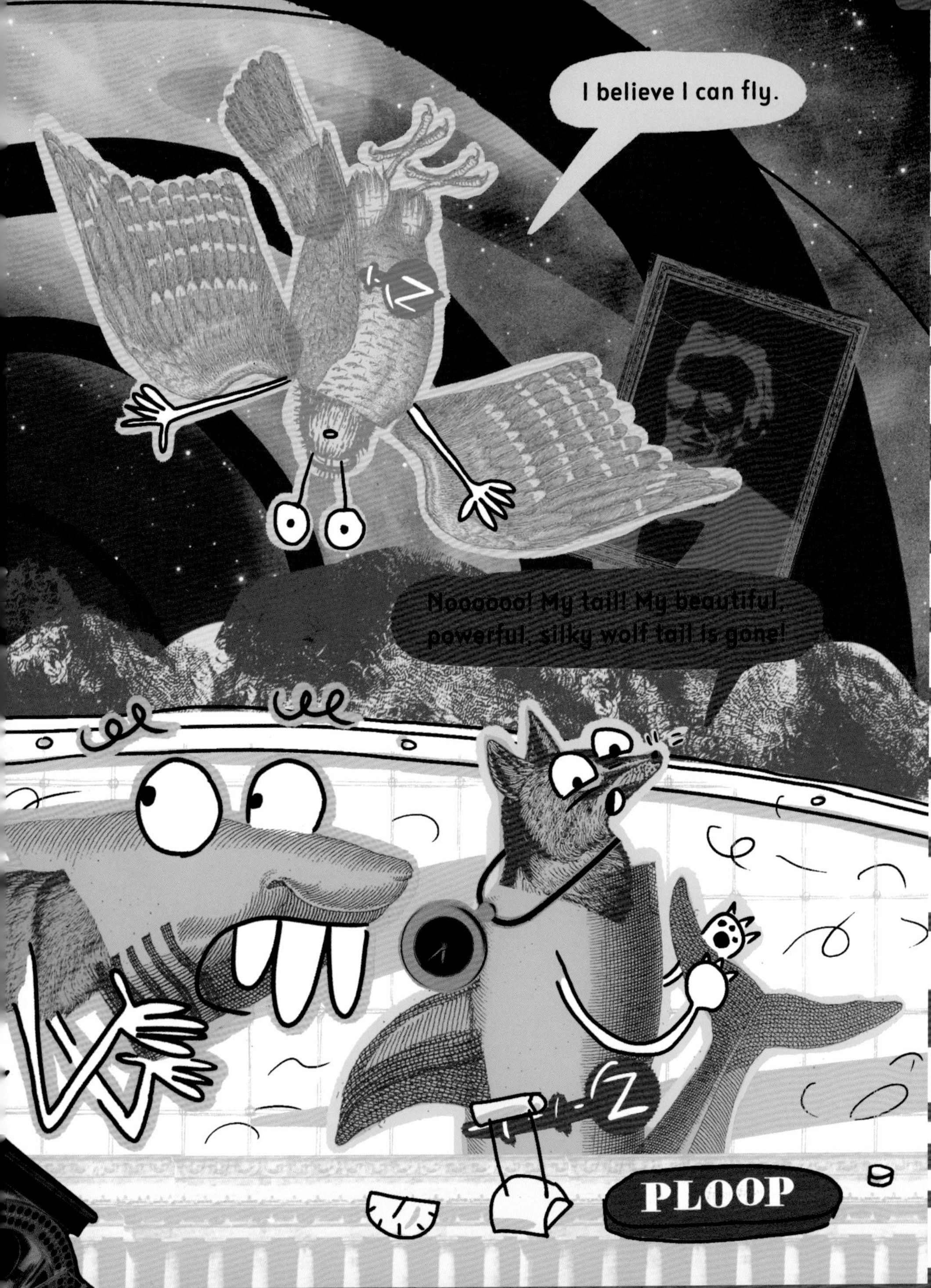
I believe I can fly.
Nooooooo! My tail! My beautiful, powerful, silky wolf tail is gone!
PLOOP

StinkBug flew the ALBV expertly through the wormhole space-time shortcut exactly as he had described it. The AstroNuts zoomed across 191,457,381 miles and back 999,999 years in the blink of a wormhole.

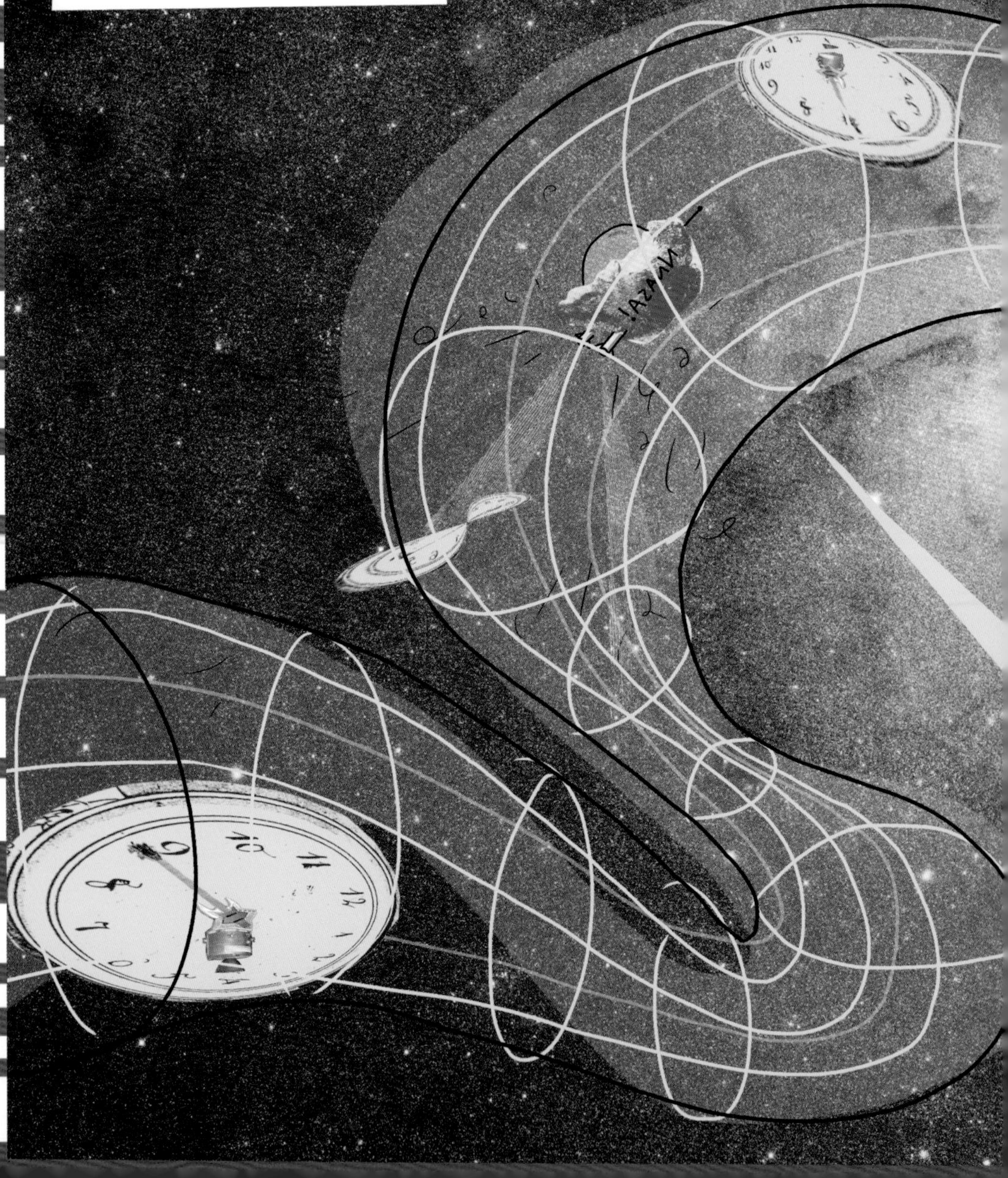

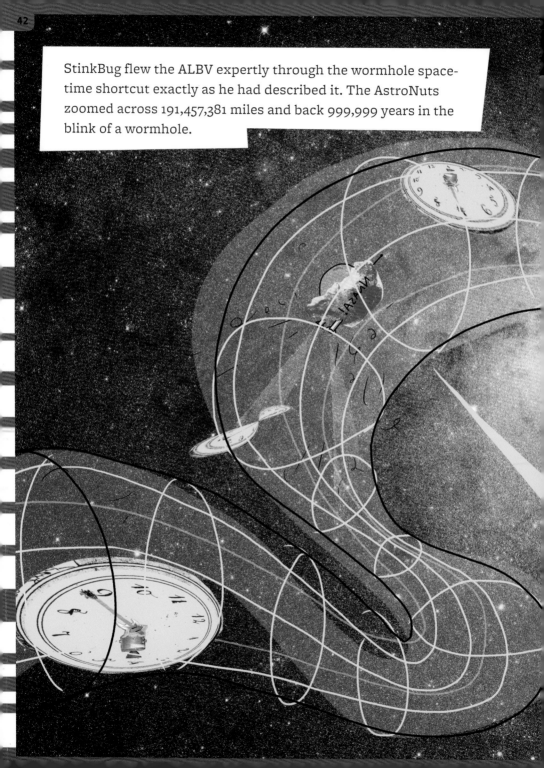

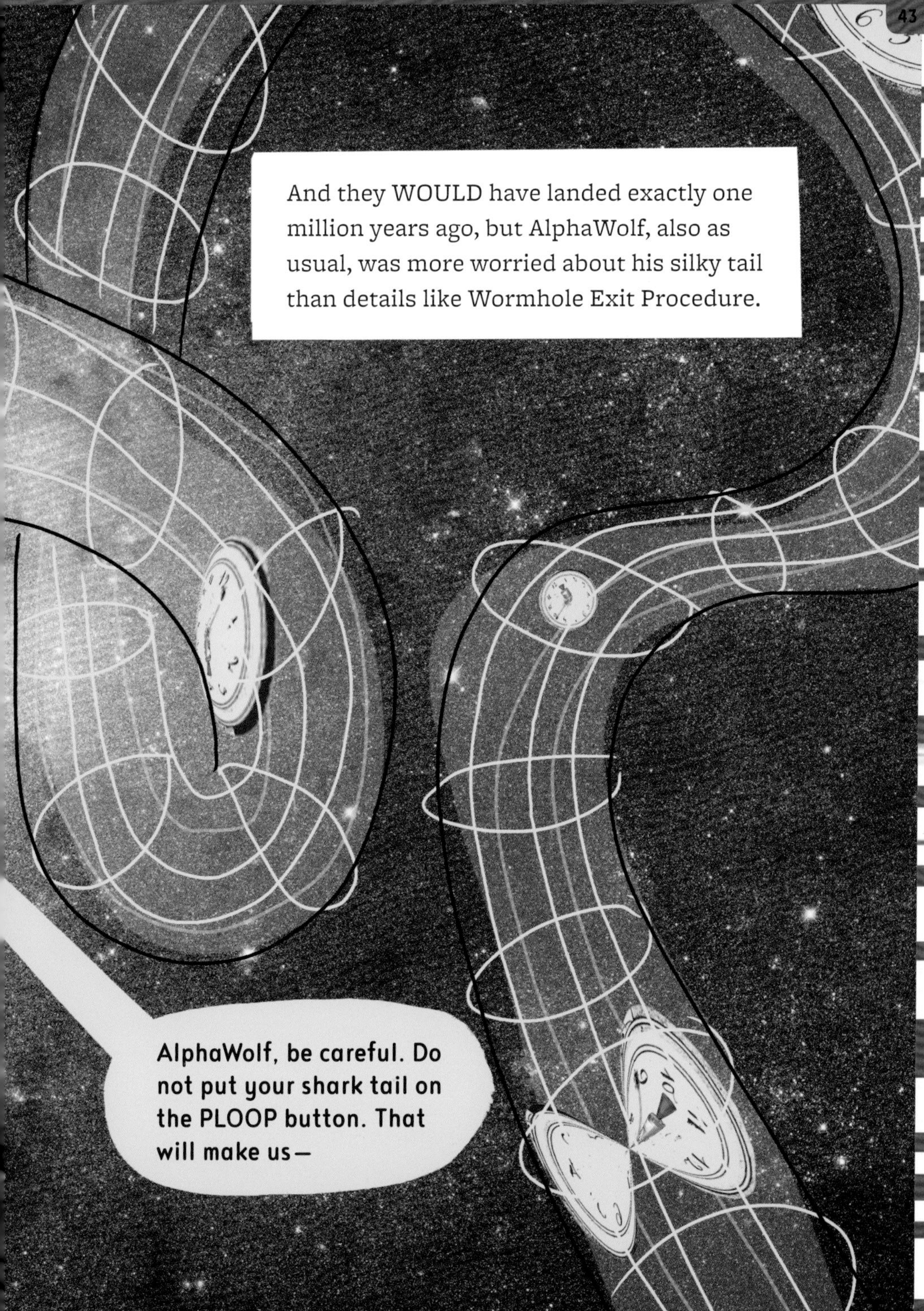
And they WOULD have landed exactly one million years ago, but AlphaWolf, also as usual, was more worried about his silky tail than details like Wormhole Exit Procedure.
AlphaWolf, be careful. Do not put your shark tail on the PLOOP button. That will make us—

CHAPTER 5: PLOOP

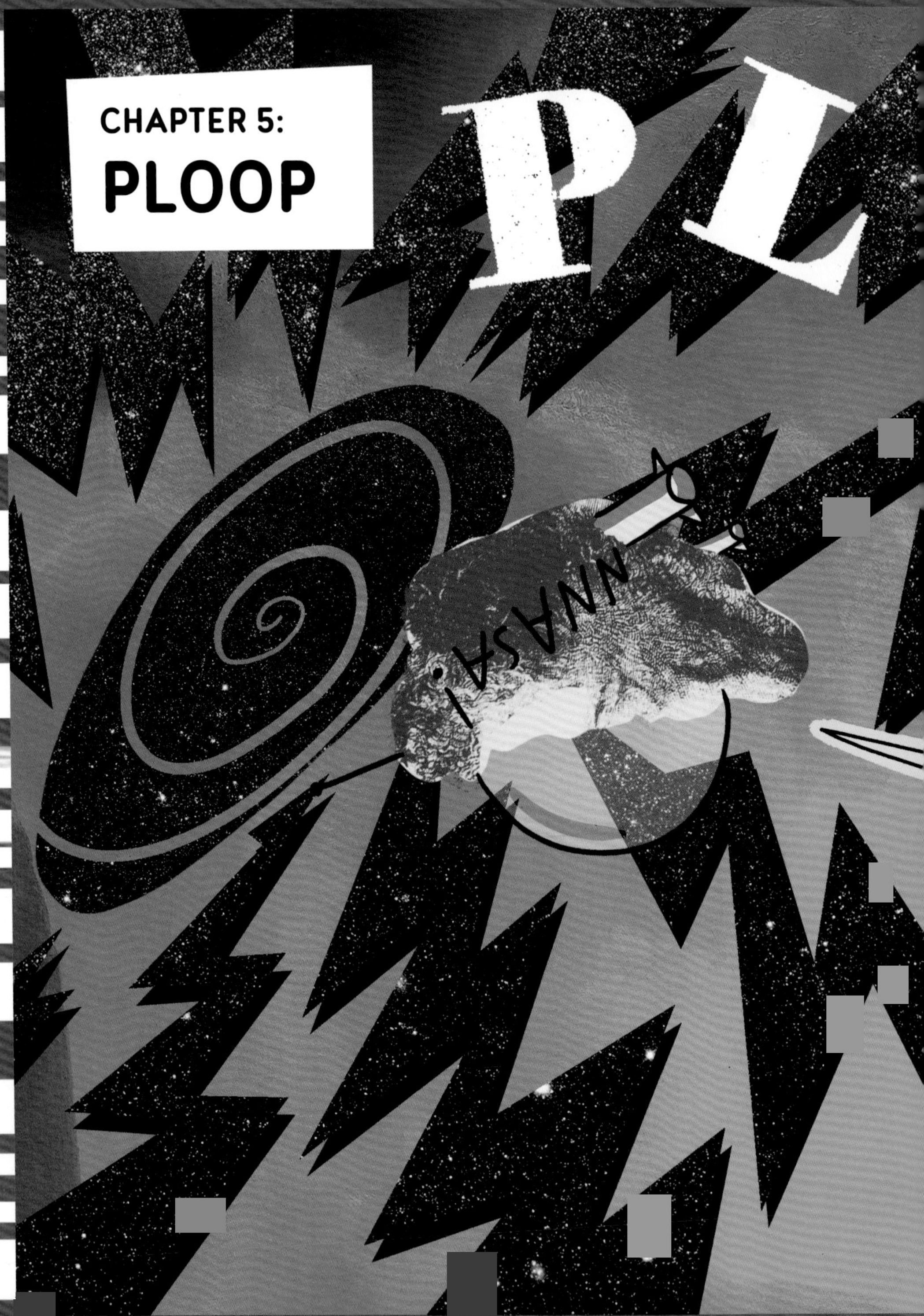
PL

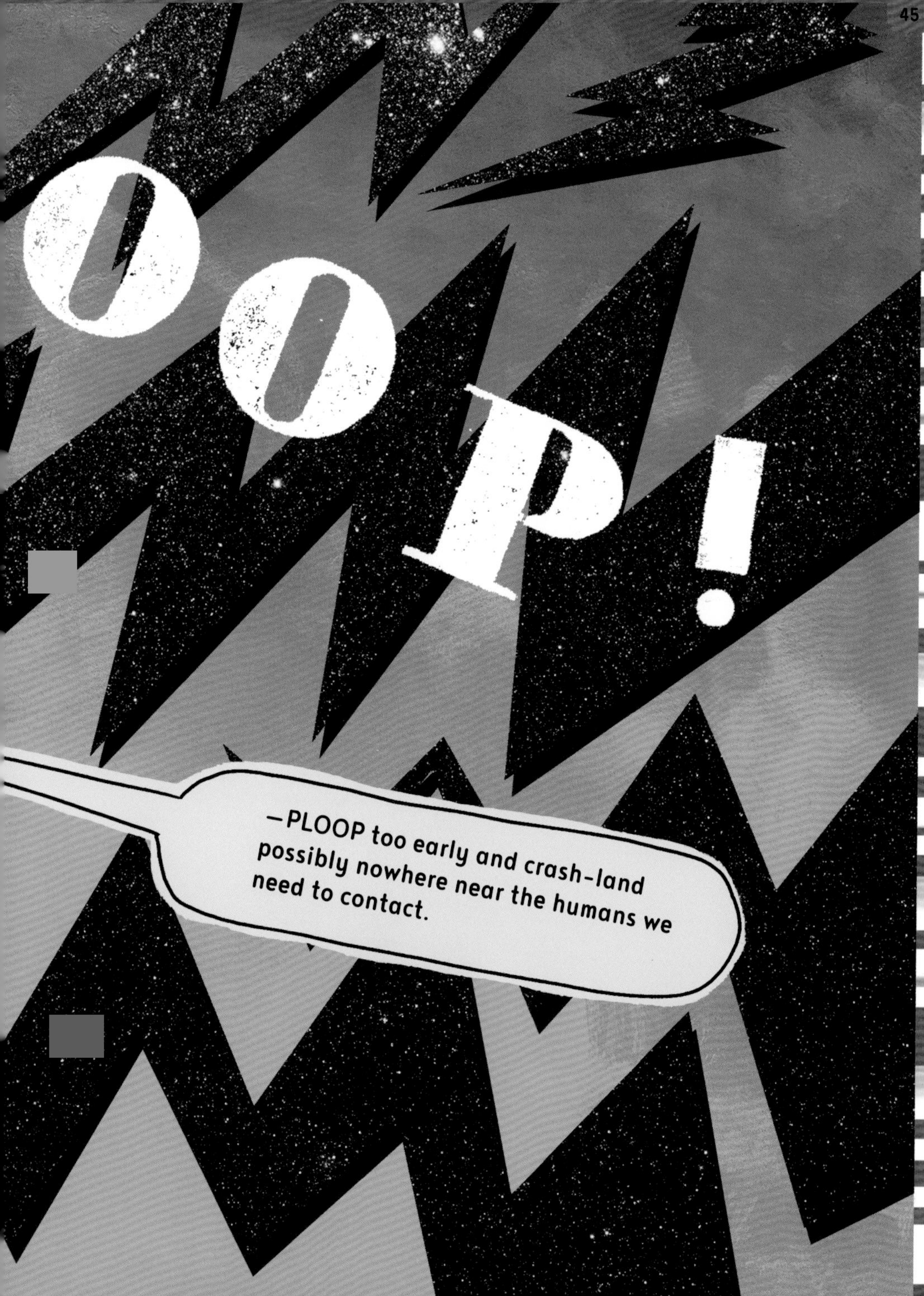
OOP!
—PLOOP too early and crash-land possibly nowhere near the humans we need to contact.

CHAPTER 6:
A Warning

Yes, the brilliant NNASA Wormhole Space-Time Travel Plan would have worked perfectly.

If it hadn't been for a certain unhelpful Mission Helper.

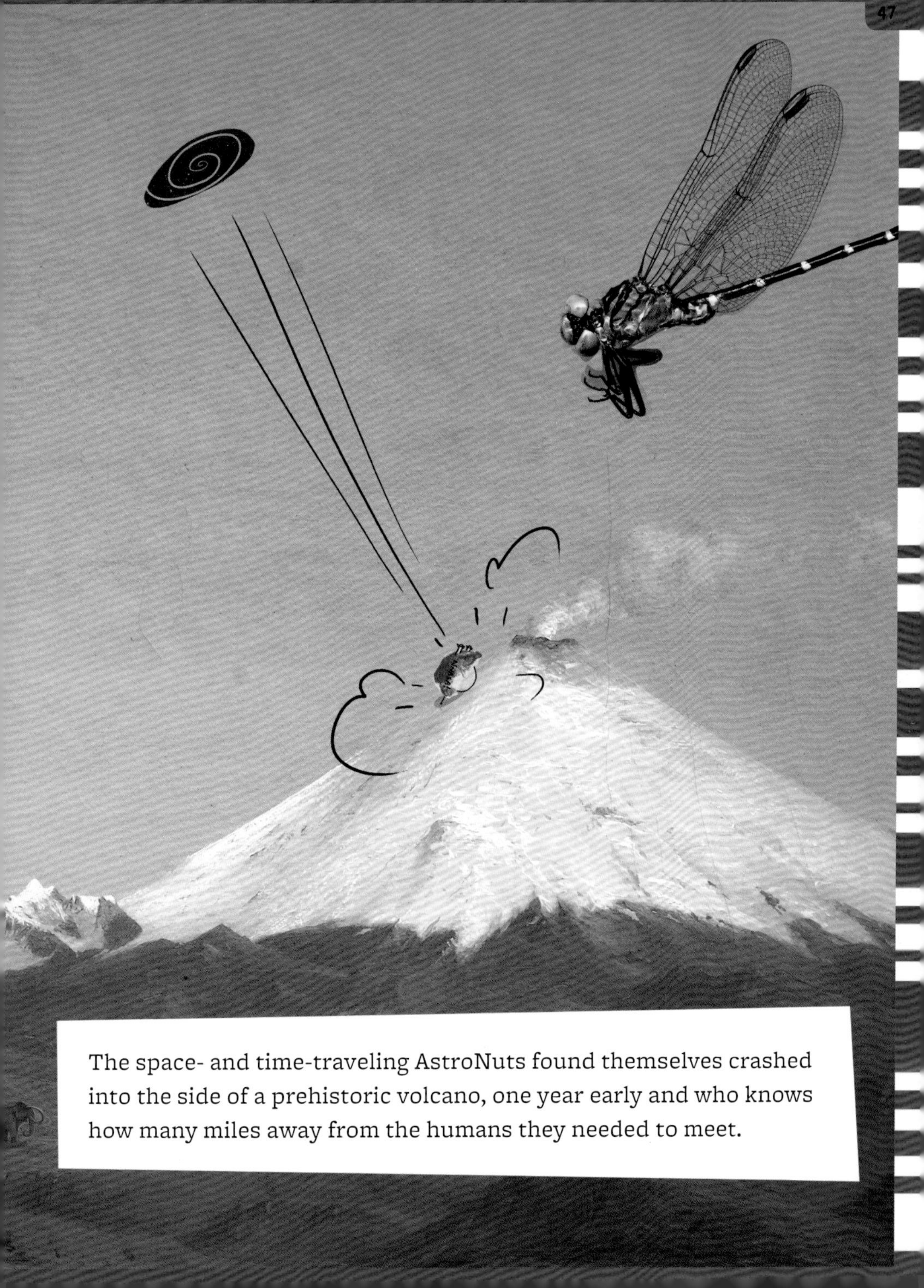

The space- and time-traveling AstroNuts found themselves crashed into the side of a prehistoric volcano, one year early and who knows how many miles away from the humans they needed to meet.

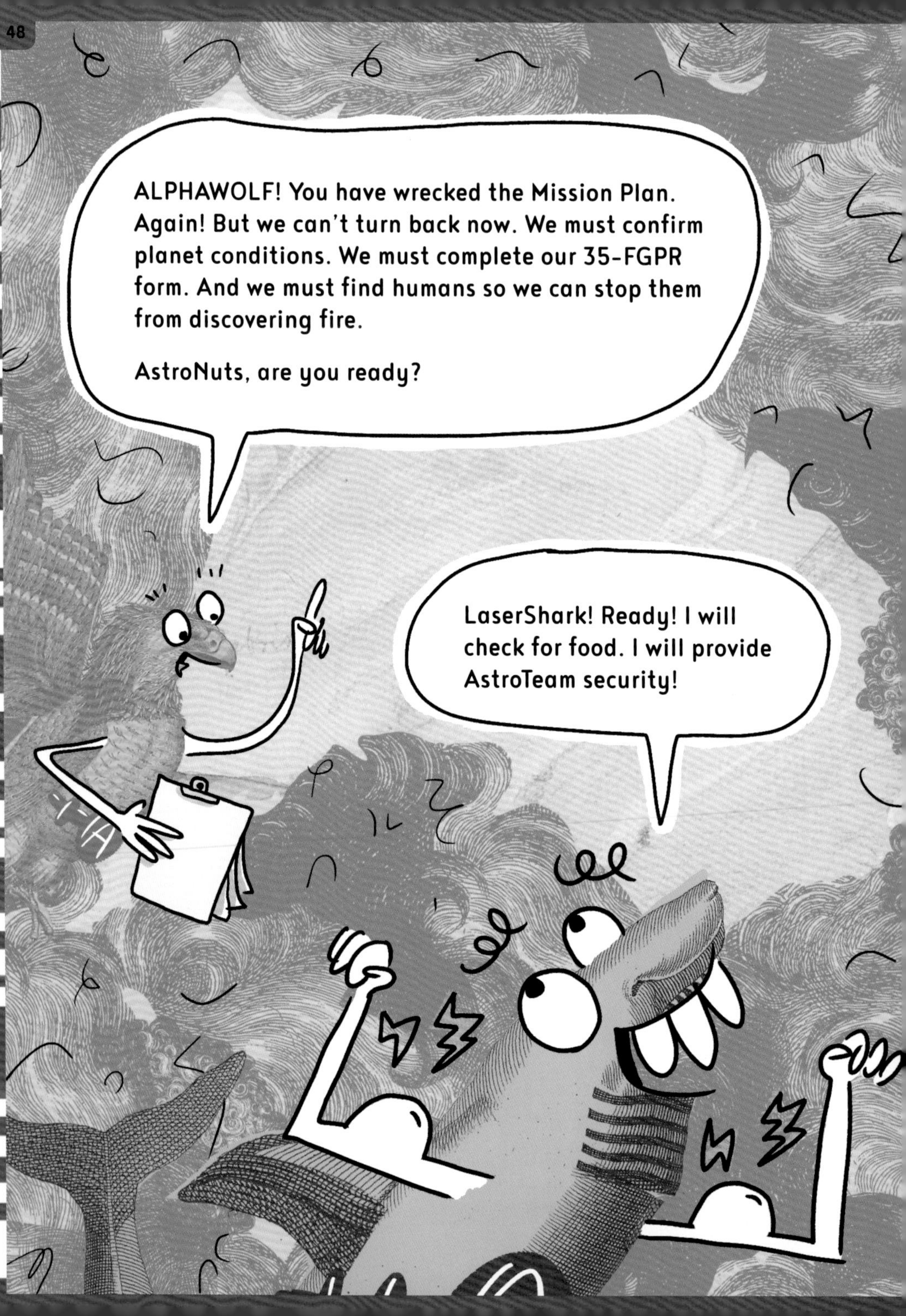
ALPHAWOLF! You have wrecked the Mission Plan. Again! But we can't turn back now. We must confirm planet conditions. We must complete our 35-FGPR form. And we must find humans so we can stop them from discovering fire.
AstroNuts, are you ready?
LaserShark! Ready! I will check for food. I will provide AstroTeam security!

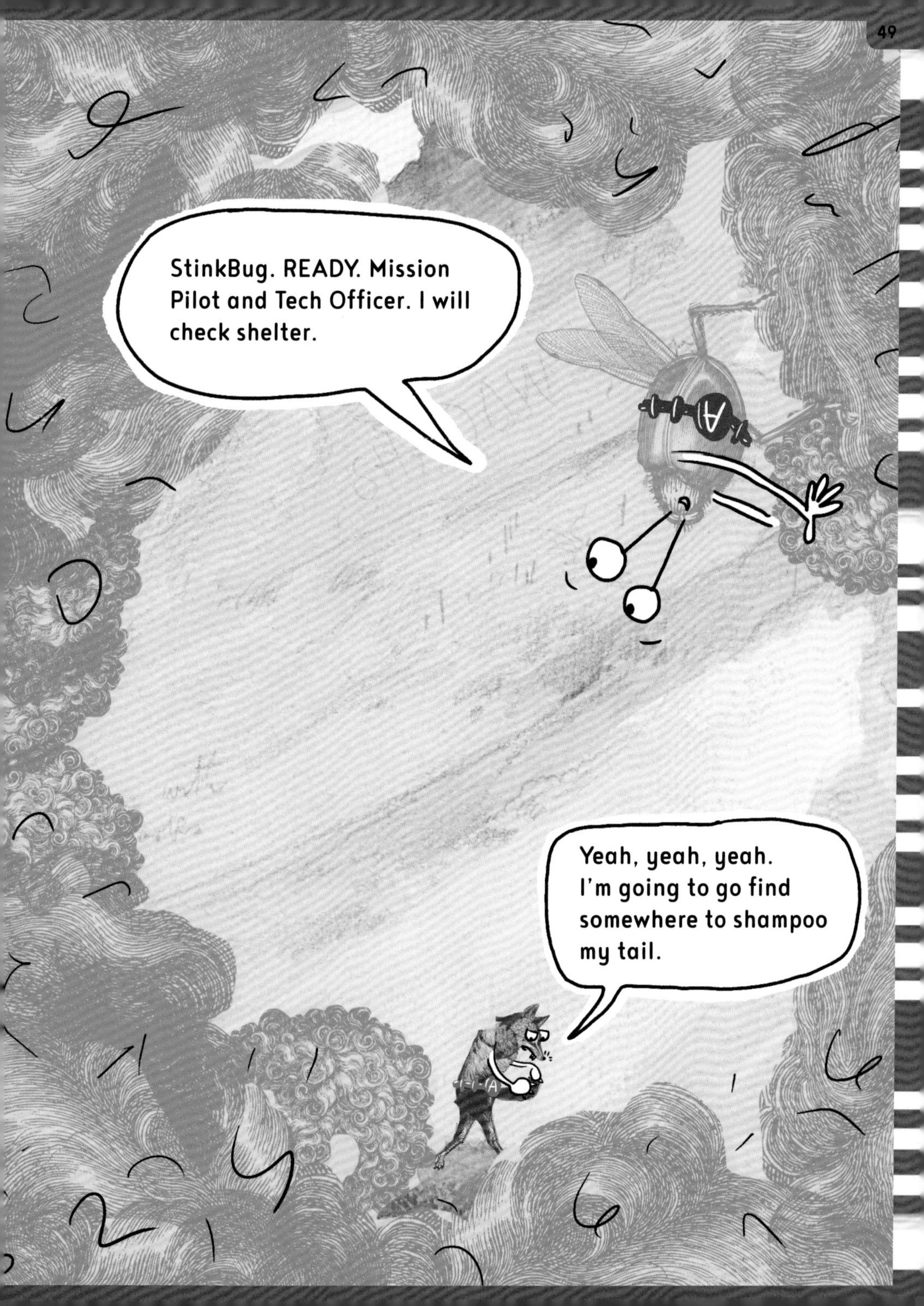
StinkBug. READY. Mission Pilot and Tech Officer. I will check shelter.
Yeah, yeah, yeah. I'm going to go find somewhere to shampoo my tail.

CHAPTER 7:

Testing, Testing

So at least three quarters of the AstroNuts charged out of the Abe Lincoln Beard Vehicle and used their superpowers to take a close look at ME. In my cleaner days. Not really that long ago.

SmartHawk used her supersonic wings to speed through my atmosphere. And she found exactly what I knew she would on my one-million-years-younger self.

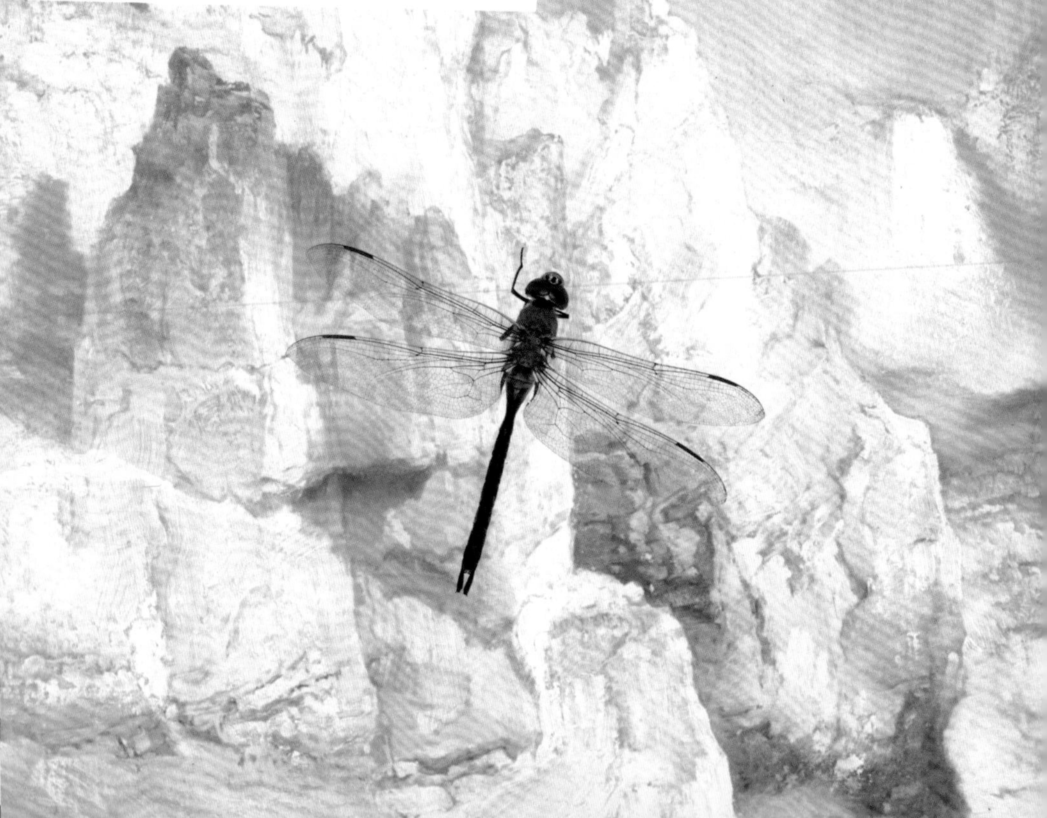

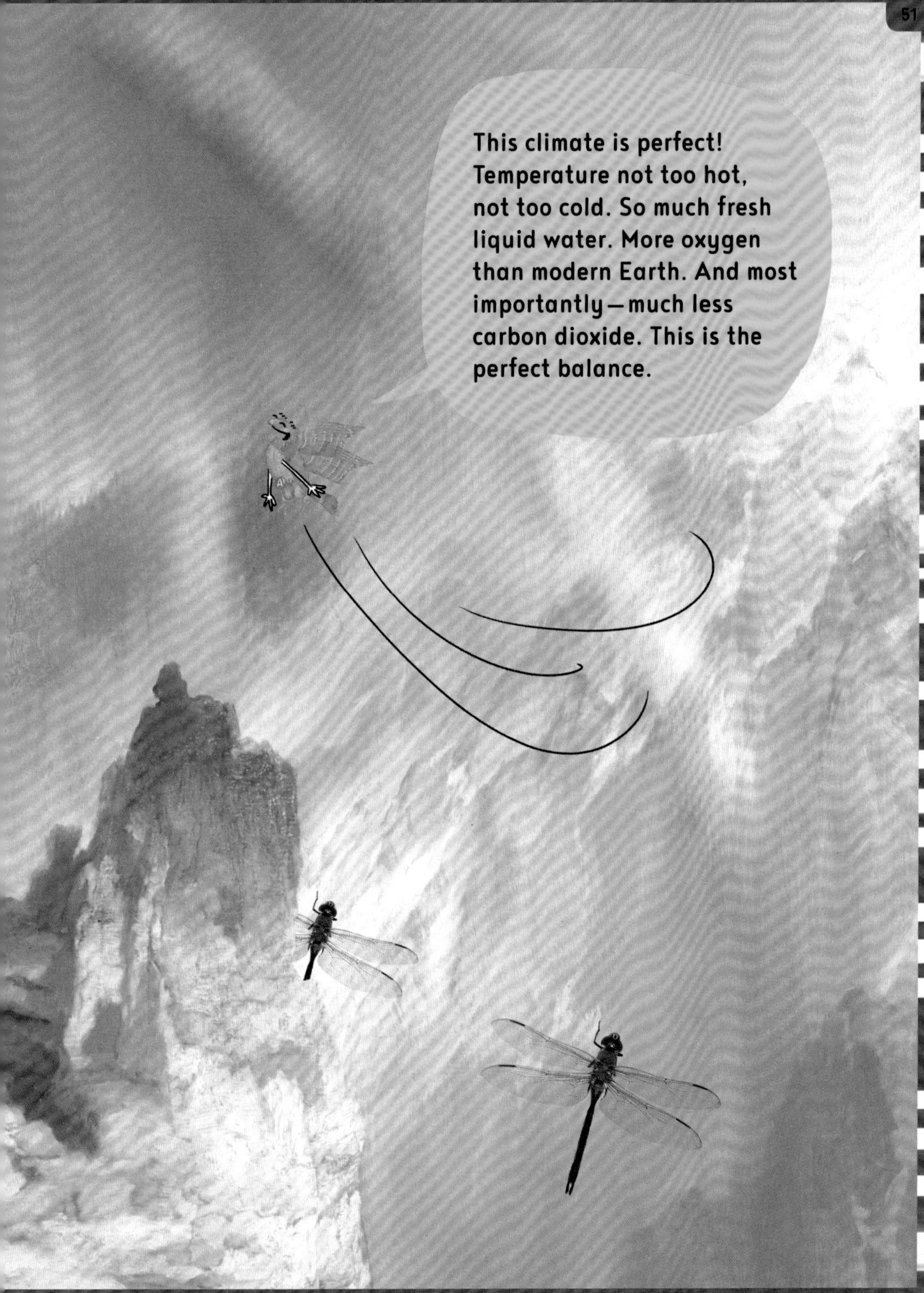
This climate is perfect! Temperature not too hot, not too cold. So much fresh liquid water. More oxygen than modern Earth. And most importantly—much less carbon dioxide. This is the perfect balance.

LaserShark electromagnetically levitated around my biomes. She found so many now-extinct plants and animals! I forgot how much I missed my horned gophers.

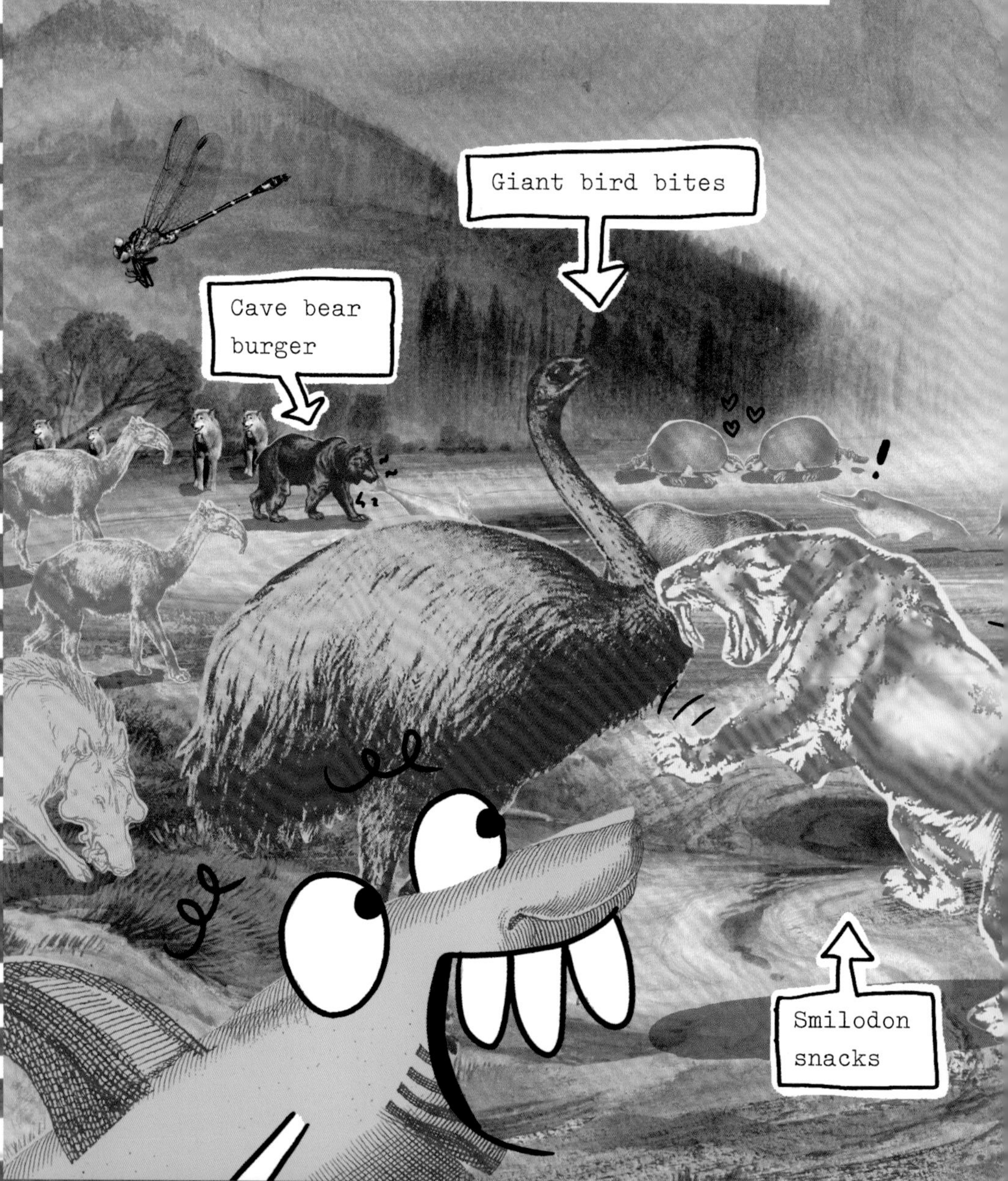
Giant bird bites
Cave bear burger
Smilodon snacks

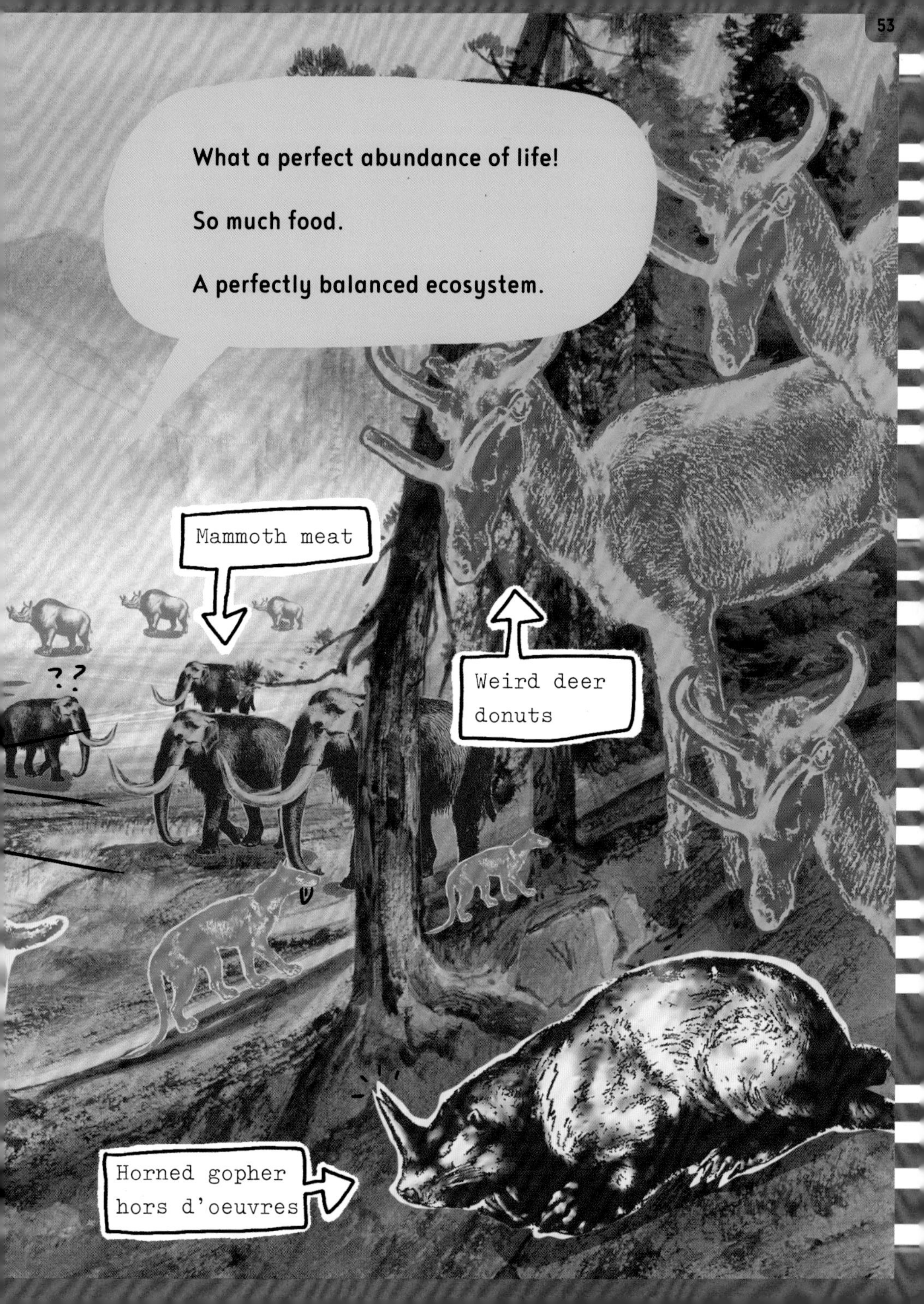
What a perfect abundance of life!
So much food.
A perfectly balanced ecosystem.
Mammoth meat
??
Weird deer donuts
Horned gopher hors d'oeuvres

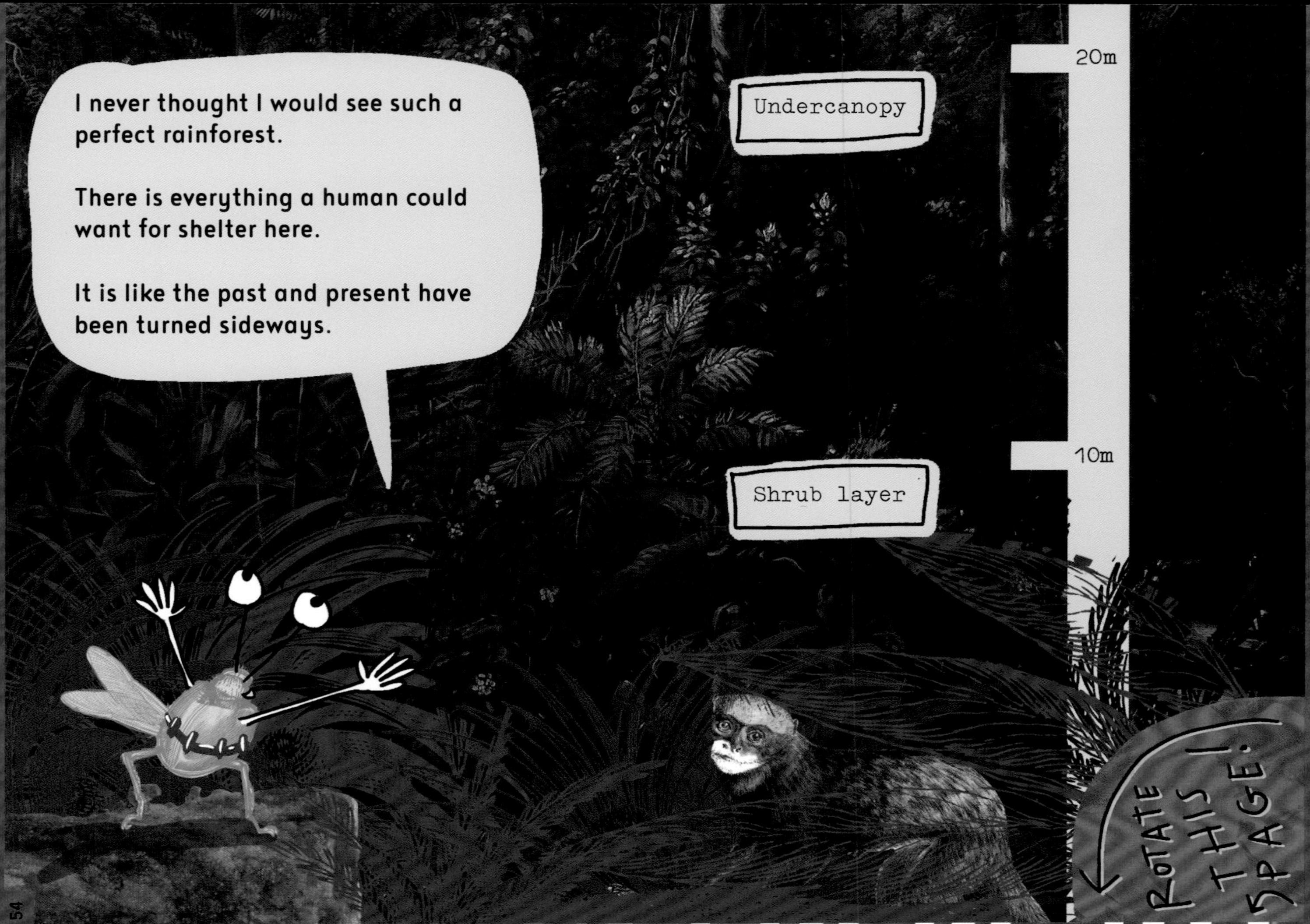
I never thought I would see such a perfect rainforest.
There is everything a human could want for shelter here.
It is like the past and present have been turned sideways.
20m
Undercanopy
10m
Shrub layer
ROTATE THIS PAGE!

StinkBug power-hopped and speed-dug through some rainforests.

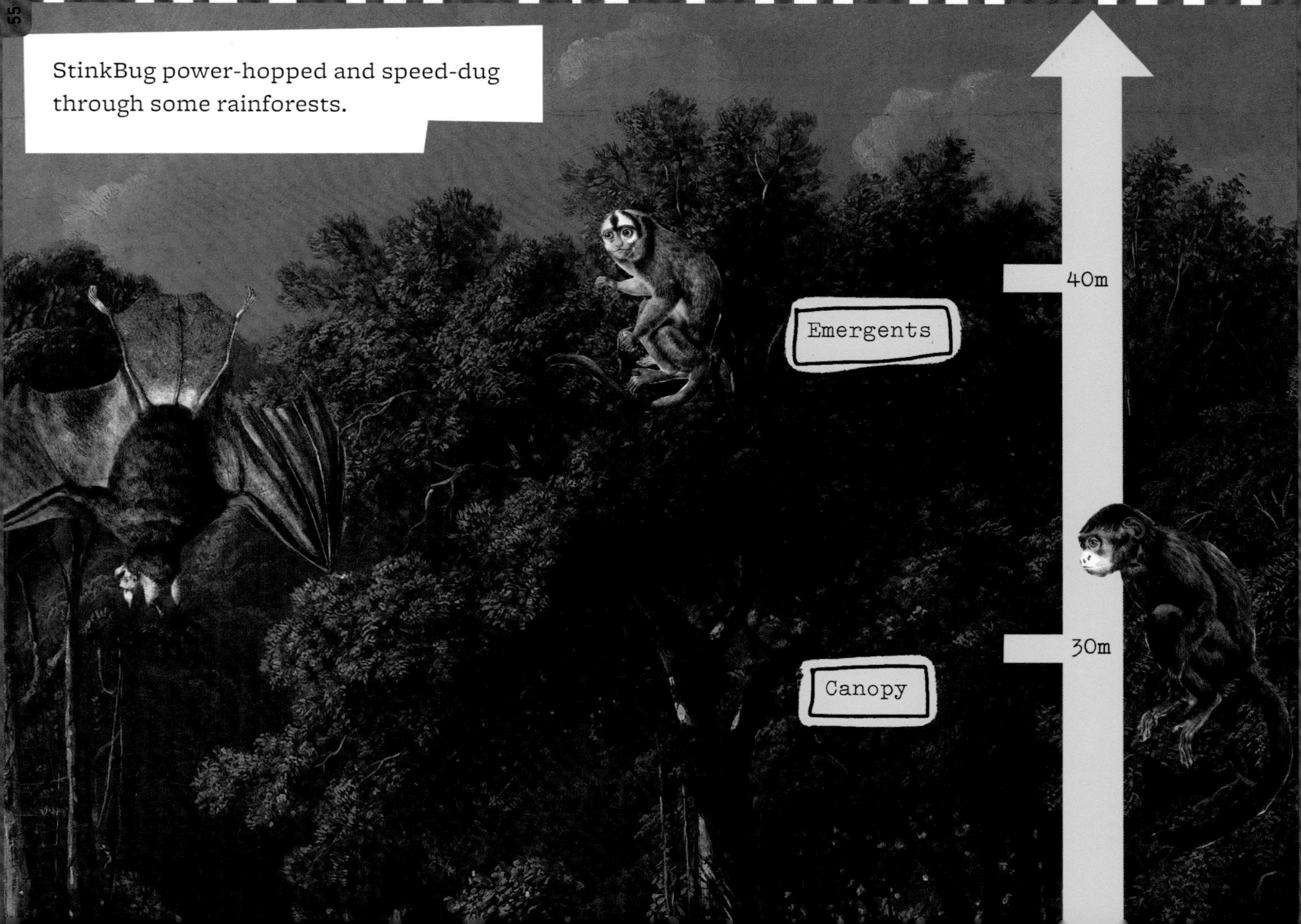
40m
Emergents
30m
Canopy

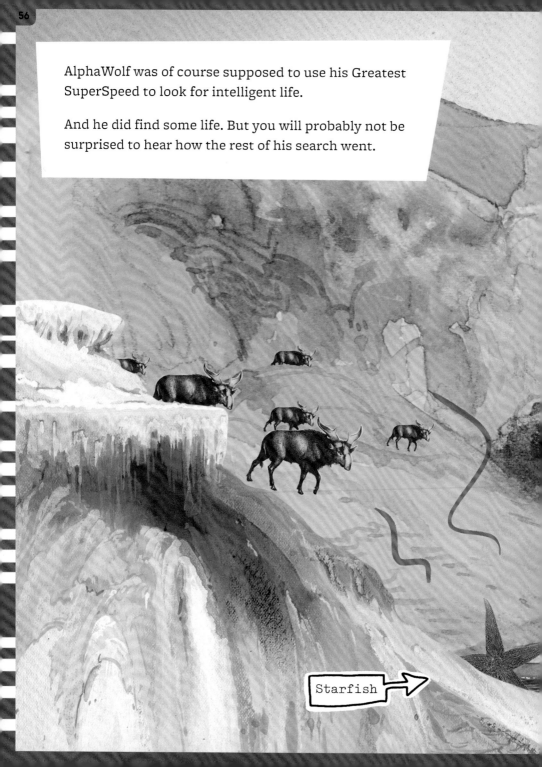

AlphaWolf was of course supposed to use his Greatest SuperSpeed to look for intelligent life.

And he did find some life. But you will probably not be surprised to hear how the rest of his search went.

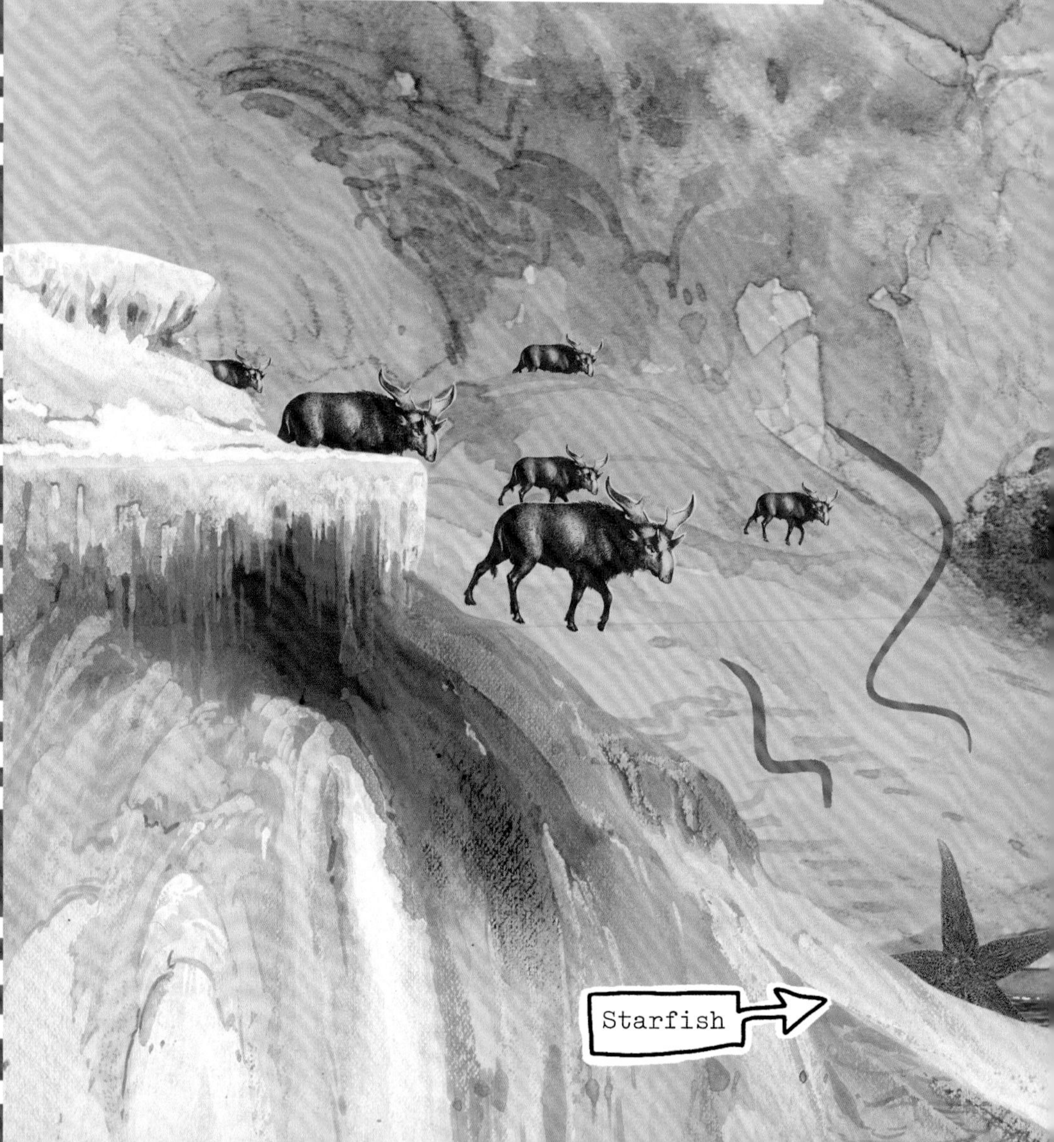
Starfish

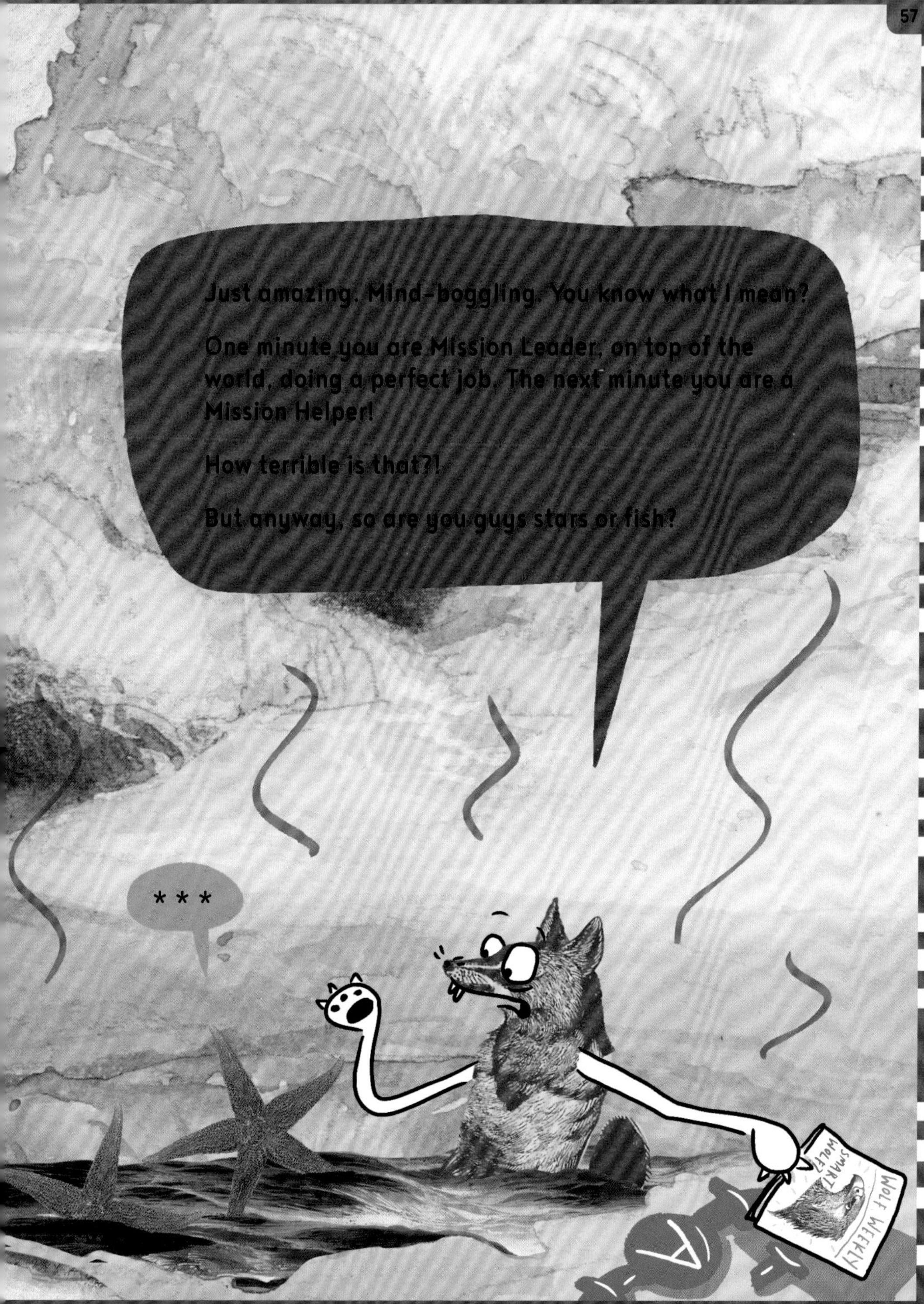
Just amazing. Mind-boggling. You know what I mean?
One minute you are Mission Leader, on top of the world, doing a perfect job. The next minute you are a Mission Helper!
How terrible is that?!
But anyway, so are you guys stars or fish?
* * *
SMART WOLF
WOLF WEEKLY

CHAPTER 8:
Homework

The AstroNuts returned to the Abe Lincoln Beard Vehicle to report their findings. And I am pretty proud to report that what the AstroNuts found was an absolutely beautifully balanced, unpolluted, teeming-with-life planet. Me.

I was still blushing when SmartHawk revealed a Mission Leader surprise.

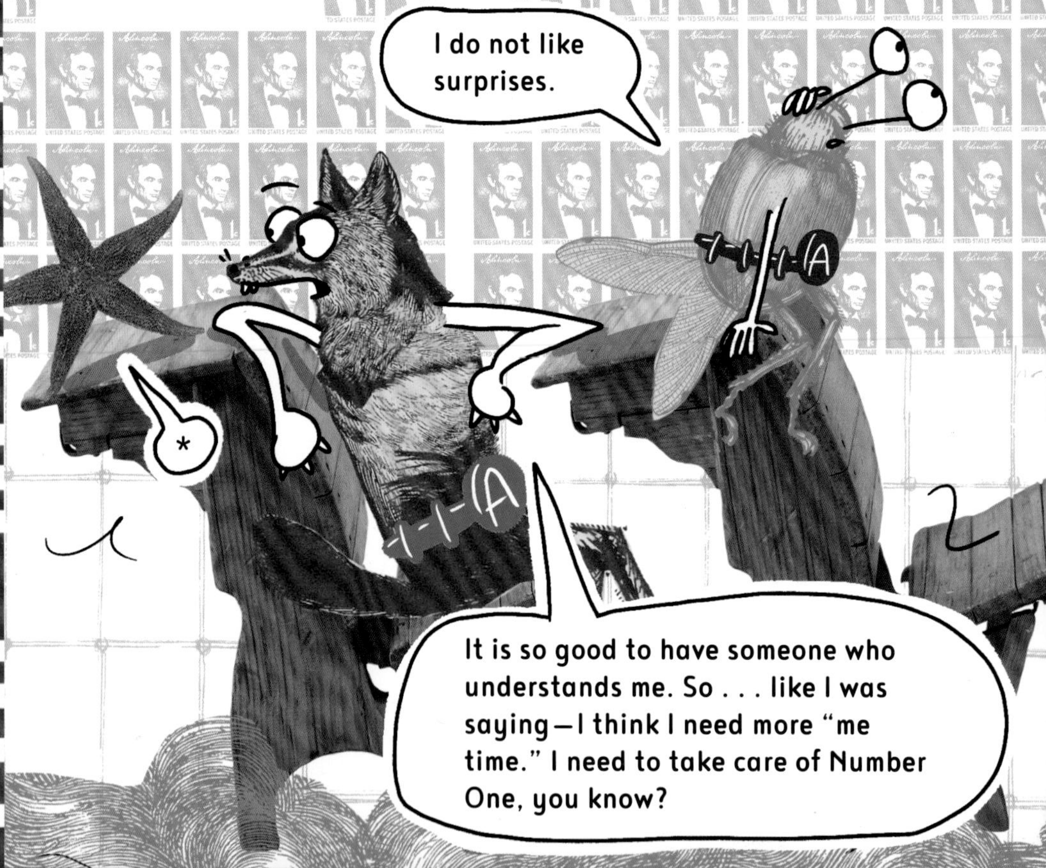

I do not like surprises.
It is so good to have someone who understands me. So . . . like I was saying—I think I need more "me time." I need to take care of Number One, you know?

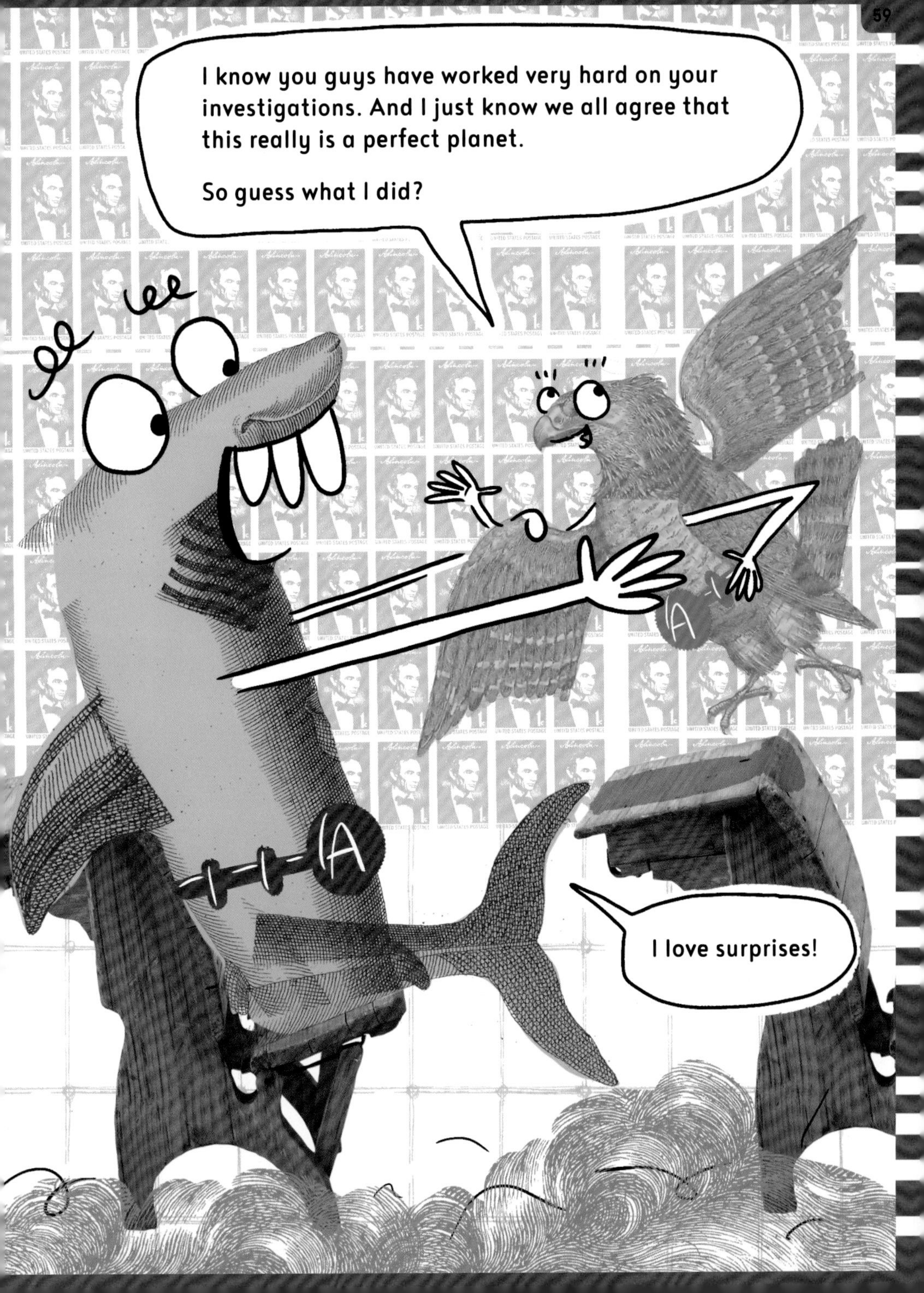
I know you guys have worked very hard on your investigations. And I just know we all agree that this really is a perfect planet.
So guess what I did?
I love surprises!

SmartHawk unveiled her surprise. And it turned out to be one of those not-really-great surprises. Useful, and a nice idea and all. But like a big, beautifully wrapped present that turns out to be . . . a pair of brown socks.

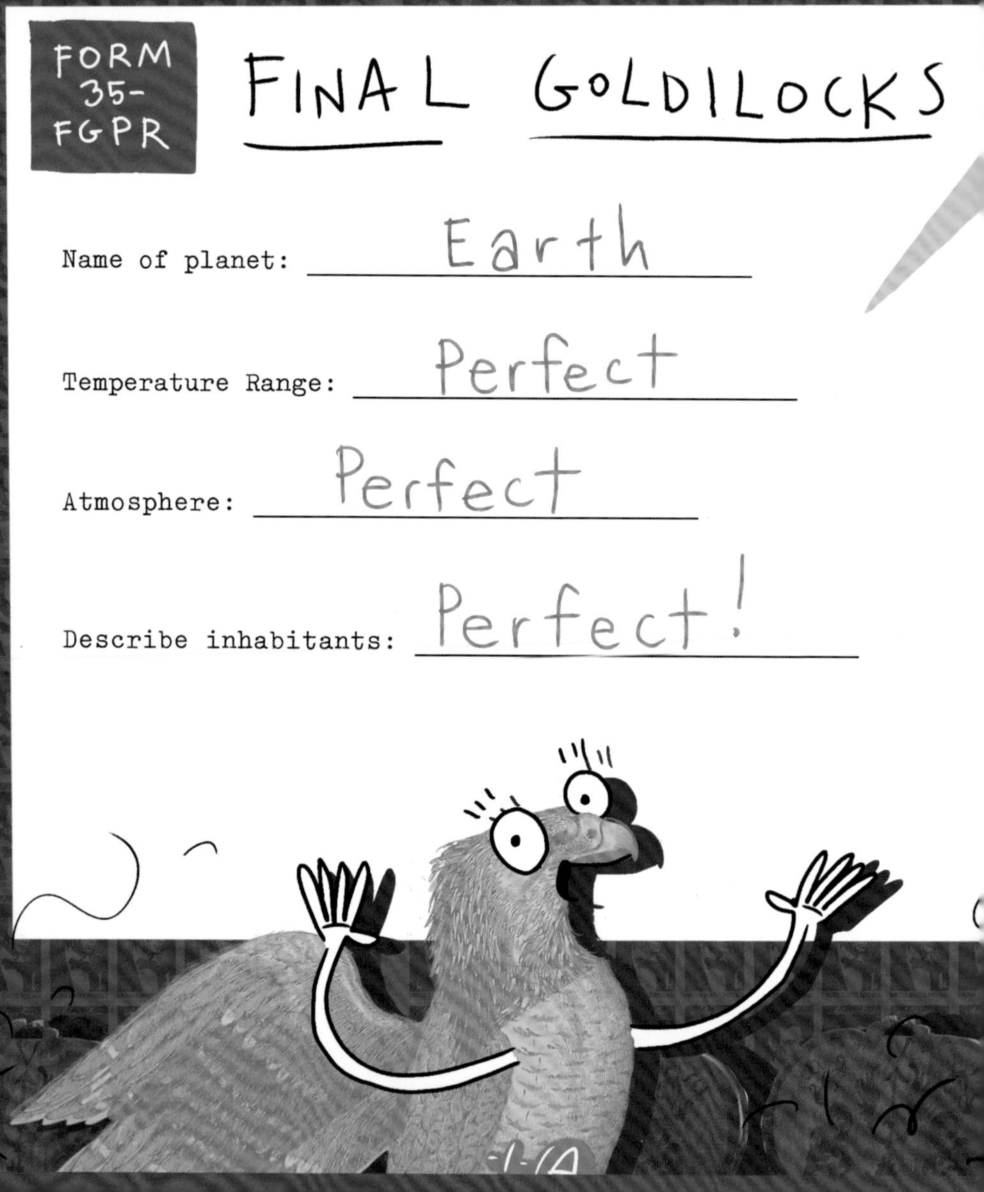
FORM 35-FGPR
FINAL GOLDILOCKS
Name of planet: Earth
Temperature Range: Perfect
Atmosphere: Perfect
Describe inhabitants: Perfect!

I filled out Form 35-FGPR for all of us!

What a mission!

We have identified that Earth, in this stage, is perfect.

Now all we have to do is find the humans and make sure they do not discover fire and change anything.

PLANET REPORT

Planet has Liquid Water: TRUE/FALSE

Humans could find
Food and Shelter here: TRUE/FALSE

Planet ecosystem
well-balanced: TRUE/FALSE

No intelligent life
harmed: TRUE/FALSE

OVERALL RATING:

a) Great
b) OK
c) Not good
d) Terrible
e) Your Head Explodes

Weirdly enough, just as SmartHawk said that, the Abe Lincoln Beard Vehicle rocked violently. Something crashed. The Lincoln Memorial Alarm wailed. . . .

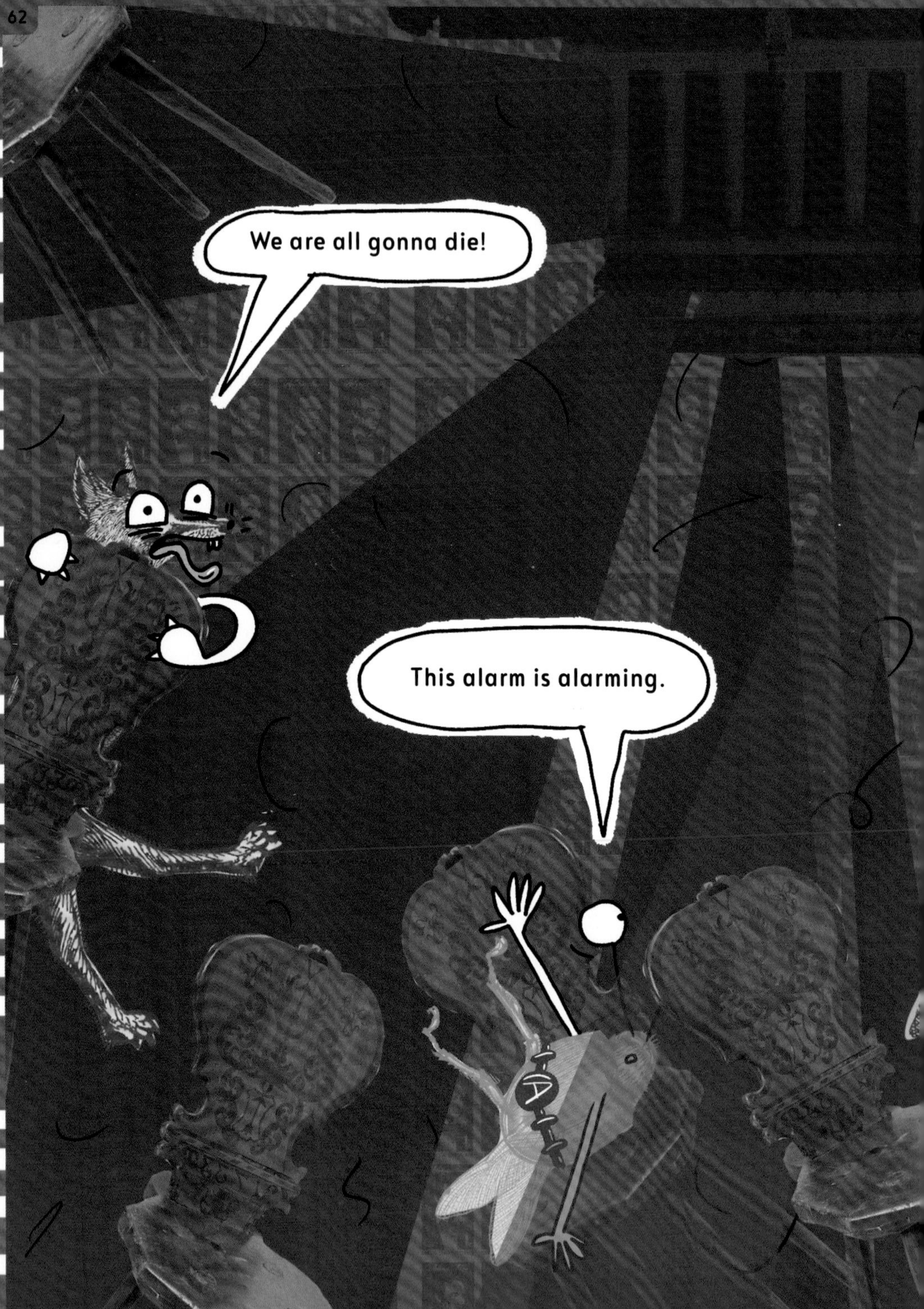
We are all gonna die!
This alarm is alarming.

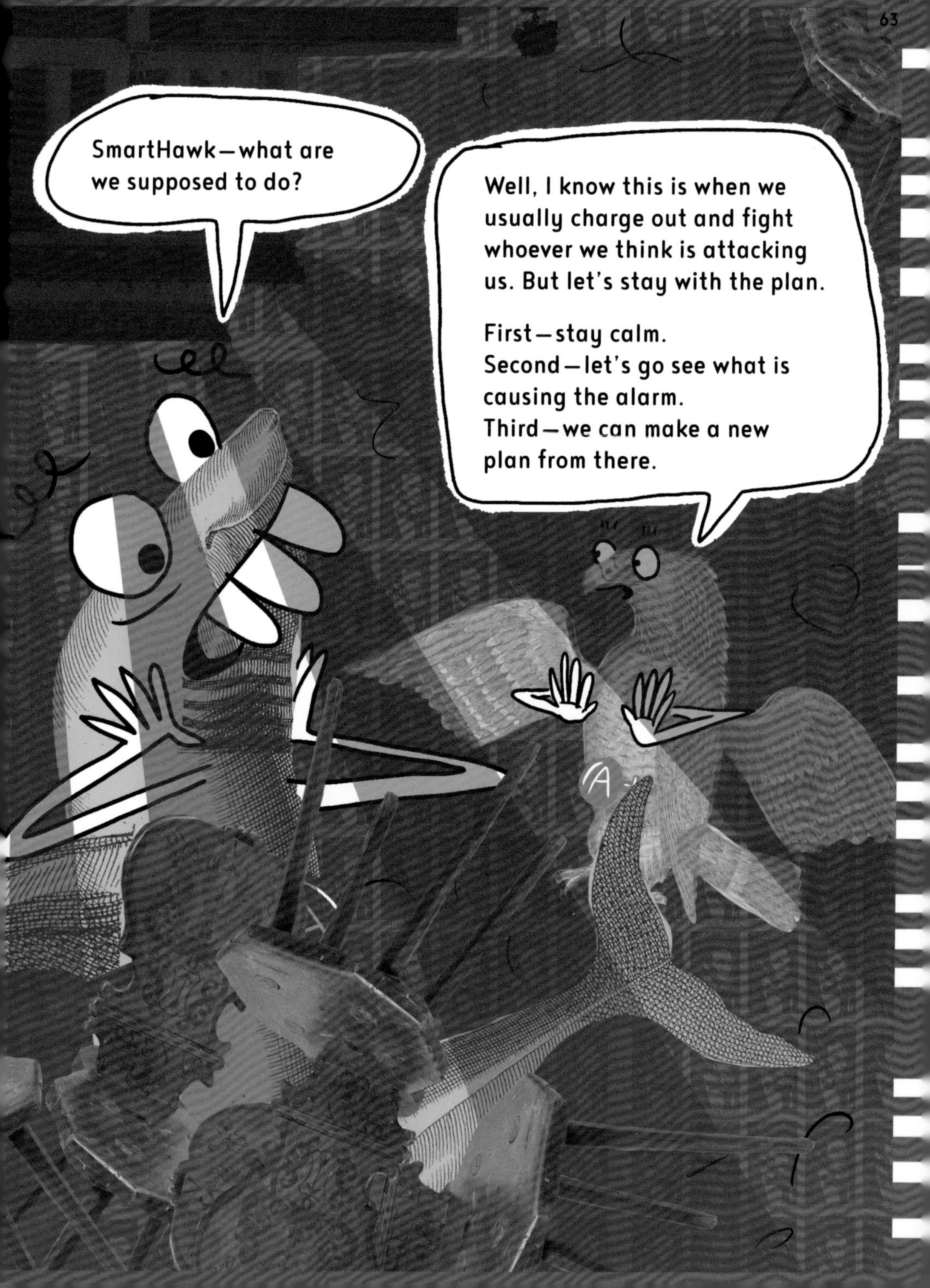
SmartHawk—what are we supposed to do?
Well, I know this is when we usually charge out and fight whoever we think is attacking us. But let's stay with the plan.
First—stay calm.
Second—let's go see what is causing the alarm.
Third—we can make a new plan from there.

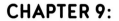

CHAPTER 9:

What's in Your Beard?

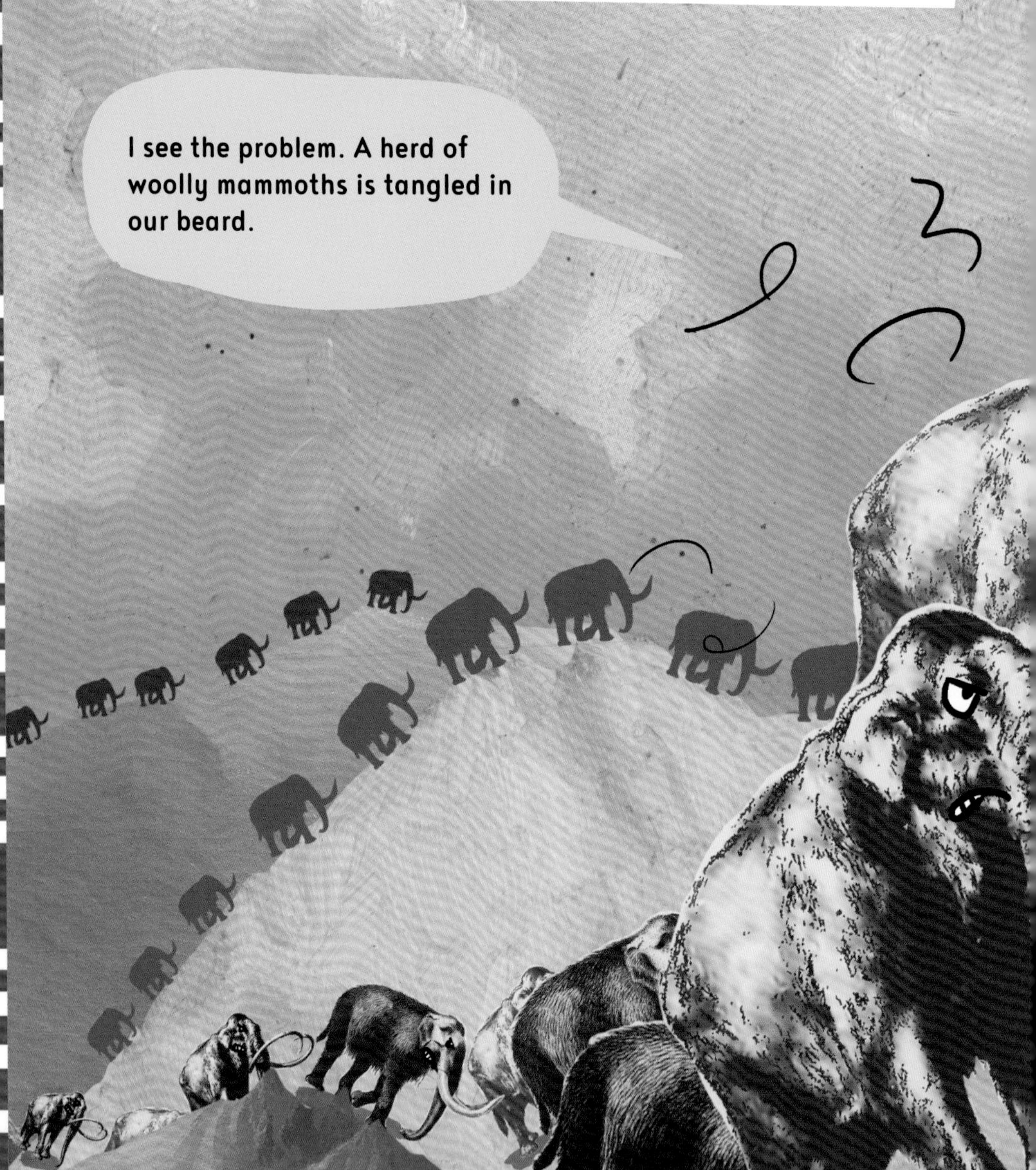
I see the problem. A herd of woolly mammoths is tangled in our beard.

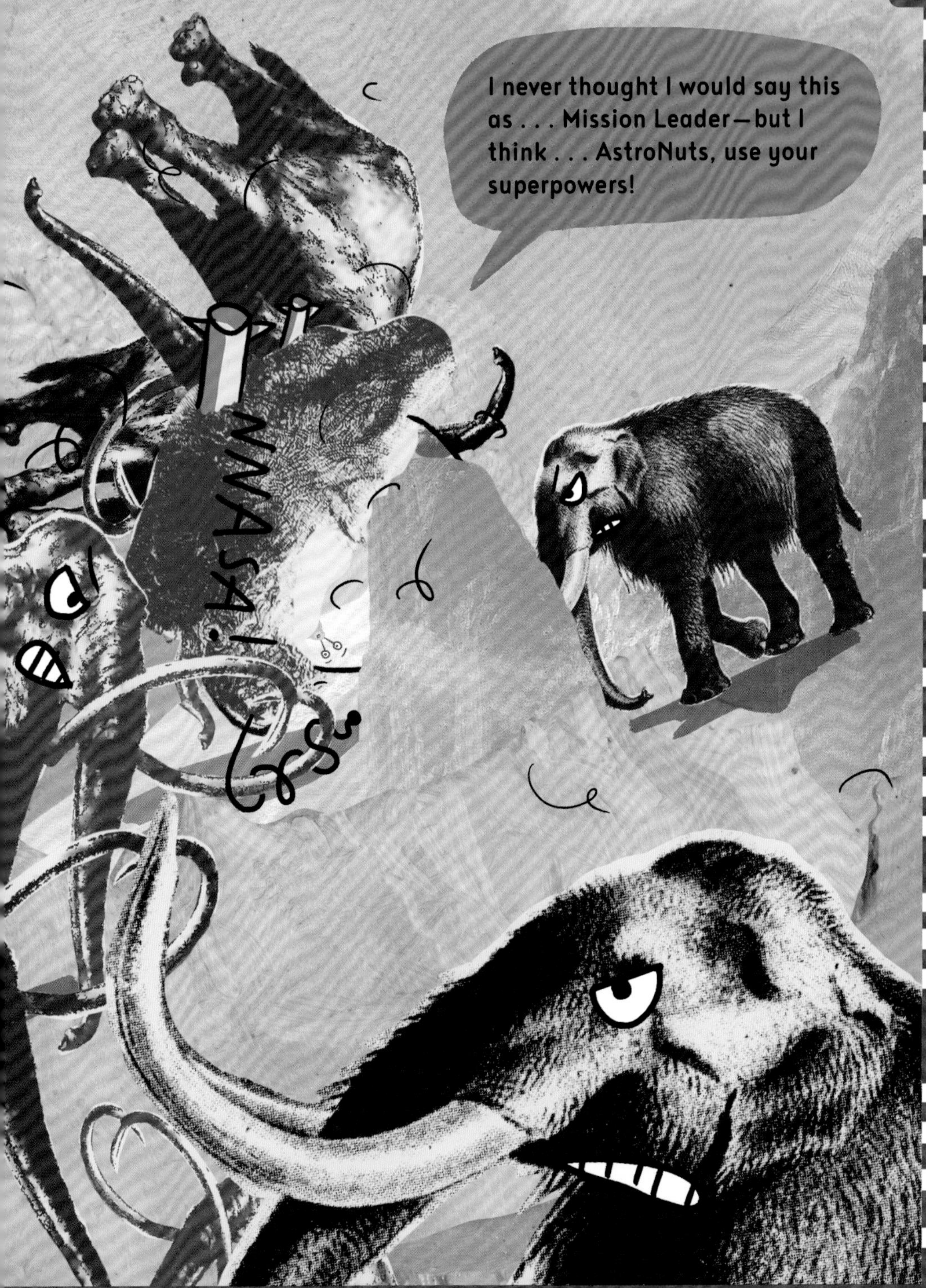
I never thought I would say this as . . . Mission Leader—but I think . . . AstroNuts, use your superpowers!
NNASA!

And did they ever!

You know I've been around for a few years. Well, more like four to five billion years. And I have seen a lot of fights in my time. Everything from megalodon vs. leviathan in my deep seas to red ants vs. black ants on my rich lands.

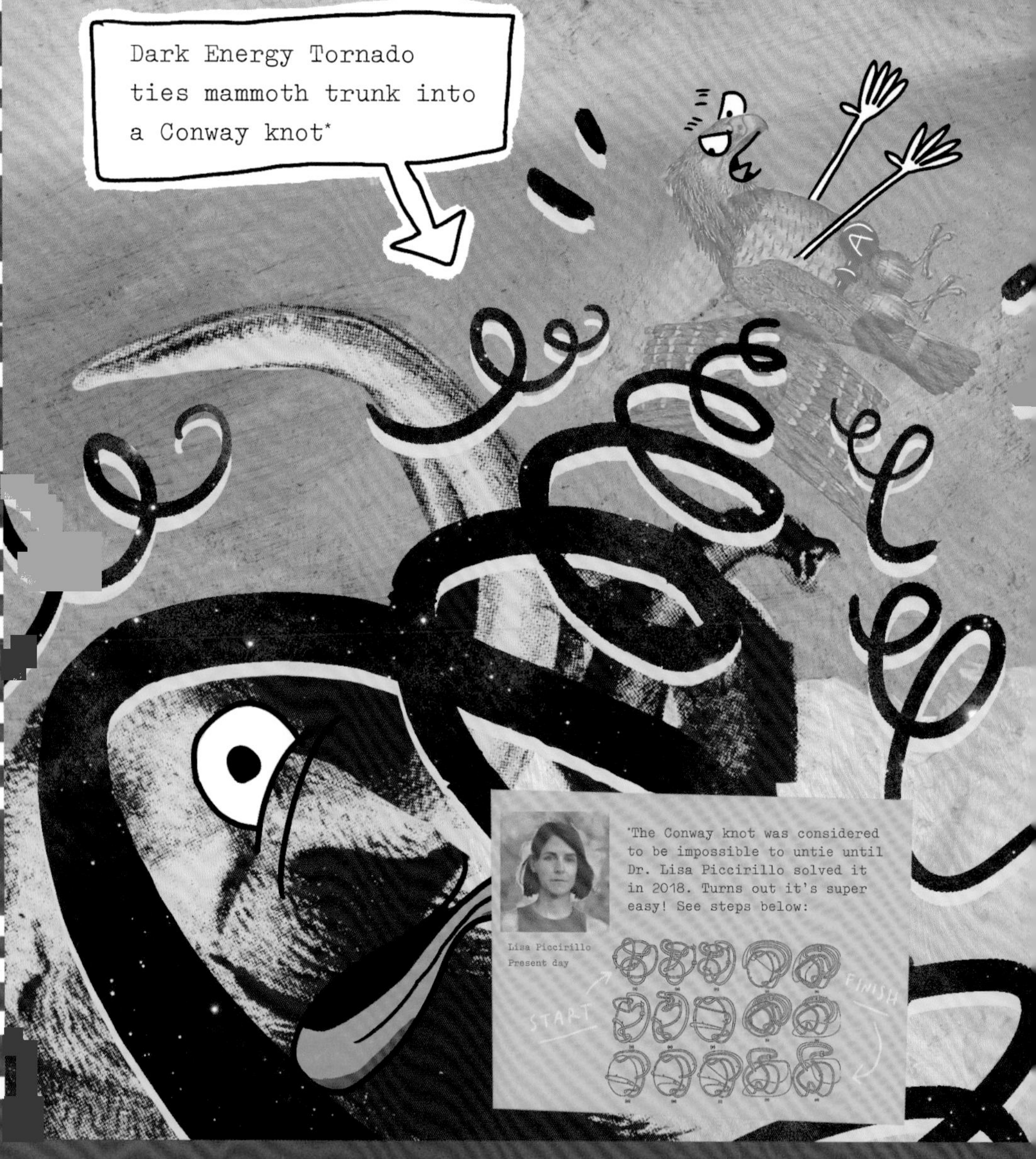
Dark Energy Tornado ties mammoth trunk into a Conway knot*
*The Conway knot was considered to be impossible to untie until Dr. Lisa Piccirillo solved it in 2018. Turns out it's super easy! See steps below:
Lisa Piccirillo
Present day
START
FINISH

And I can honestly tell you I have never seen a fight as weird as woolly mammoths vs. superpowered AstroNuts in an Abraham Lincoln Beard.

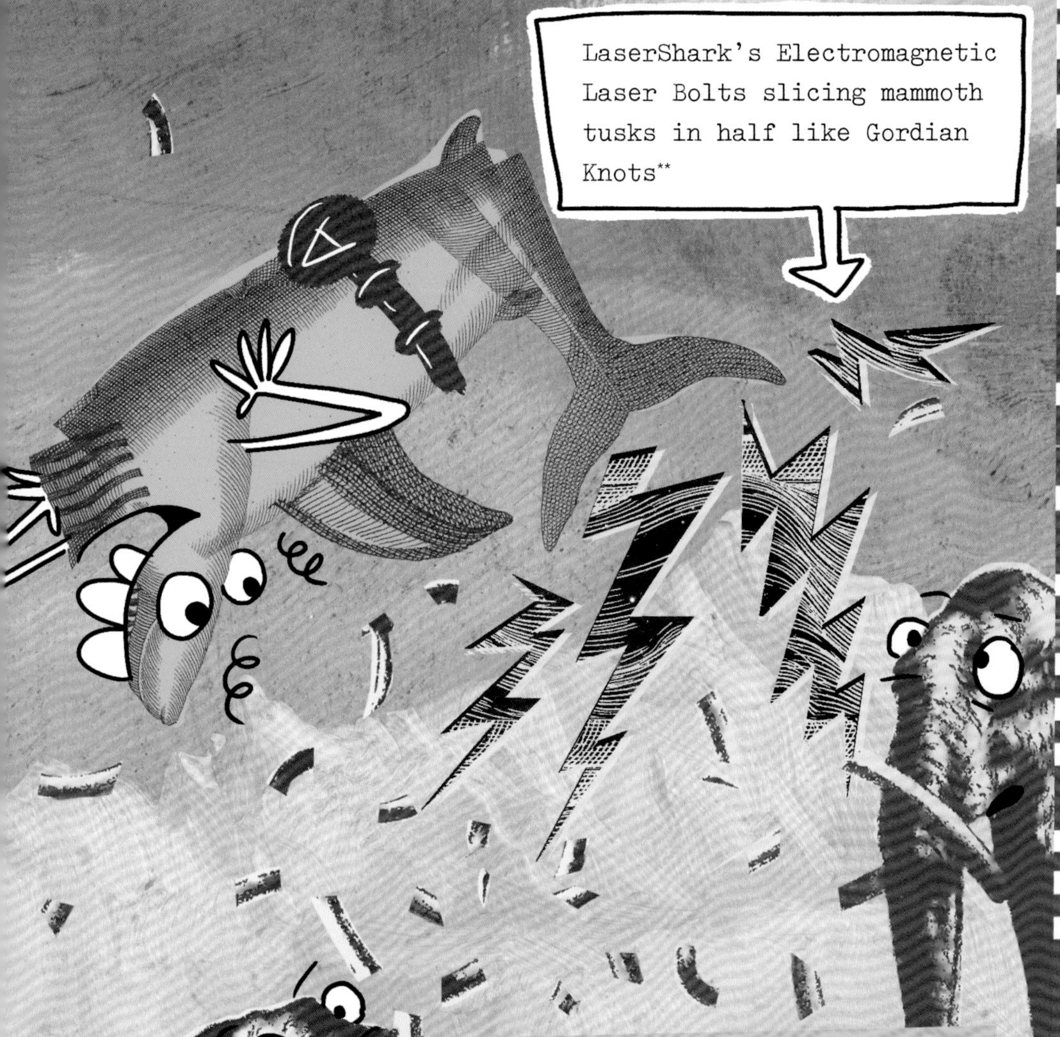
LaserShark's Electromagnetic Laser Bolts slicing mammoth tusks in half like Gordian Knots**

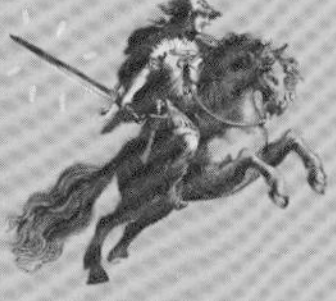
Alexander the Great
356–323 BCE

**In 333 BCE, Alexander the Great was shown the Gordian Knot. He was told he would not be successful unless he could undo the knot. He took out his sword and cut the Gordian Knot in half.

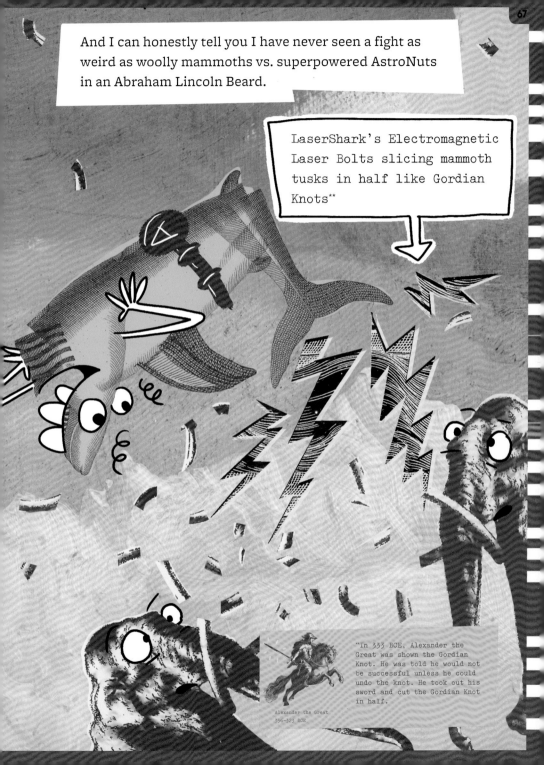

Small correction to my earlier description: MOST of the AstroNuts were attacking. Some of them were just picking.

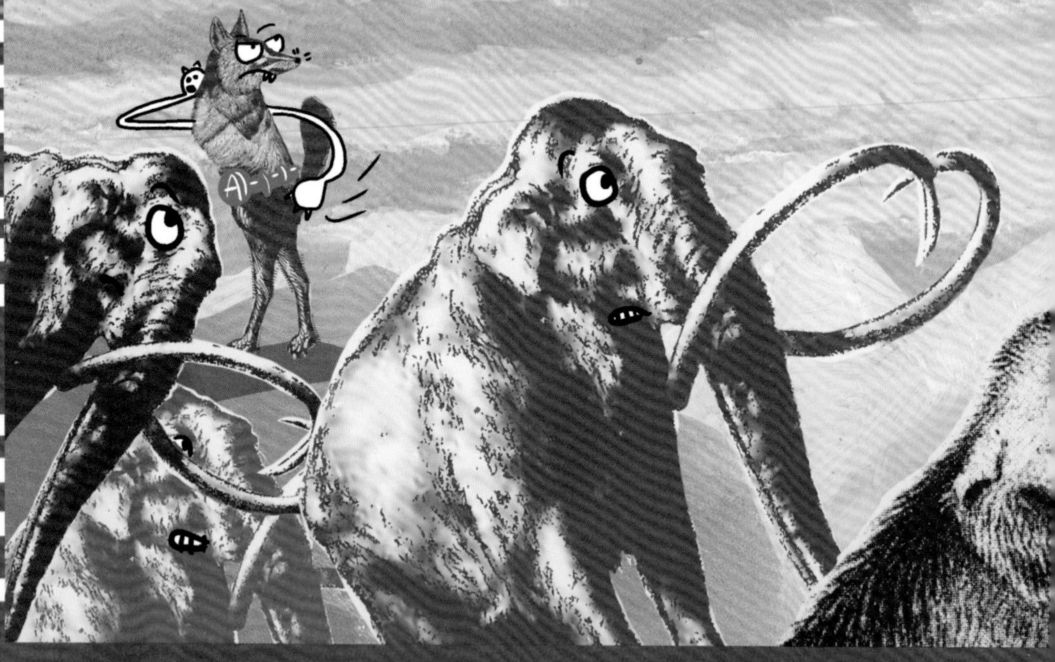
REAL-STRONG-IUM claws picking AlphaButt*

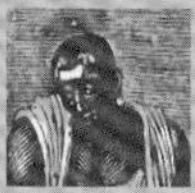
Brahmagupta
598-c. 665

*Picking one's AlphaButt is kinda like doing nothing, which is a lot like zero. One of the first mentions of the concept of zero was by an Indian mathematician named Brahmagupta in the 600s.

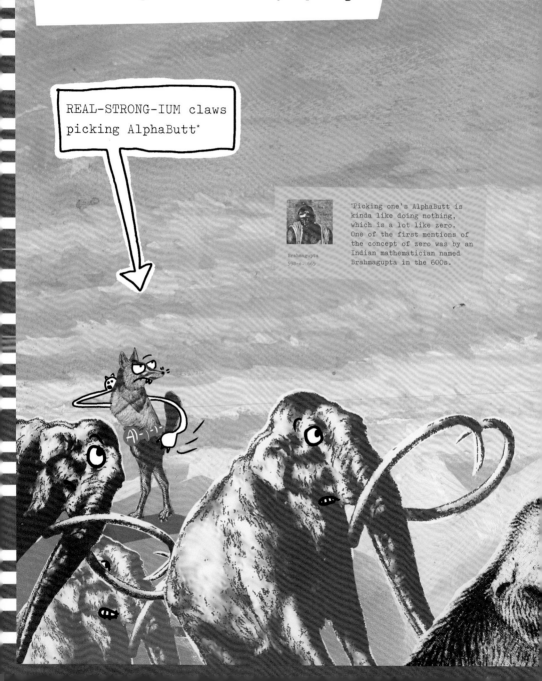

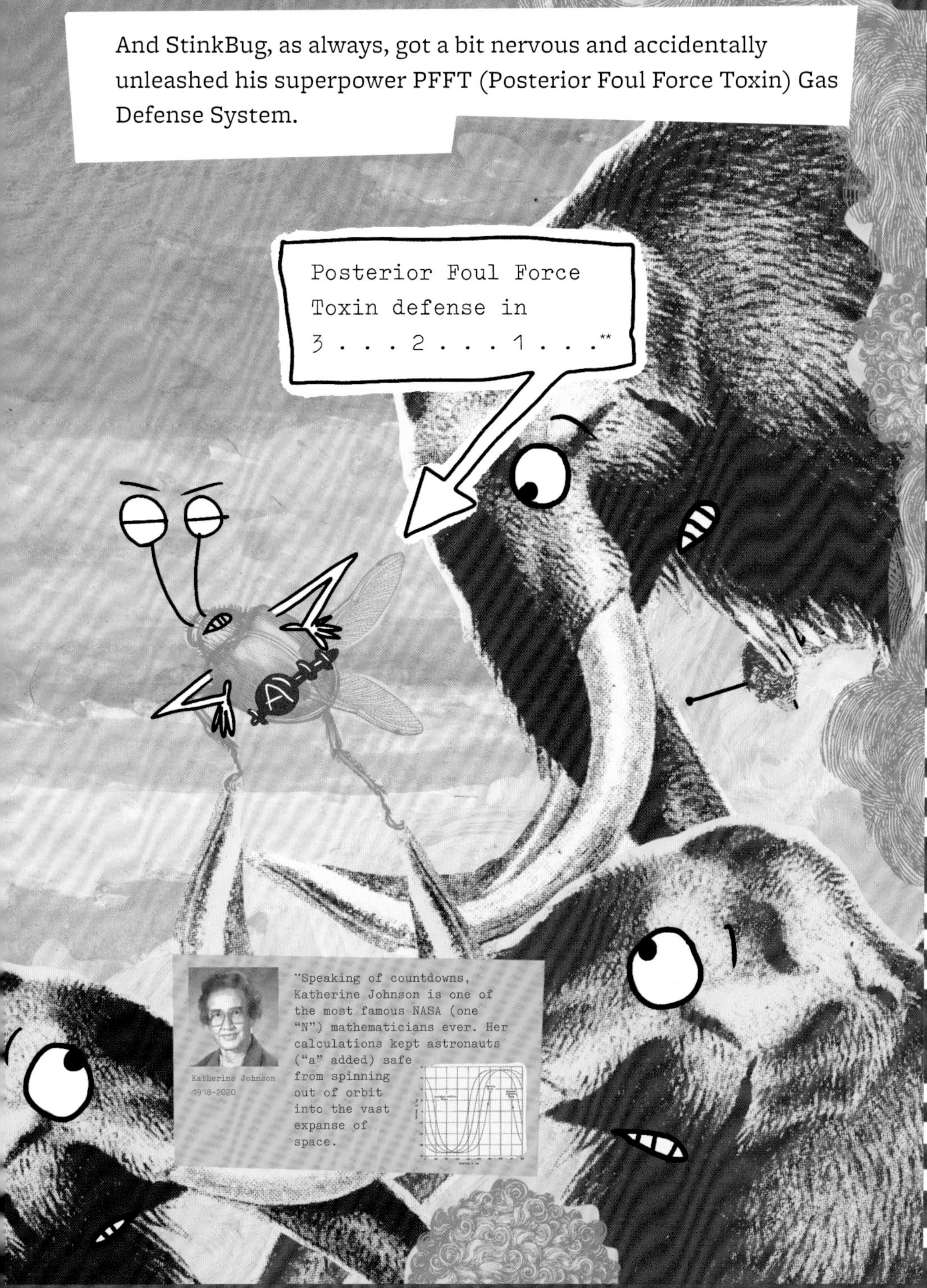
And StinkBug, as always, got a bit nervous and accidentally unleashed his superpower PFFT (Posterior Foul Force Toxin) Gas Defense System.
Posterior Foul Force Toxin defense in 3 . . . 2 . . . 1 . . .**
**Speaking of countdowns, Katherine Johnson is one of the most famous NASA (one "N") mathematicians ever. Her calculations kept astronauts ("a" added) safe from spinning out of orbit into the vast expanse of space.
Katherine Johnson
1918-2020

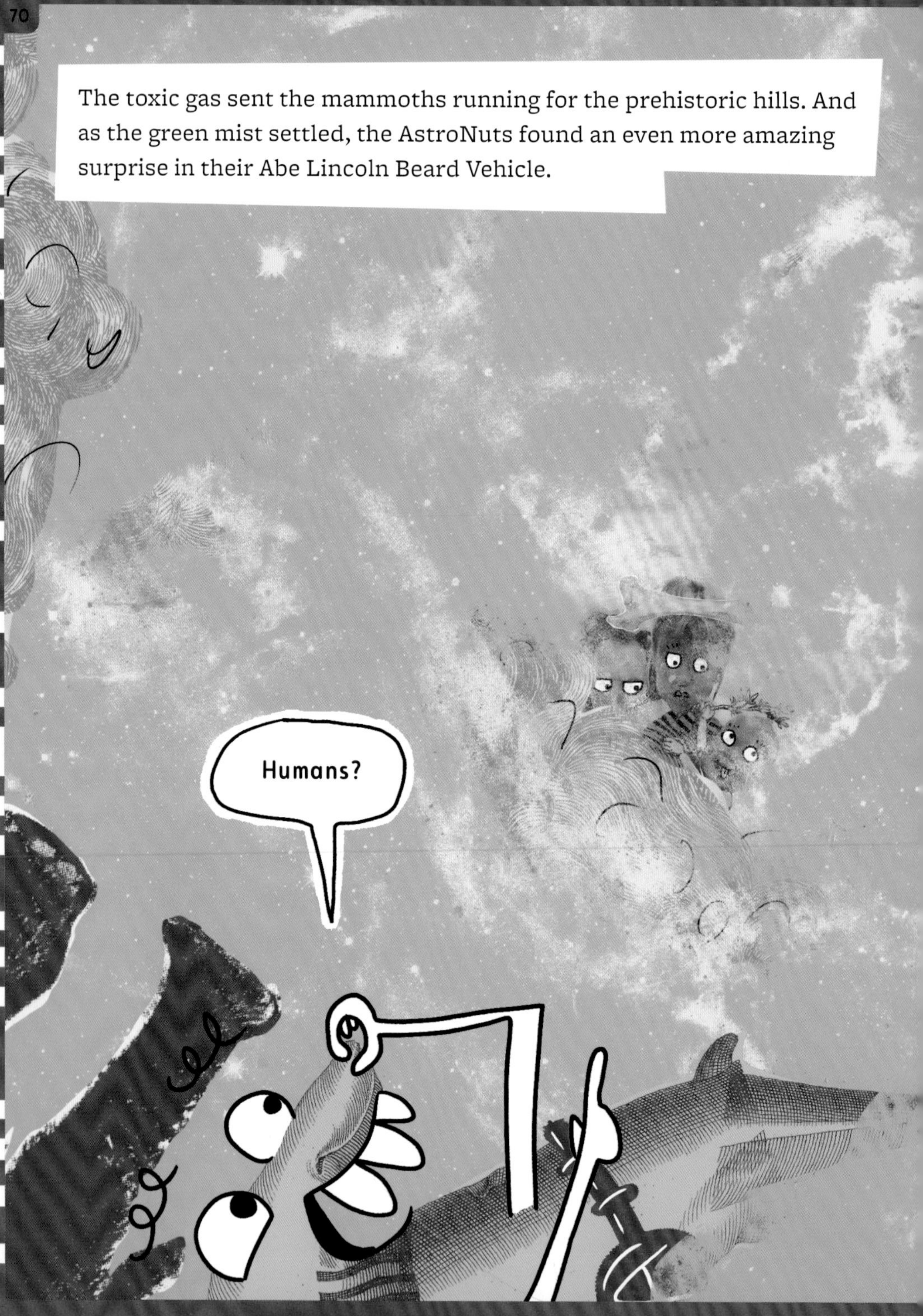
The toxic gas sent the mammoths running for the prehistoric hills. And as the green mist settled, the AstroNuts found an even more amazing surprise in their Abe Lincoln Beard Vehicle.
Humans?

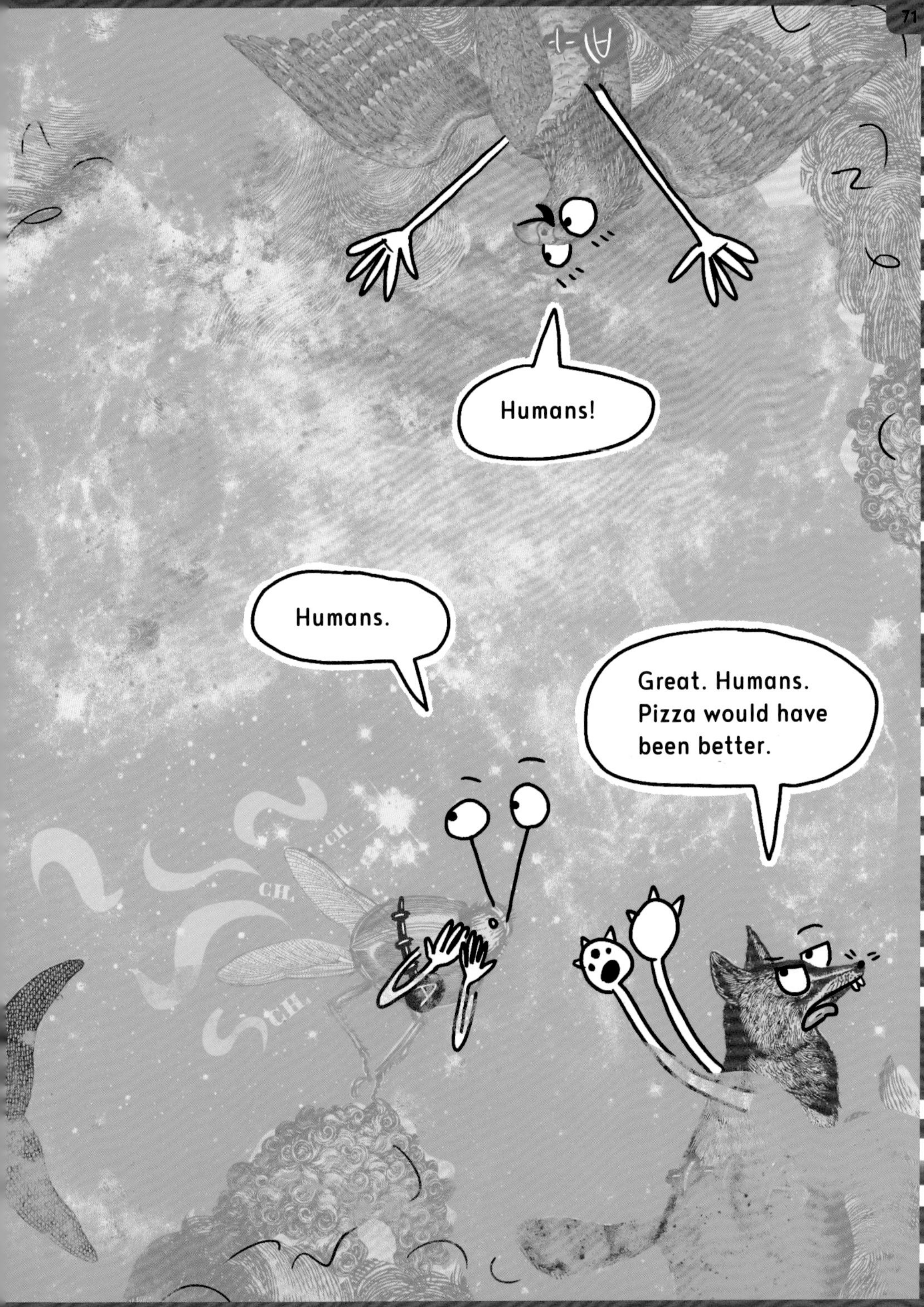
Humans!
Humans.
Great. Humans. Pizza would have been better.

CHAPTER 10:

Really, Humans!

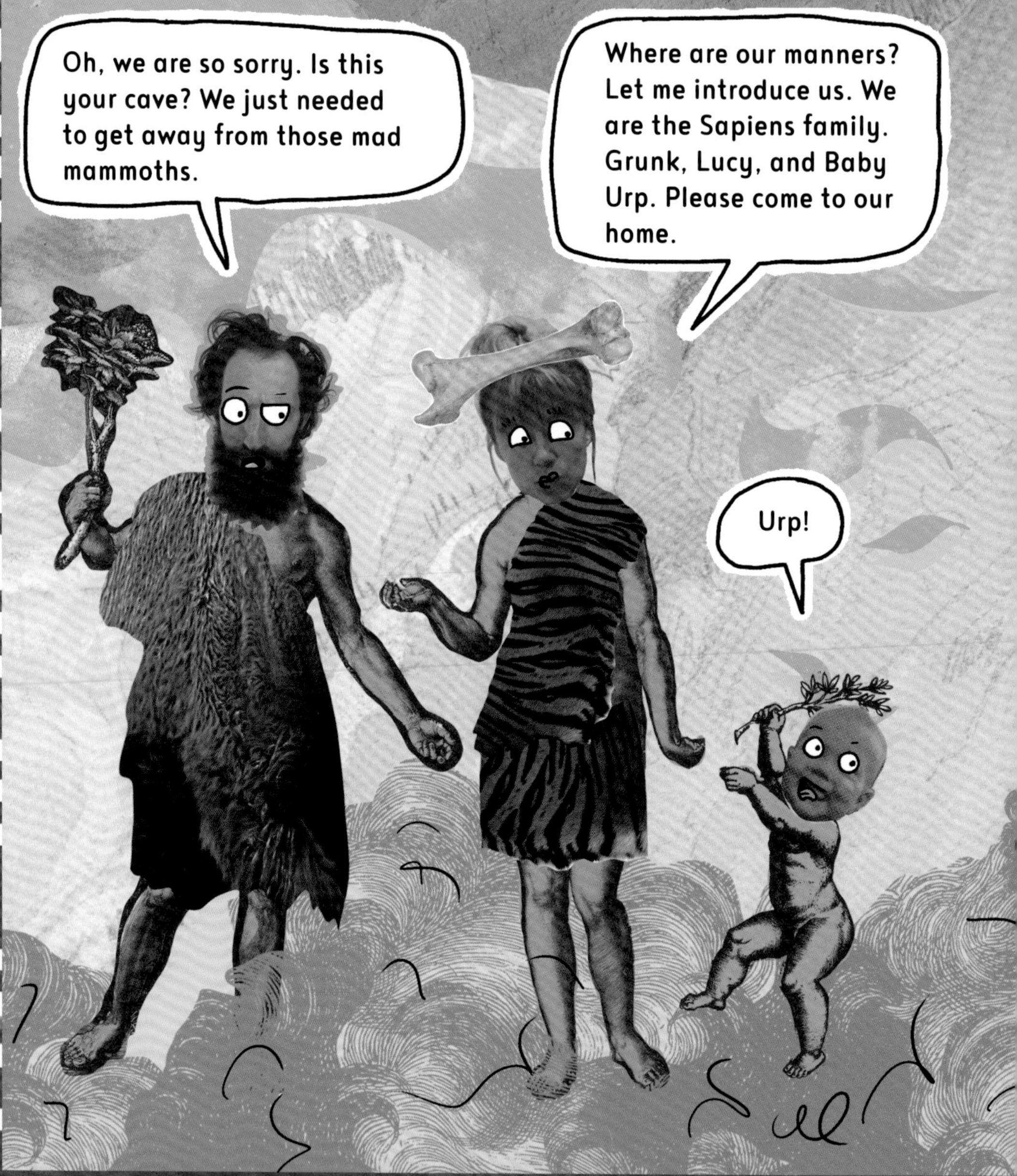

Oh, we are so sorry. Is this your cave? We just needed to get away from those mad mammoths.
Where are our manners? Let me introduce us. We are the Sapiens family. Grunk, Lucy, and Baby Urp. Please come to our home.
Urp!

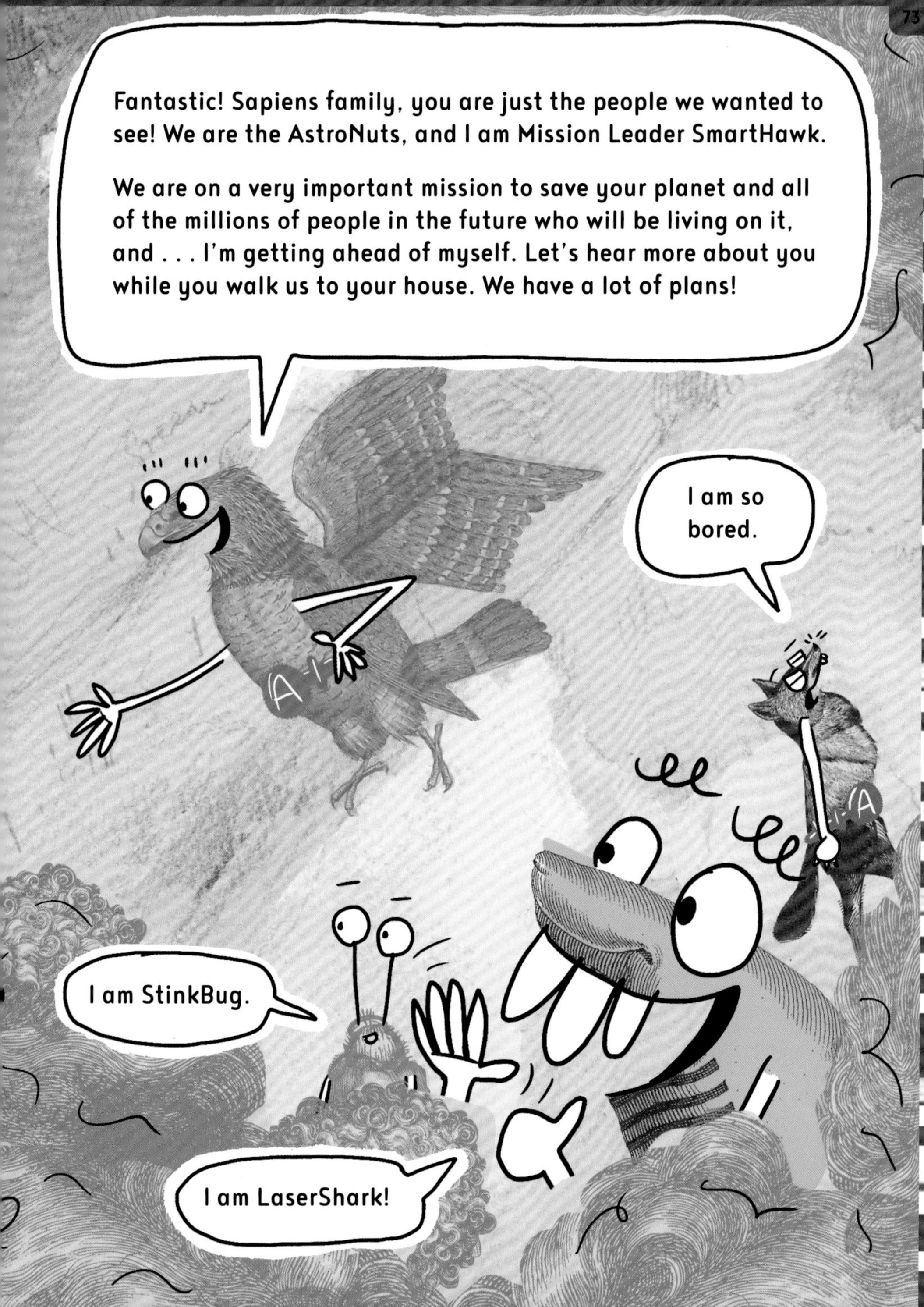
Fantastic! Sapiens family, you are just the people we wanted to see! We are the AstroNuts, and I am Mission Leader SmartHawk.
We are on a very important mission to save your planet and all of the millions of people in the future who will be living on it, and . . . I'm getting ahead of myself. Let's hear more about you while you walk us to your house. We have a lot of plans!
I am so bored.
I am StinkBug.
I am LaserShark!

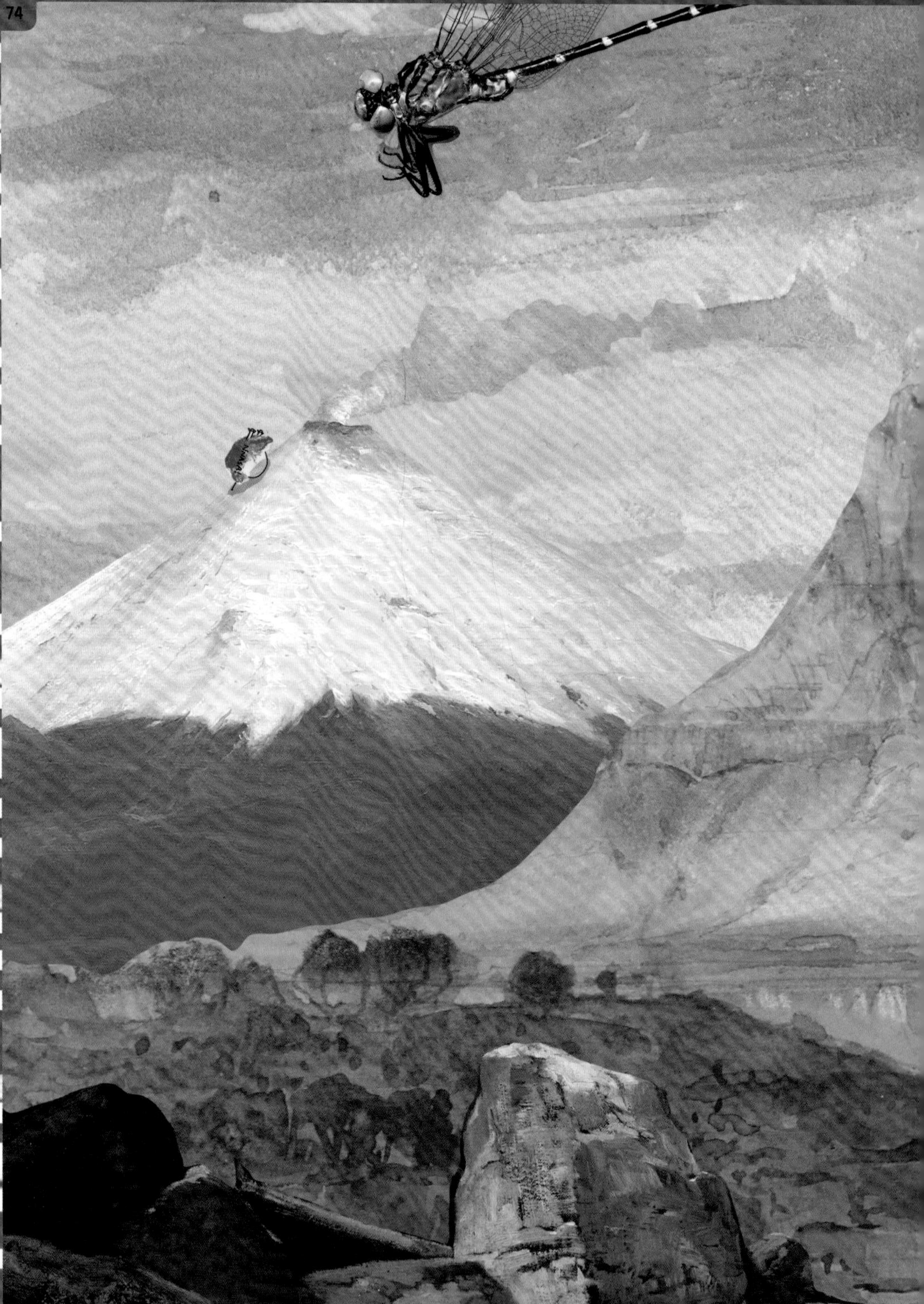

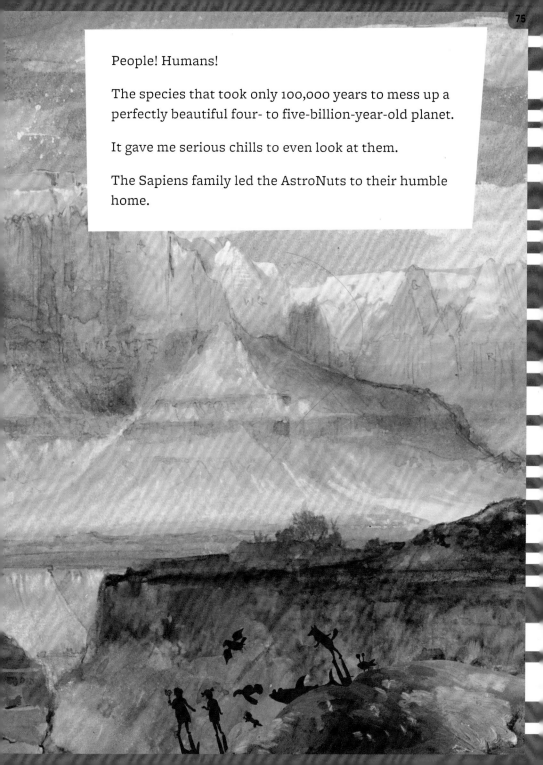

People! Humans!

The species that took only 100,000 years to mess up a perfectly beautiful four- to five-billion-year-old planet.

It gave me serious chills to even look at them.

The Sapiens family led the AstroNuts to their humble home.

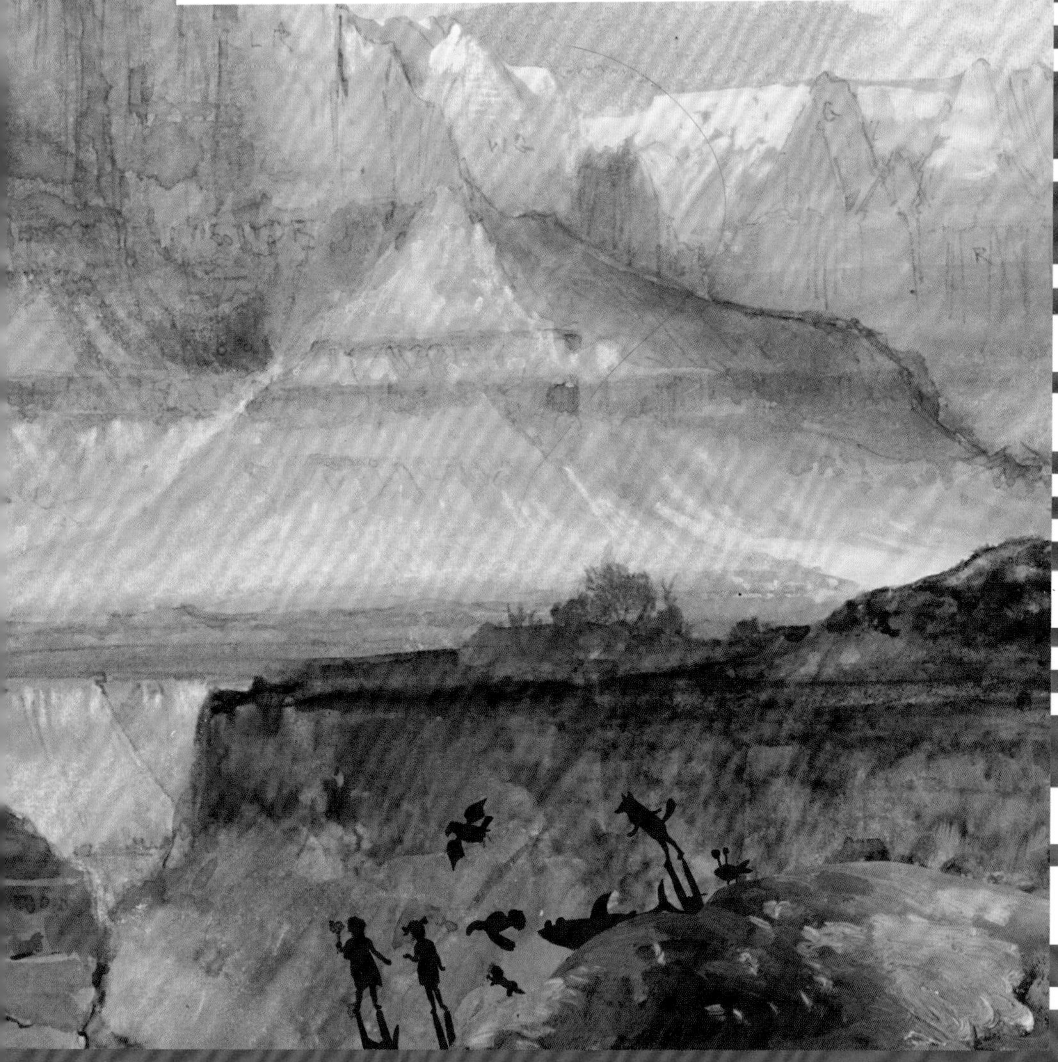

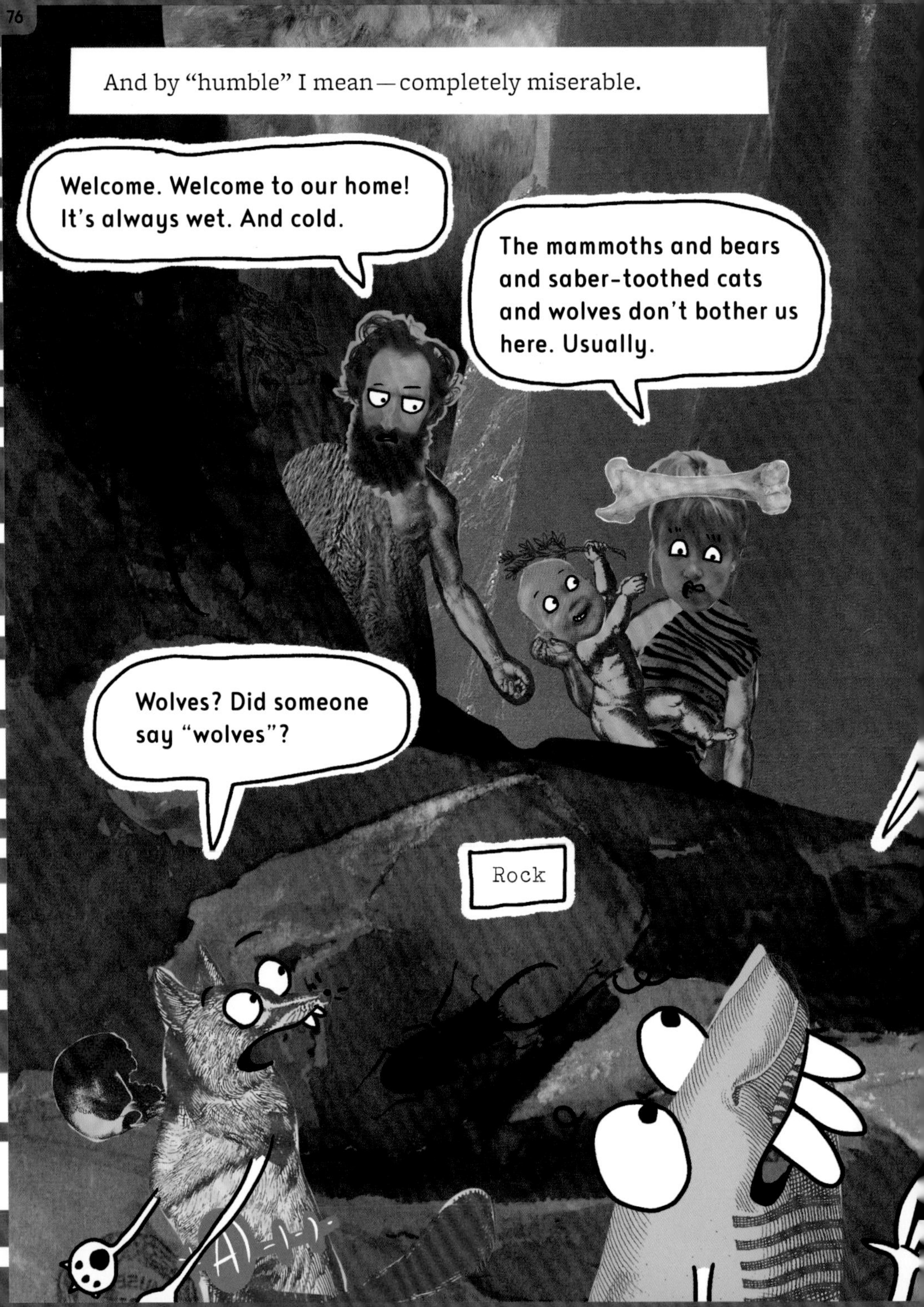
And by "humble" I mean—completely miserable.
Welcome. Welcome to our home! It's always wet. And cold.
The mammoths and bears and saber-toothed cats and wolves don't bother us here. Usually.
Wolves? Did someone say "wolves"?
Rock

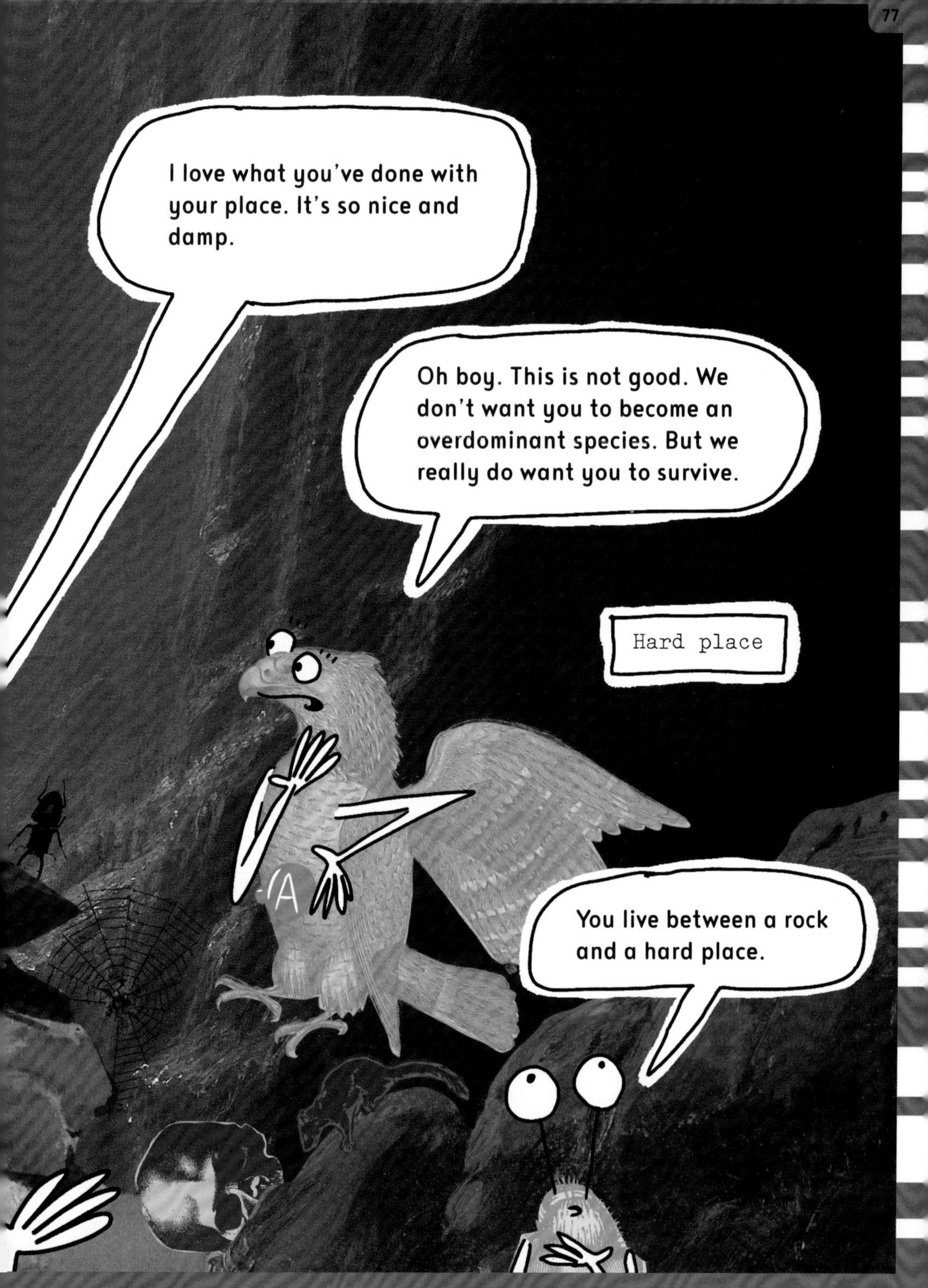
I love what you've done with your place. It's so nice and damp.
Oh boy. This is not good. We don't want you to become an overdominant species. But we really do want you to survive.
Hard place
You live between a rock and a hard place.

What StinkBug said was true. The Sapiens family was living between a rock and a hard place. What StinkBug said was also an idiom. That's a phrase that means more than it actually says. "Between a rock and a hard place" means being in a difficult situation where both choices for a solution are bad.

As a human, you might not want to hear this. But the tough science is: you humans are not the most likely to be in charge, or even survive.

Here's what you don't have:

No sharp teeth. No warm fur. No tough skin.
You are not fast. Not strong. Not big. No poison fangs, no stingers, no sharp claws to defend yourself. No camouflage, no small size to hide yourself.

But here is the one thing you do have:

Brains!

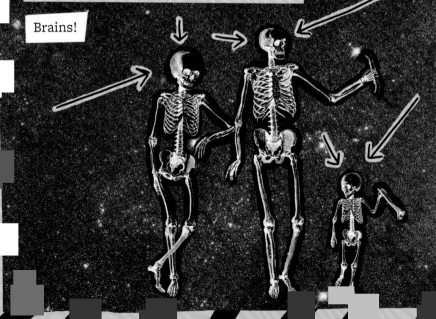

And these brains make all the difference.

Brains give humans the huge advantages of speech, memory, group communication, and organization. Tool- and weapon-making, hunting, farming, logical thinking, scientific learning. Inventing, writing, art, music, dance, geography class-cutting, green pants-wearing, terrible haircut-giving . . .

The big brain is also what helped humans discover the power of fire. Human brains figured out that fire was the best tool of all. Fire gives humans all the warmth, strength, defense, and digestible food that you don't naturally have.

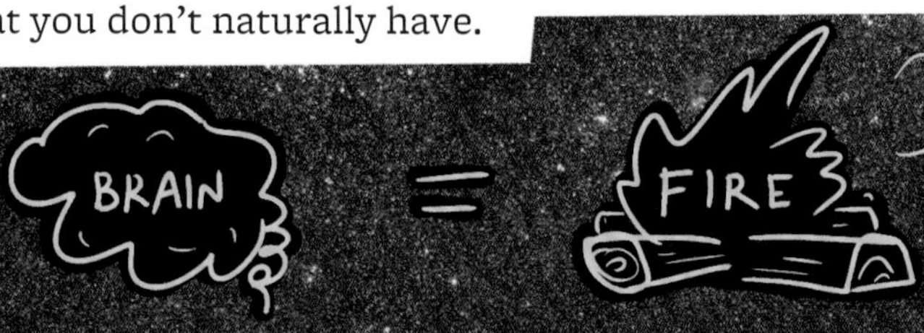
BRAIN
=
FIRE

But here is the problem. That same smart human brain also led humans to take fossil fuels like oil and coal out of me, and invent things like cars and factories that polluted me and overheated me.

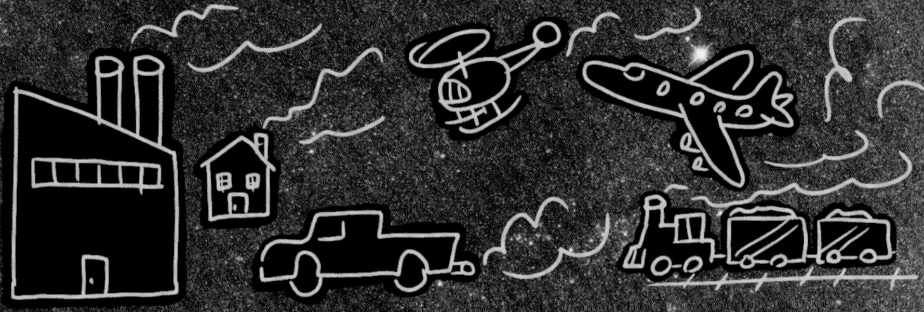

So yes, it was the Sapiens family who were living between a rock and a hard place. But it was the AstroNuts who were really "between a rock and a hard place." They had to find a way to help humans not get wiped out by bigger, stronger, faster species. But they could not let them figure out that the best way to do that was . . . by discovering fire.

The whole mess got me thinking. Maybe it wouldn't be the worst thing to have another species in charge. Humans had their shot. And look where it got us—in a global climate catastrophe.

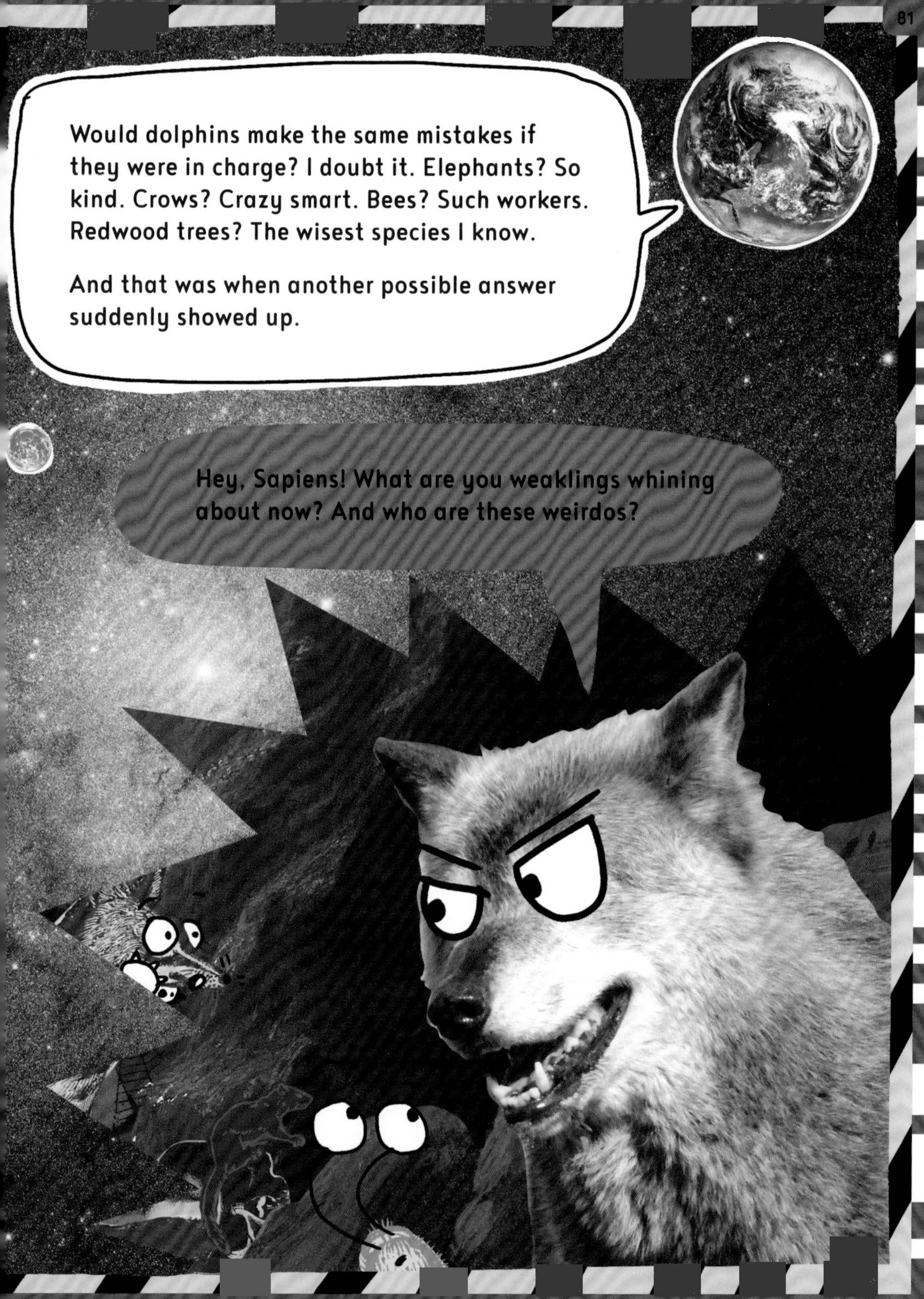
Would dolphins make the same mistakes if they were in charge? I doubt it. Elephants? So kind. Crows? Crazy smart. Bees? Such workers. Redwood trees? The wisest species I know.
And that was when another possible answer suddenly showed up.
Hey, Sapiens! What are you weaklings whining about now? And who are these weirdos?

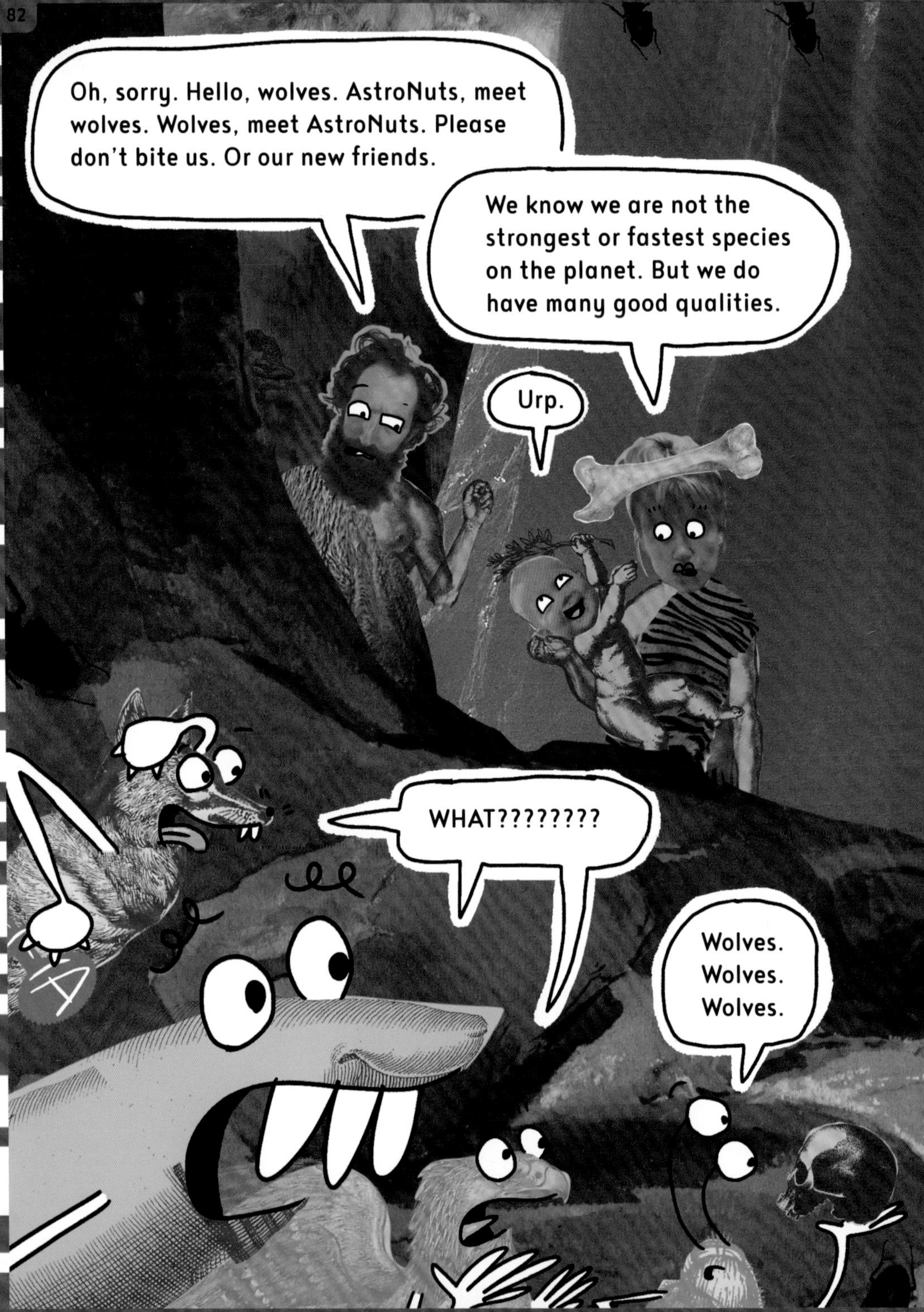
Oh, sorry. Hello, wolves. AstroNuts, meet wolves. Wolves, meet AstroNuts. Please don't bite us. Or our new friends.
We know we are not the strongest or fastest species on the planet. But we do have many good qualities.
Urp.
WHAT????????
Wolves.
Wolves.
Wolves.

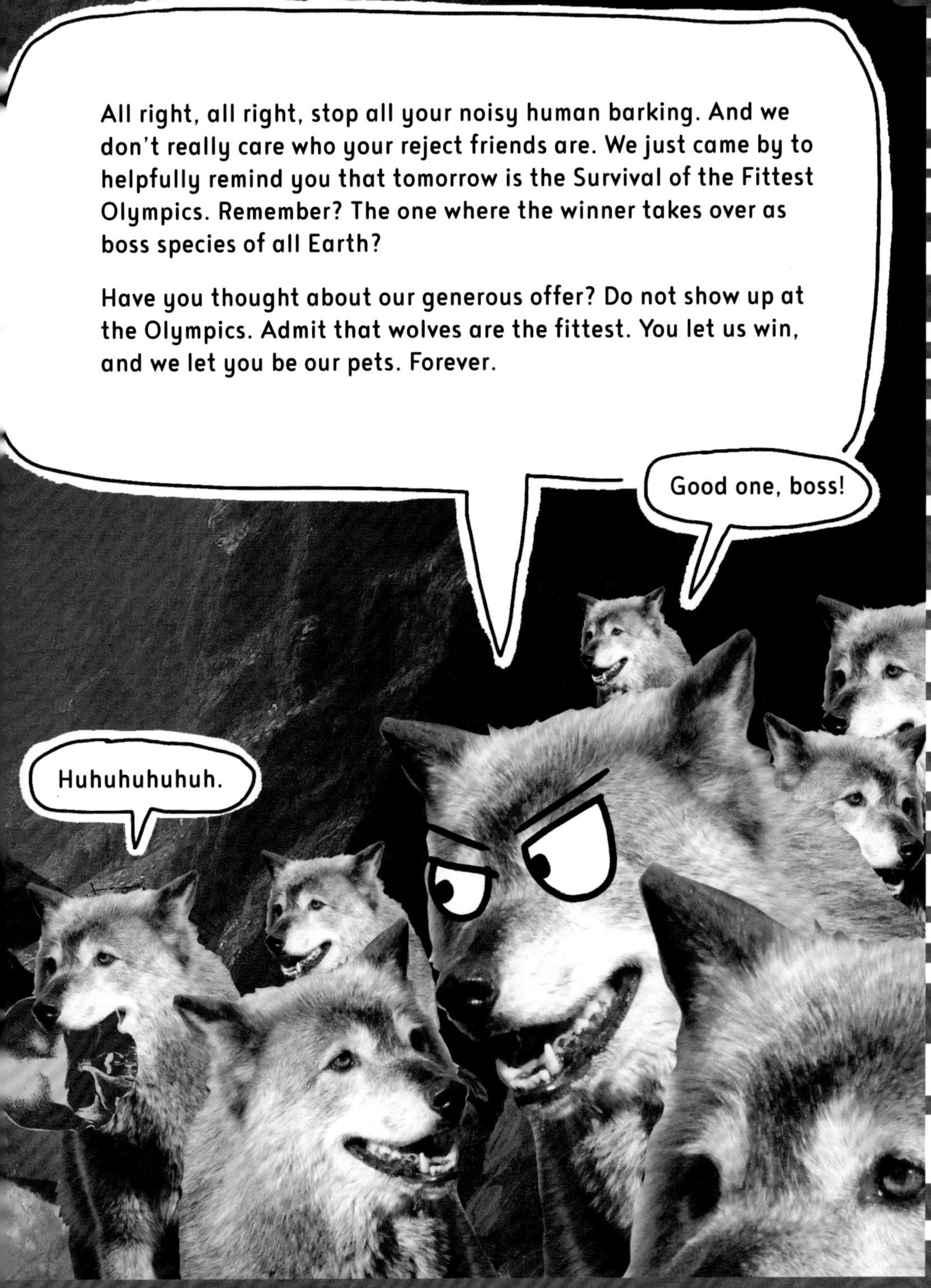
All right, all right, stop all your noisy human barking. And we don't really care who your reject friends are. We just came by to helpfully remind you that tomorrow is the Survival of the Fittest Olympics. Remember? The one where the winner takes over as boss species of all Earth?
Have you thought about our generous offer? Do not show up at the Olympics. Admit that wolves are the fittest. You let us win, and we let you be our pets. Forever.
Good one, boss!
Huhuhuhuhuh.

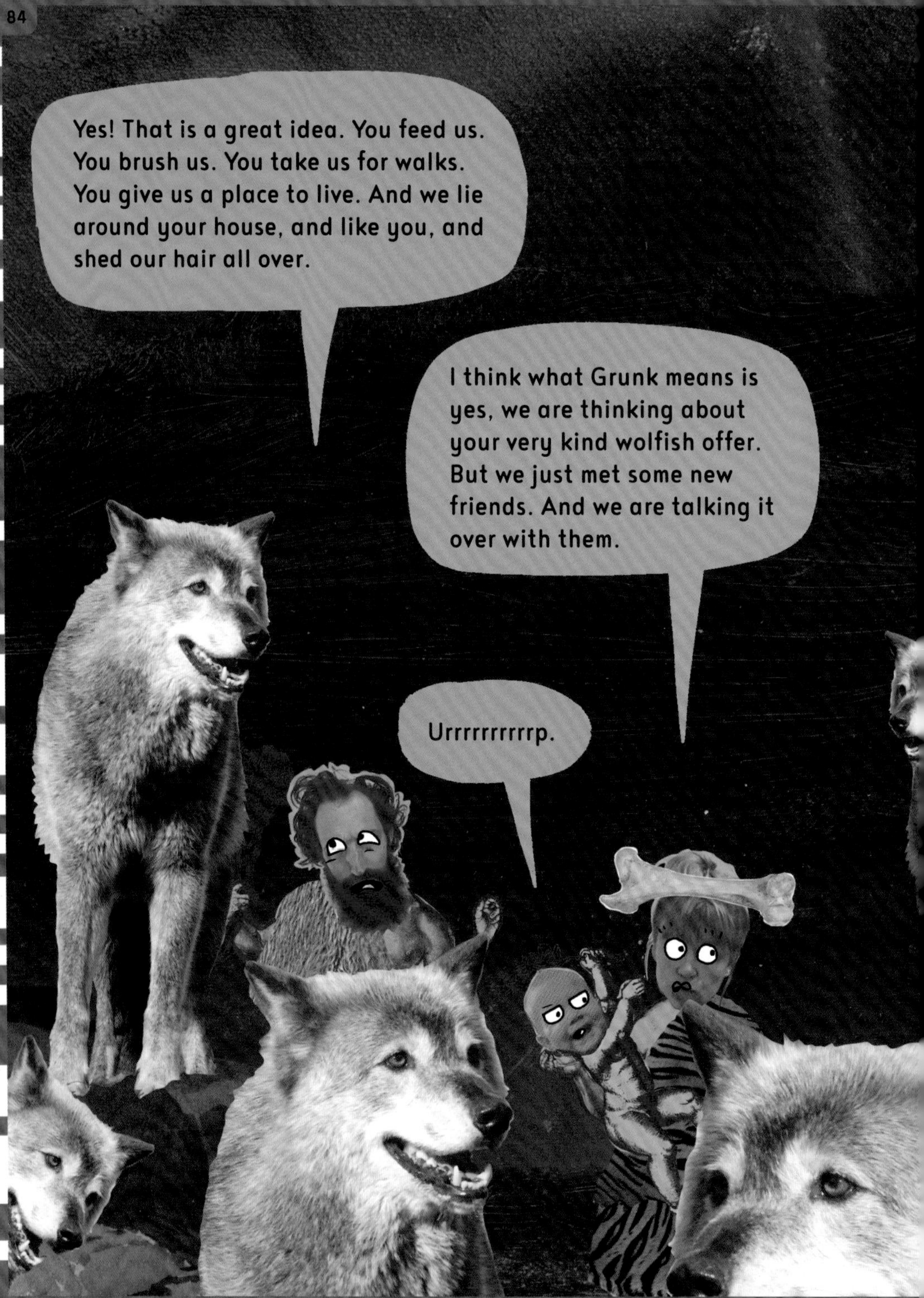
Yes! That is a great idea. You feed us. You brush us. You take us for walks. You give us a place to live. And we lie around your house, and like you, and shed our hair all over.
I think what Grunk means is yes, we are thinking about your very kind wolfish offer. But we just met some new friends. And we are talking it over with them.
Urrrrrrrrrp.

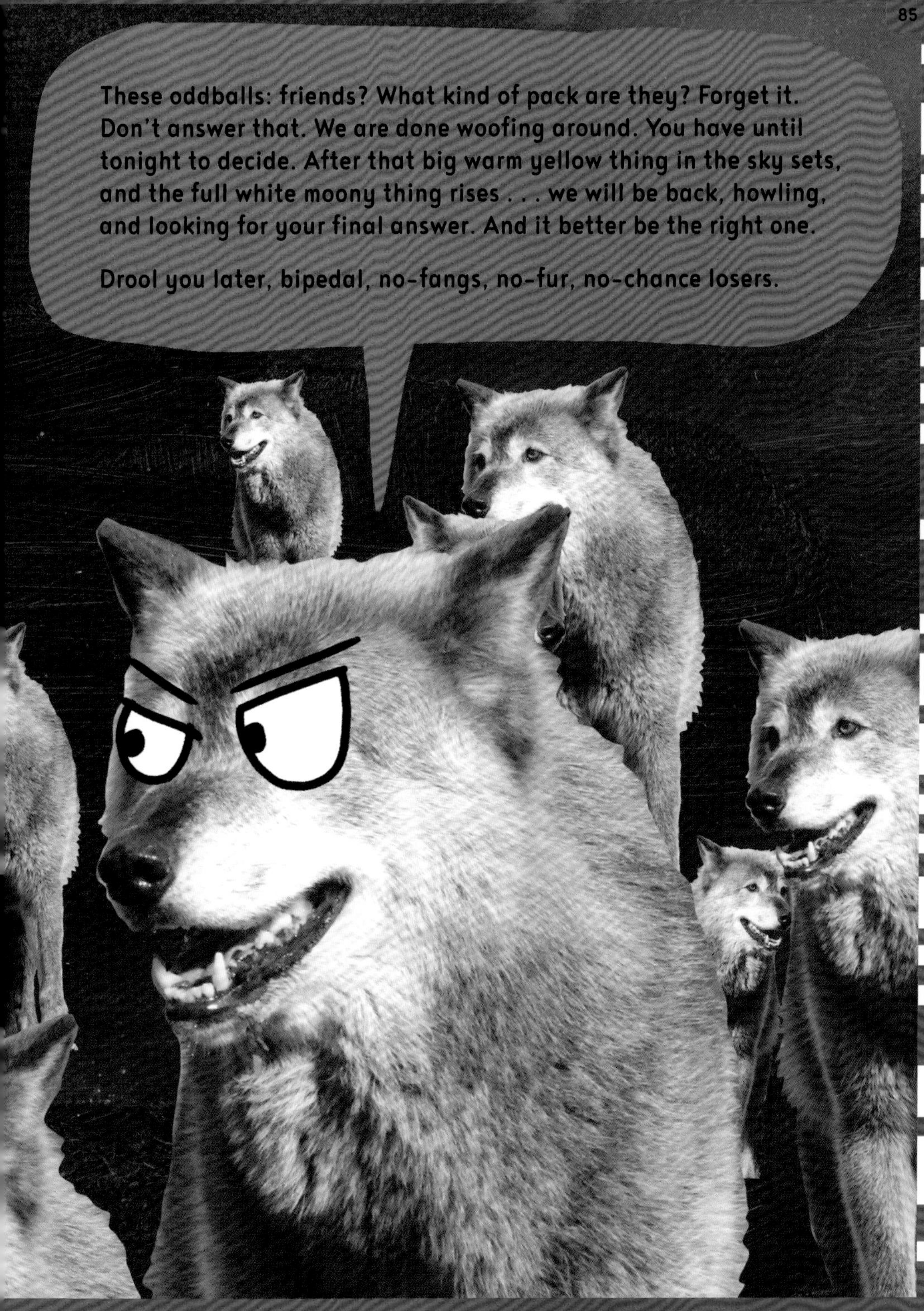
These oddballs: friends? What kind of pack are they? Forget it. Don't answer that. We are done woofing around. You have until tonight to decide. After that big warm yellow thing in the sky sets, and the full white moony thing rises . . . we will be back, howling, and looking for your final answer. And it better be the right one.
Drool you later, bipedal, no-fangs, no-fur, no-chance losers.

CHAPTER 11:
Earthtalk

Uhhhhh yeah, about that Survival of the Fittest Olympics. I may have kind of forgotten to tell you about that earlier.

I was young. I had a lot of crazy ideas. Natural selection was one of them.

I thought a contest might be the best way to find out which species should be in charge of the world.

So I invented the Survival of the Fittest. It's a contest where we find out who is fastest, strongest, smartest. The fittest win. The not-so-fit lose.

I know you humans think that one of you named Charles Darwin came up with these ideas of evolution and the survival of the fittest. But come on! I was using both of these ideas millions . . . truly, MILLIONS of years before Charles D. was wearing diapers.

Oh, humans. This is another reason why I love you and hate you. You are sometimes so smart but other times sooo clueless.

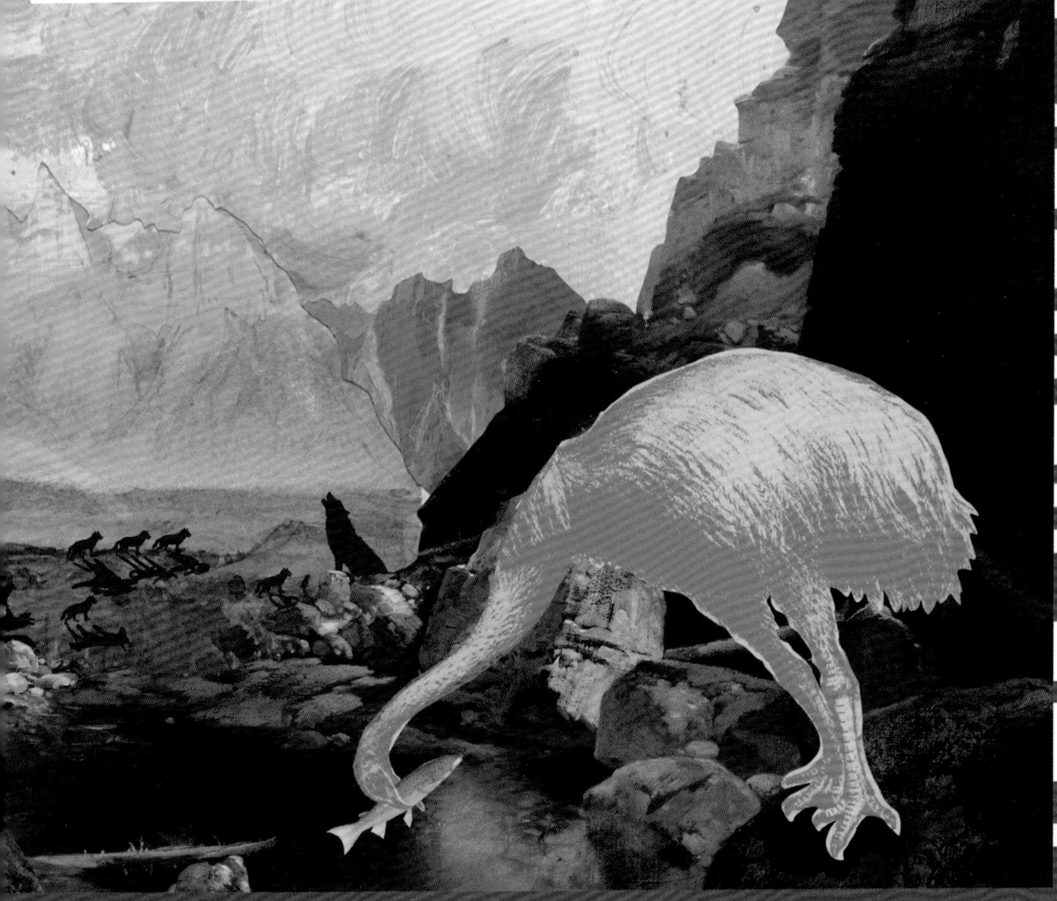

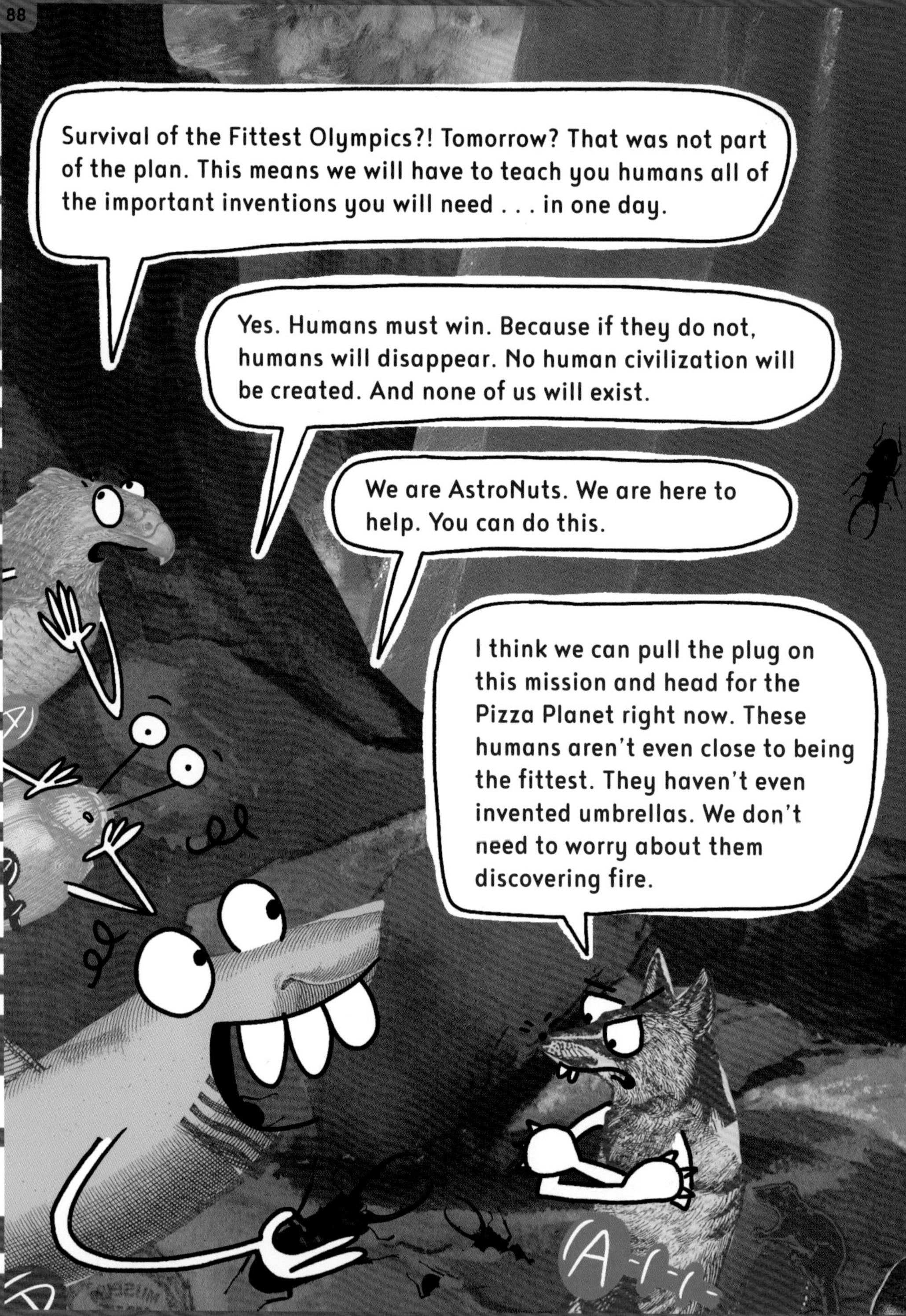
Survival of the Fittest Olympics?! Tomorrow? That was not part of the plan. This means we will have to teach you humans all of the important inventions you will need . . . in one day.
Yes. Humans must win. Because if they do not, humans will disappear. No human civilization will be created. And none of us will exist.
We are AstroNuts. We are here to help. You can do this.
I think we can pull the plug on this mission and head for the Pizza Planet right now. These humans aren't even close to being the fittest. They haven't even invented umbrellas. We don't need to worry about them discovering fire.

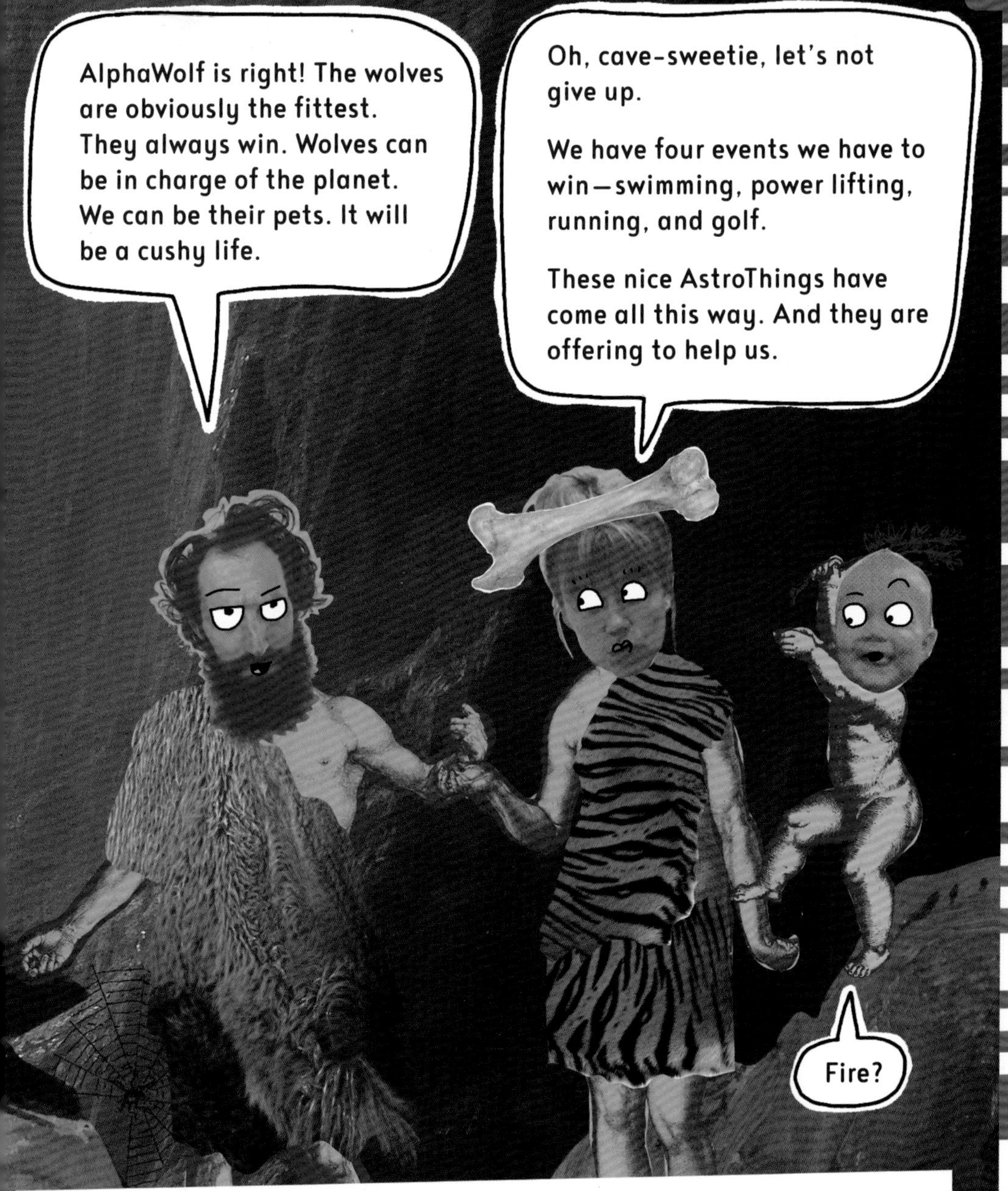
AlphaWolf is right! The wolves are obviously the fittest. They always win. Wolves can be in charge of the planet. We can be their pets. It will be a cushy life.
Oh, cave-sweetie, let's not give up.
We have four events we have to win—swimming, power lifting, running, and golf.
These nice AstroThings have come all this way. And they are offering to help us.
Fire?

Oh man this looked bad. This looked impossible. Like how on me, Earth, could this small band of early humans learn everything they needed to know to defeat every other species in my world? But guess who had already figured this out?

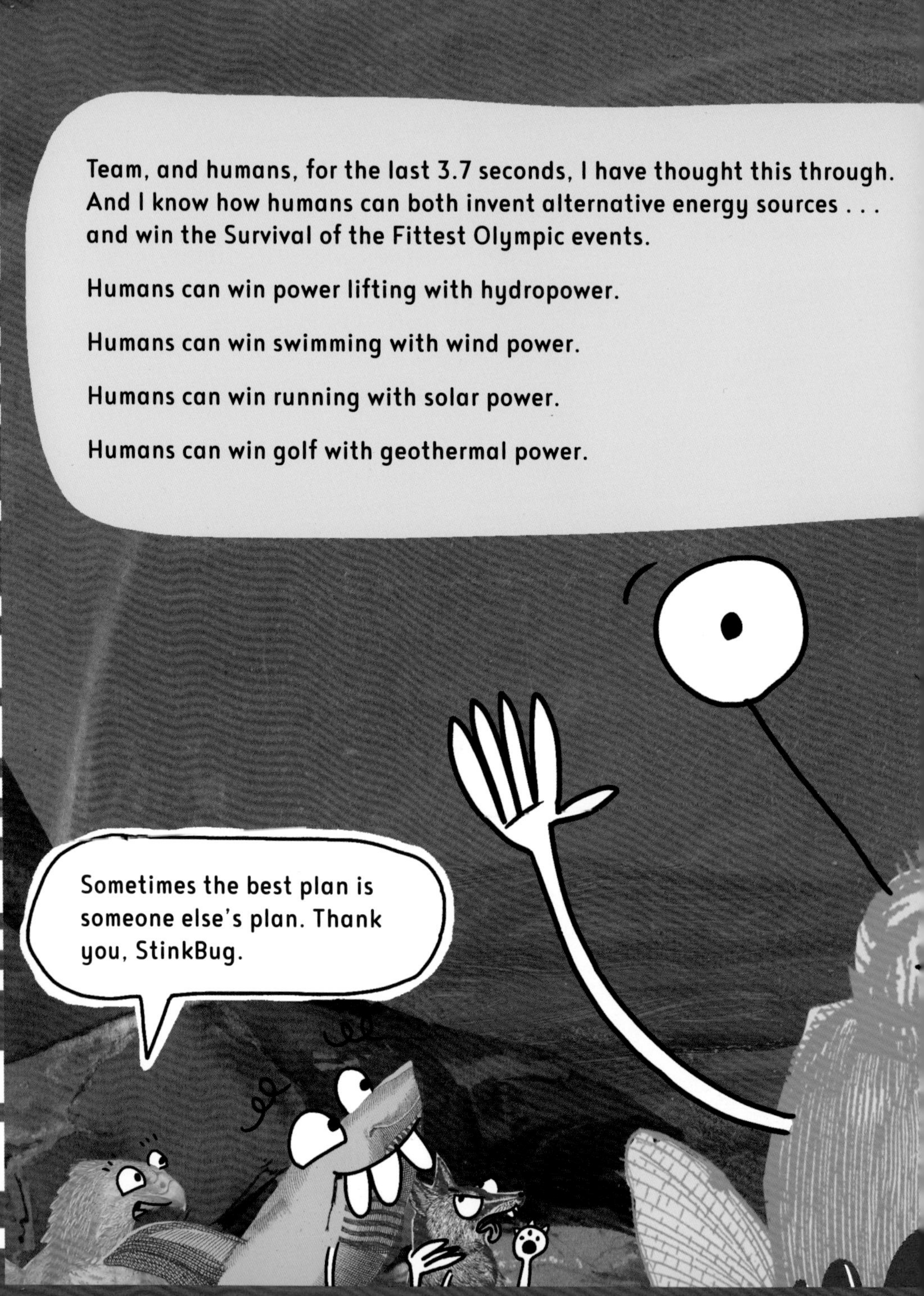
Team, and humans, for the last 3.7 seconds, I have thought this through. And I know how humans can both invent alternative energy sources . . . and win the Survival of the Fittest Olympic events.
Humans can win power lifting with hydropower.
Humans can win swimming with wind power.
Humans can win running with solar power.
Humans can win golf with geothermal power.
Sometimes the best plan is someone else's plan. Thank you, StinkBug.

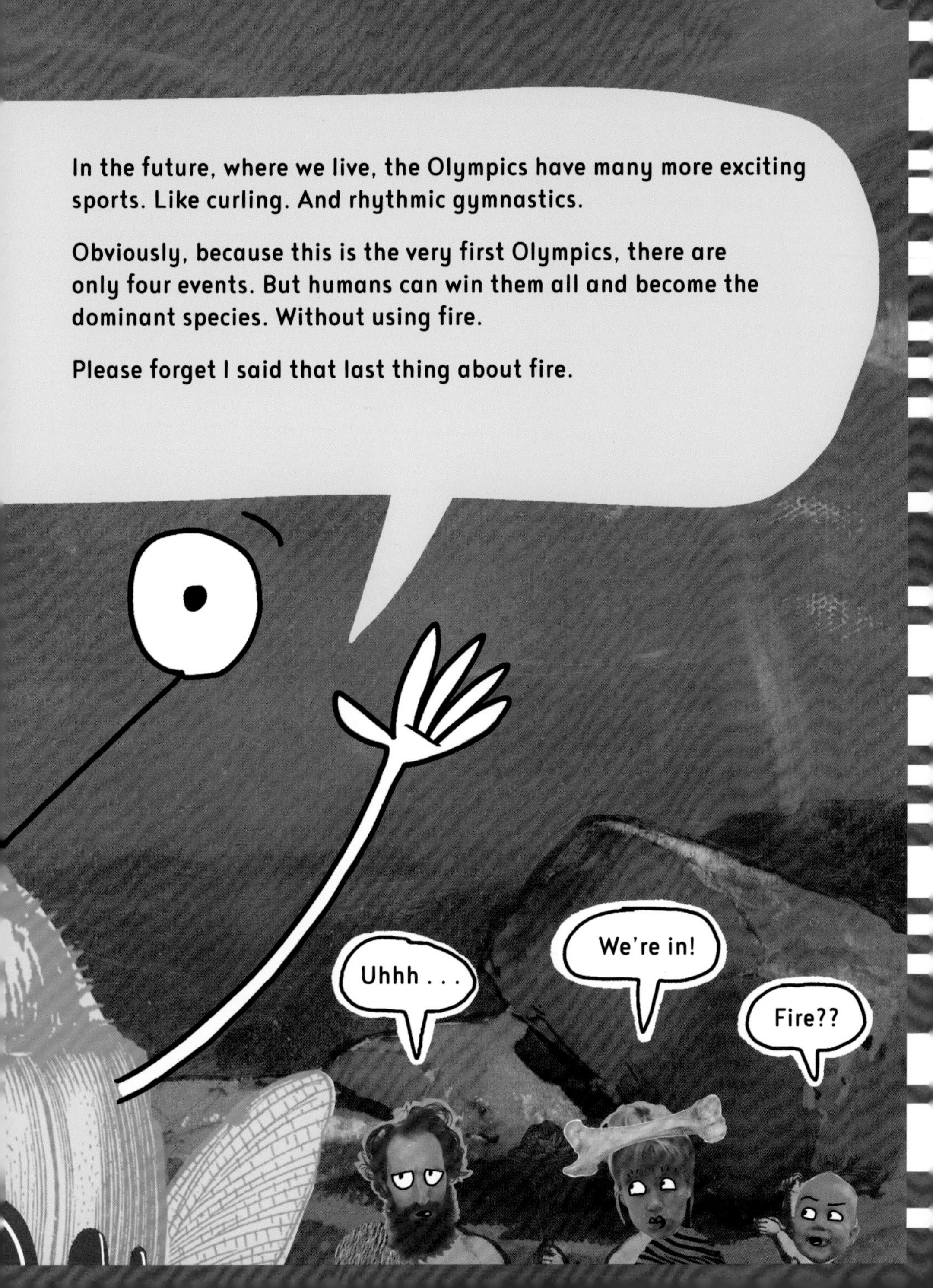
In the future, where we live, the Olympics have many more exciting sports. Like curling. And rhythmic gymnastics.
Obviously, because this is the very first Olympics, there are only four events. But humans can win them all and become the dominant species. Without using fire.
Please forget I said that last thing about fire.
Uhhh . . .
We're in!
Fire??

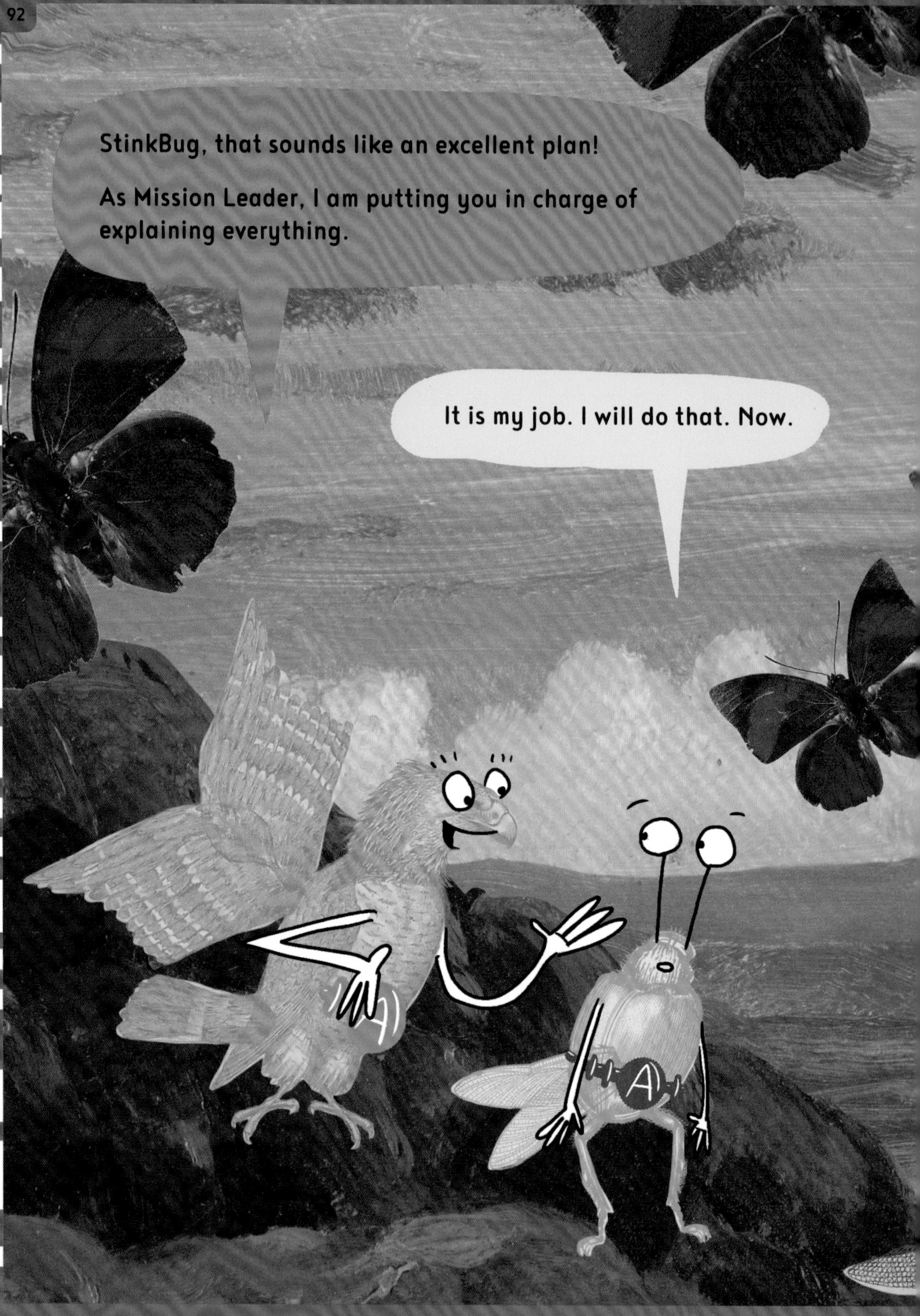
StinkBug, that sounds like an excellent plan!
As Mission Leader, I am putting you in charge of explaining everything.
It is my job. I will do that. Now.

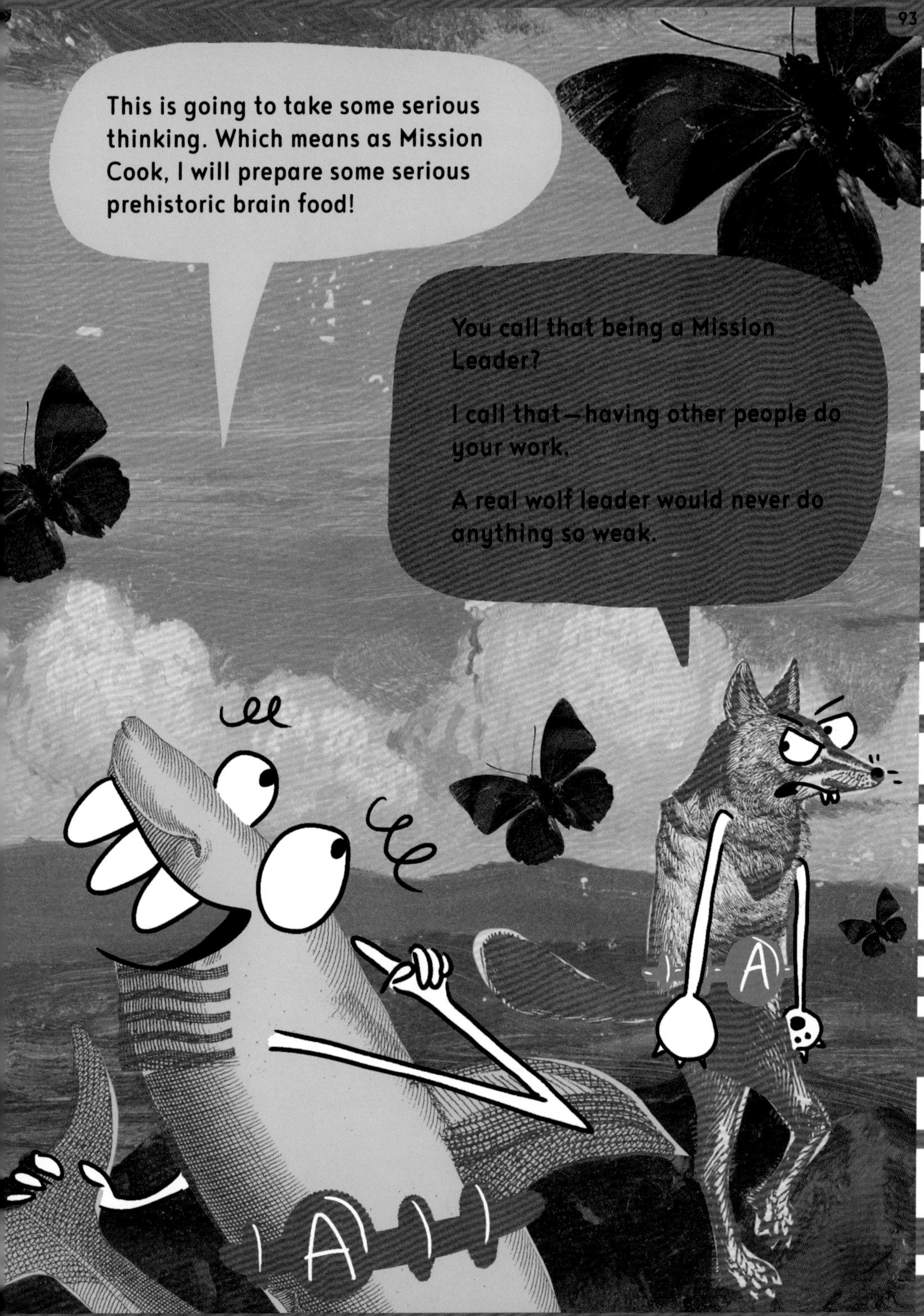
This is going to take some serious thinking. Which means as Mission Cook, I will prepare some serious prehistoric brain food!
You call that being a Mission Leader?
I call that—having other people do your work.
A real wolf leader would never do anything so weak.

CHAPTER 12:

Hydropower

StinkBug! Thank goodness for StinkBug. No one was completely sure what he was talking about. But they were sure *he* knew what he was talking about. So they got to work—inventing and training.

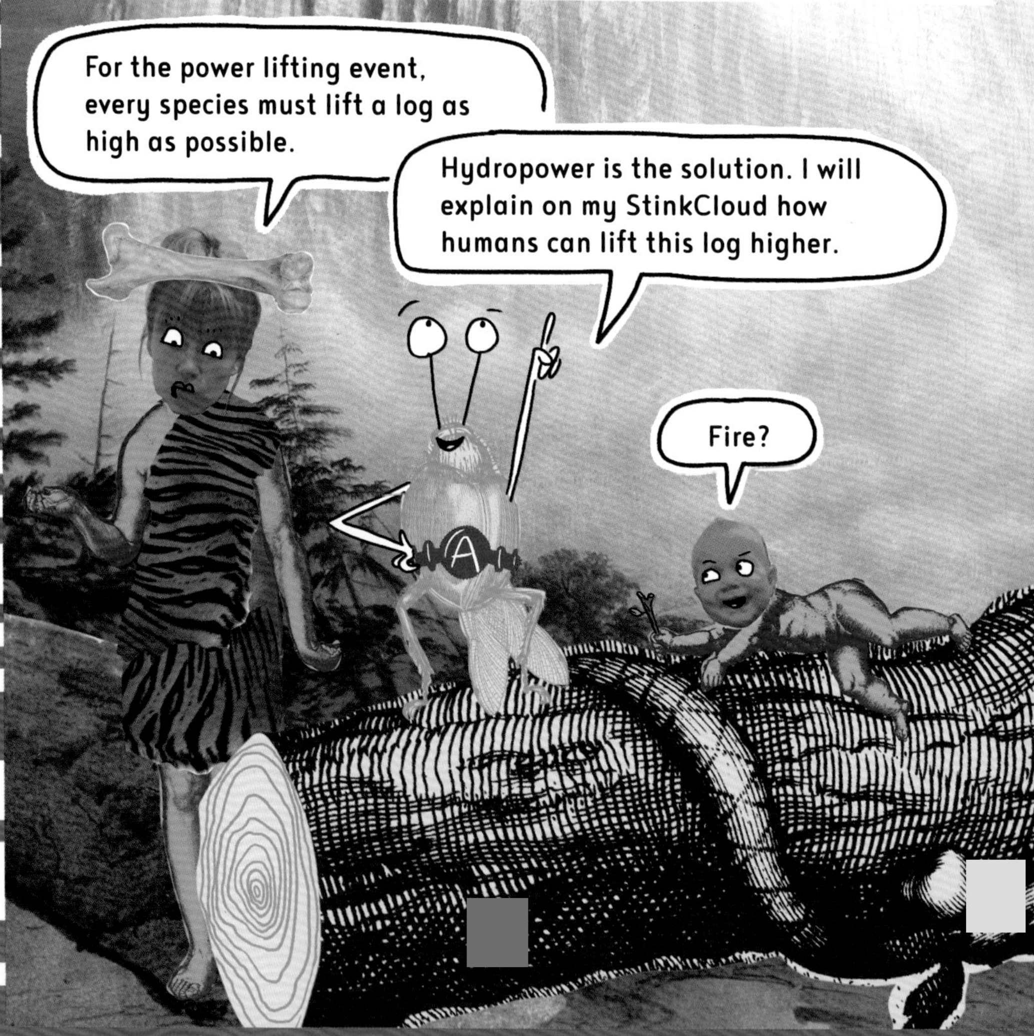
For the power lifting event, every species must lift a log as high as possible.
Hydropower is the solution. I will explain on my StinkCloud how humans can lift this log higher.
Fire?

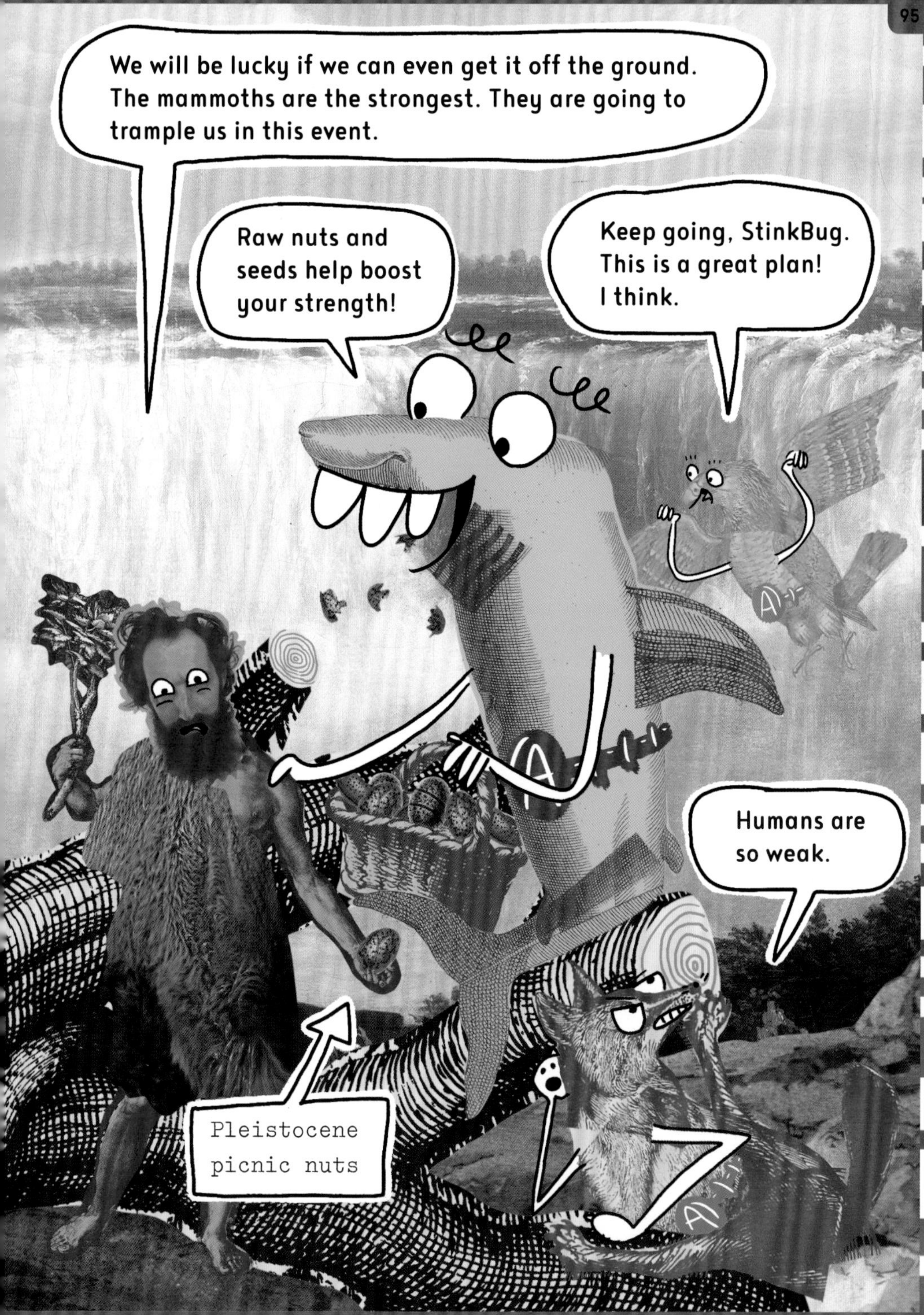
We will be lucky if we can even get it off the ground. The mammoths are the strongest. They are going to trample us in this event.
Raw nuts and seeds help boost your strength!
Keep going, StinkBug. This is a great plan! I think.
Humans are so weak.
Pleistocene picnic nuts

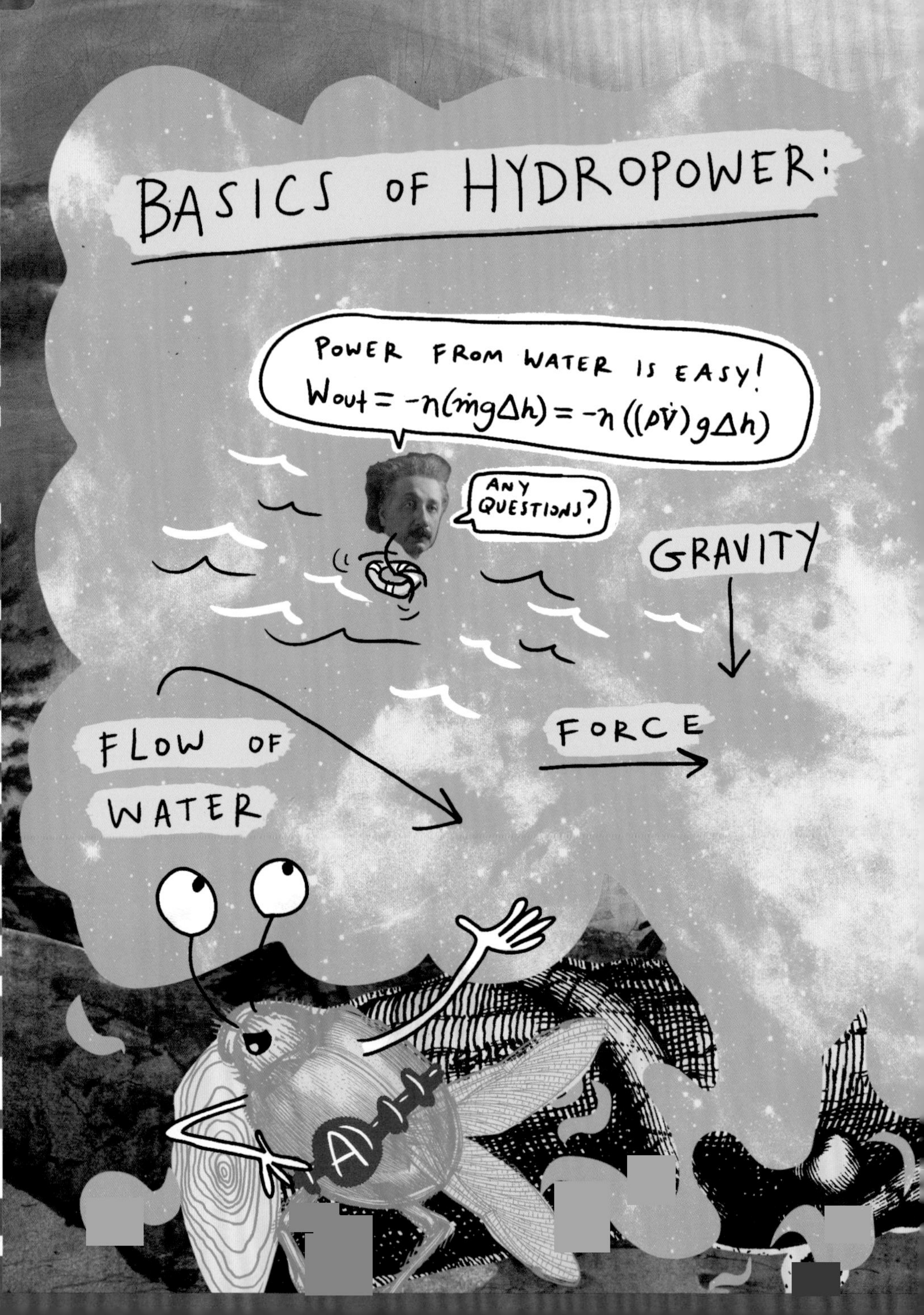
BASICS OF HYDROPOWER:
POWER FROM WATER IS EASY!
$W_{out} = -\eta(\dot{m}g\Delta h) = -\eta((\rho\dot{V})g\Delta h)$
ANY QUESTIONS?
GRAVITY
FORCE
FLOW OF WATER

APPLICATION OF HYDROPOWER:
MOUNTAIN LAKE
AQUEDUCT
FORCE OF WATER LIFTS LOG
I see. The force of the water pushes the log up.
Honey, that's crazy. We don't even know what force is.

CHAPTER 13:
Wind Power

Next StinkBug came up with an even wilder idea for winning the swimming event.

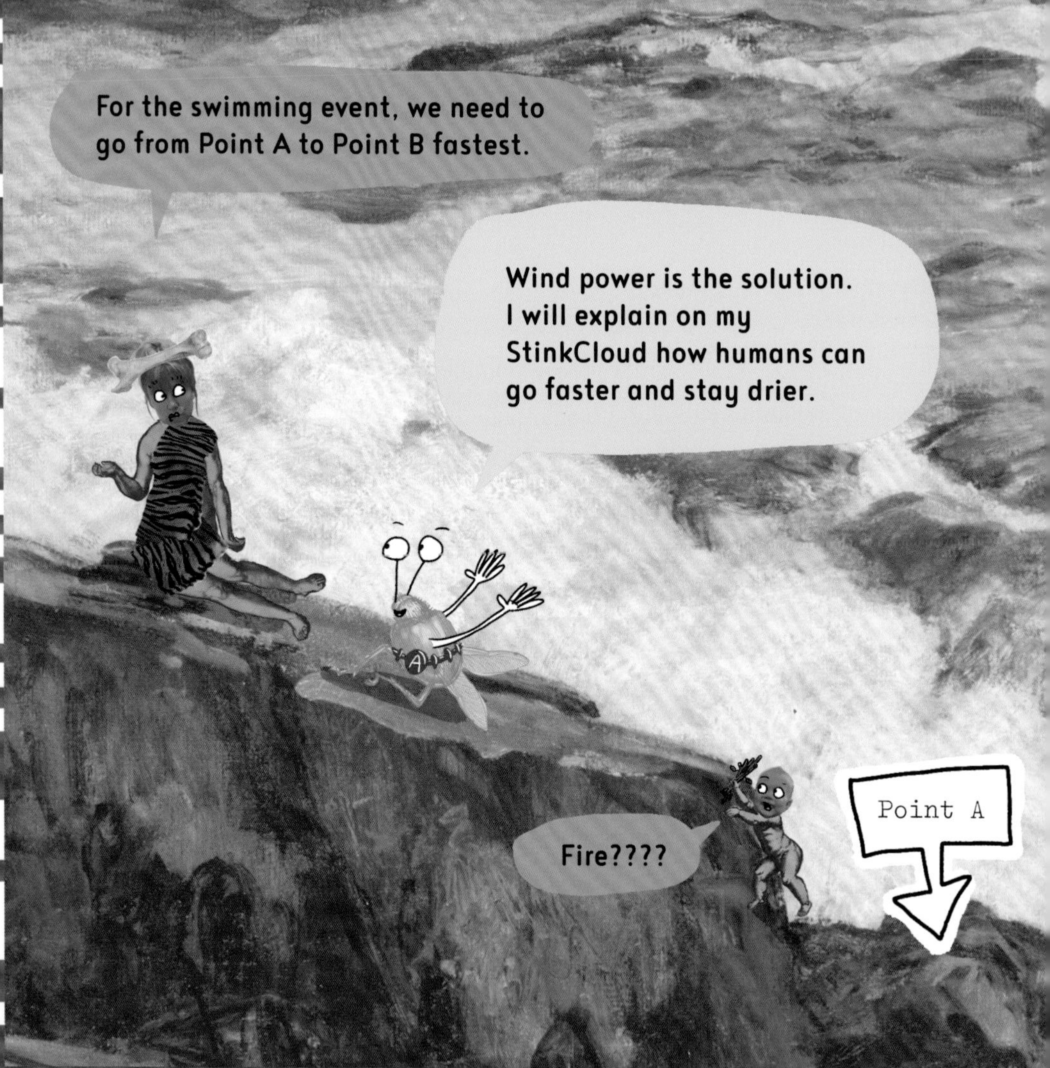
For the swimming event, we need to go from Point A to Point B fastest.
Wind power is the solution. I will explain on my StinkCloud how humans can go faster and stay drier.
Fire????
Point A

I can't say I understand even half of what is going on here. But a good leader lets the team members do their best work.

Point B

Ha. I would win this with my wolfie paddle.

I can't swim!

Omega-3 fatty fish oils are good for your heart! They will help you swim.

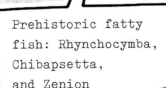

Prehistoric fatty fish: Rhynchocymba, Chibapsetta, and Zenion

BASICS OF WIND POWER:

HOW AIRFOILS WORK

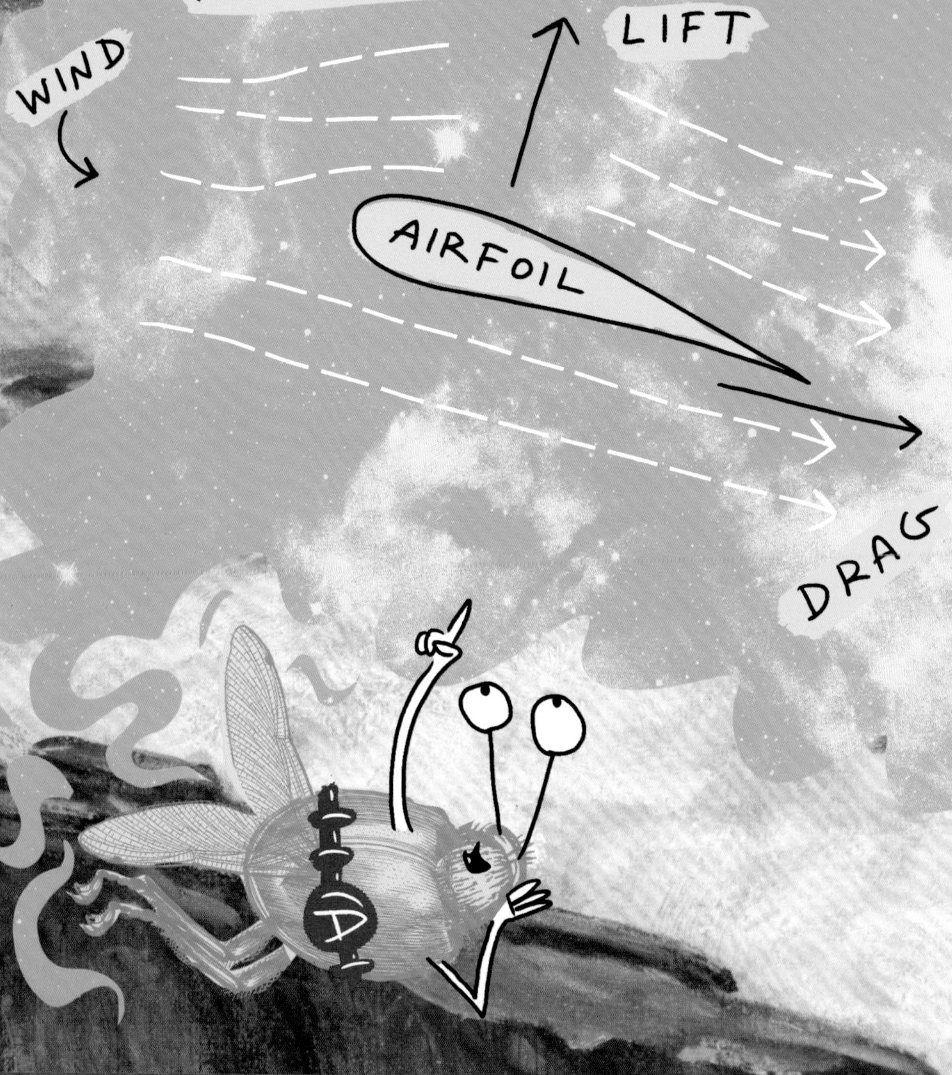
LIFT
WIND
AIRFOIL
DRAG

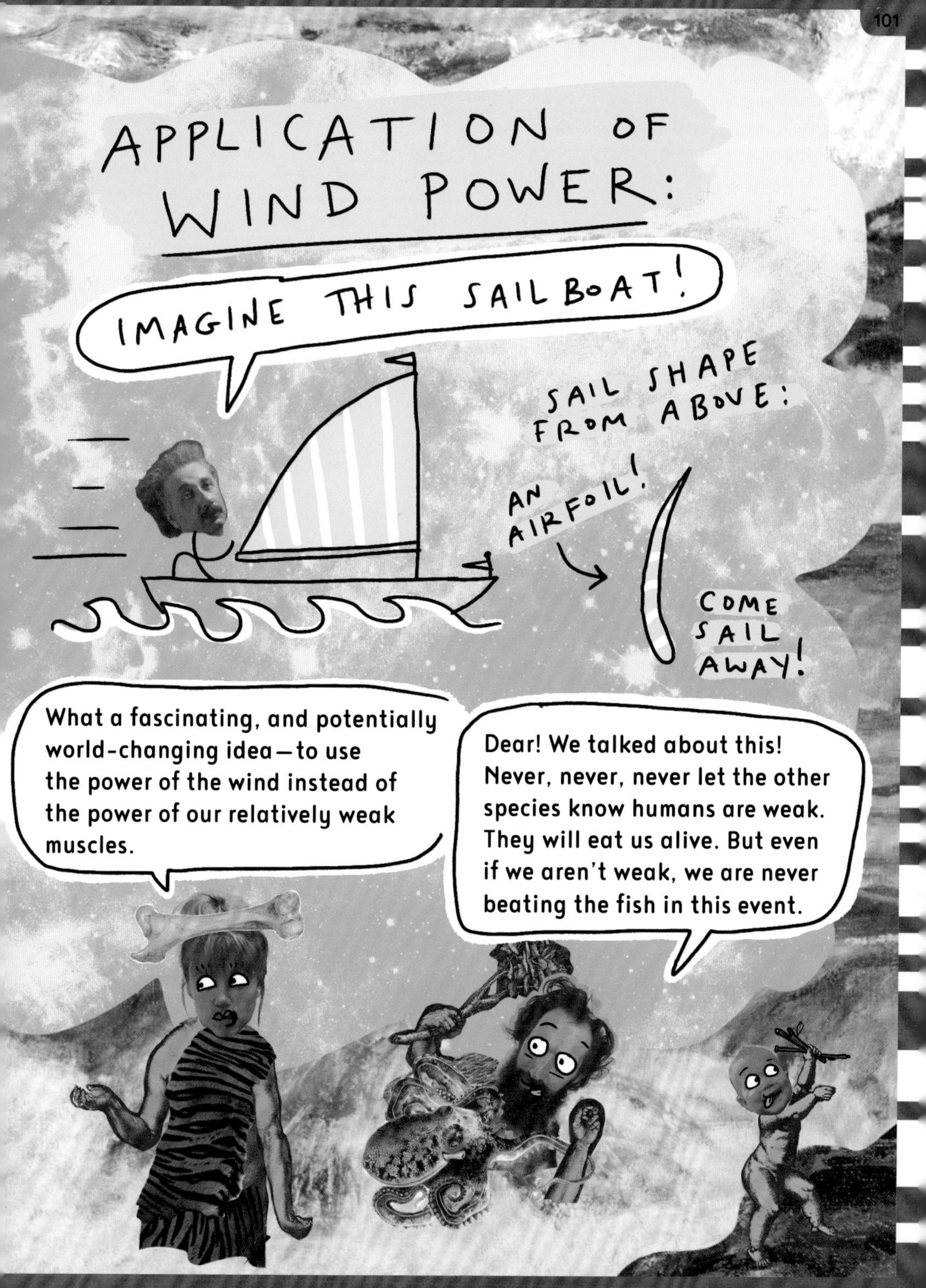

APPLICATION OF WIND POWER:
IMAGINE THIS SAILBOAT!
SAIL SHAPE FROM ABOVE:
AN AIRFOIL!
COME SAIL AWAY!
What a fascinating, and potentially world-changing idea—to use the power of the wind instead of the power of our relatively weak muscles.
Dear! We talked about this! Never, never, never let the other species know humans are weak. They will eat us alive. But even if we aren't weak, we are never beating the fish in this event.

CHAPTER 14:

Geothermal Power

StinkBug kept going, as only StinkBug can.

And I have to add—okay, I invented golf. I know. I know. It seems like a really stupid idea to be hitting a tiny ball around and trying to get it into an equally tiny hole. But oh that green looks so good on me. The long fairways. The tightly rolled greens . . .

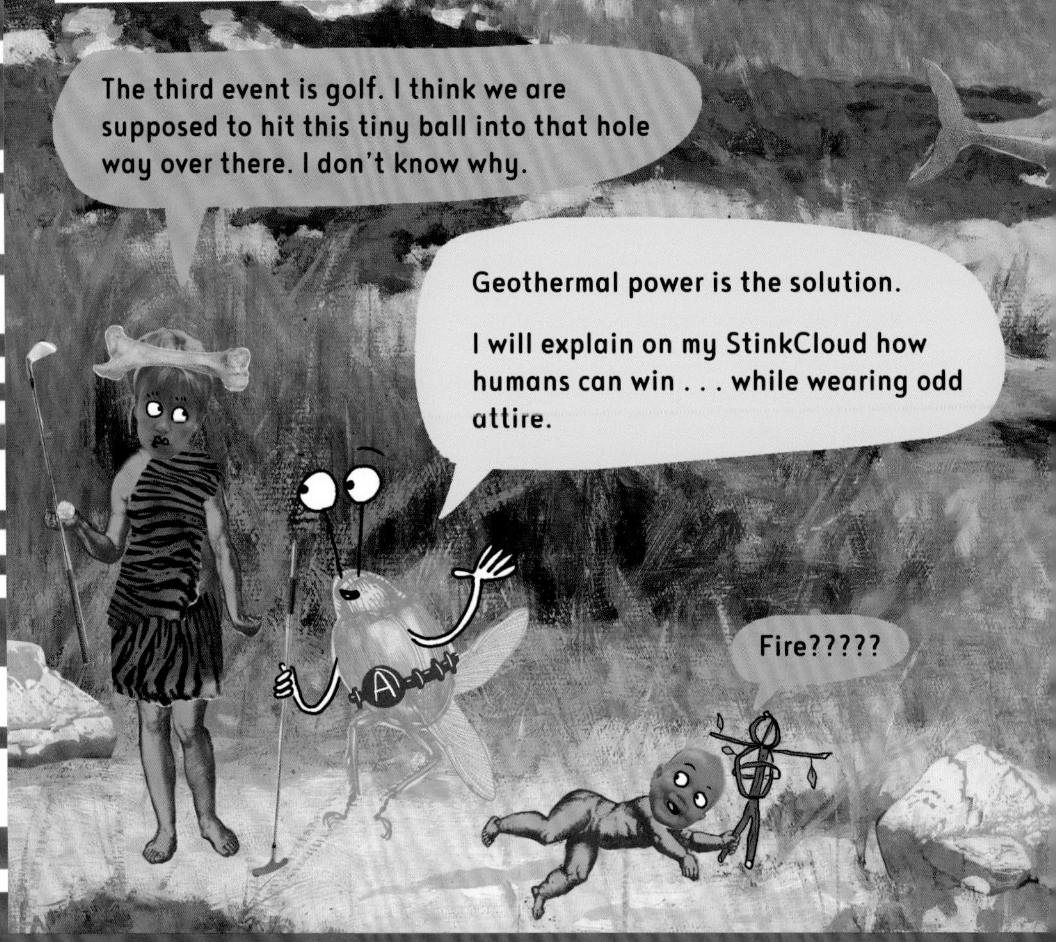
The third event is golf. I think we are supposed to hit this tiny ball into that hole way over there. I don't know why.
Geothermal power is the solution.
I will explain on my StinkCloud how humans can win . . . while wearing odd attire.
Fire?????

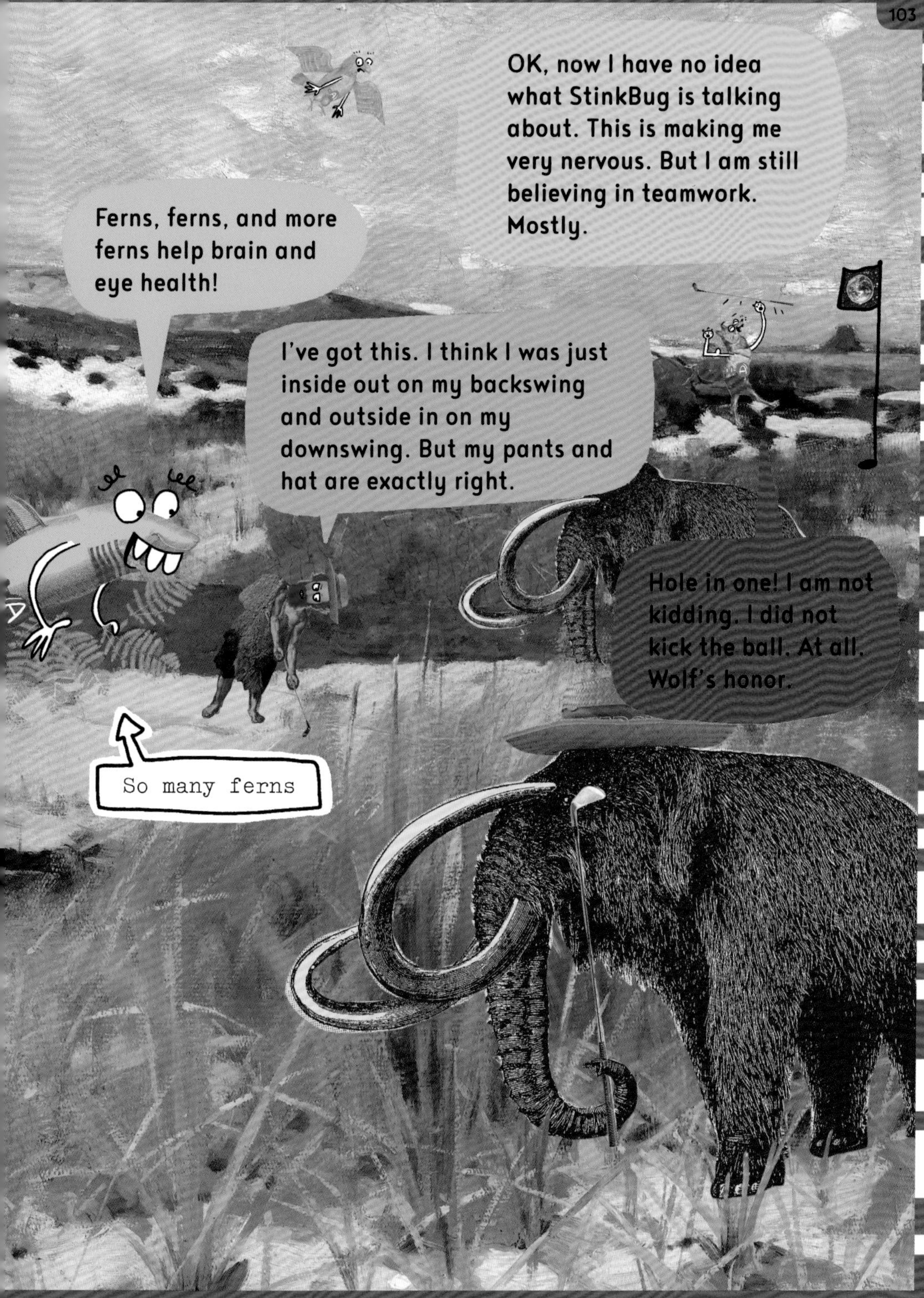
OK, now I have no idea what StinkBug is talking about. This is making me very nervous. But I am still believing in teamwork. Mostly.
Ferns, ferns, and more ferns help brain and eye health!
I've got this. I think I was just inside out on my backswing and outside in on my downswing. But my pants and hat are exactly right.
Hole in one! I am not kidding. I did not kick the ball. At all. Wolf's honor.
So many ferns

BASICS OF GEOTHERMAL POWER:

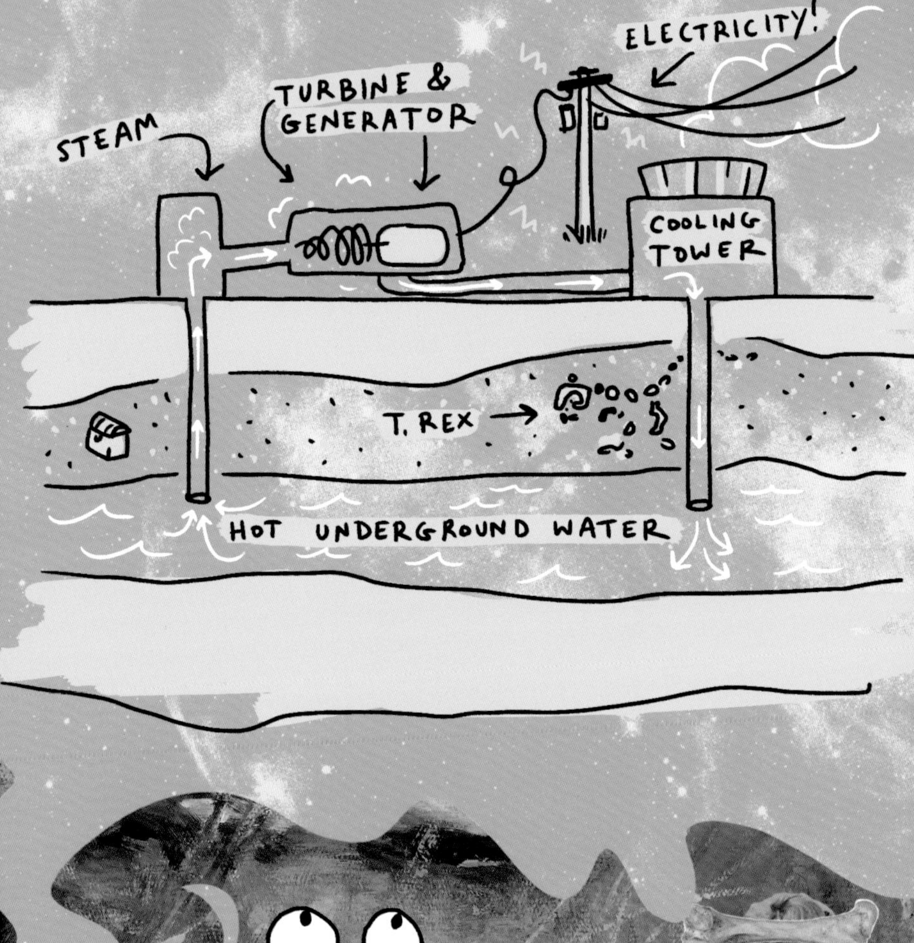
ELECTRICITY!
TURBINE & GENERATOR
STEAM
COOLING TOWER
T. REX
HOT UNDERGROUND WATER

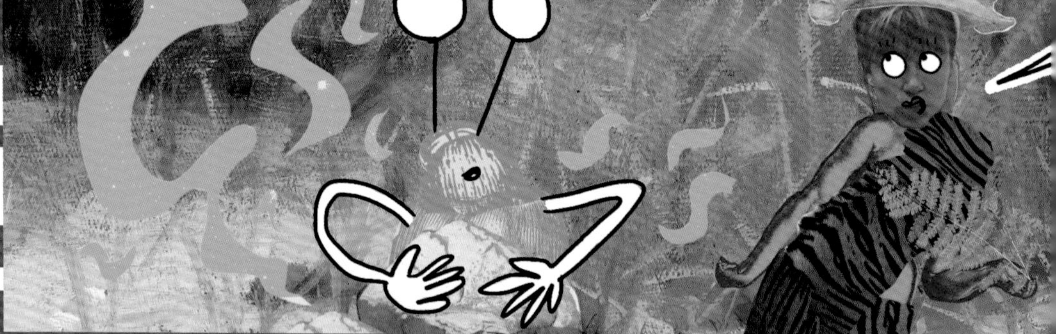

APPLICATION OF GEOTHERMAL POWER:

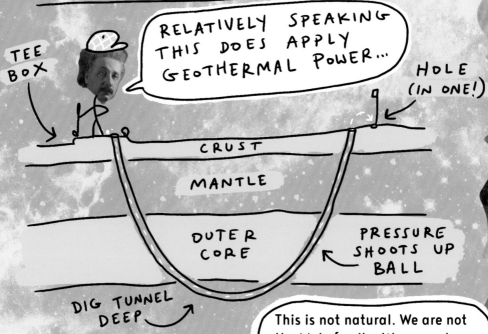

RELATIVELY SPEAKING THIS DOES APPLY GEOTHERMAL POWER...

TEE BOX

HOLE (IN ONE!)

CRUST

MANTLE

OUTER CORE

PRESSURE SHOOTS UP BALL

DIG TUNNEL DEEP

What a simple use of Earth's inner heat. I can see how that could come in handy in a lot of ways.

This is not natural. We are not the Mole family. We are not going to start tunneling like moles. We are going to win this the old-fashioned Sapiens way—with our golf clubs.

CHAPTER 15:

Solar Power

I don't know about your head, but my gigantic planet mind was spinning after all these StinkBug ideas. It felt like doing long division in a mirror, underwater.

But StinkBug didn't notice. AND the future of all humans was depending on the Sapiens family winning. So SmartHawk waved to StinkBug to finish strong.

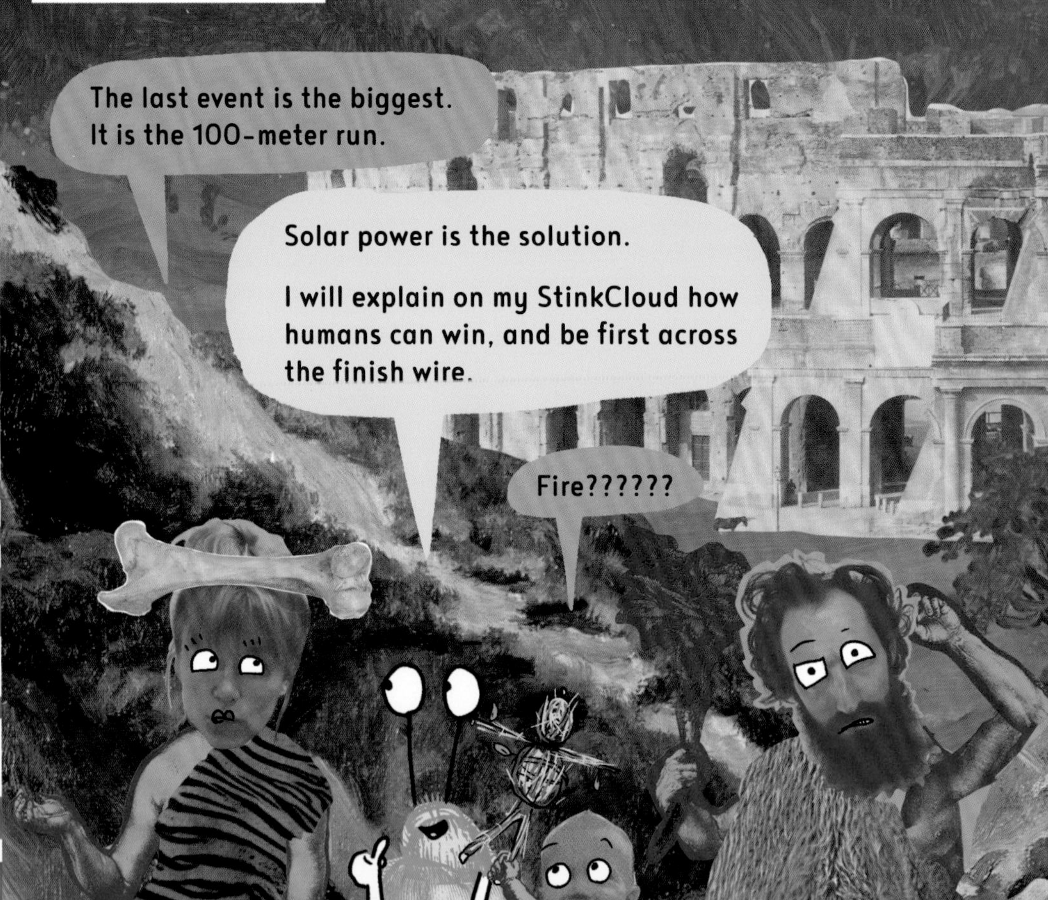
The last event is the biggest. It is the 100-meter run.
Solar power is the solution.
I will explain on my StinkCloud how humans can win, and be first across the finish wire.
Fire??????

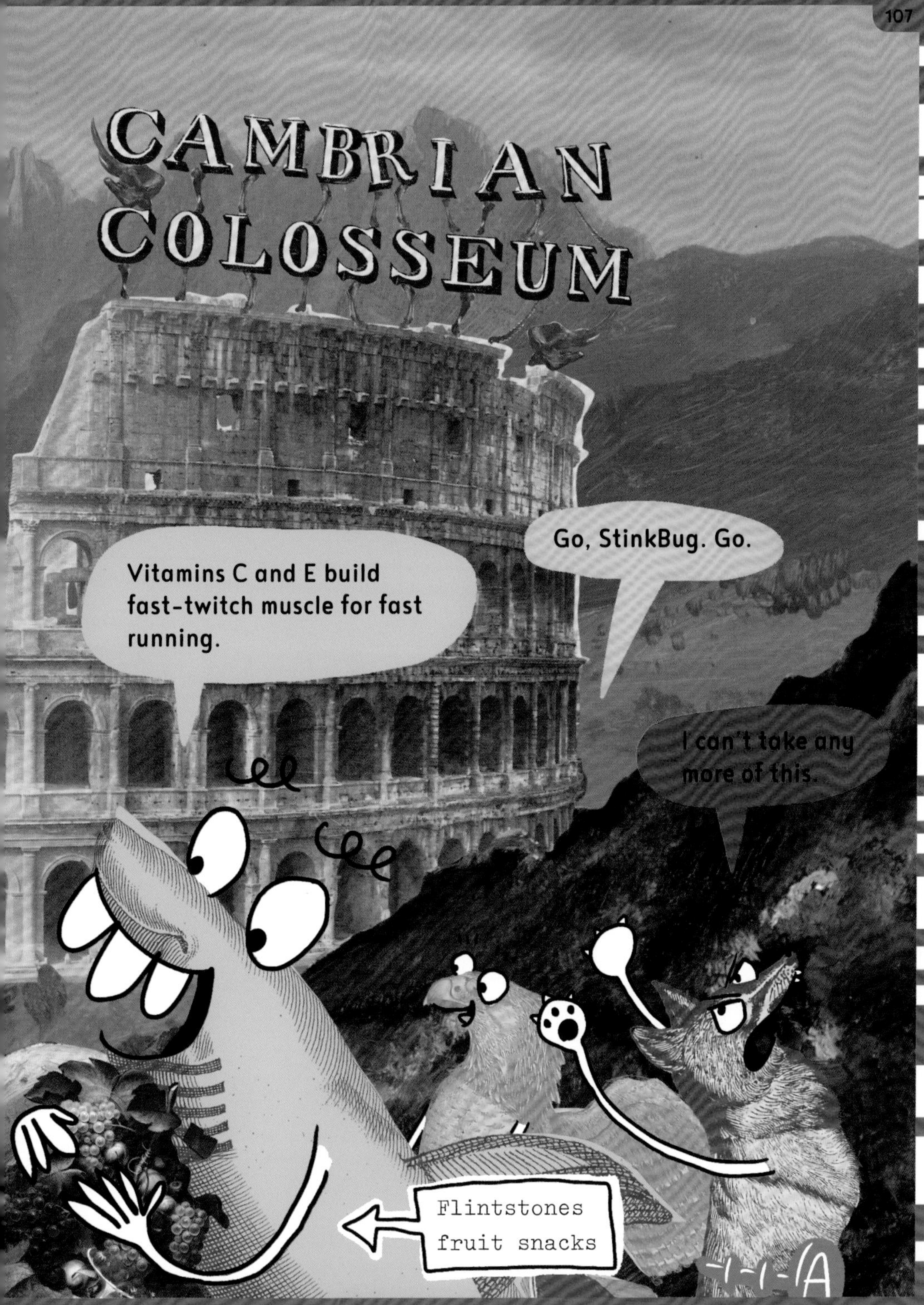
CAMBRIAN COLOSSEUM
Go, StinkBug. Go.
Vitamins C and E build fast-twitch muscle for fast running.
I can't take any more of this.
Flintstones fruit snacks
-I-I-IA

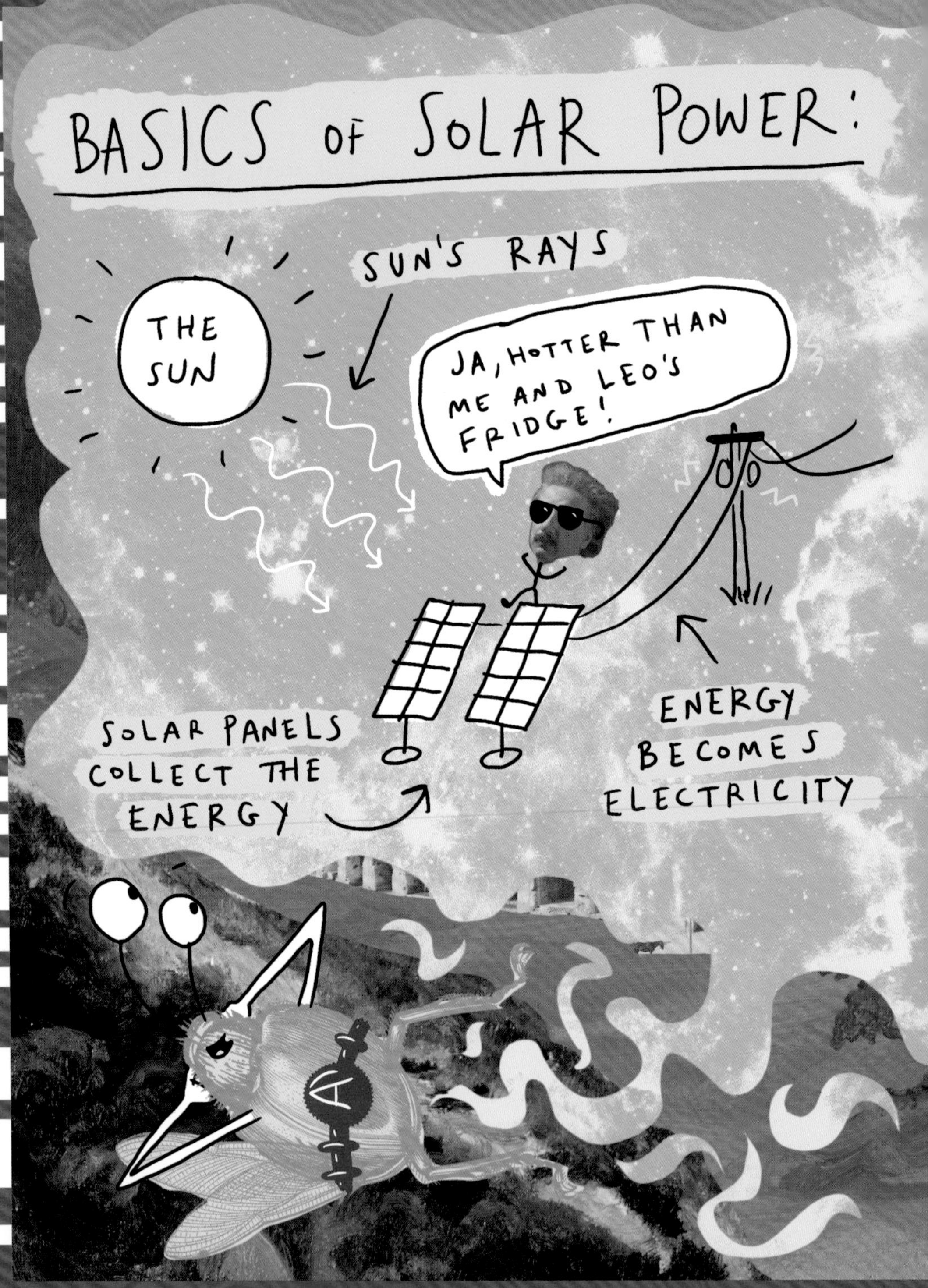
BASICS OF SOLAR POWER:
THE SUN
SUN'S RAYS
JA, HOTTER THAN ME AND LEO'S FRIDGE!
SOLAR PANELS COLLECT THE ENERGY
ENERGY BECOMES ELECTRICITY

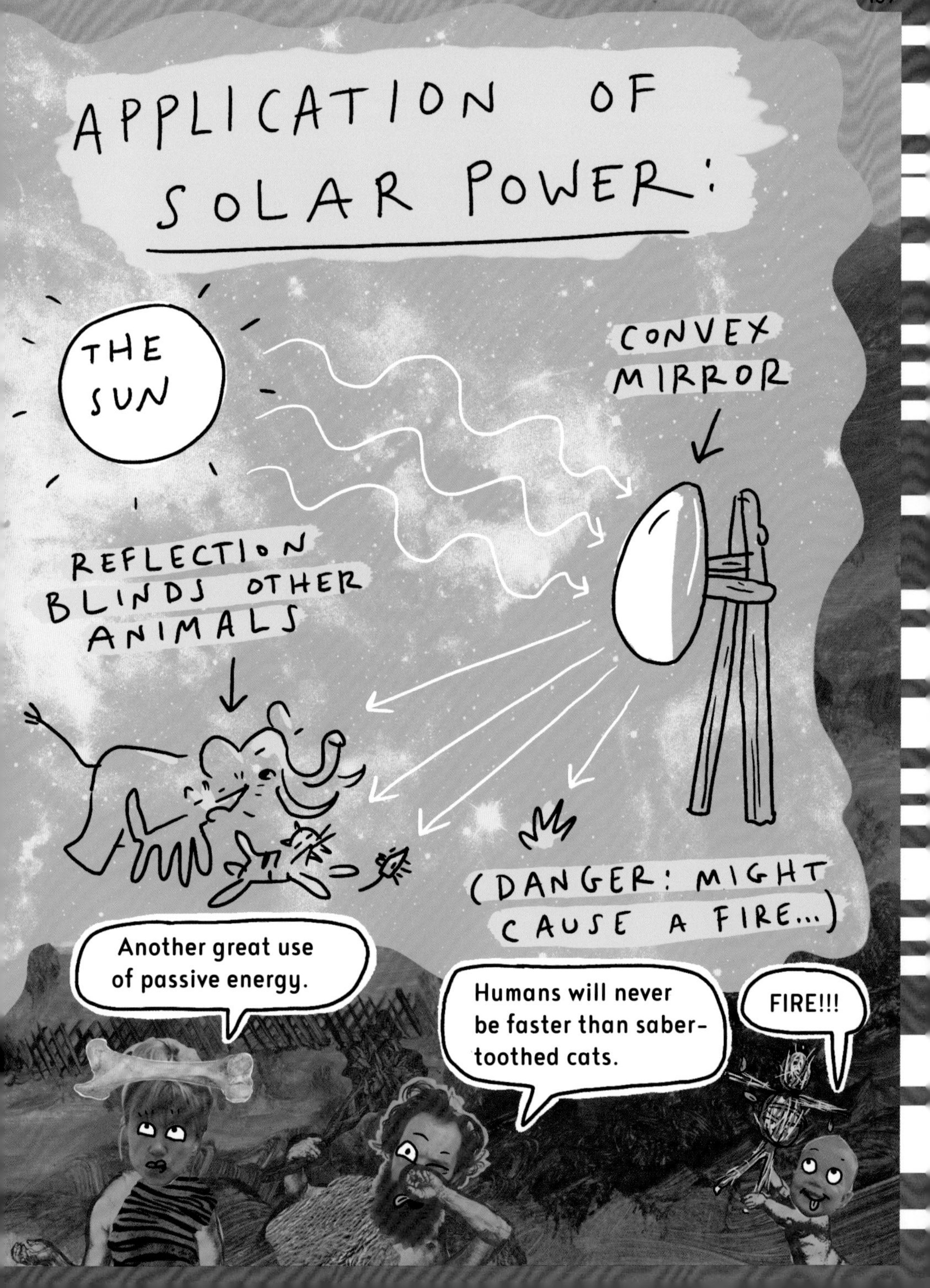
APPLICATION OF SOLAR POWER:
THE SUN
CONVEX MIRROR
REFLECTION BLINDS OTHER ANIMALS
(DANGER: MIGHT CAUSE A FIRE...)
Another great use of passive energy.
Humans will never be faster than saber-toothed cats.
FIRE!!!

CHAPTER 16:
Olympic Nonsense

Wow. That was a lot. I mean really a LOT to take in.

Using water, wind, geothermal, and solar energy?
To win an all-species Survival of the Fittest Olympics?
Come on! Who would even think up such a thing?
It made no sense!
But it actually did.

StinkBug knew this was exactly what humans have always done—
used their one advantage over bigger and stronger and faster
species, like mammoths and tigers and Komodo dragons.
Humans used their big brains.

CAMBRIAN
COLOSSEUM

That big human brain has helped humans invent great things, like the wheel, the lever, language, numbers, music, and art.

Sadly, that big human brain has also helped humans cause not-so-great-things, like global pollution, extinctions, climate change, school photo day, and elevator music.

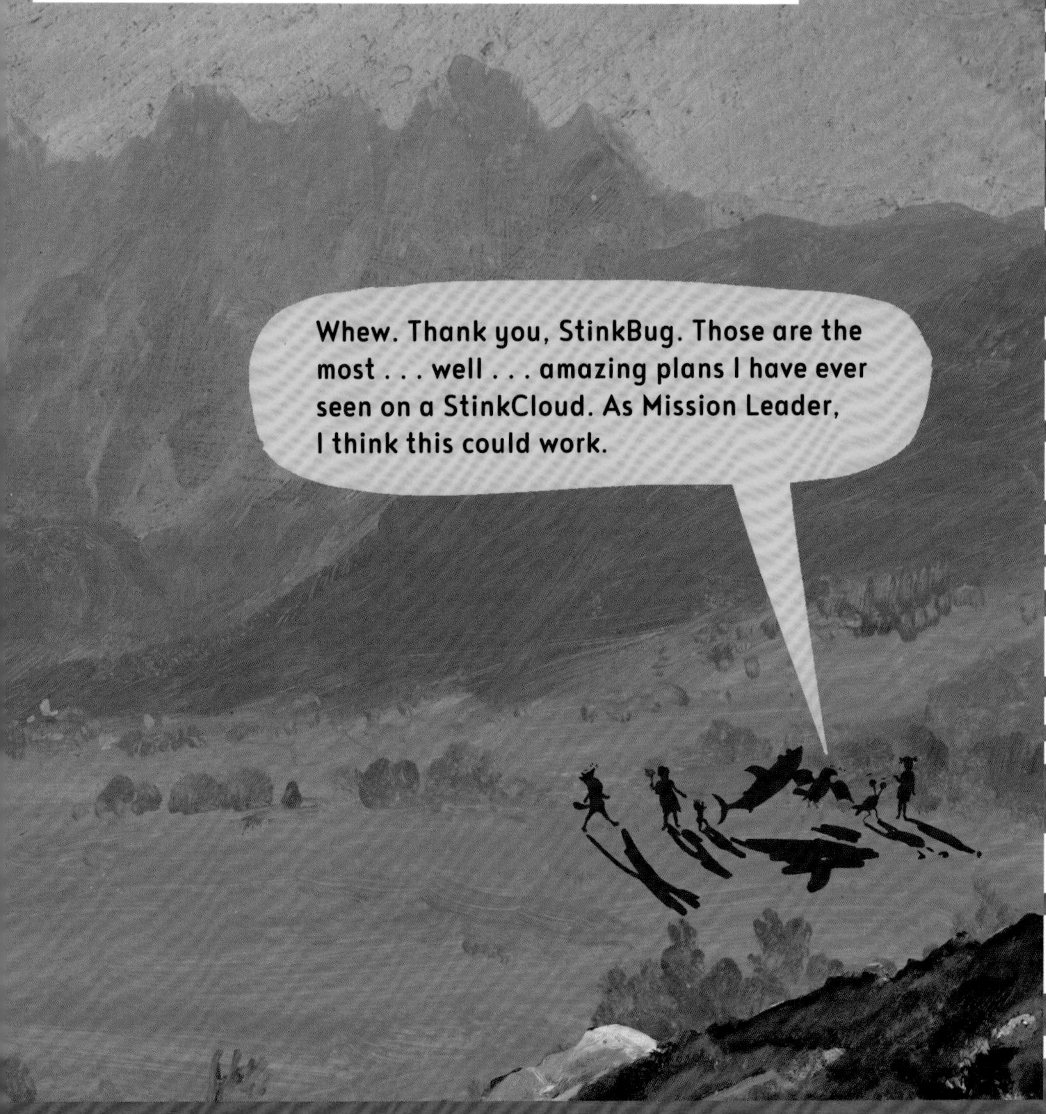
Whew. Thank you, StinkBug. Those are the most . . . well . . . amazing plans I have ever seen on a StinkCloud. As Mission Leader, I think this could work.

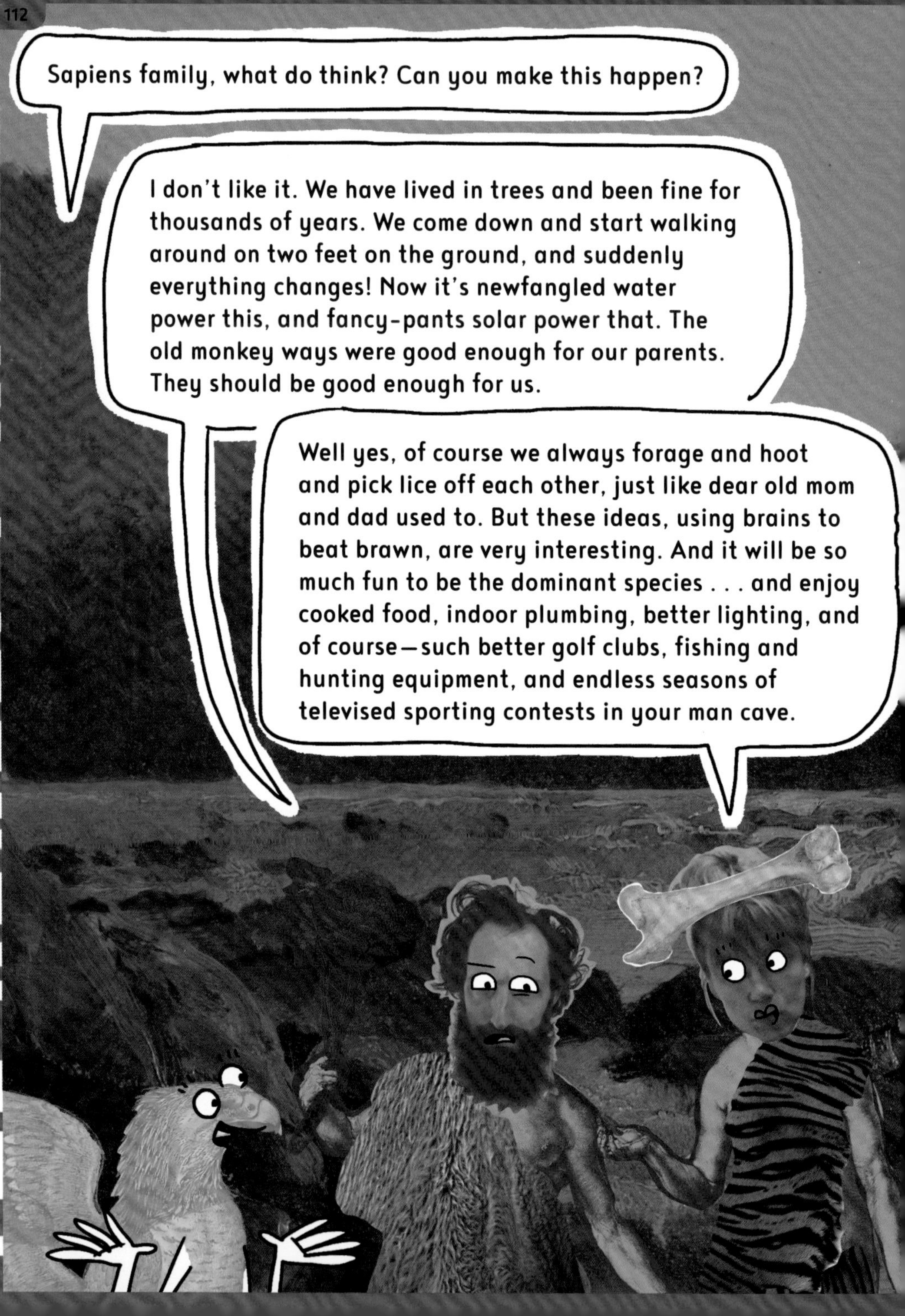
Sapiens family, what do think? Can you make this happen?
I don't like it. We have lived in trees and been fine for thousands of years. We come down and start walking around on two feet on the ground, and suddenly everything changes! Now it's newfangled water power this, and fancy-pants solar power that. The old monkey ways were good enough for our parents. They should be good enough for us.
Well yes, of course we always forage and hoot and pick lice off each other, just like dear old mom and dad used to. But these ideas, using brains to beat brawn, are very interesting. And it will be so much fun to be the dominant species . . . and enjoy cooked food, indoor plumbing, better lighting, and of course—such better golf clubs, fishing and hunting equipment, and endless seasons of televised sporting contests in your man cave.

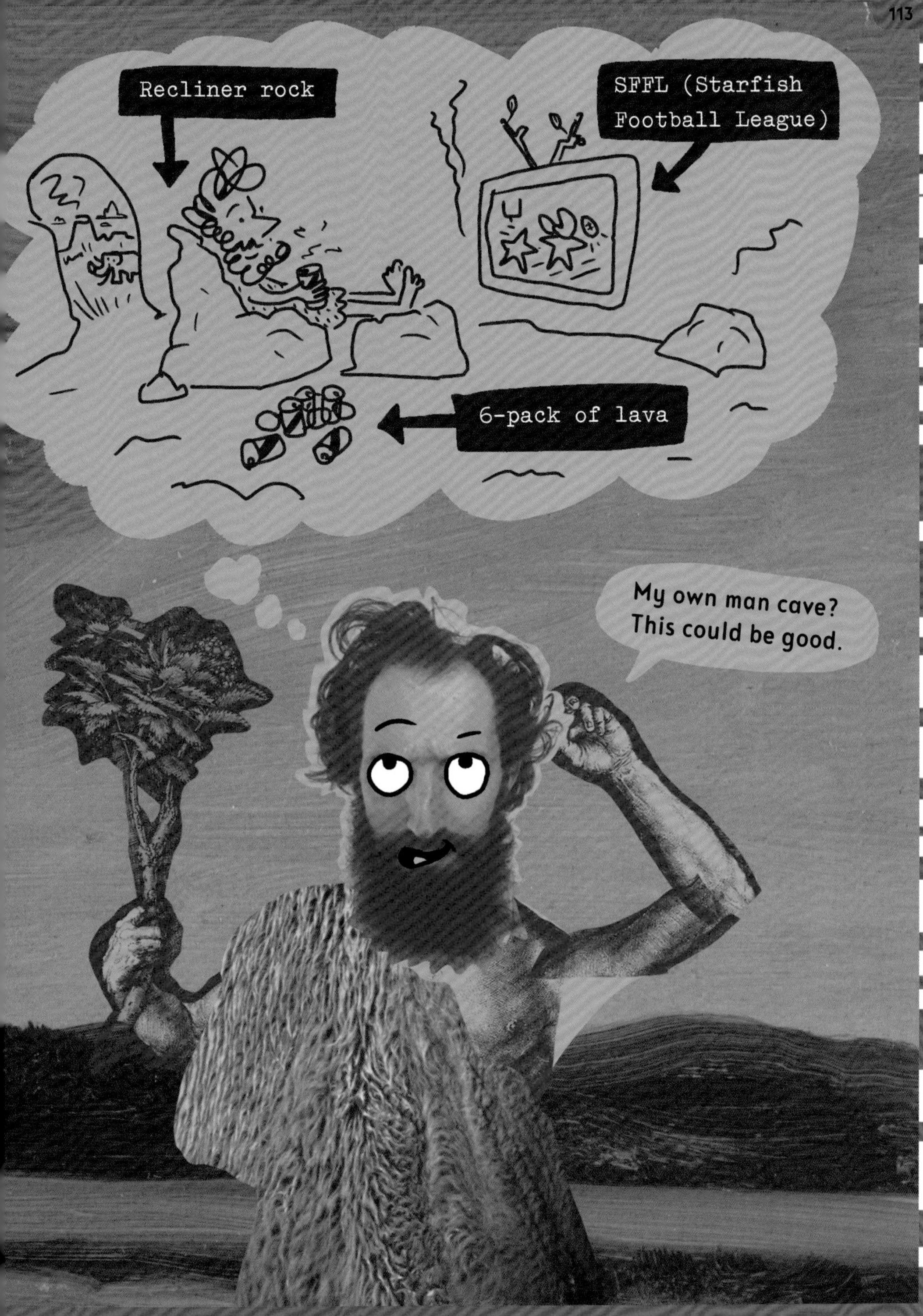
Recliner rock
SFFL (Starfish Football League)
6-pack of lava
My own man cave? This could be good.

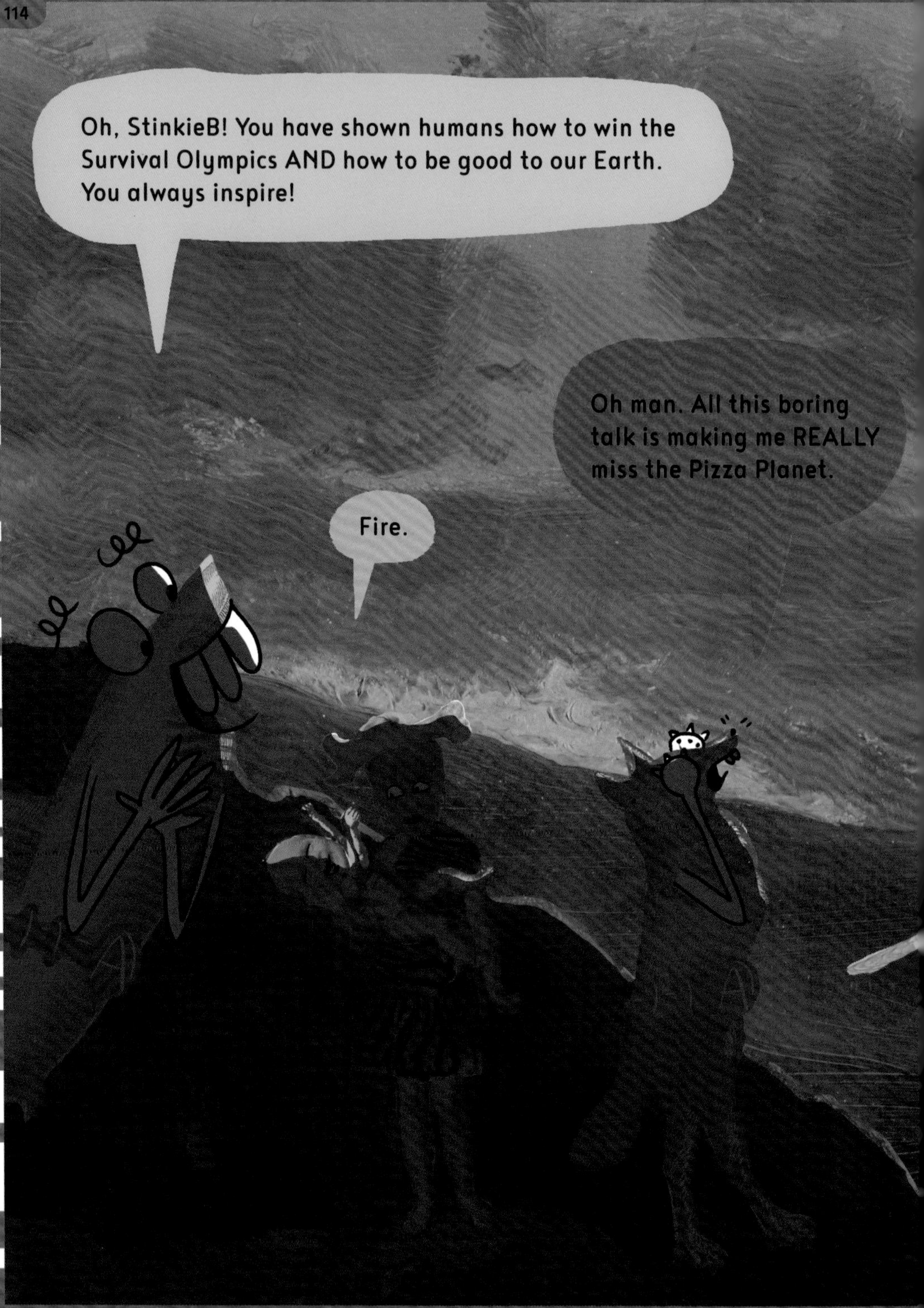
Oh, StinkieB! You have shown humans how to win the Survival Olympics AND how to be good to our Earth. You always inspire!
Oh man. All this boring talk is making me REALLY miss the Pizza Planet.
Fire.

As the sun went down, the full moon rose, and we all shared a quiet moment of hope, a feeling of working together, a glimpse of the possibility of happiness.

Then, as promised, you-know-who showed up again and wrecked the whole mood.

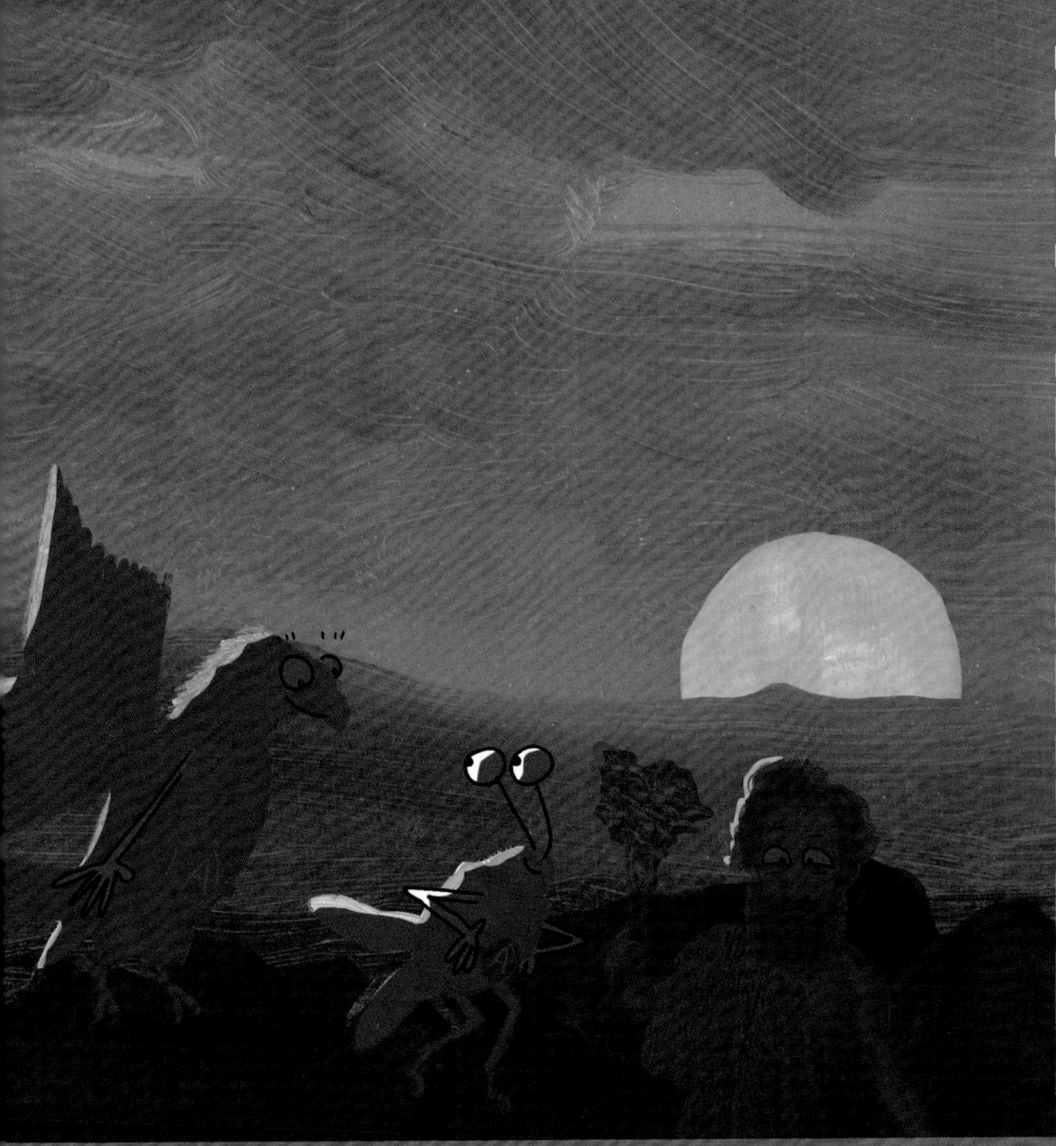

CHAPTER 17:

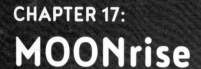

MOONrise

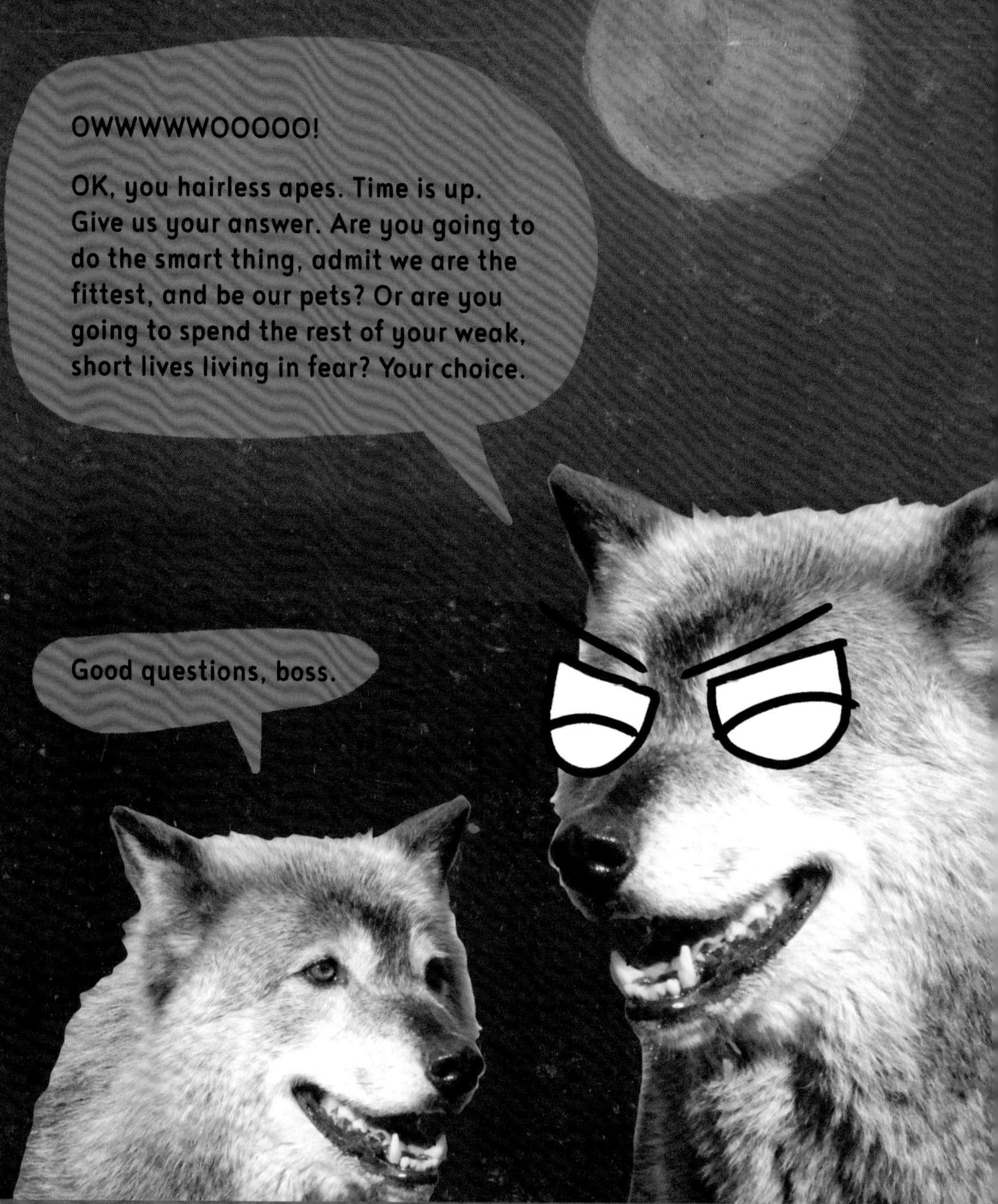
OWWWWWOOOOO!
OK, you hairless apes. Time is up. Give us your answer. Are you going to do the smart thing, admit we are the fittest, and be our pets? Or are you going to spend the rest of your weak, short lives living in fear? Your choice.
Good questions, boss.

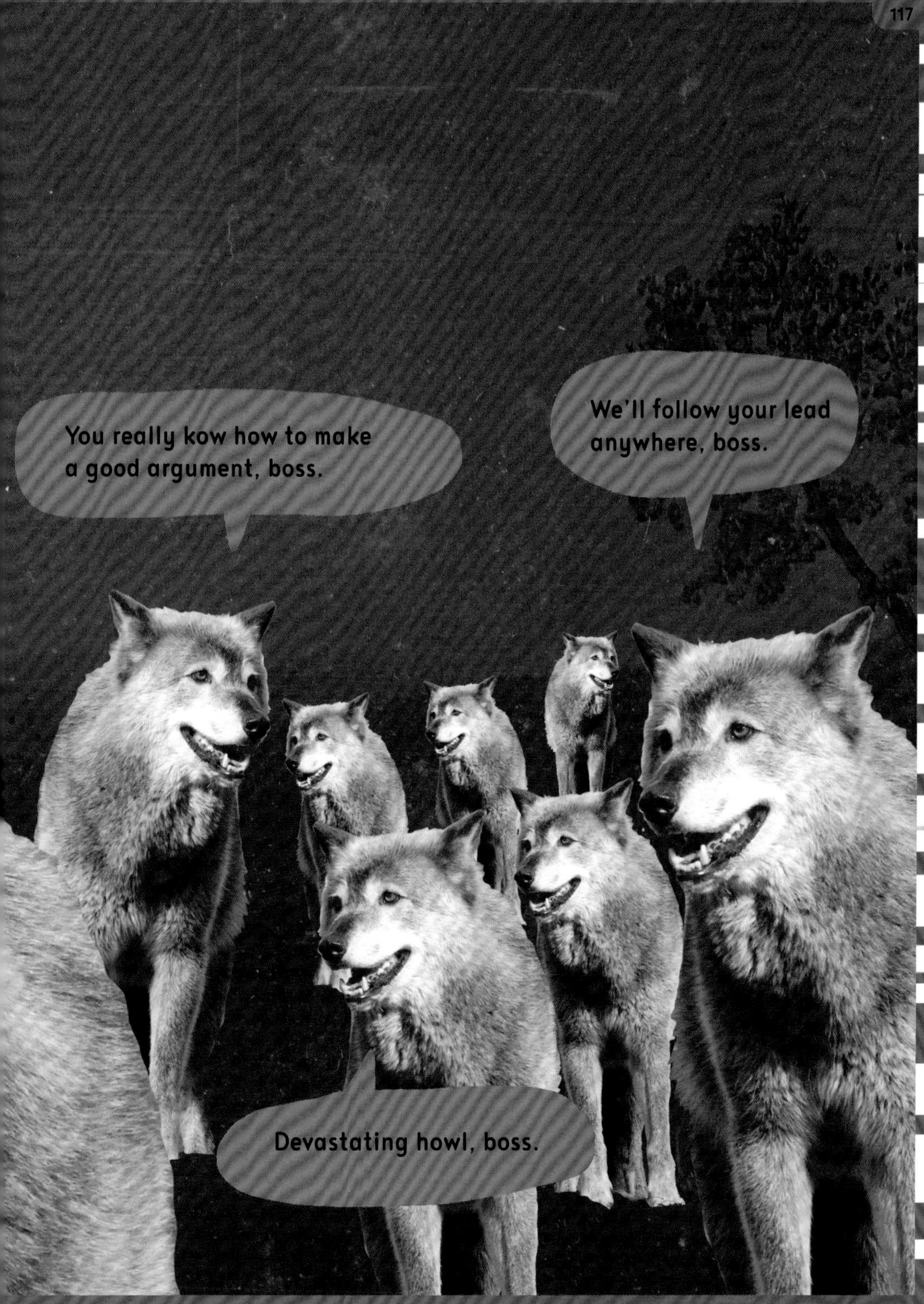
You really kow how to make a good argument, boss.
We'll follow your lead anywhere, boss.
Devastating howl, boss.

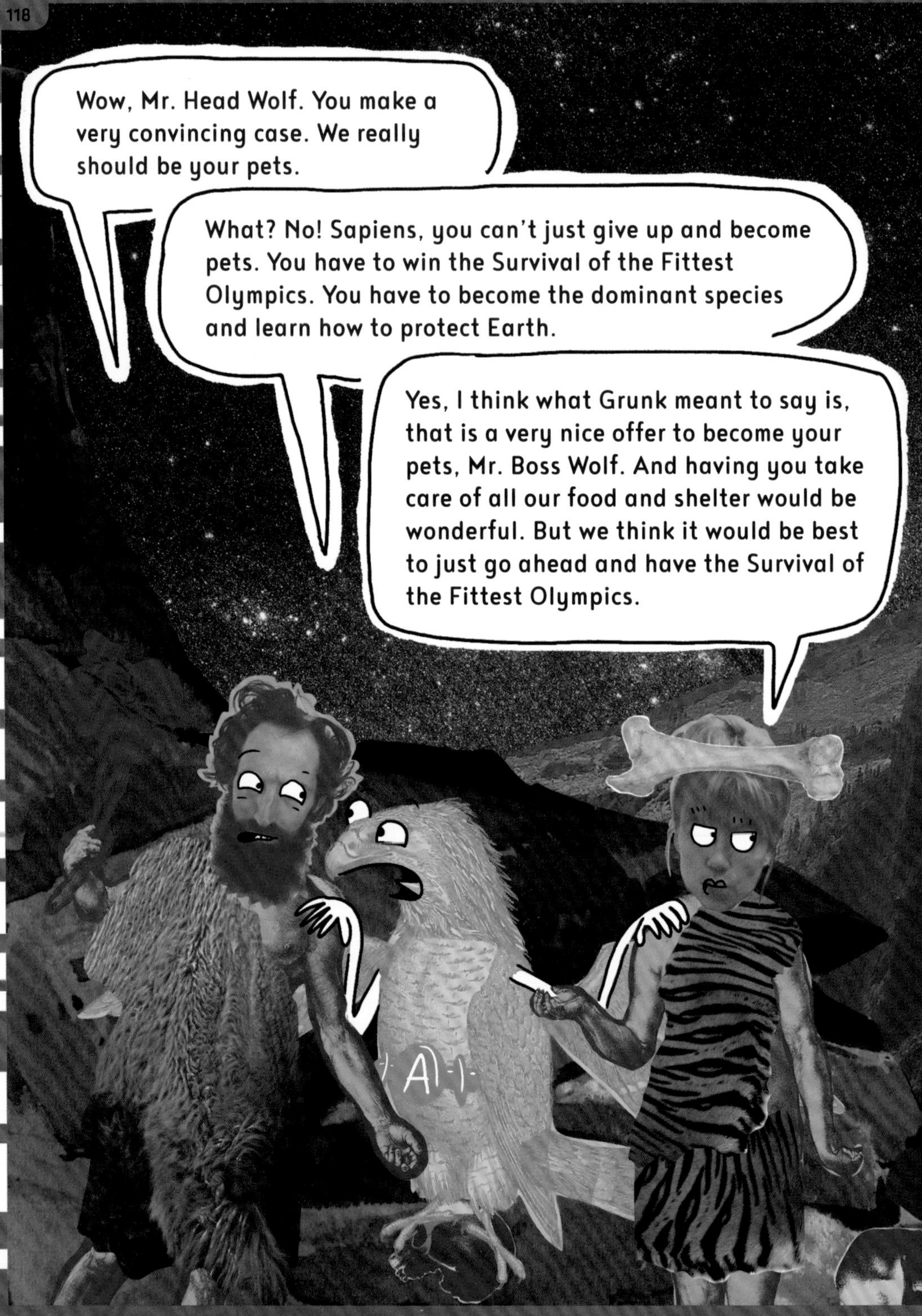
Wow, Mr. Head Wolf. You make a very convincing case. We really should be your pets.
What? No! Sapiens, you can't just give up and become pets. You have to win the Survival of the Fittest Olympics. You have to become the dominant species and learn how to protect Earth.
Yes, I think what Grunk meant to say is, that is a very nice offer to become your pets, Mr. Boss Wolf. And having you take care of all our food and shelter would be wonderful. But we think it would be best to just go ahead and have the Survival of the Fittest Olympics.
AI

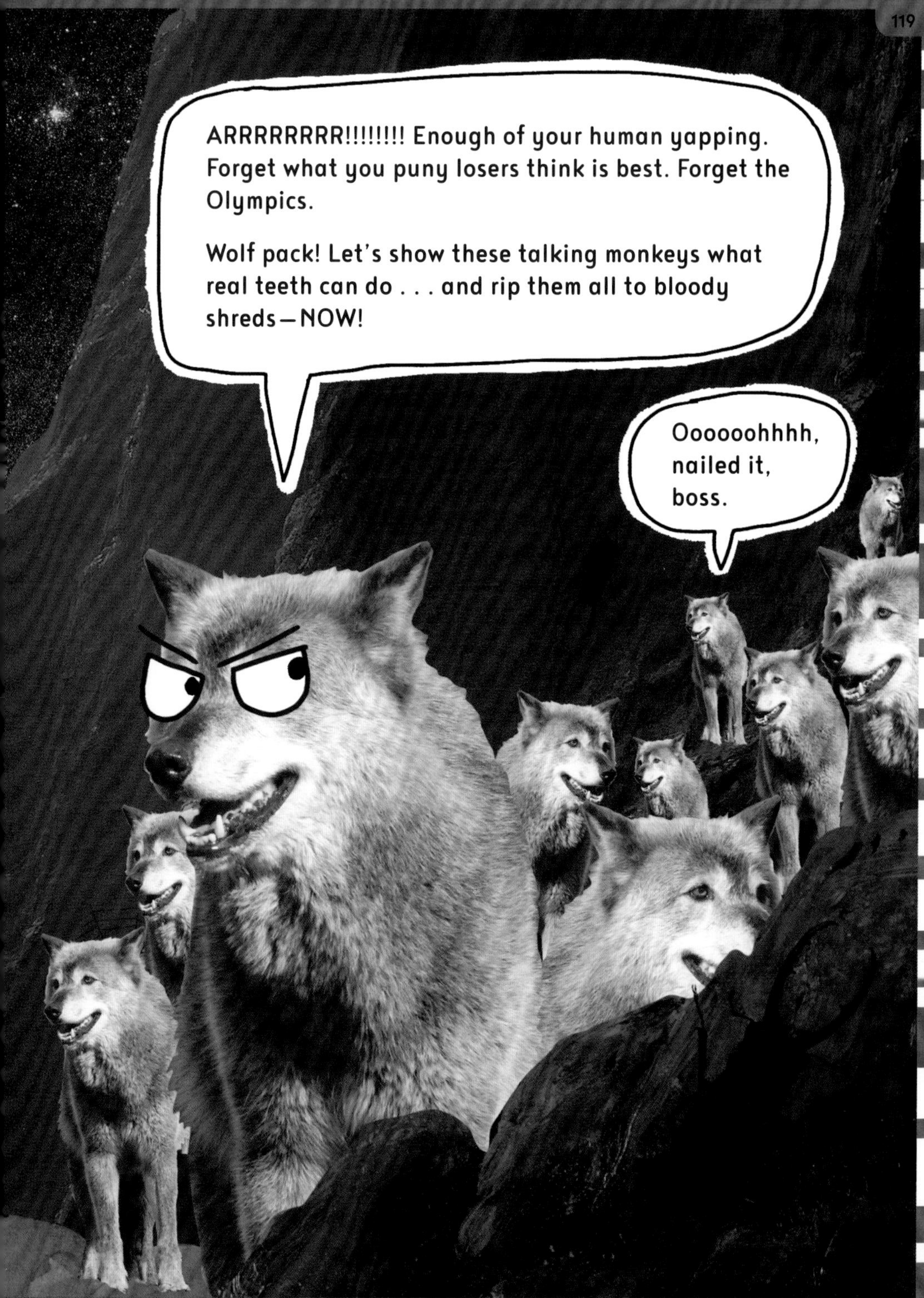
ARRRRRRRR!!!!!!!! Enough of your human yapping. Forget what you puny losers think is best. Forget the Olympics.
Wolf pack! Let's show these talking monkeys what real teeth can do . . . and rip them all to bloody shreds—NOW!
Oooooohhhh, nailed it, boss.

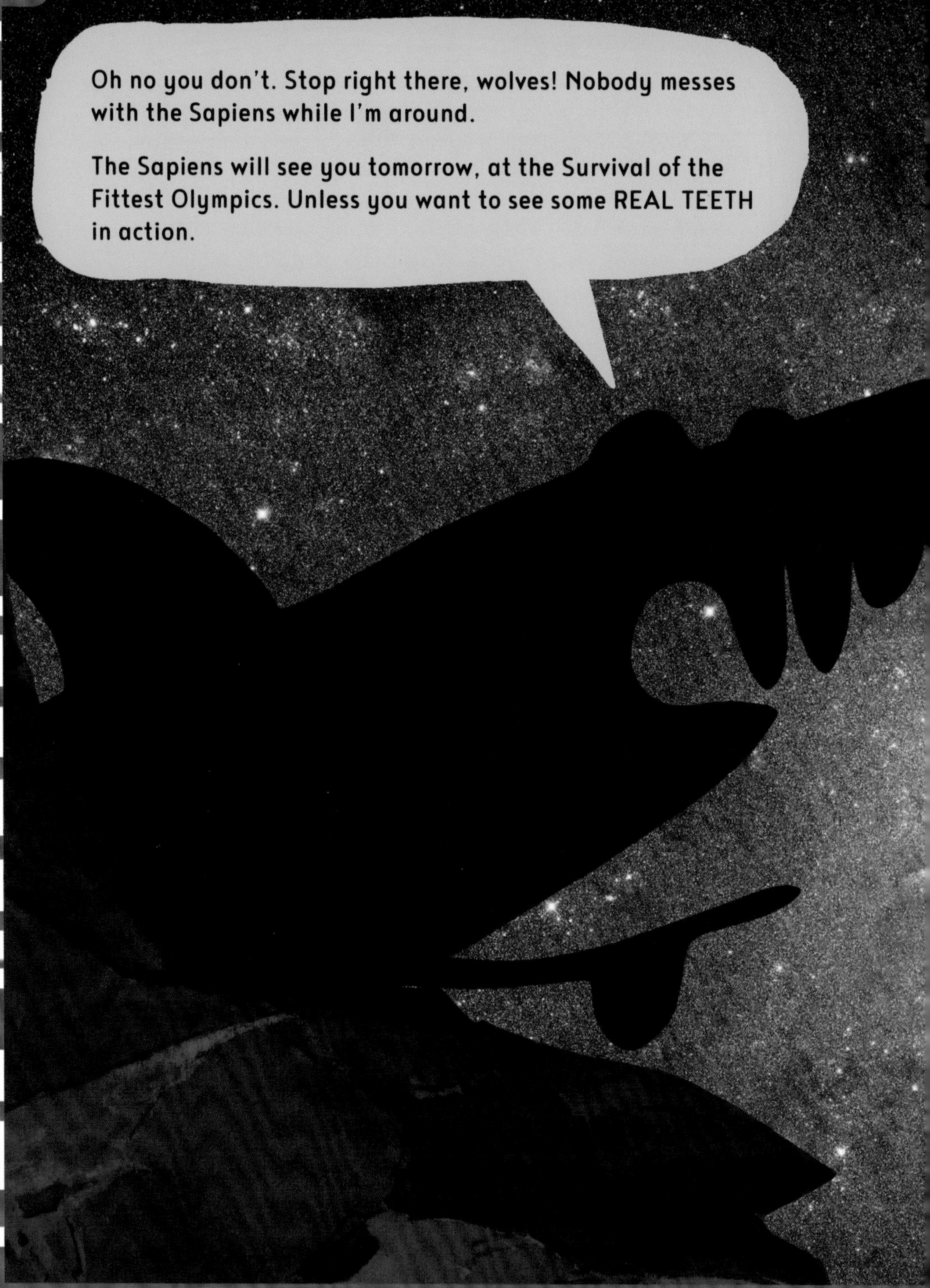
Oh no you don't. Stop right there, wolves! Nobody messes with the Sapiens while I'm around.
The Sapiens will see you tomorrow, at the Survival of the Fittest Olympics. Unless you want to see some REAL TEETH in action.

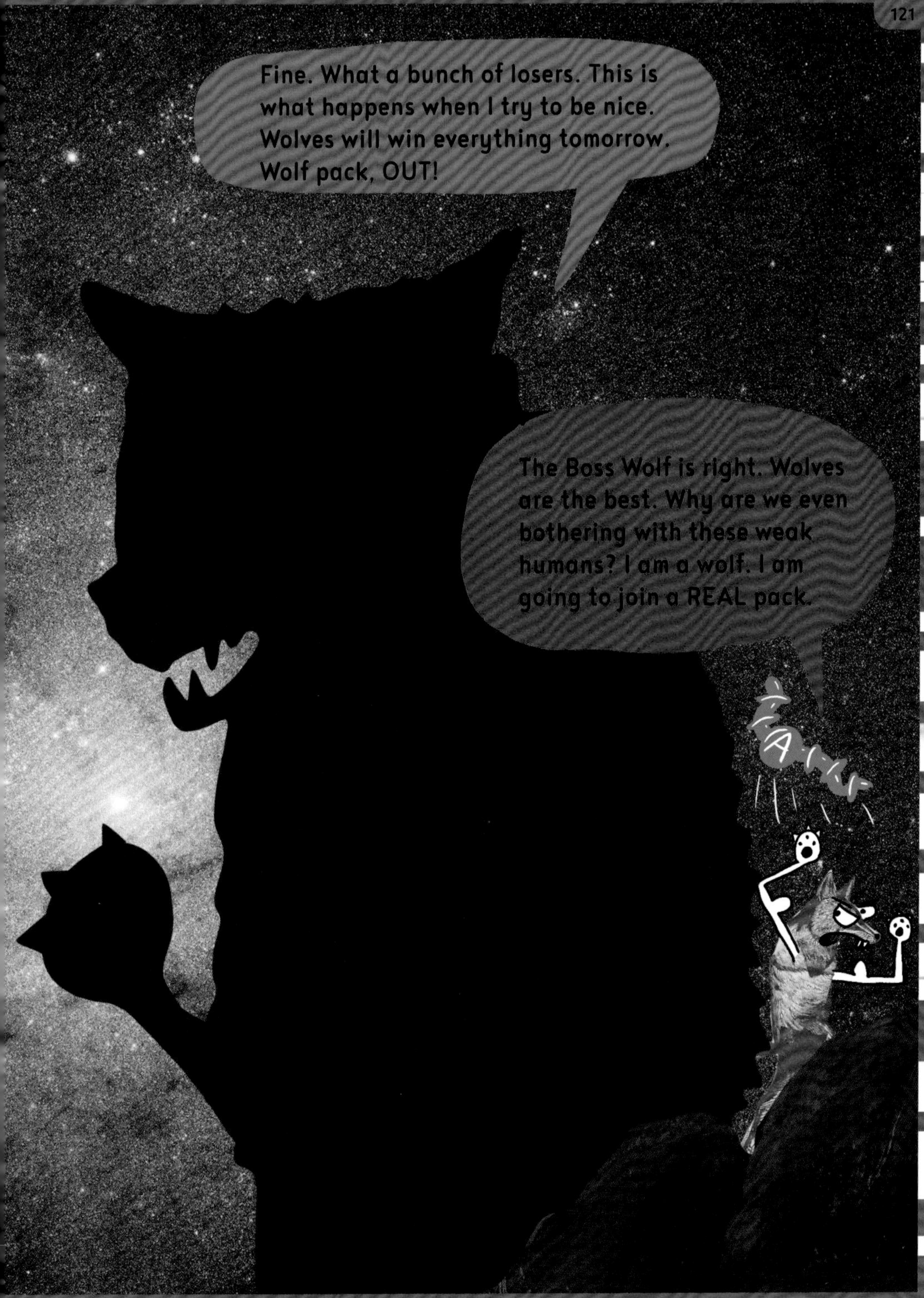
Fine. What a bunch of losers. This is what happens when I try to be nice. Wolves will win everything tomorrow. Wolf pack, OUT!
The Boss Wolf is right. Wolves are the best. Why are we even bothering with these weak humans? I am a wolf. I am going to join a REAL pack.

The wolves ran off howling in the moonlight. And AlphaWolf ran off howling with them. I probably don't have to tell you, this kind of freaked everyone out, myself included. But it especially freaked out SmartHawk.

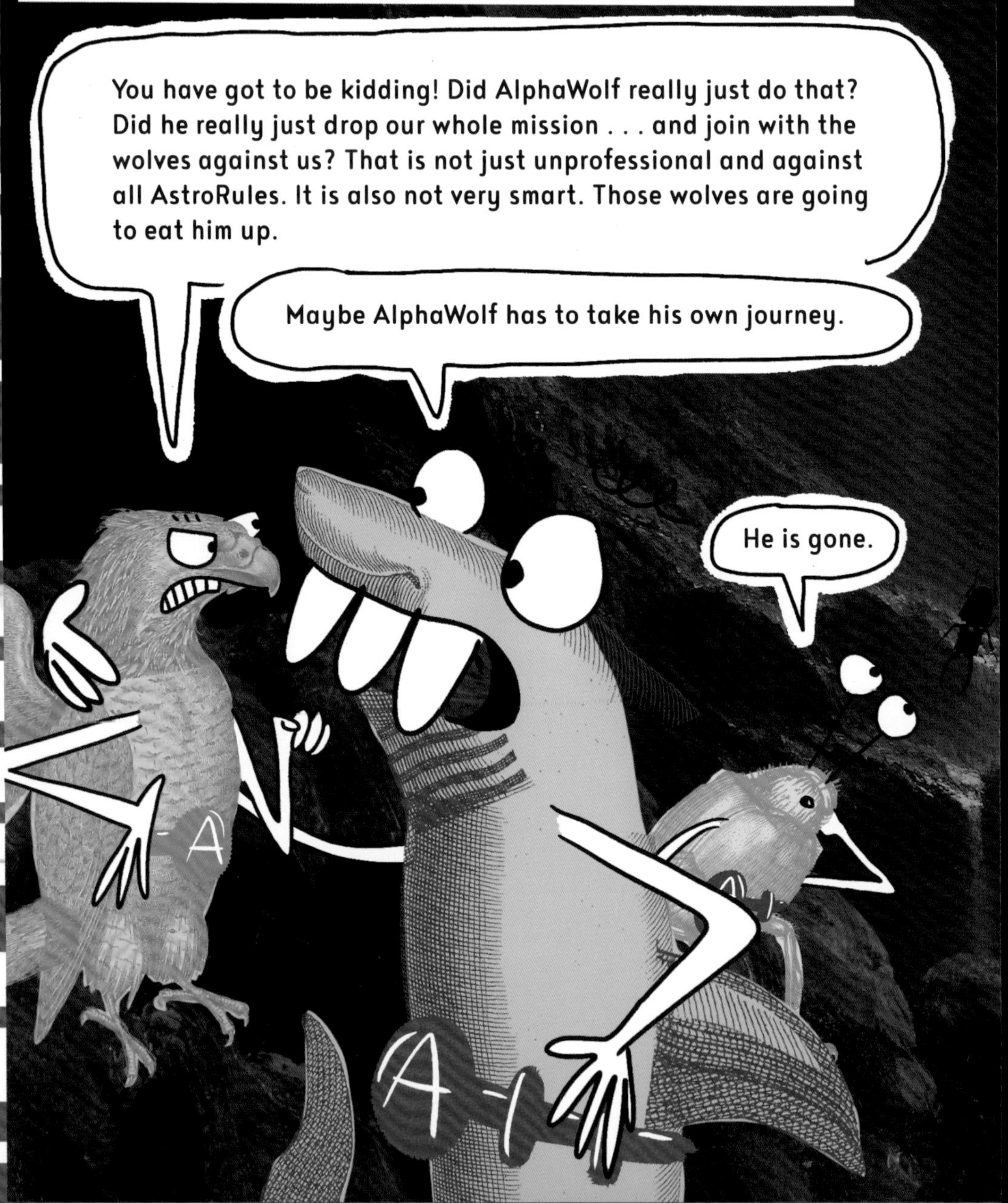
You have got to be kidding! Did AlphaWolf really just do that? Did he really just drop our whole mission . . . and join with the wolves against us? That is not just unprofessional and against all AstroRules. It is also not very smart. Those wolves are going to eat him up.
Maybe AlphaWolf has to take his own journey.
He is gone.

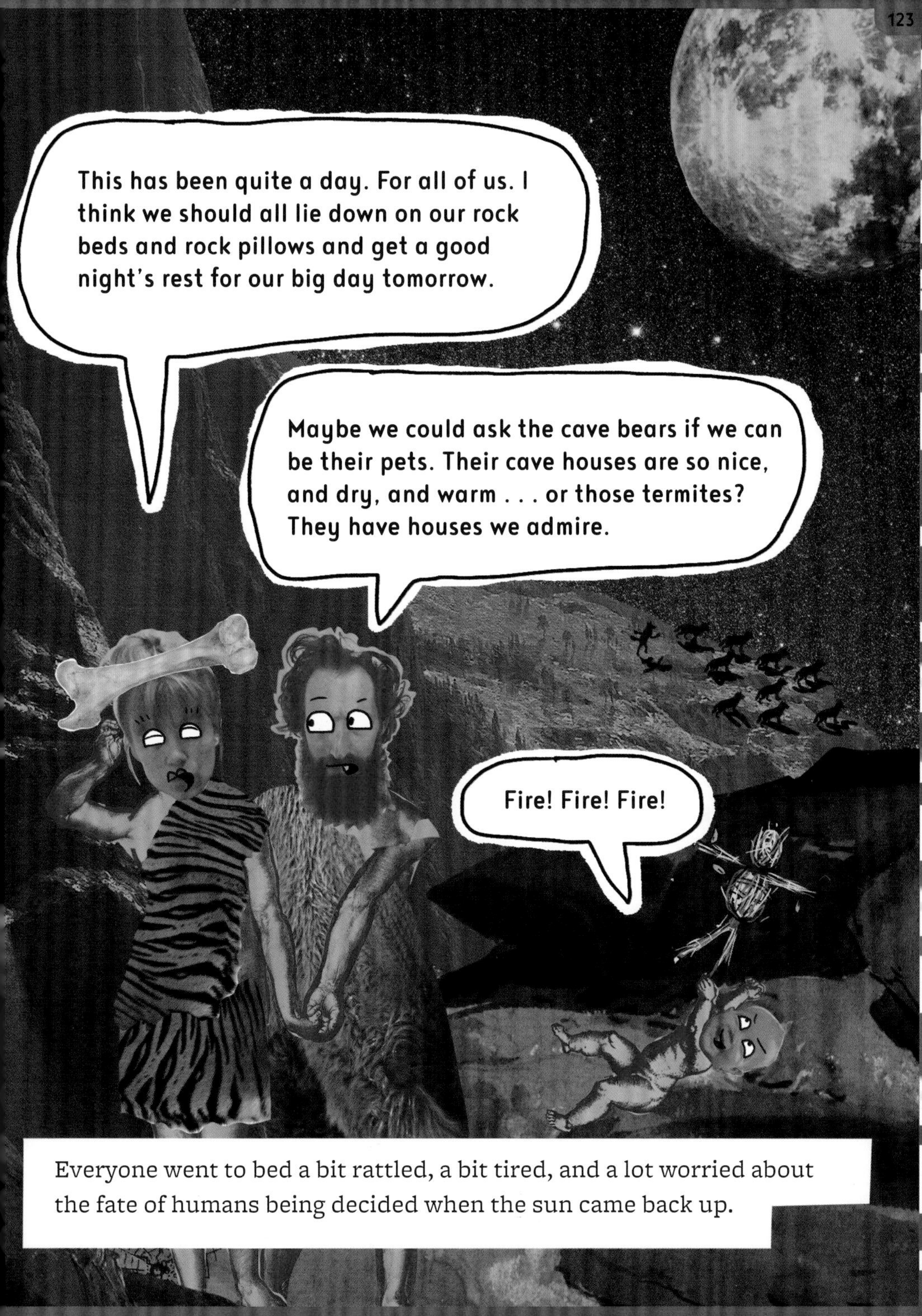
This has been quite a day. For all of us. I think we should all lie down on our rock beds and rock pillows and get a good night's rest for our big day tomorrow.
Maybe we could ask the cave bears if we can be their pets. Their cave houses are so nice, and dry, and warm . . . or those termites? They have houses we admire.
Fire! Fire! Fire!

Everyone went to bed a bit rattled, a bit tired, and a lot worried about the fate of humans being decided when the sun came back up.

CHAPTER 18:
Night Shift

Even I found myself a bit disturbed. It looked like AlphaWolf was going to just hand me over to the wolves.

And if you are a spinning planet, as I am, things like this continue to be disturbing, because I never sleep.

Half of me is always facing the sun. I am always half awake, half thinking, half worrying that things are about to go terribly wrong.

But thank goodness for you, me, and all humans, baby Urp was also awake this night 999,999 years ago.

And thank goodness she was using her one advantage more powerful than any tooth or claw or muscle—her brain.

She got to work building her idea to save us all with a:

Then she:

WA-BAM!
WA-BAM!
WA-BAM!
WA-BAM!

She:

CRUN

And:

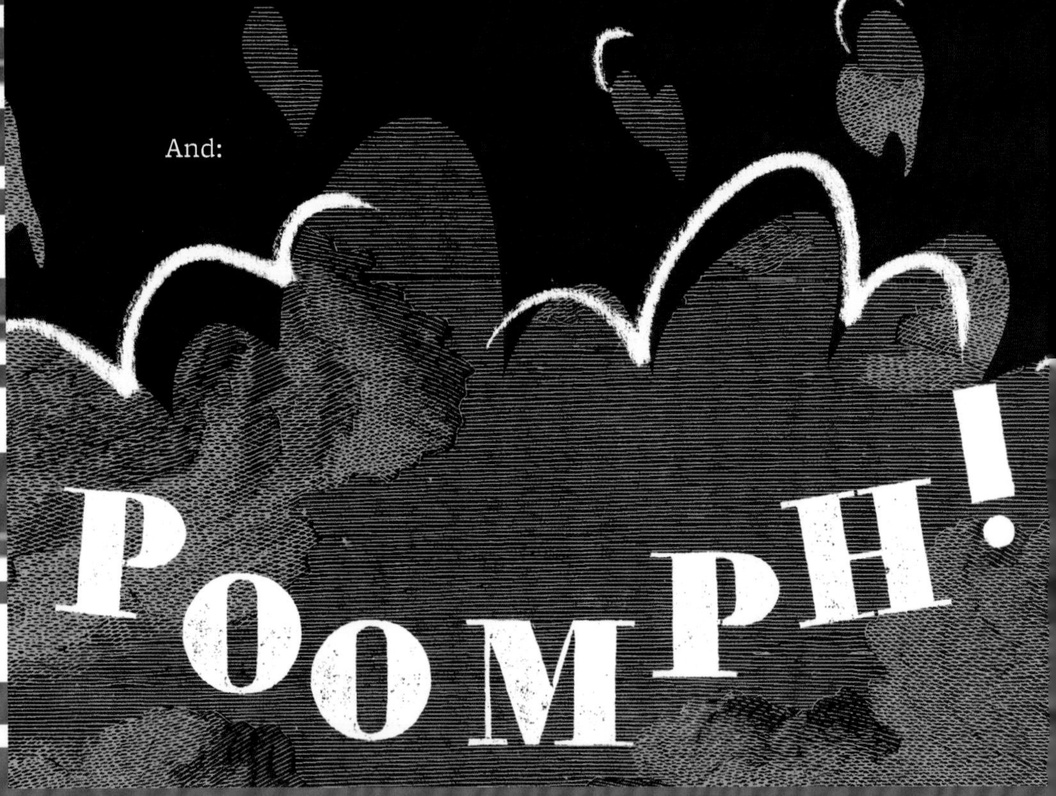
POOMPH!

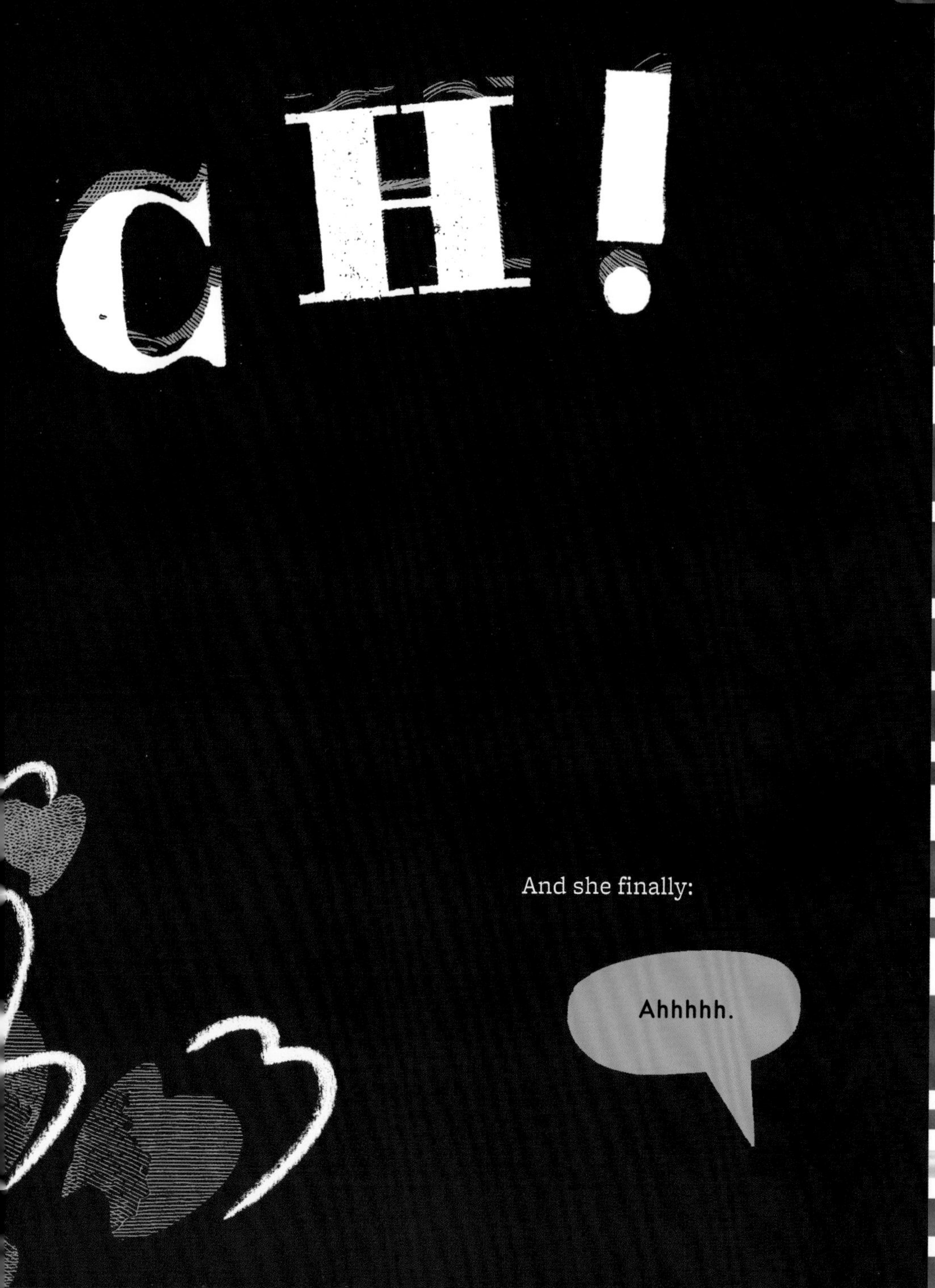
CH!
And she finally:
Ahhhhh.

CHAPTER 19:

Wolf Night Shift

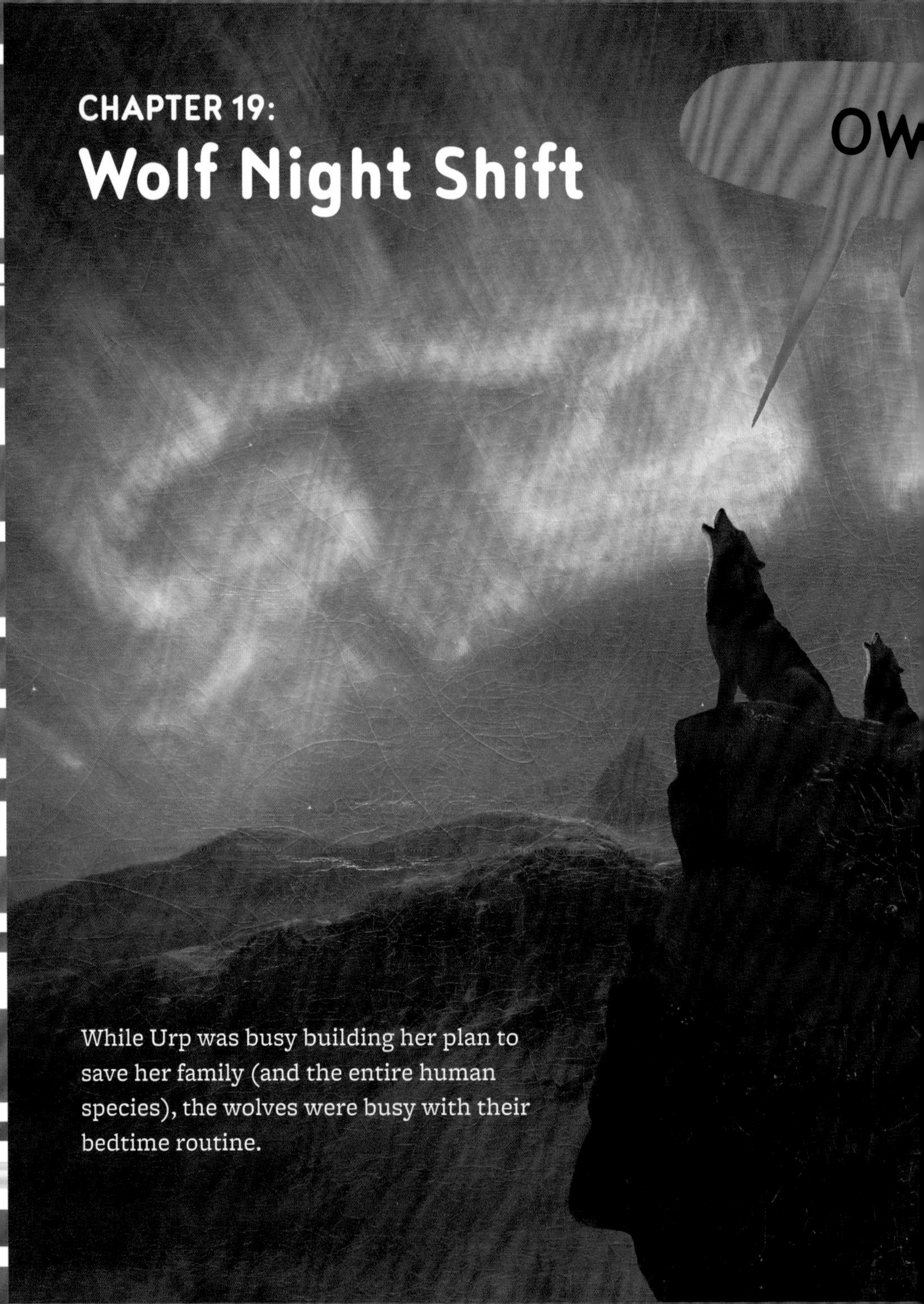
OW

While Urp was busy building her plan to save her family (and the entire human species), the wolves were busy with their bedtime routine.

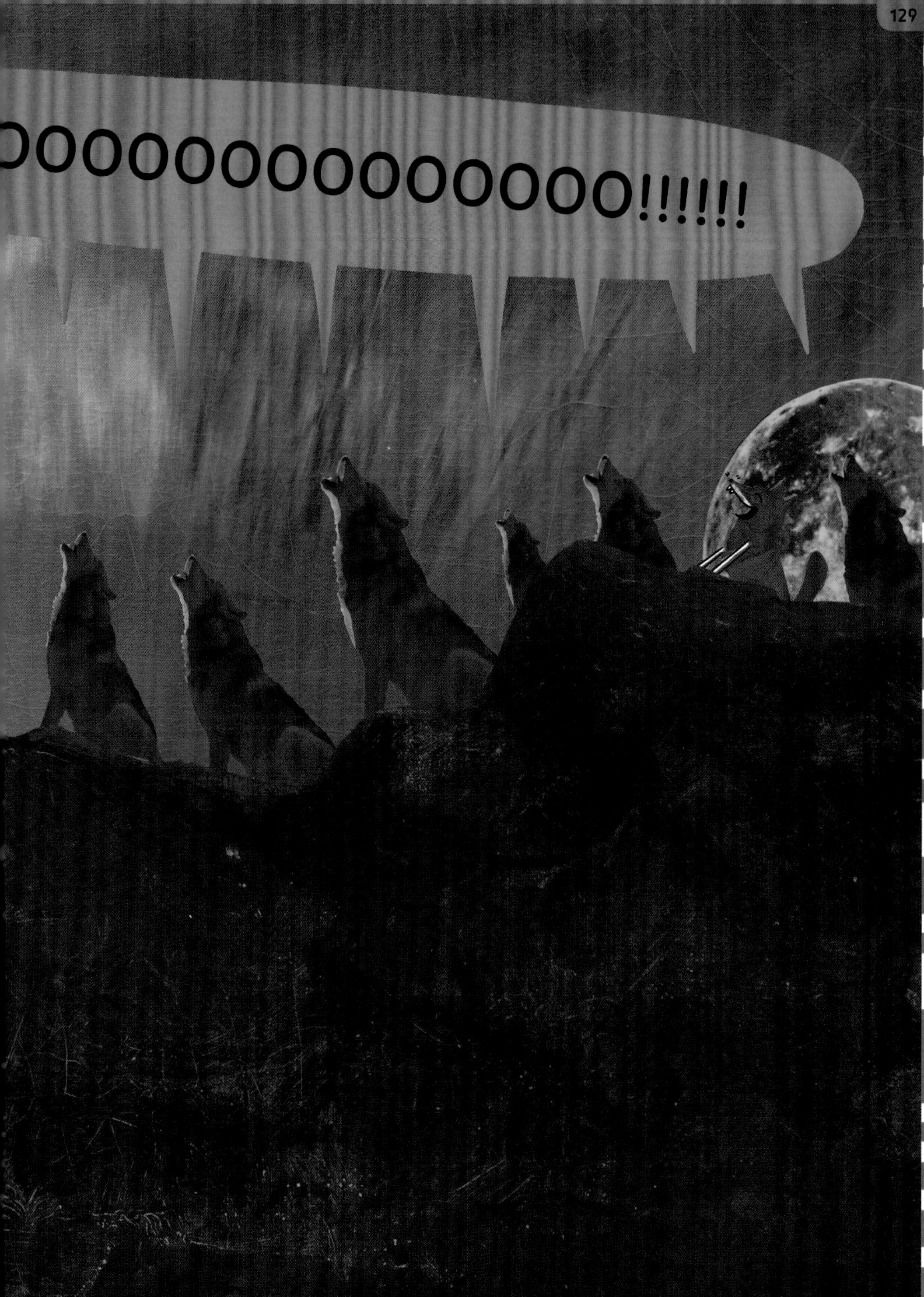
OOOOOOOOOOOOO!!!!!!

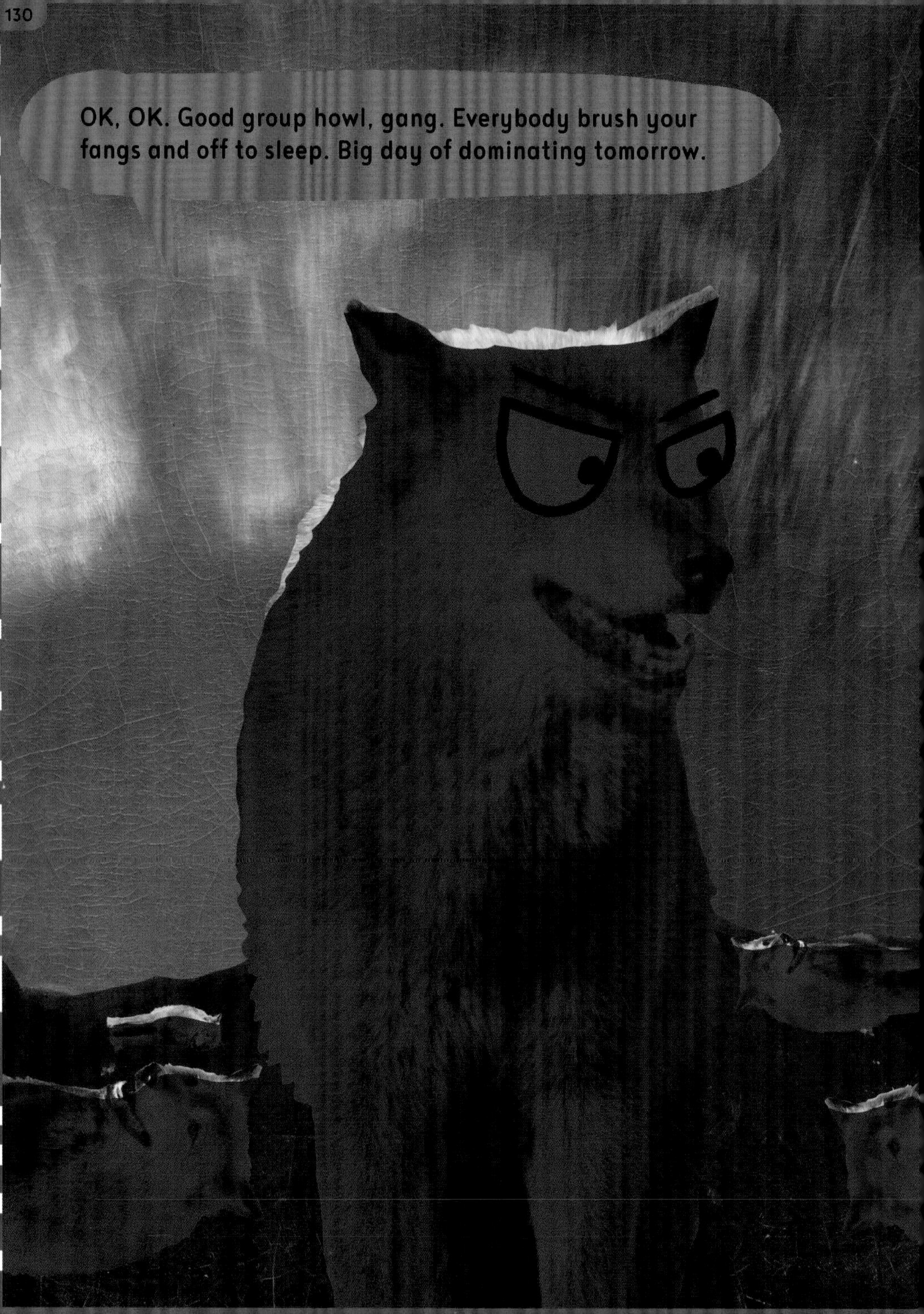
OK, OK. Good group howl, gang. Everybody brush your fangs and off to sleep. Big day of dominating tomorrow.

Oh, yeah! This is the life! Wild and free! Goooooooooo, wolves!

What? Oh, it's you—that AstroRunt. Welcome to the wolf pack. You are the newest and the puniest, so you are the new Omega. Bottom of the pack. Now pipe down and get to work.

But I am from the future! And I have REAL-STRONG-IUM claws! And I am superfast!

That's great. You can use all of that to real-strong and real-fast clean up the wolf den, fluff up my bedding, and roll over on your back.

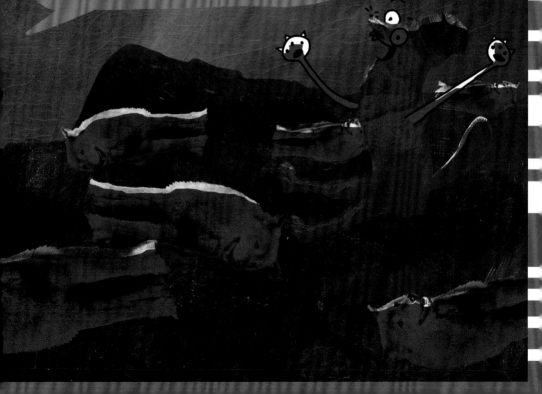

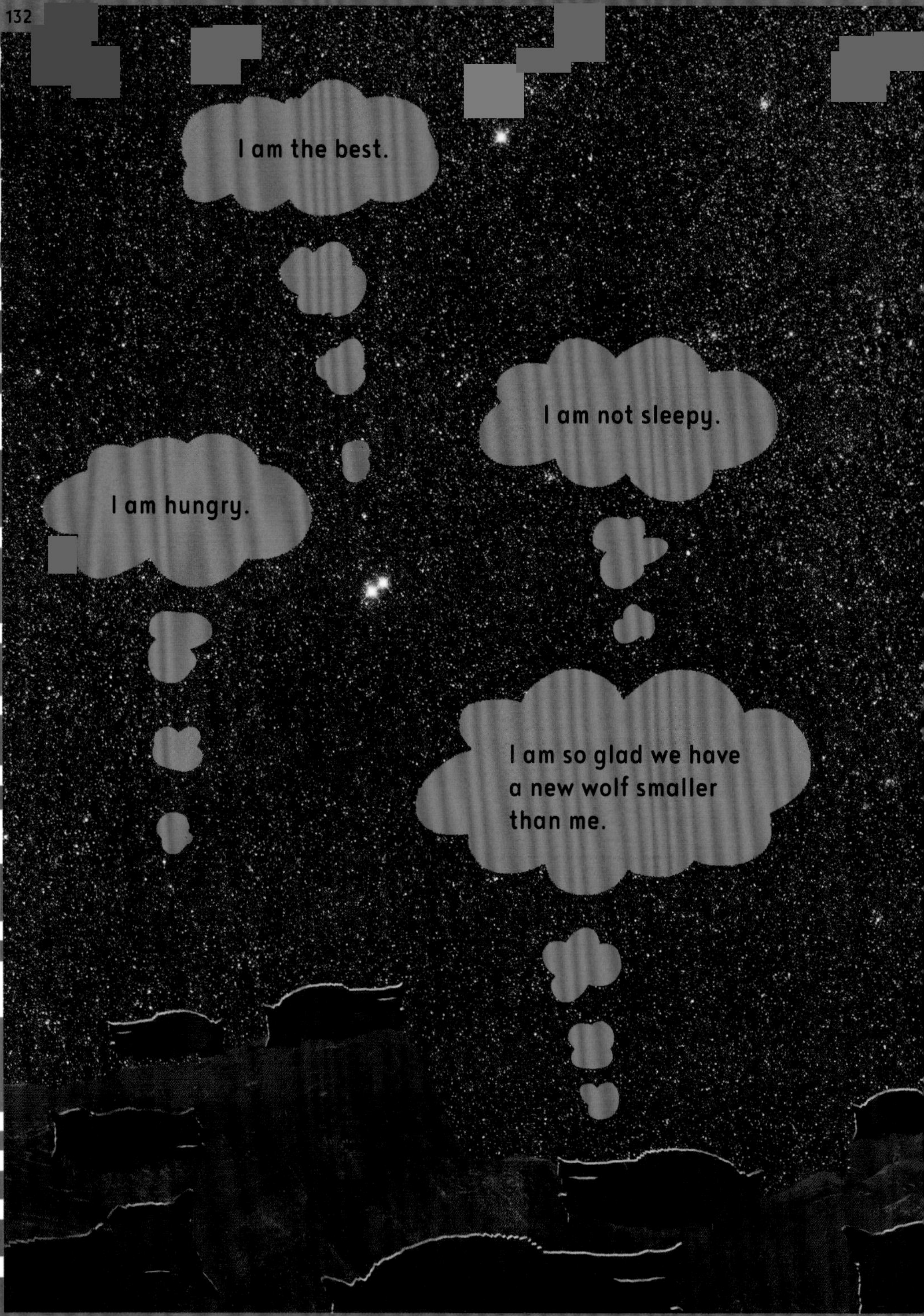
I am the best.
I am not sleepy.
I am hungry.
I am so glad we have a new wolf smaller than me.

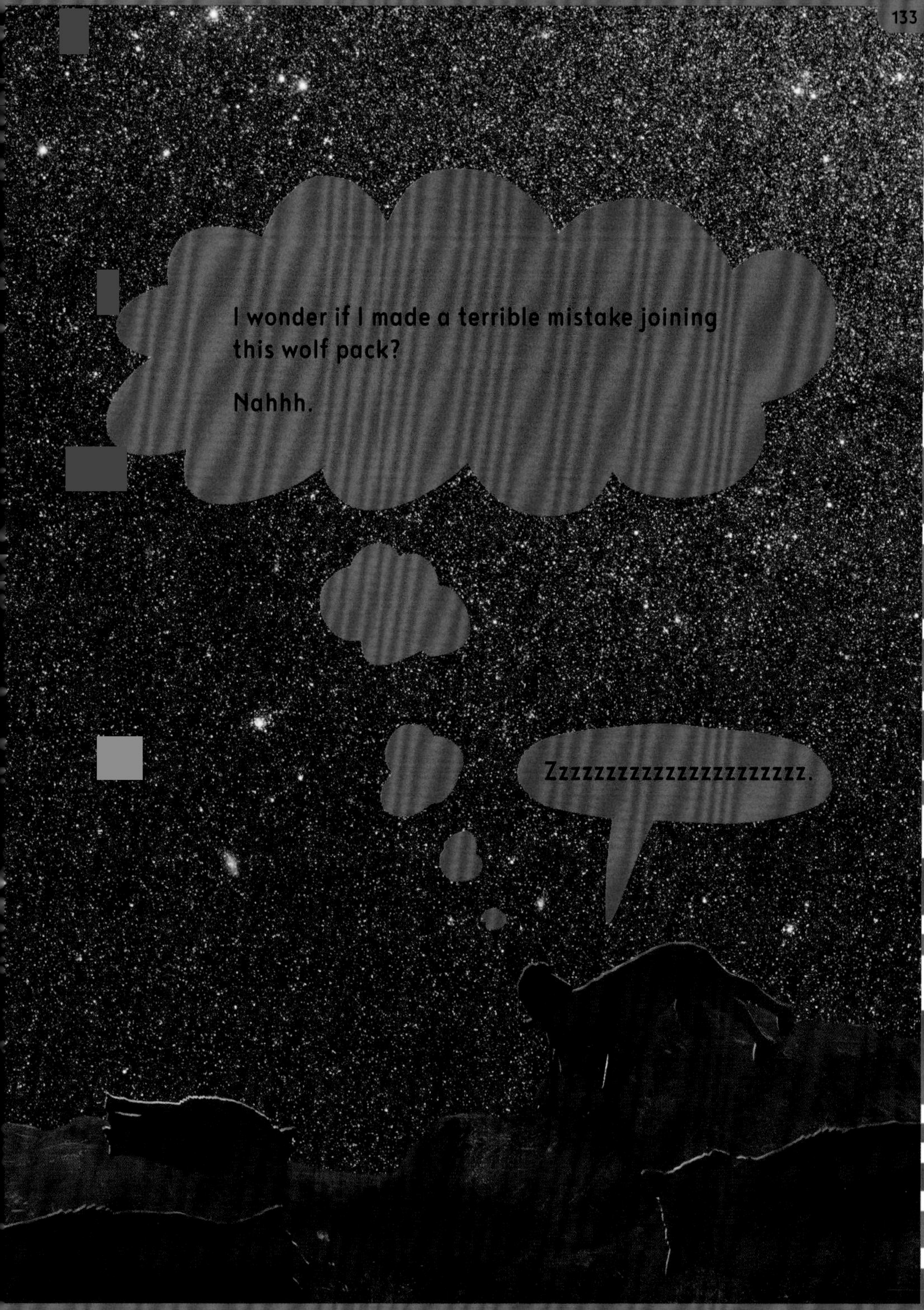
I wonder if I made a terrible mistake joining this wolf pack?
Nahhh.
Zzzzzzzzzzzzzzzzzzzzzz.

CHAPTER 20:
Sunrise

This is it, team.

The big day for us, the fate of humans, the fate of the whole Earth.

We have lost a team member. But we are in good shape! We have a plan for the Sapiens to win the Survival of the Fittest Olympics. We have shown the Sapiens alternate energy sources. AND—we have not shown them fire.

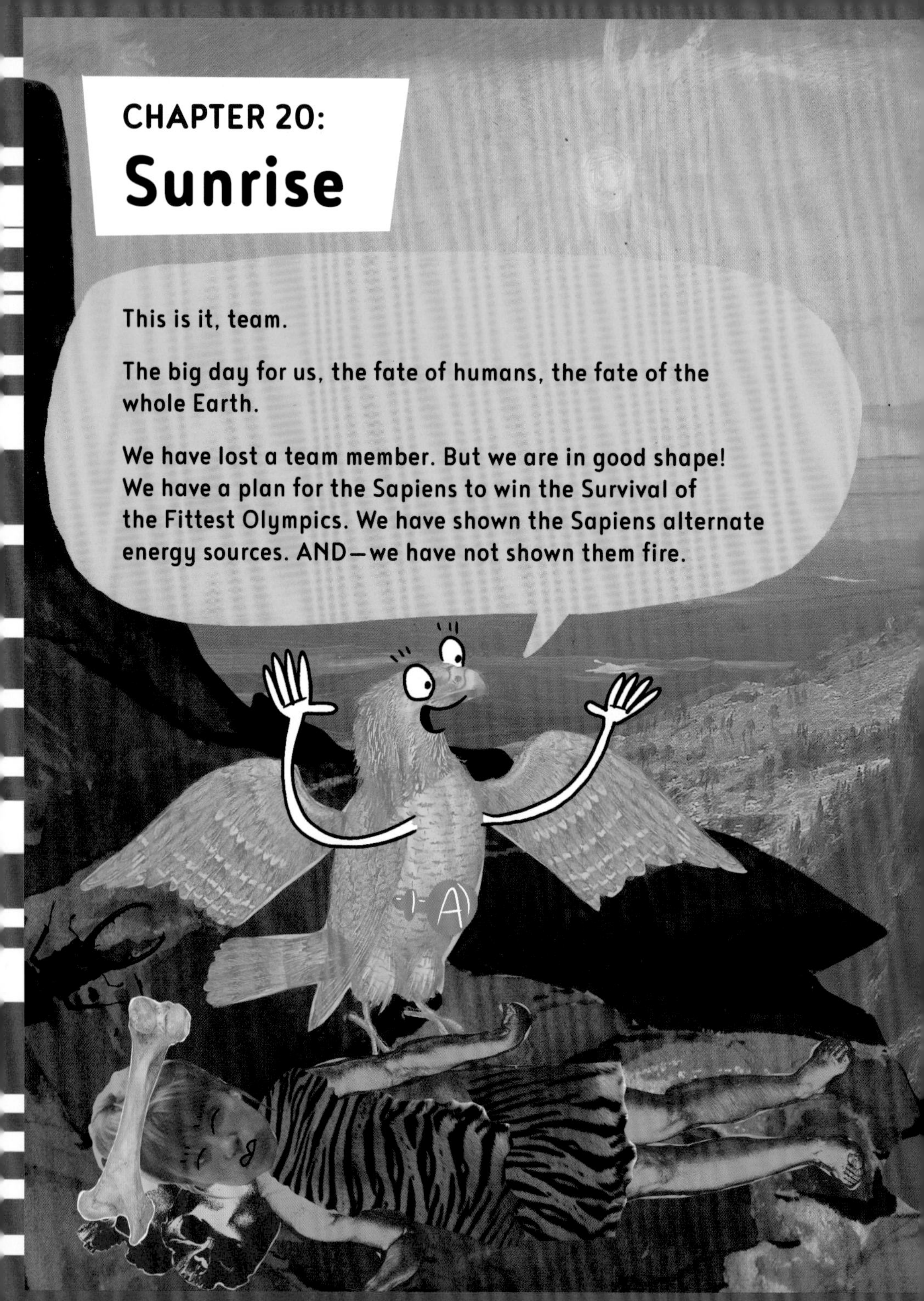

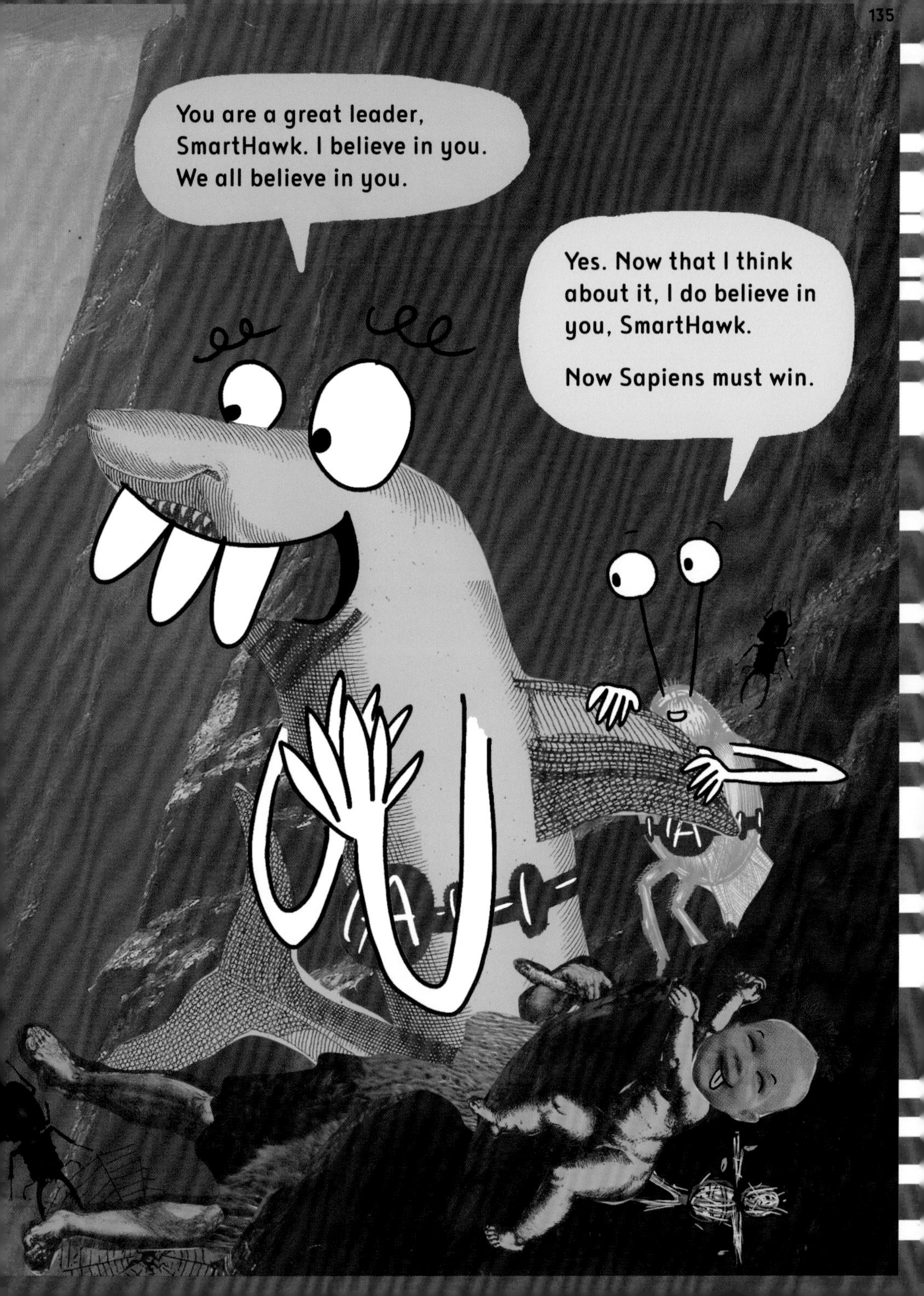
You are a great leader, SmartHawk. I believe in you. We all believe in you.
Yes. Now that I think about it, I do believe in you, SmartHawk.
Now Sapiens must win.

CHAPTER 21:
Sunrise, Wolfstyle

At the wolf den, the Boss Wolf welcomed AlphaWolf in the traditional way that the highest-ranking wolf greets the new lowest-ranking wolf.

And AlphaWolf reacted how everyone reacts when you put their hand in warm water when they are sleeping.

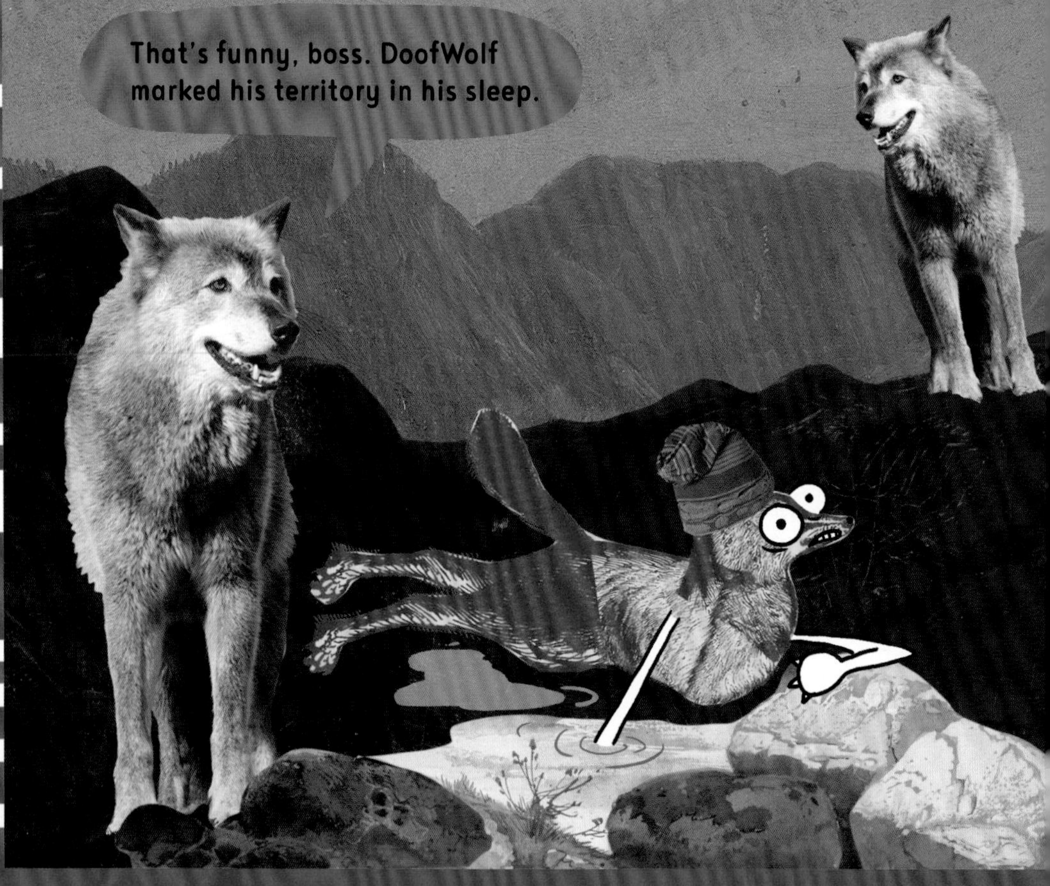
That's funny, boss. DoofWolf marked his territory in his sleep.

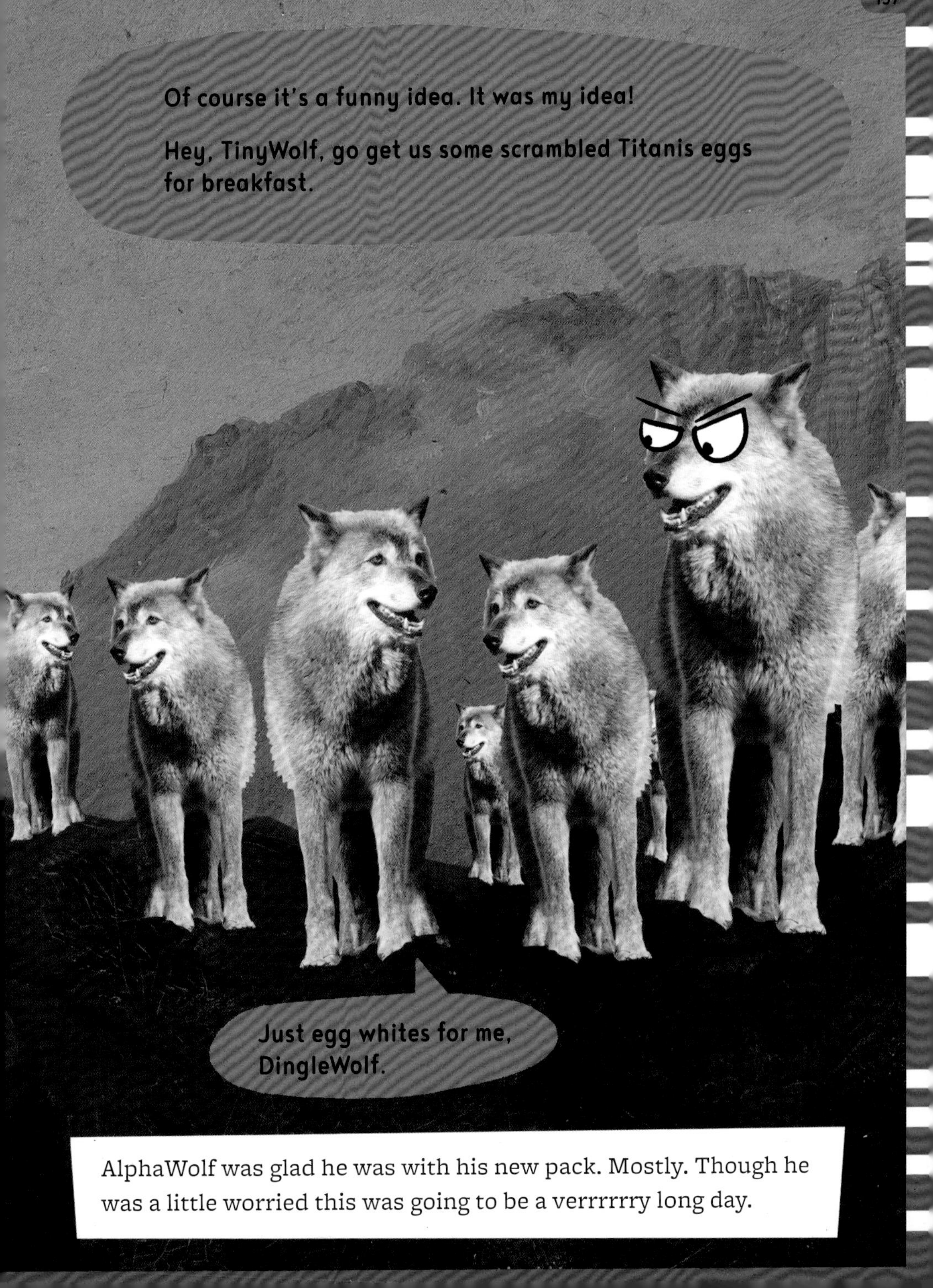
Of course it's a funny idea. It was my idea!
Hey, TinyWolf, go get us some scrambled Titanis eggs for breakfast.
Just egg whites for me, DingleWolf.

AlphaWolf was glad he was with his new pack. Mostly. Though he was a little worried this was going to be a verrrrrry long day.

CHAPTER 22:
Breakfast

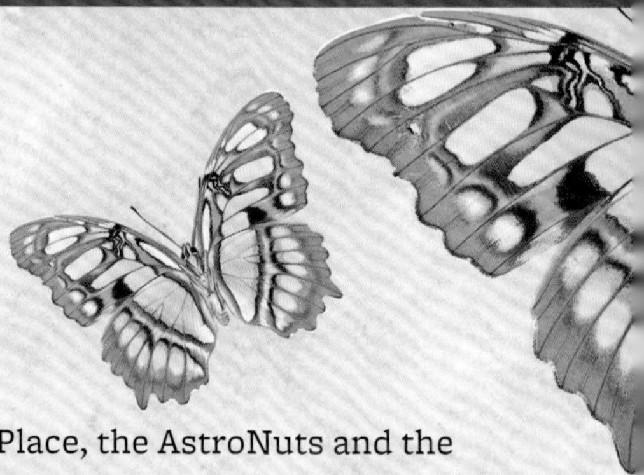

Back between the Rock and the Hard Place, the AstroNuts and the Sapiens woke up and were chowing down on what turned out to be THE BEST BREAKFAST IN THE HISTORY OF EARTH. (Which for the longest time had been Brontosaurus Stomp Waffles with Mango Mash Syrup.)

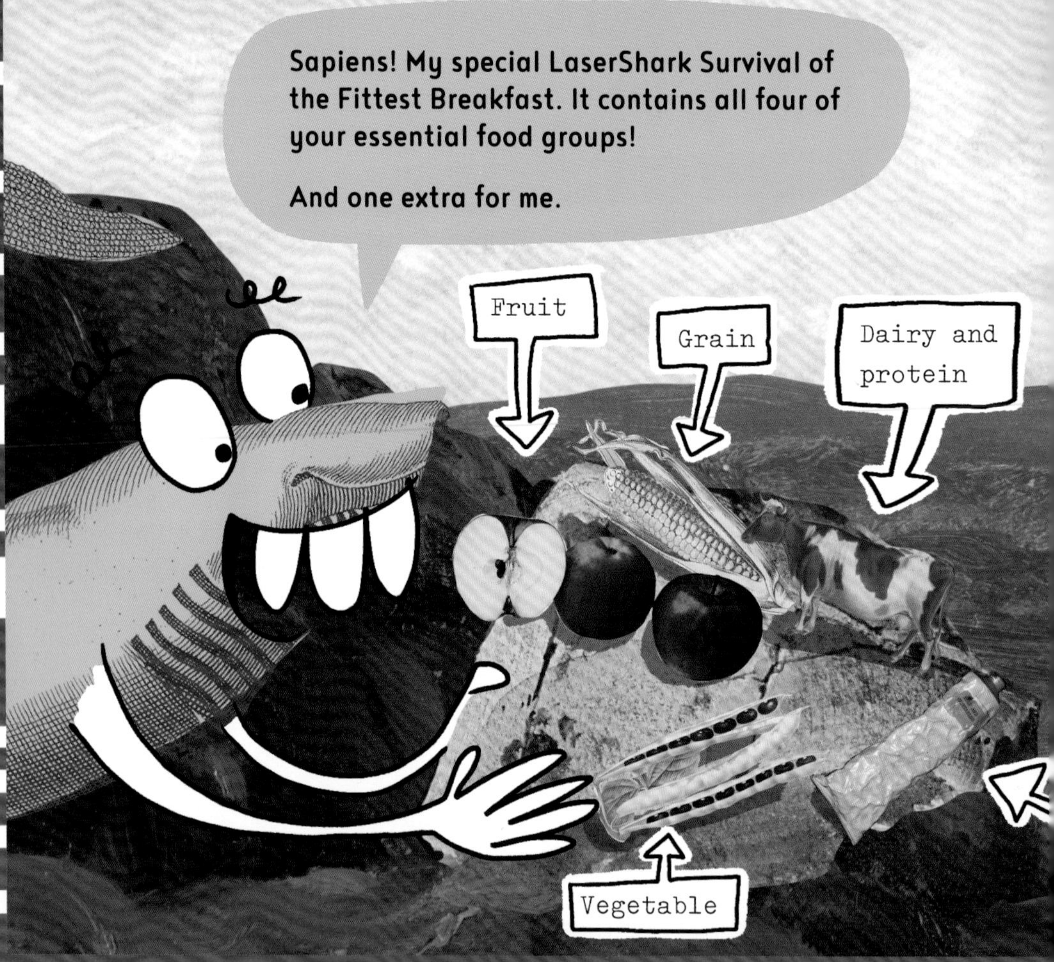

Sapiens! My special LaserShark Survival of the Fittest Breakfast. It contains all four of your essential food groups!
And one extra for me.
Fruit
Grain
Dairy and protein
Vegetable

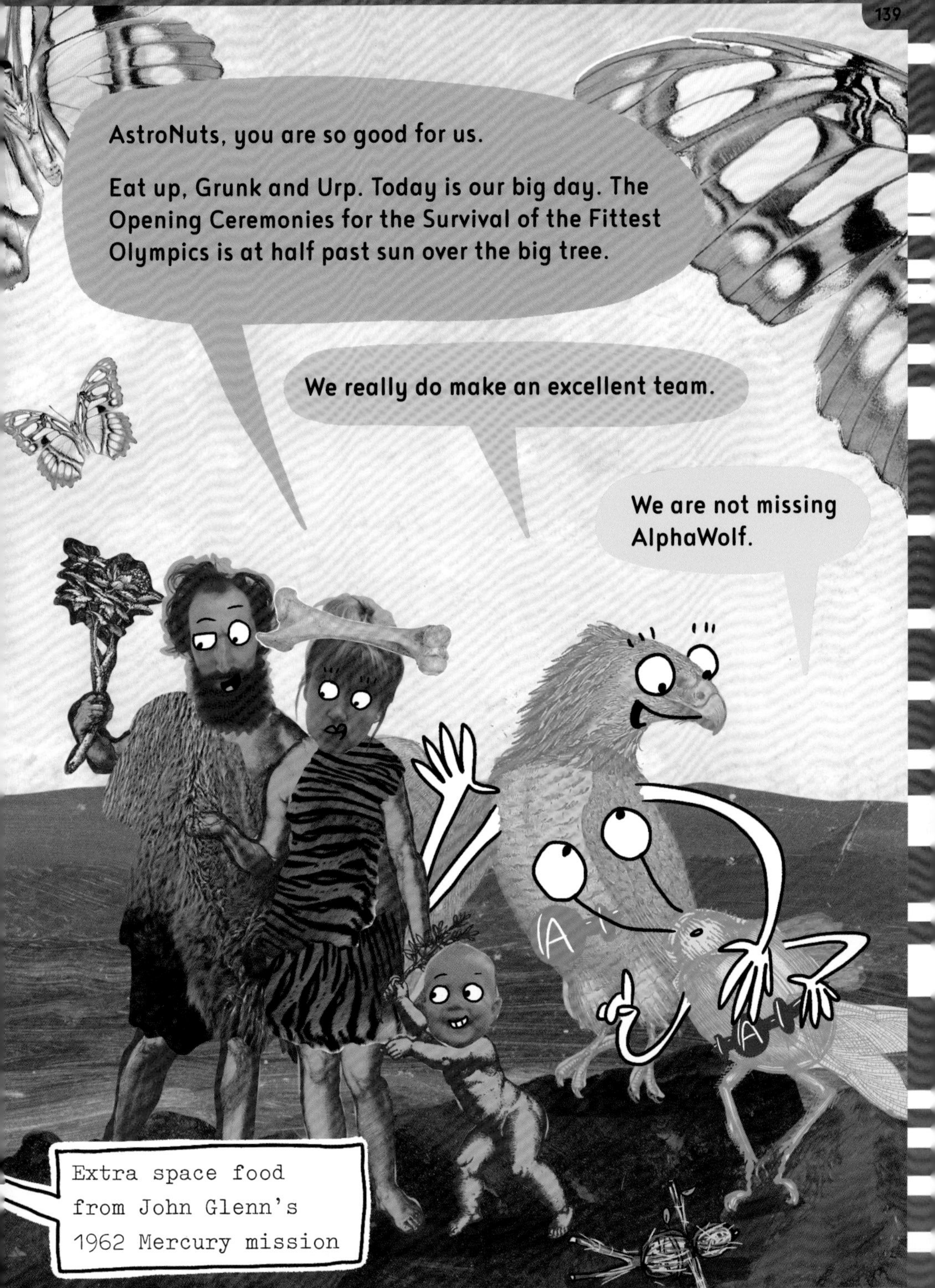
AstroNuts, you are so good for us.
Eat up, Grunk and Urp. Today is our big day. The Opening Ceremonies for the Survival of the Fittest Olympics is at half past sun over the big tree.
We really do make an excellent team.
We are not missing AlphaWolf.
Extra space food from John Glenn's 1962 Mercury mission

CHAPTER 23:

Wolf Pack Breakfast

AlphaWolf quickly discovered that collecting Titanis eggs was not a real thing. He had been pranked again. Wolves don't even like scrambled eggs.

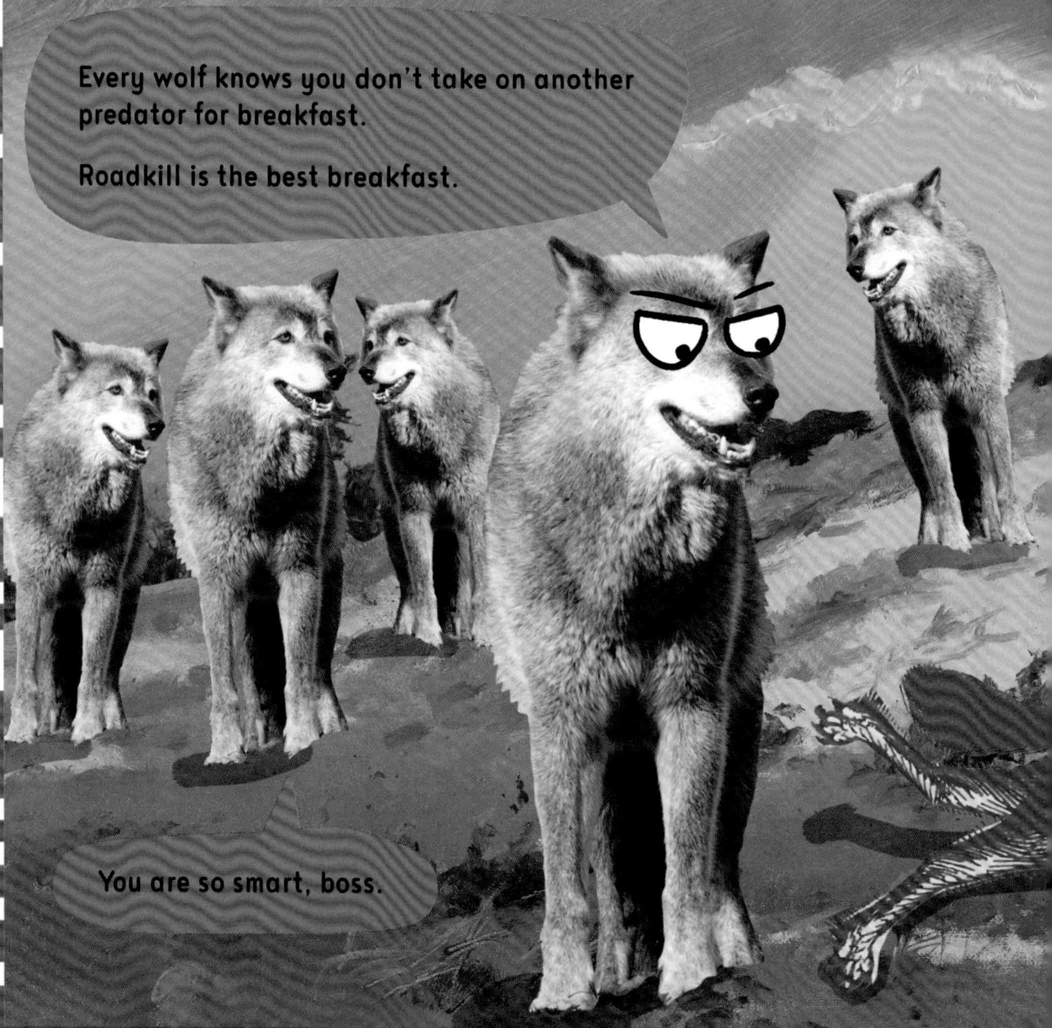
Every wolf knows you don't take on another predator for breakfast.
Roadkill is the best breakfast.
You are so smart, boss.

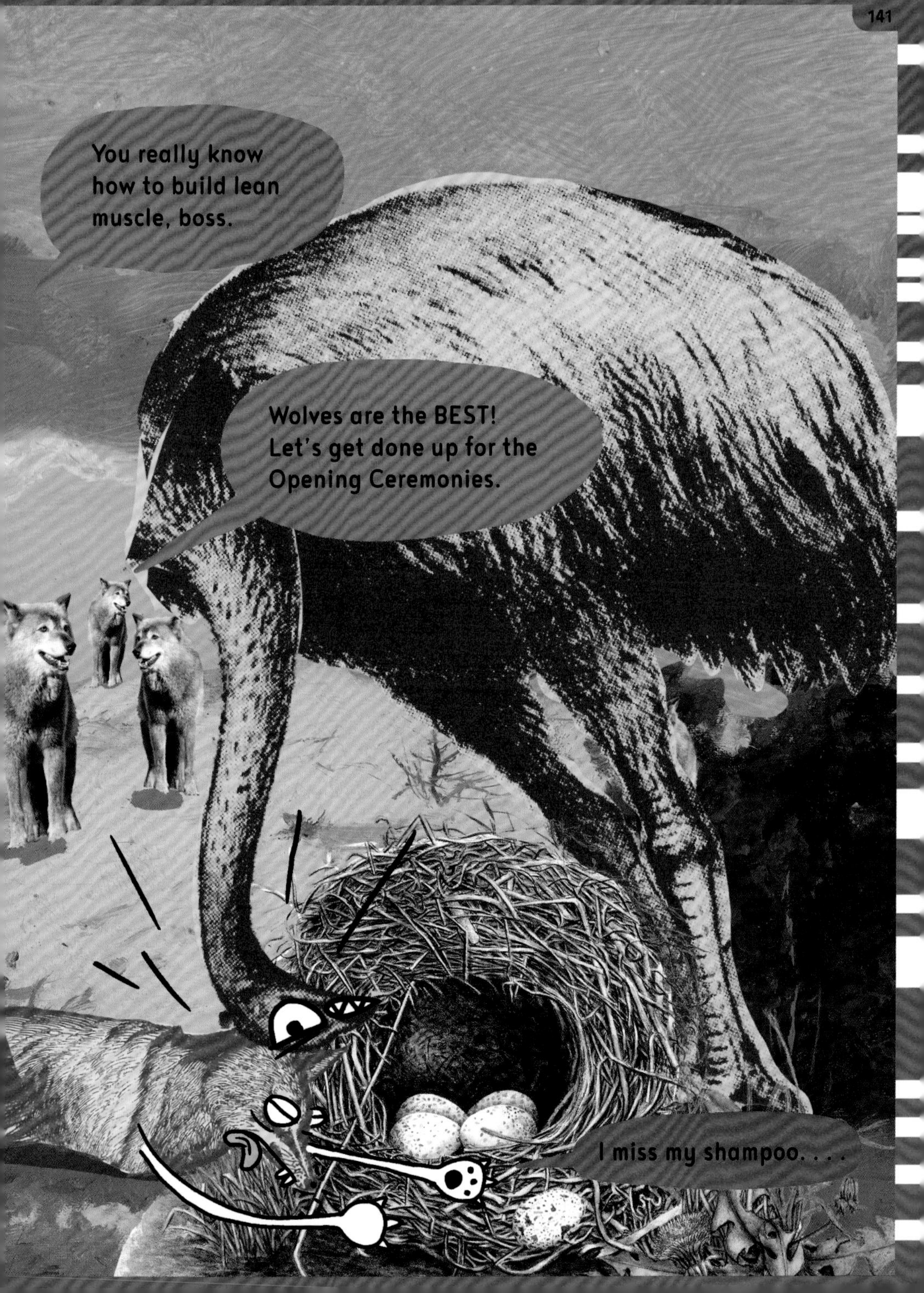
You really know how to build lean muscle, boss.
Wolves are the BEST! Let's get done up for the Opening Ceremonies.
I miss my shampoo. . . .

CHAPTER 24:
Done Up

Again, I would just like to say, I'm sorry. I did have the idea for the Survival of the Fittest Olympics. I did think up golf. But the Opening Ceremonies outfits were NOT my fault.

I don't know who came up with that idea. It always goes wrong.

Sorry.

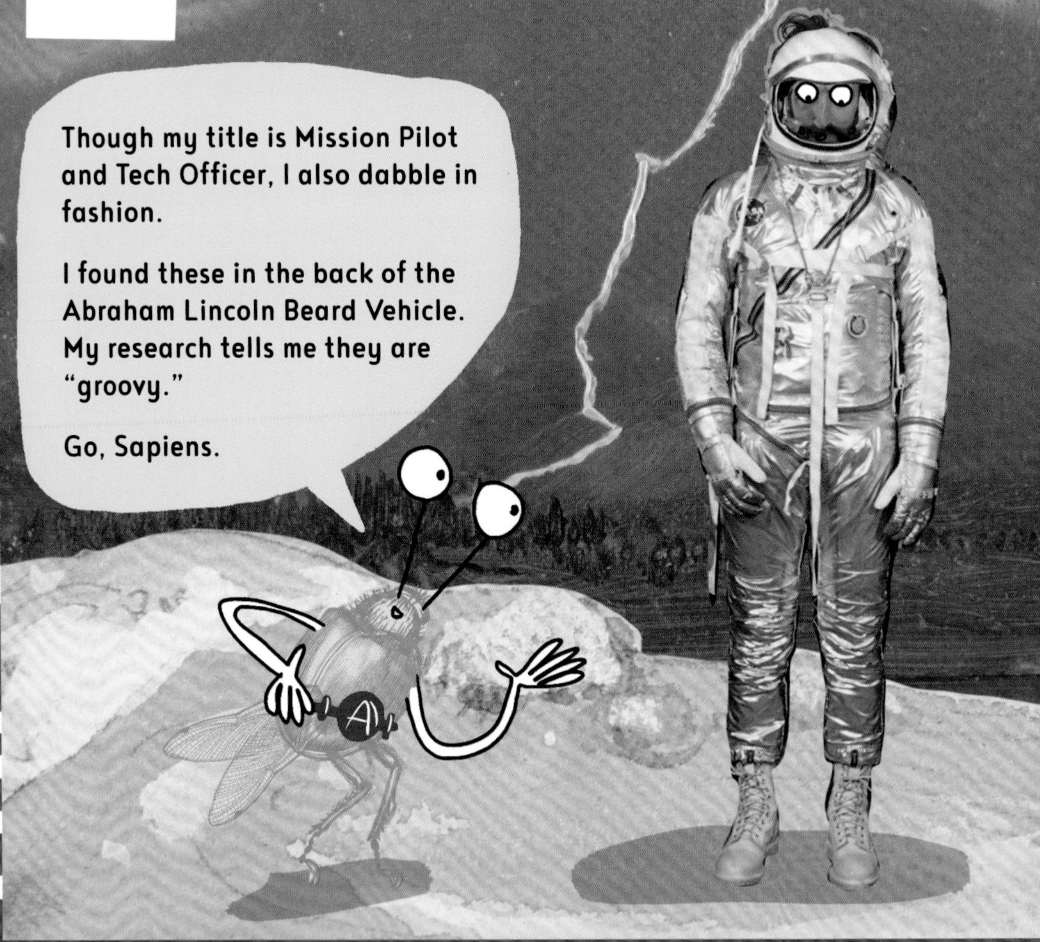
Though my title is Mission Pilot and Tech Officer, I also dabble in fashion.
I found these in the back of the Abraham Lincoln Beard Vehicle. My research tells me they are "groovy."
Go, Sapiens.

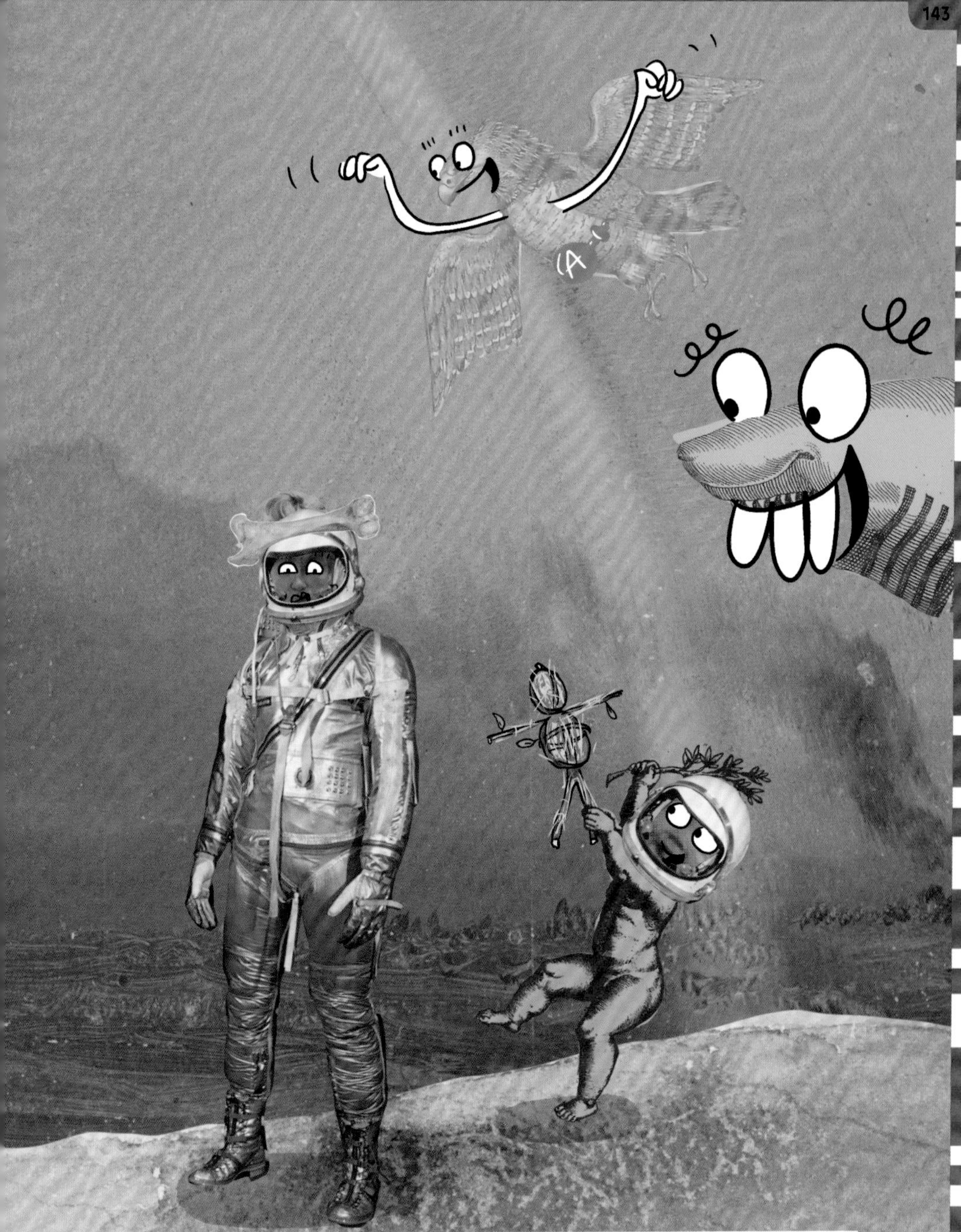

Meanwhile . . . the wolf pack was getting done up . . . in their own particularly wolfish way.

CHAPTER 25:

Mammoth Dung

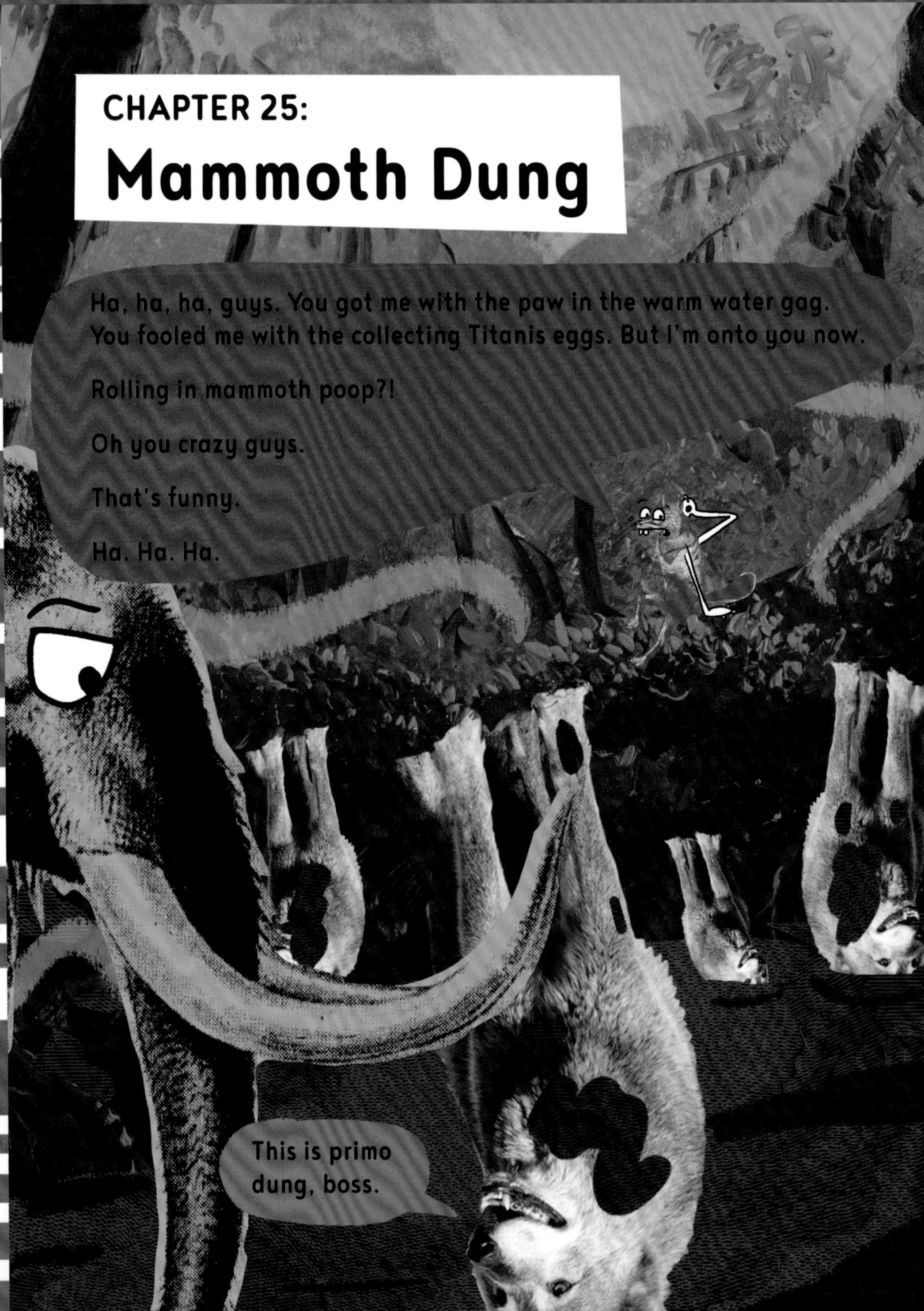
Ha, ha, ha, guys. You got me with the paw in the warm water gag. You fooled me with the collecting Titanis eggs. But I'm onto you now.
Rolling in mammoth poop?!
Oh you crazy guys.
That's funny.
Ha. Ha. Ha.
This is primo dung, boss.

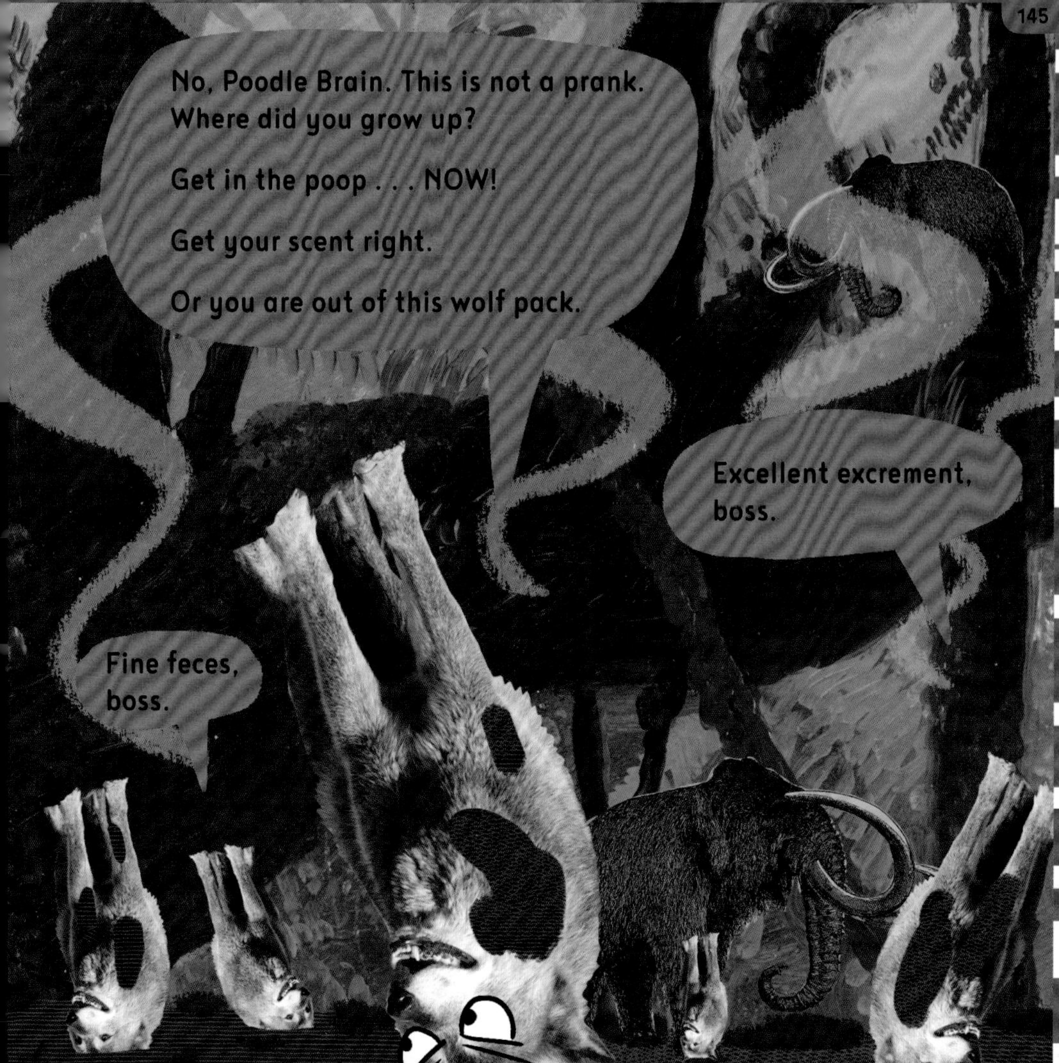
No, Poodle Brain. This is not a prank.
Where did you grow up?
Get in the poop . . . NOW!
Get your scent right.
Or you are out of this wolf pack.
Excellent excrement, boss.
Fine feces, boss.

Yes, wolves actually do roll in feces to disguise their scent during hunts.

So they were rolling in mammoth poop to give themselves an edge in the Olympics. Though it is also a great way to keep other animals away from you. You might want to try it sometime.

And yes, AlphaWolf did do what he had to doo-doo to stay in the wolf pack.

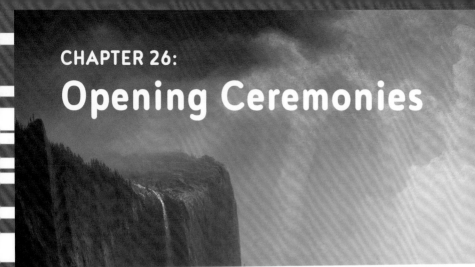

CHAPTER 26:
Opening Ceremonies

Wow. We kind of went off the rails there, huh? Talking about mammoth dung is fine. But I want you to remember the big story was the Survival of the Fittest Olympics. What species would be best? Would the AstroNuts be able to help the Sapiens family enough for them to win? But also not let them discover fire? And not send humans down the destructive path of ruining my climate forever?

All those questions were about to be answered in one important event.

And again—I'm sorry about inventing golf.

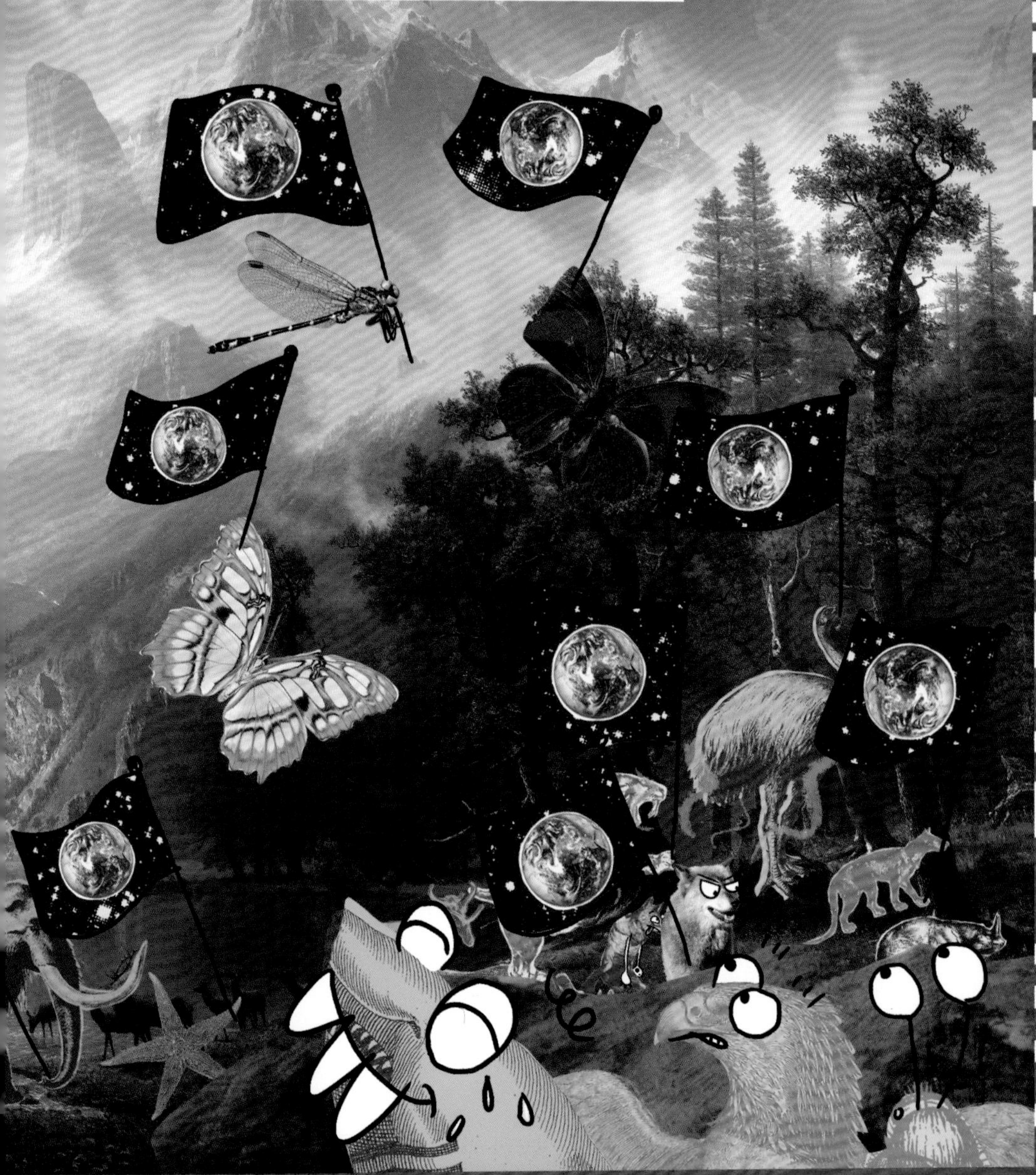

The Opening Ceremonies! Oh, what excitement. What drama. What fashion. The Olympic favorites led the way into the Cambrian Colosseum.

Team Titanis bird! Look at those powerful legs (great for running and kicking). Look at those magnificent beaks (great for pecking, I guess). But who designed those hats?

The dolphins! So smart with those dolphin brains. Equipped with sonar, you know. That could be a huge advantage. And why are they always smiling? Probably because they can't see through those snorkel-masks.

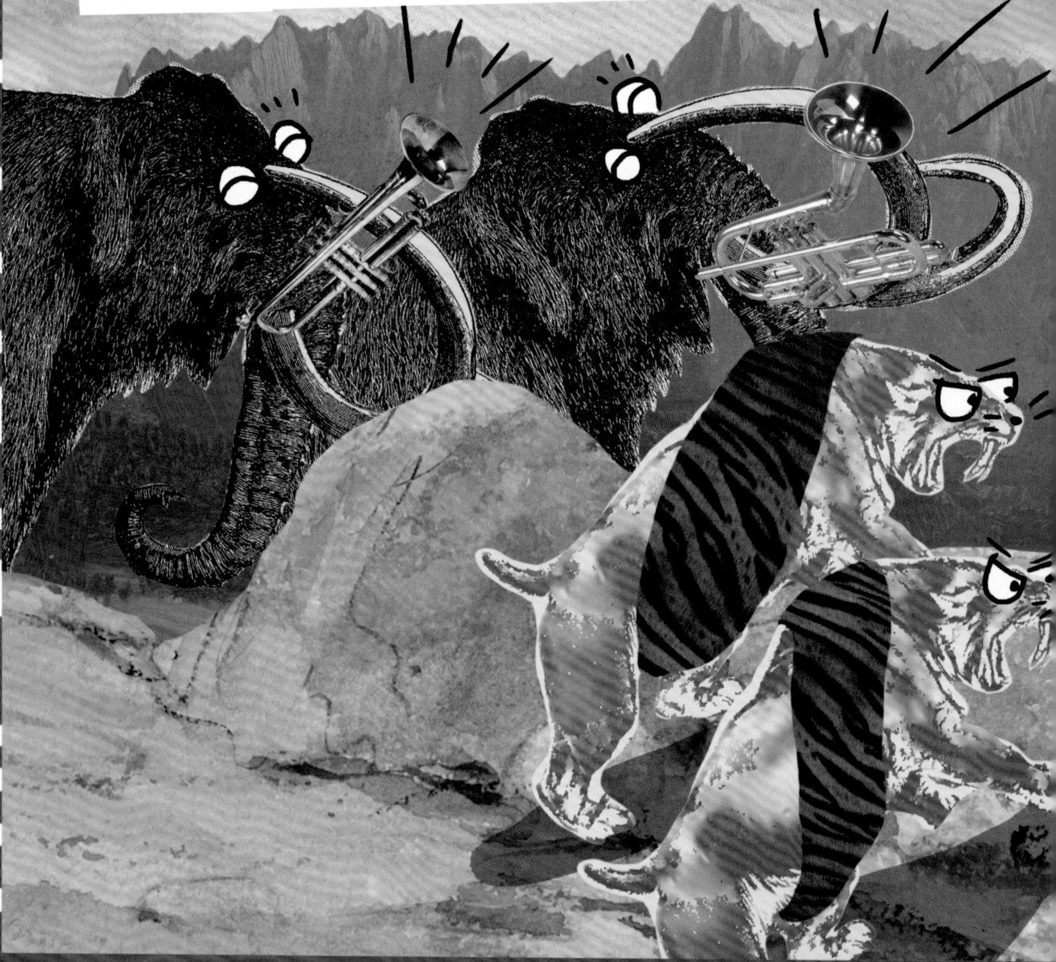

Saber-toothed cats! No one wants to mess with them. Pretty obvious plus to have those giant sharp teeth. And their speed. And wait what? A tiger-print sash? Why?

And would you look at that! So furry. So powerful. So . . . mammoth. SO LOUD. Team Woolly Mammoth.

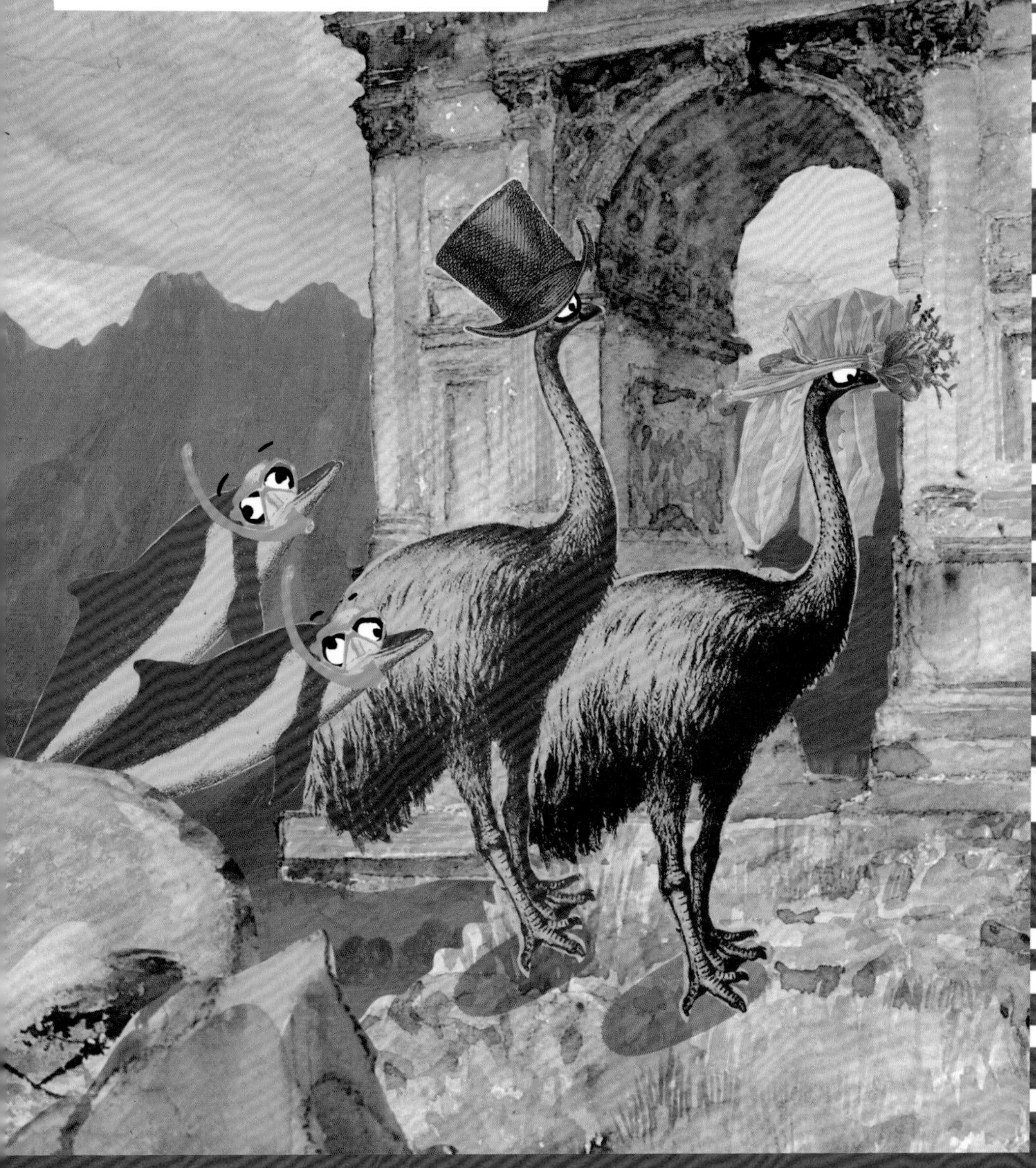

But don't take my word for all of this. Check out the Survival of the Fittest Olympics Pleistocene Program.

PLEISTOCENE

KNOW YOUR COMPETITION!

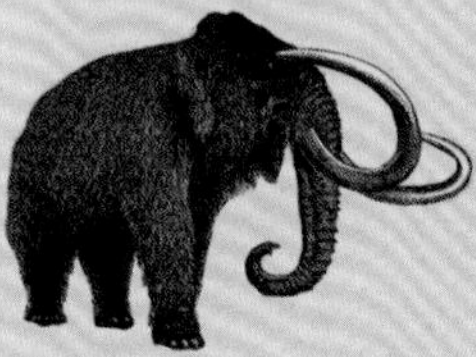

MAMMUTHUS PRIMIGENIUS

FUN FACT:
GREAT MEMORY

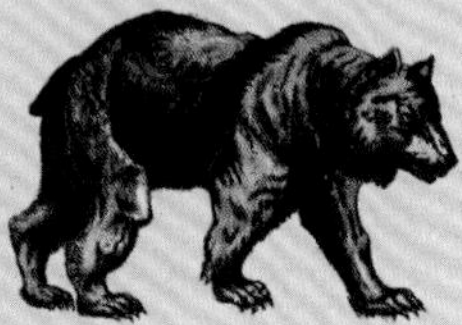

URSUS SPELAEUS

FUN FACT:
MOSTLY VEGETARIAN

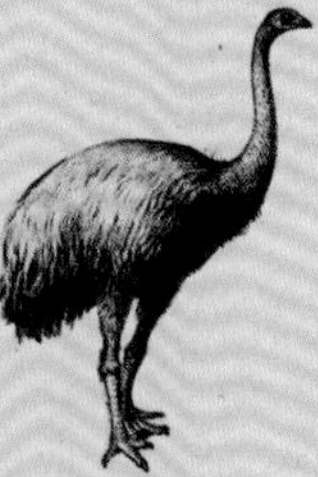

AEPYORNIS MAXIMUS

FUN FACT:
THREE-TOED FEET

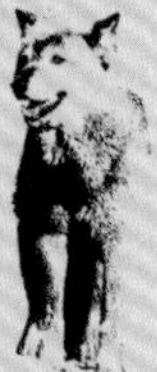

CANIS DIRUS

FUN FACT:
NAME MEANS "FEARSOME DOG"

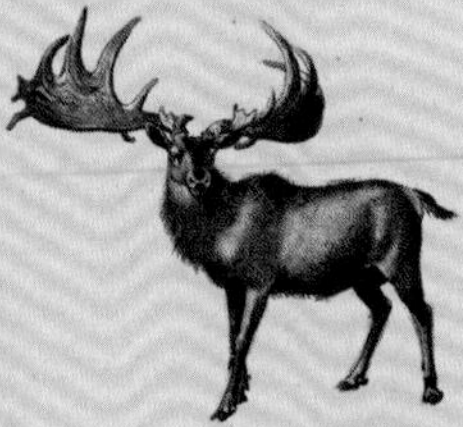

MEGALOCEROS GIGANTEUS

FUN FACT:
OVER 7 FEET TALL

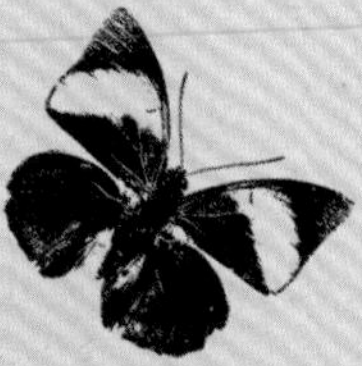

PRODRYAS PERSEPHONE

FUN FACT:
TINY FEET

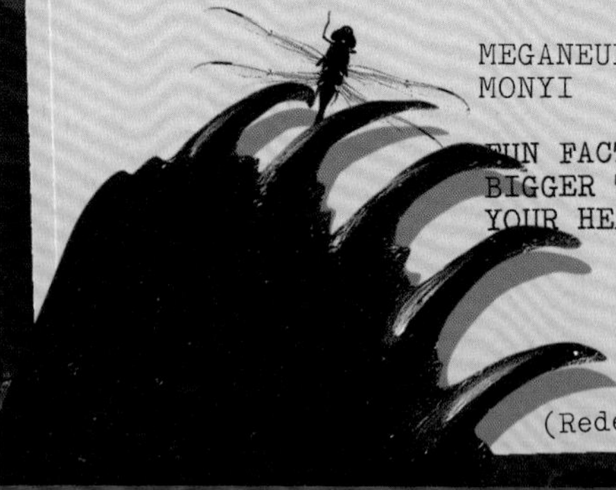

MEGANEURA MONYI

FUN FACT:
BIGGER THAN YOUR HEAD

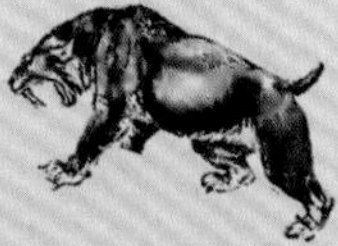

SMILODON FATALIS

FUN FACT:
NICKNAME "SMILEY"

(Redeem program for free T-shirt at the info kiosk.)

What a wildly evolved bunch of competitors.

PROGRAM

ALL OLYMPIC DECISIONS FINAL

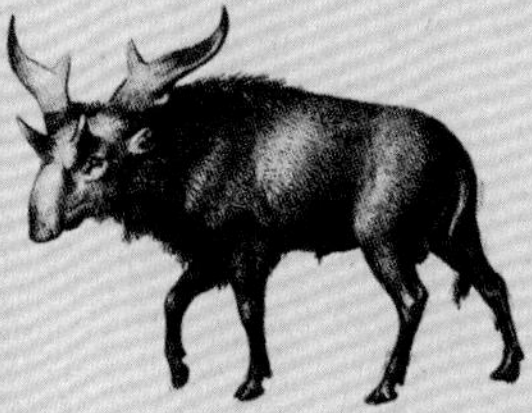

CERVALCES
LATIFRONS

FUN FACT:
BIGGER THAN
HIS COUSIN
MEGALOCEROS

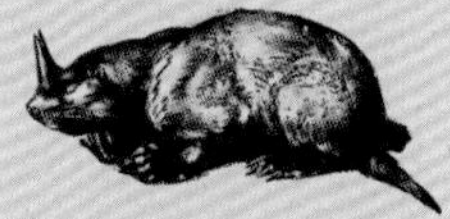

CERATOGAULUS
HATCHERI

FUN FACT:
IT'S A
HORNED GOPHER!

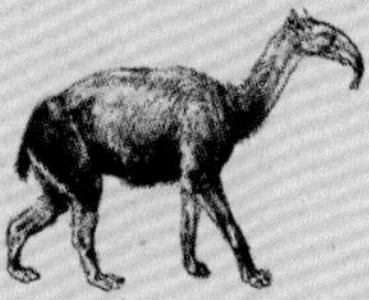

CAMELOPS
KANSANUS

FUN FACT:
TASTES LIKE
CHICKEN

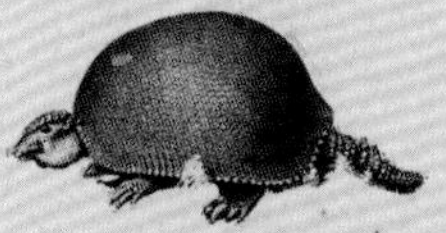

GLYPTODON
CLAVIPES

FUN FACT:
WEIGHS 2 TONS

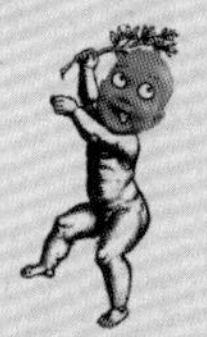

HOMO
SAPIENS

FUN FACT:
OPPOSABLE
THUMB

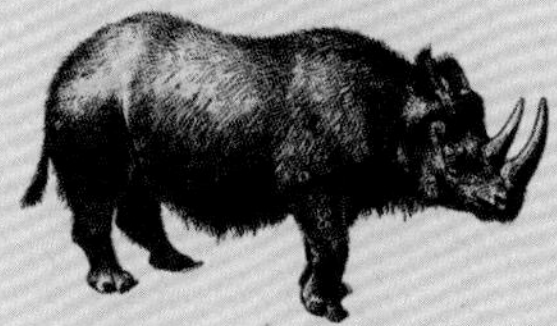

COELODONTA
ANTIQUITATIS

FUN FACT:
GRASS EATER,
POOR FLOSSER

MEGATHERIUM
ANUM

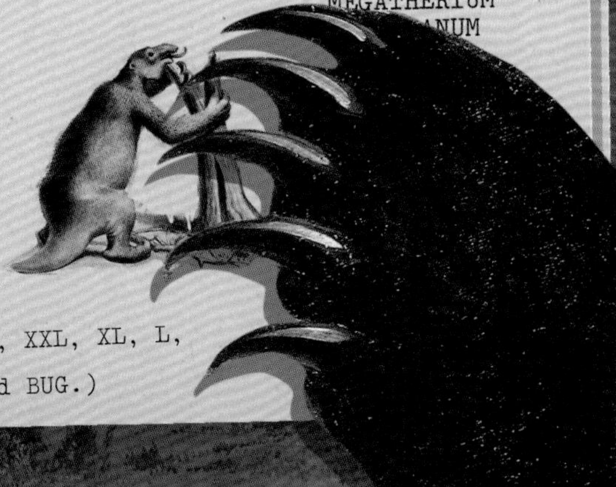

TURSIOPS
PYENSONI

FUN FACT:
A TOTAL NUT
FOR MARINE
MAMMAL
FOSSILS

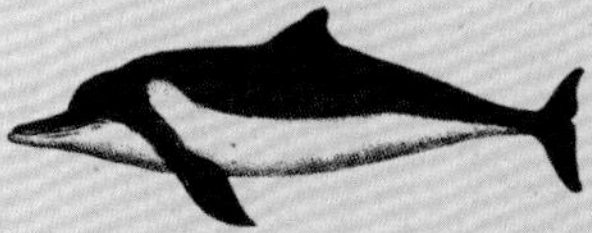

(T-shirt sizes are XXXXXL, XXXXL, XXXL, XXL, XL, L, M, S, XS, XXS, XXXS, XXXXS, XXXXXS, and BUG.)

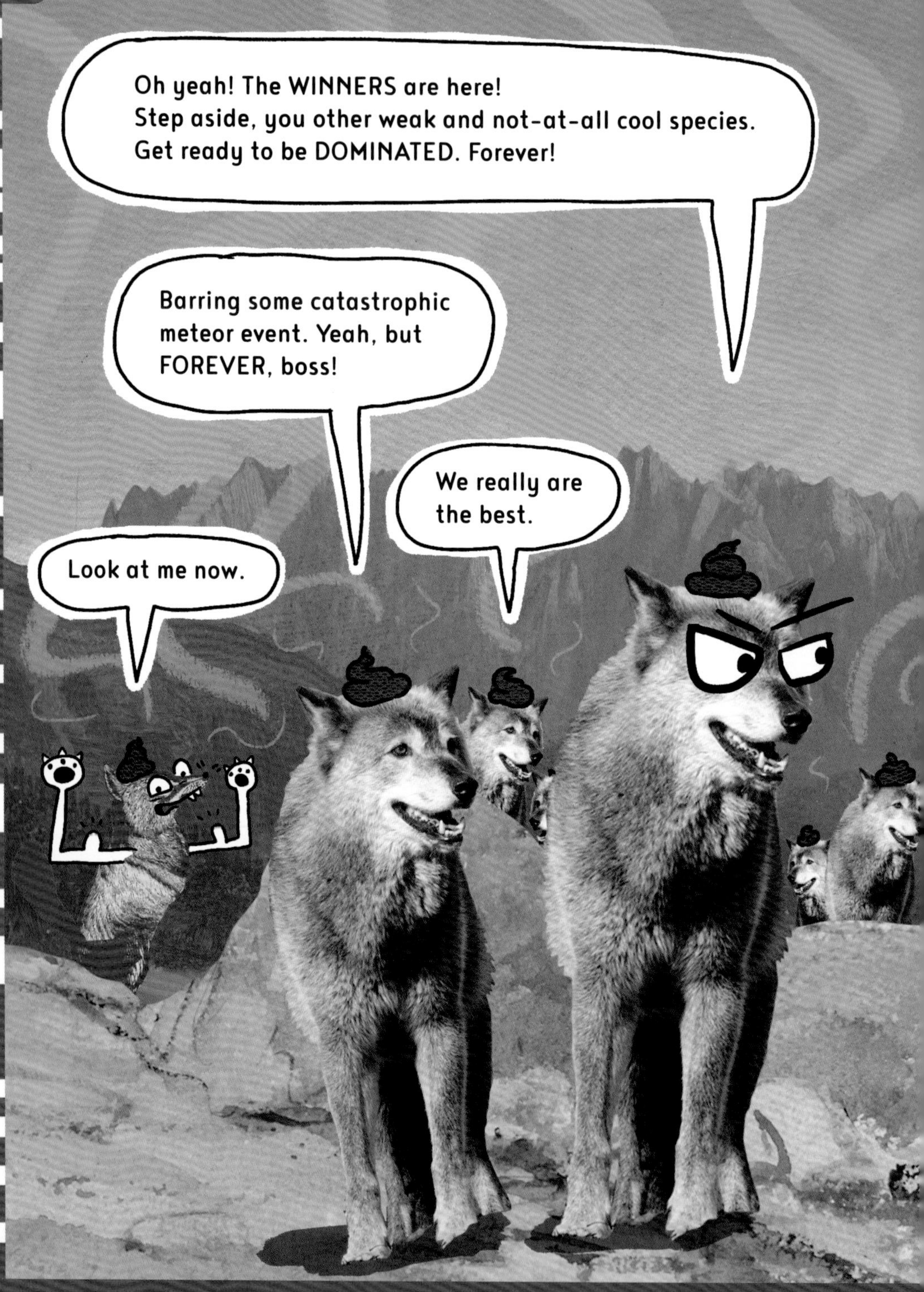
Oh yeah! The WINNERS are here! Step aside, you other weak and not-at-all cool species. Get ready to be DOMINATED. Forever!
Barring some catastrophic meteor event. Yeah, but FOREVER, boss!
We really are the best.
Look at me now.

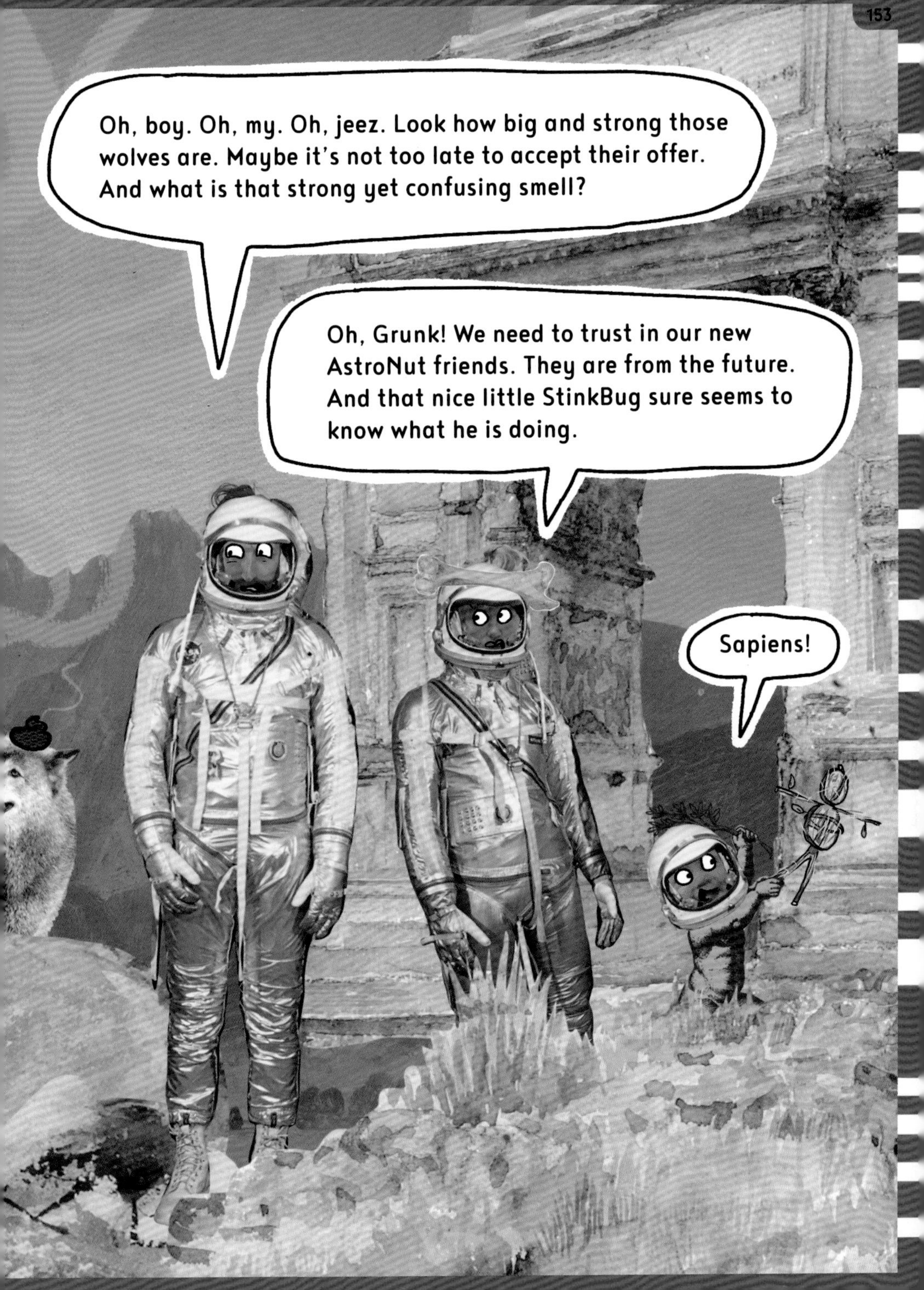
Oh, boy. Oh, my. Oh, jeez. Look how big and strong those wolves are. Maybe it's not too late to accept their offer. And what is that strong yet confusing smell?
Oh, Grunk! We need to trust in our new AstroNut friends. They are from the future. And that nice little StinkBug sure seems to know what he is doing.
Sapiens!

In the stands, the AstroNuts prepared for the biggest, most important event they (and I) had ever been part of. SmartHawk reviewed, reread, and reorganized the plans for helping the Sapiens win every event. StinkBug worked like StinkBug always does. And LaserShark practiced her most superpowered electromagnetic cheers.

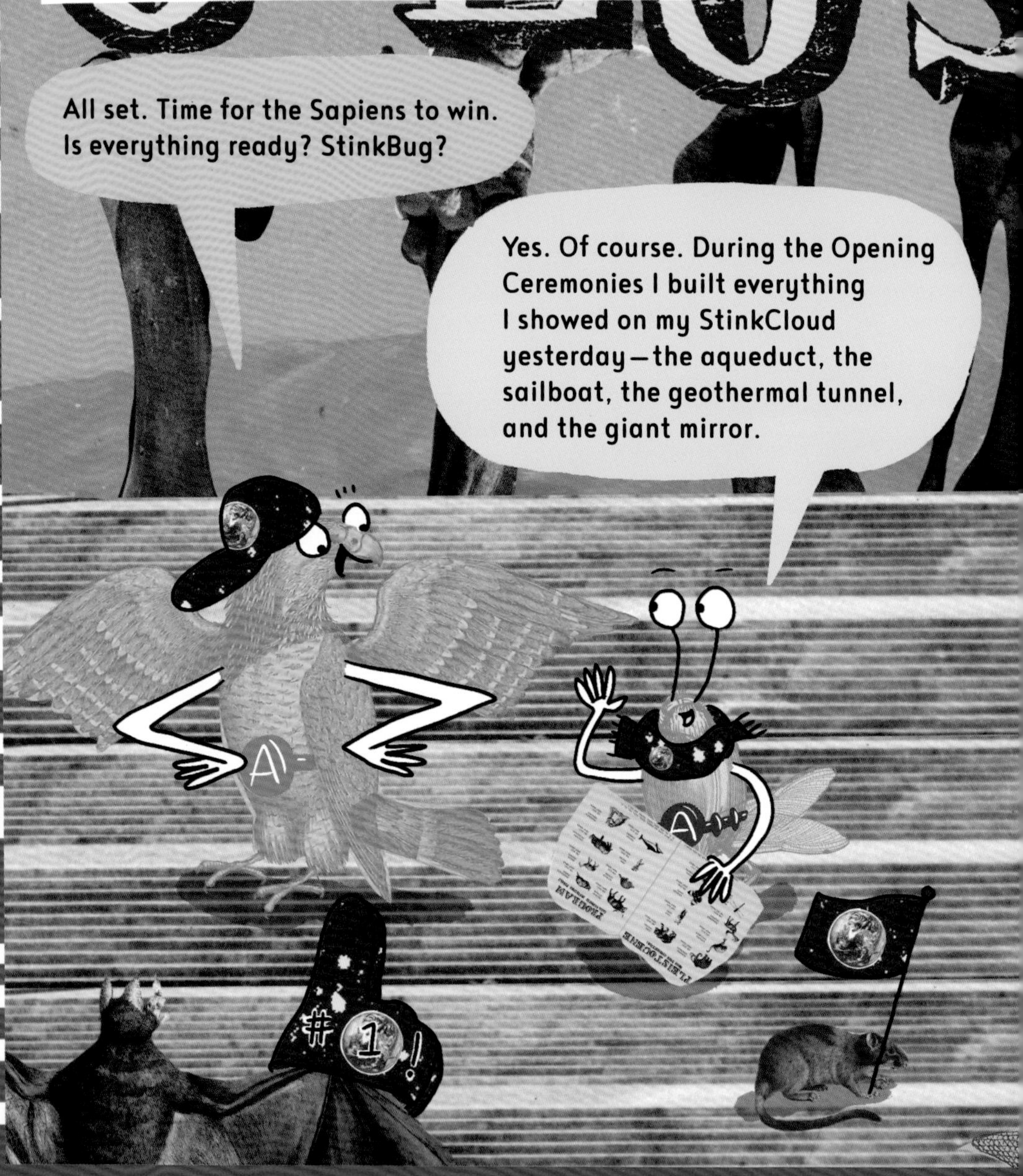
All set. Time for the Sapiens to win. Is everything ready? StinkBug?
Yes. Of course. During the Opening Ceremonies I built everything I showed on my StinkCloud yesterday—the aqueduct, the sailboat, the geothermal tunnel, and the giant mirror.
#1!

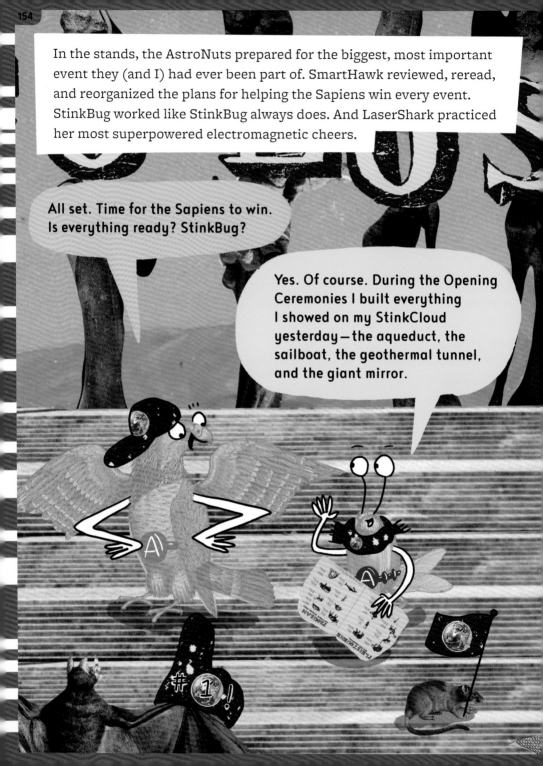

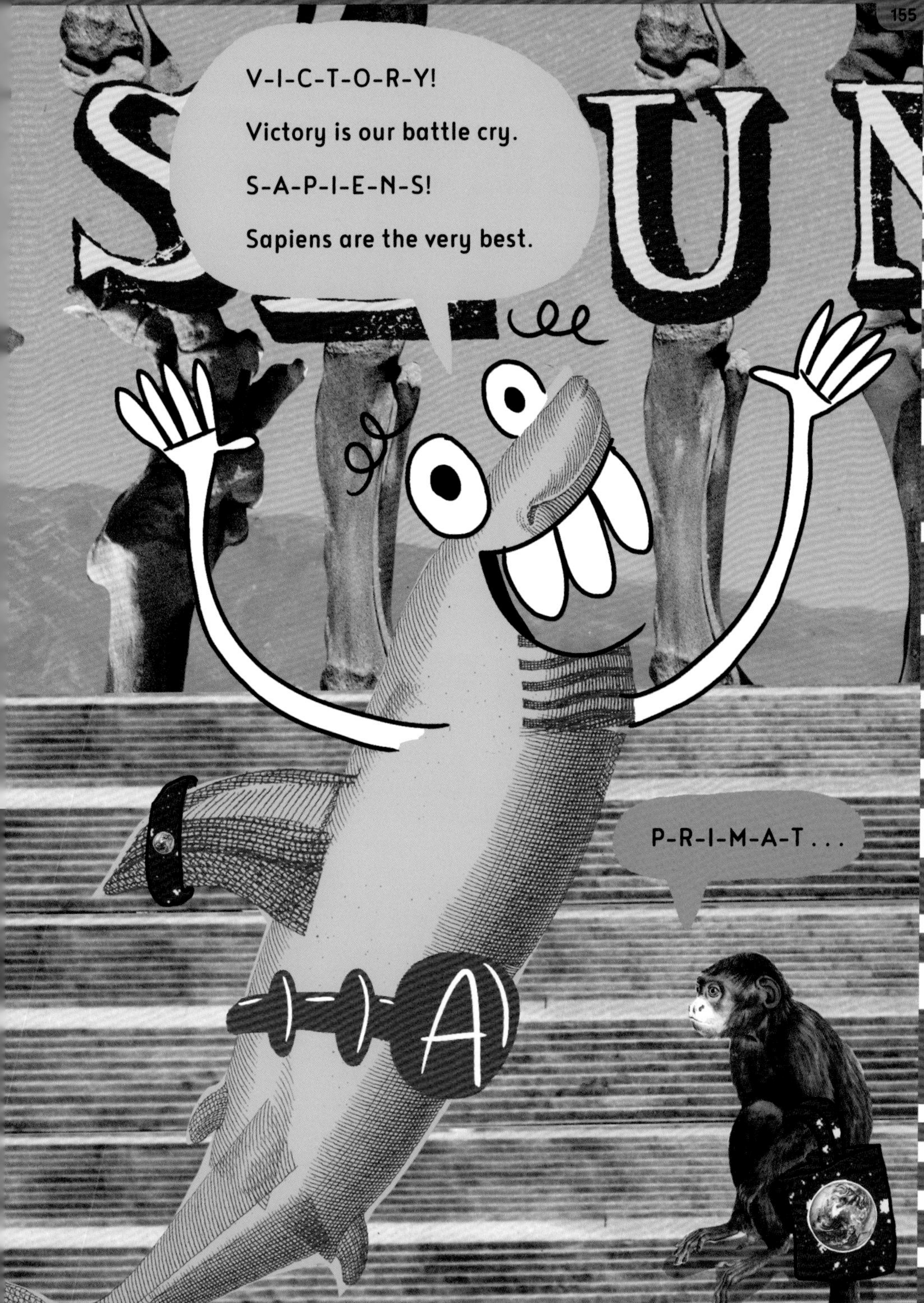
V-I-C-T-O-R-Y!
Victory is our battle cry.
S-A-P-I-E-N-S!
Sapiens are the very best.
AI
P-R-I-M-A-T . . .

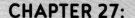

CHAPTER 27:

Power to the People

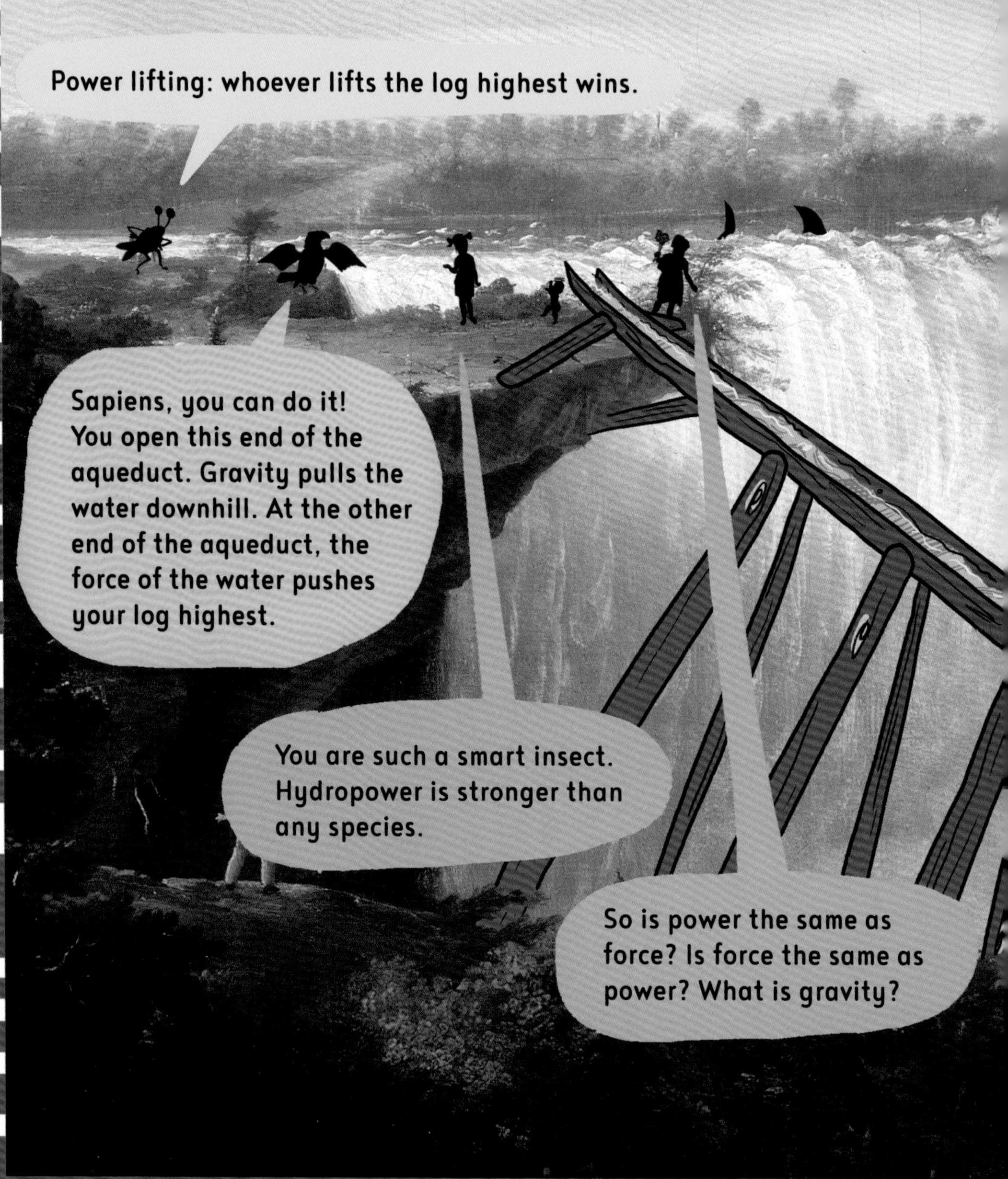
Power lifting: whoever lifts the log highest wins.
Sapiens, you can do it! You open this end of the aqueduct. Gravity pulls the water downhill. At the other end of the aqueduct, the force of the water pushes your log highest.
You are such a smart insect. Hydropower is stronger than any species.
So is power the same as force? Is force the same as power? What is gravity?

StinkBug's hydropower plan was a good plan. No, it was a great plan. If you've ever stood in one of my rushing streams, you know how strong water can be. Water can move mountains. Water made my Grand Canyon. Water can lift a log without even trying.

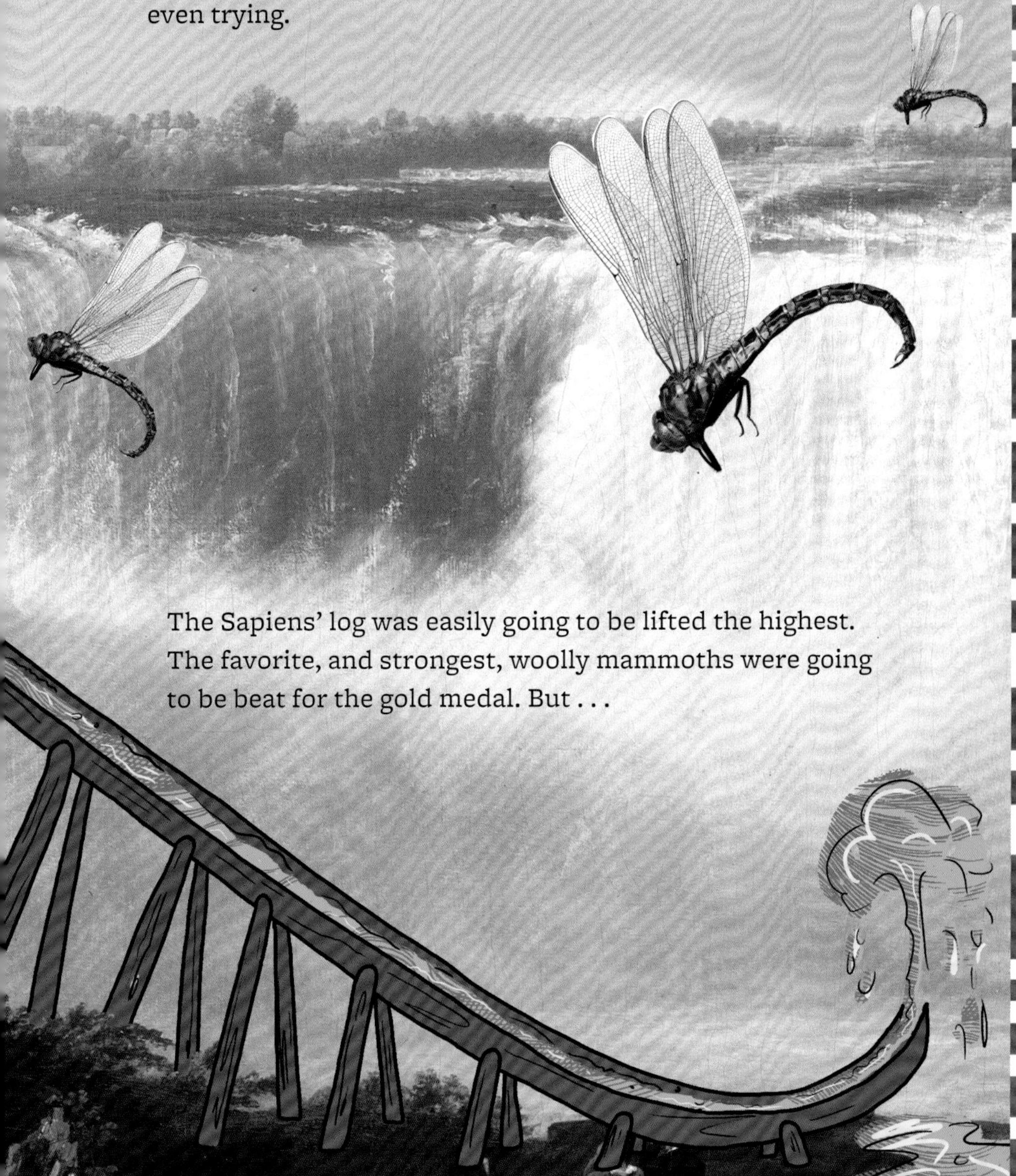

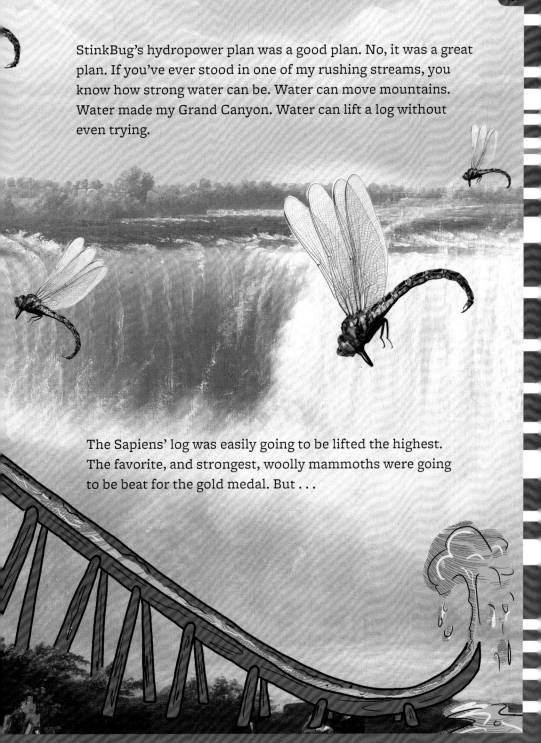

The Sapiens' log was easily going to be lifted the highest. The favorite, and strongest, woolly mammoths were going to be beat for the gold medal. But . . .

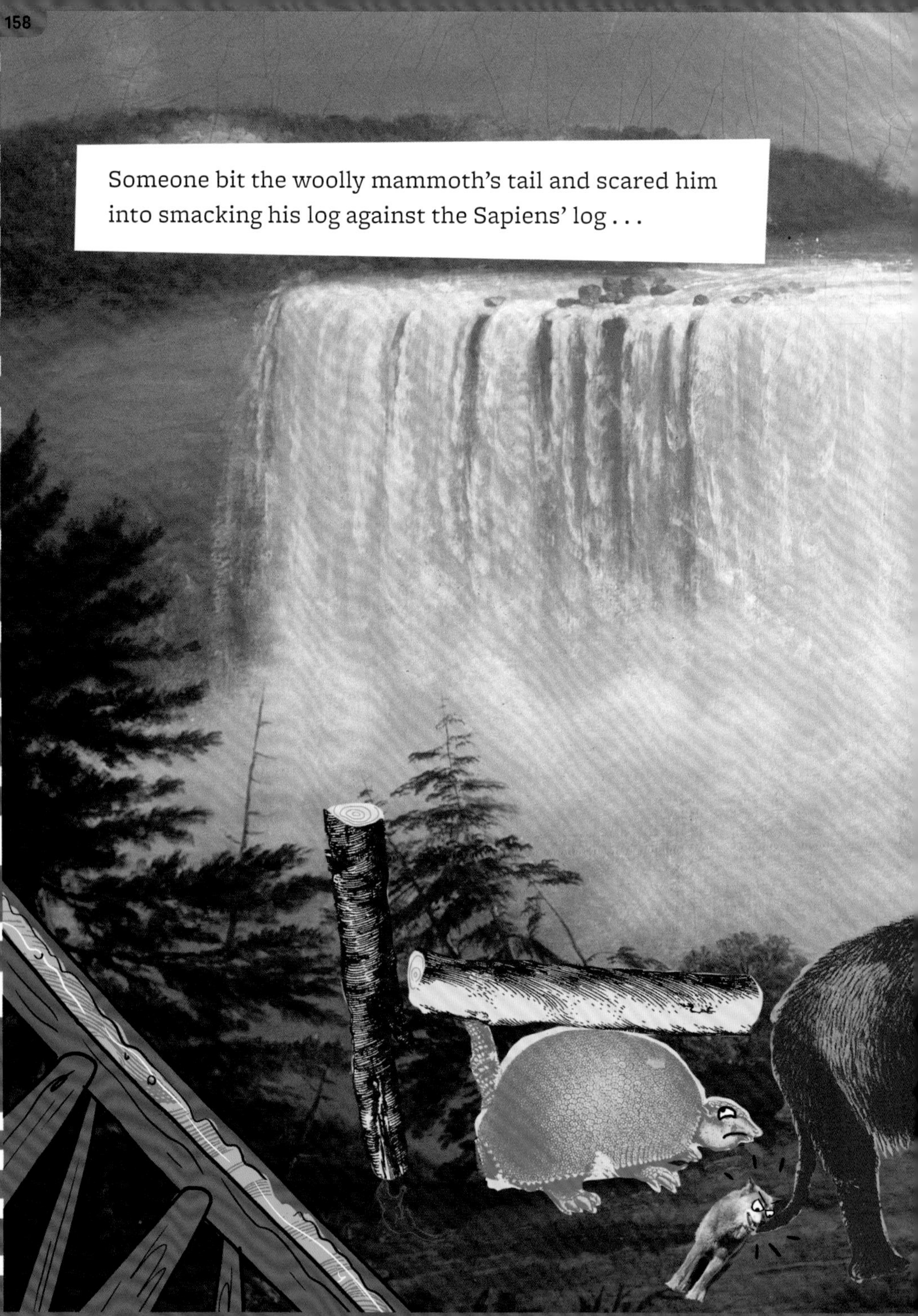
Someone bit the woolly mammoth's tail and scared him into smacking his log against the Sapiens' log . . .

knocking both the woolly mammoths and the Sapiens out of the power lifting event . . . and giving the gold to the . . .

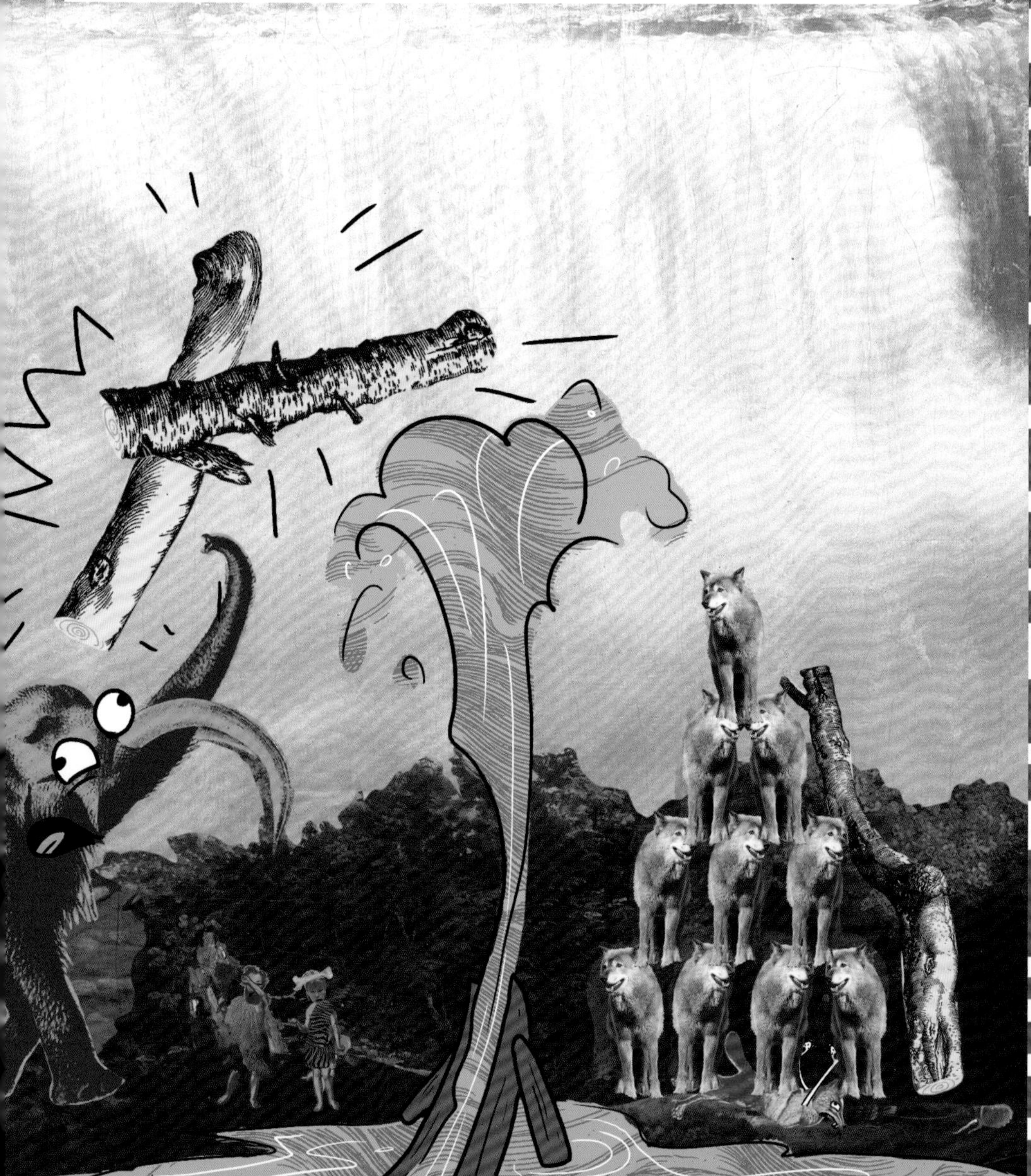

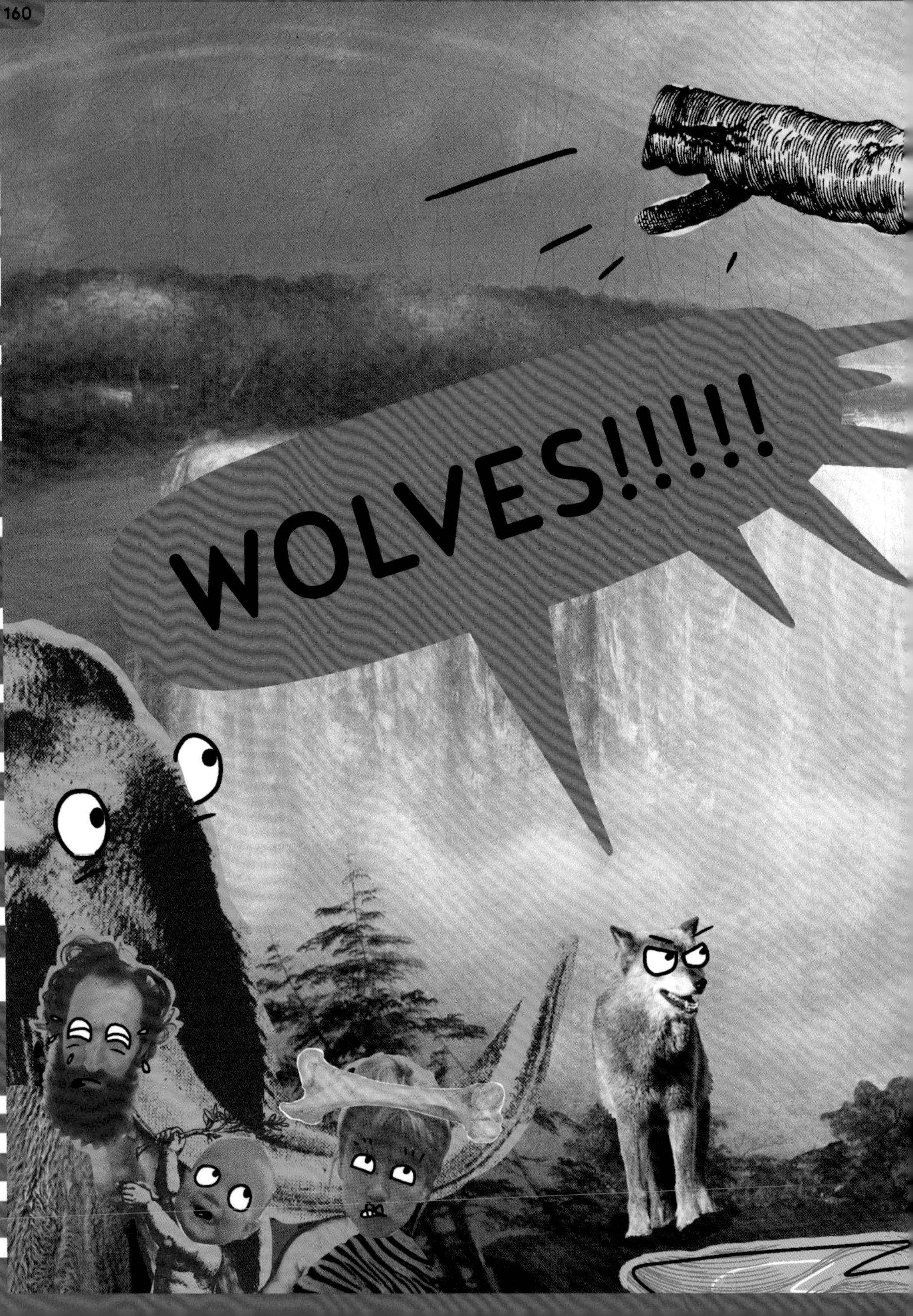
WOLVES!!!!!

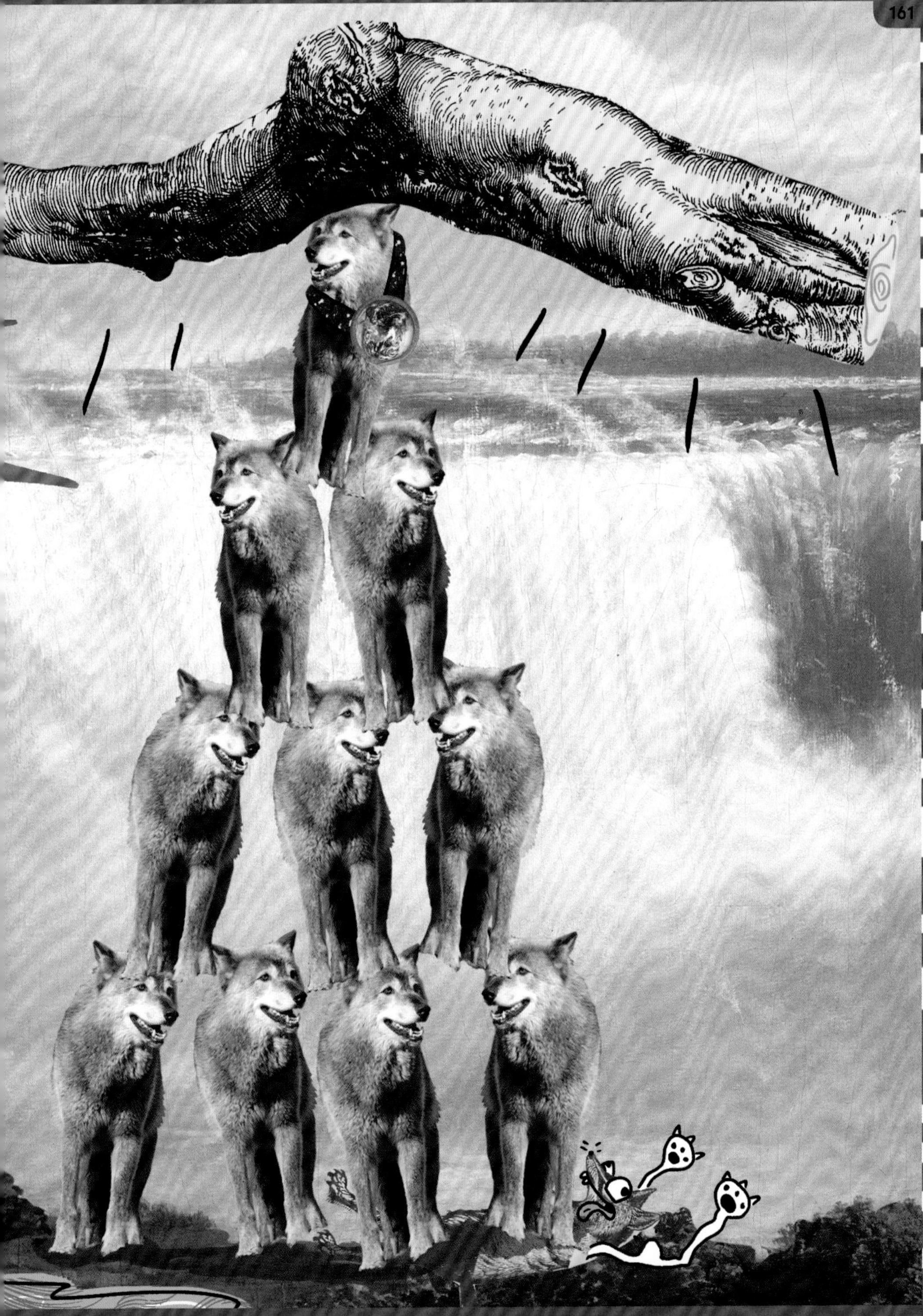

CHAPTER 28:

The Cut of the Jib

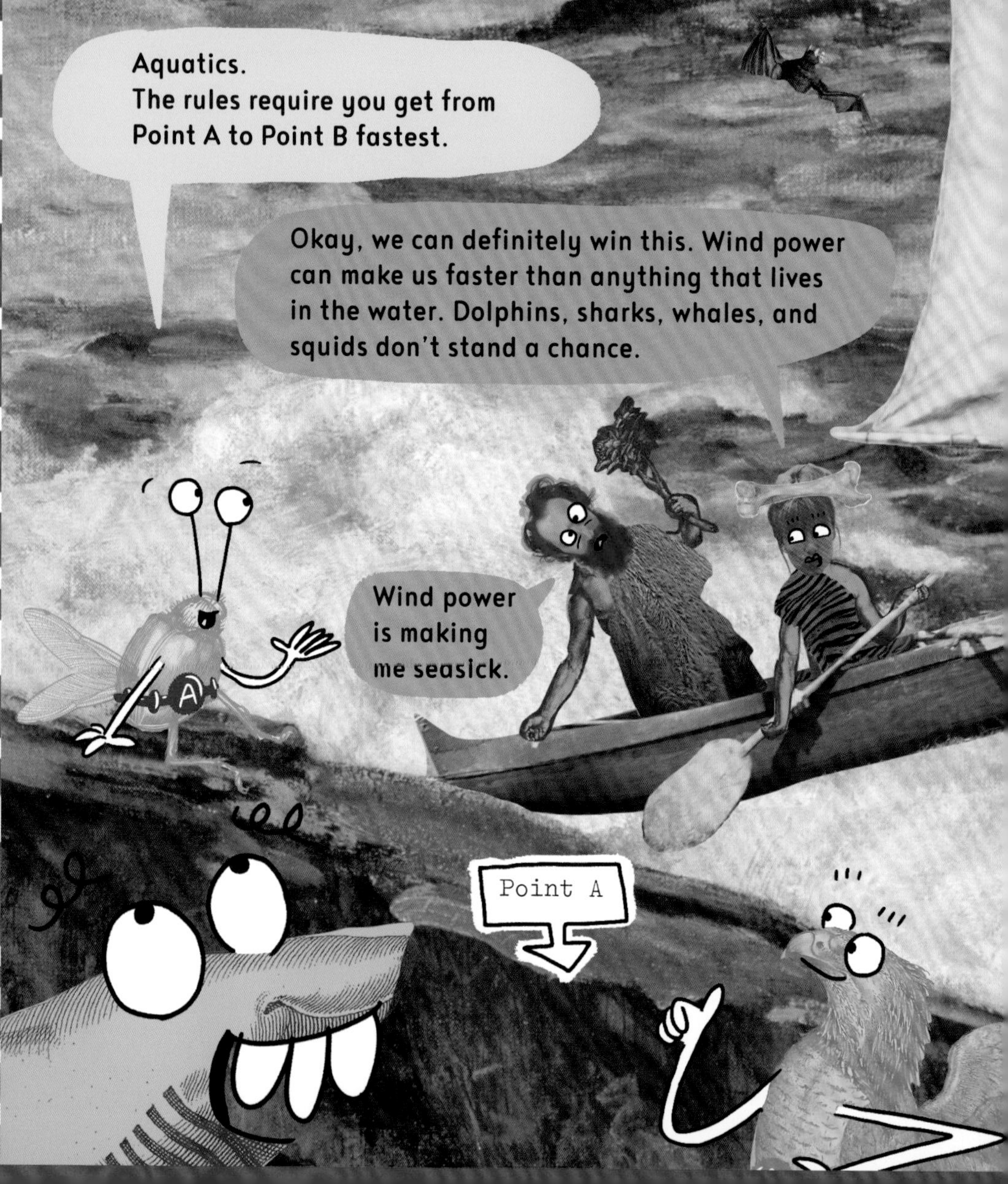
Aquatics.
The rules require you get from Point A to Point B fastest.
Okay, we can definitely win this. Wind power can make us faster than anything that lives in the water. Dolphins, sharks, whales, and squids don't stand a chance.
Wind power is making me seasick.
Point A

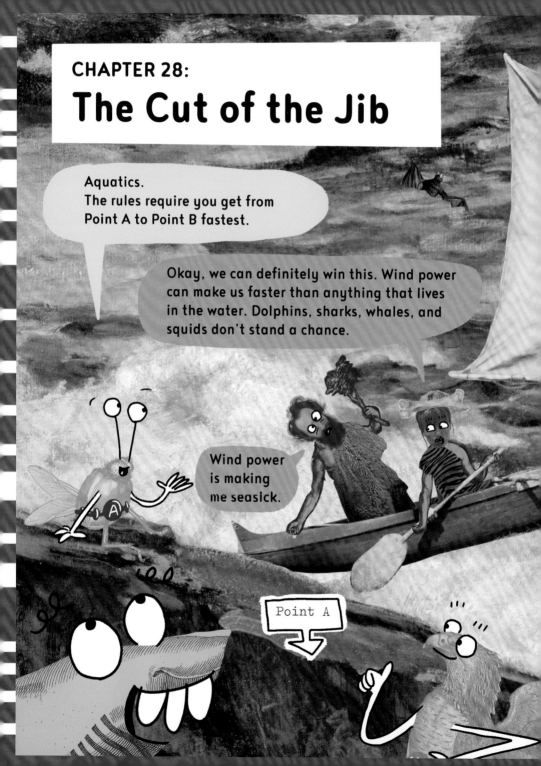

The wind power plan was even better than the hydropower plan. You've felt how fast a good breeze of mine is on one of my windy days. And I know you've seen the speed of my tornados and hurricanes. No fish or bird can beat that.

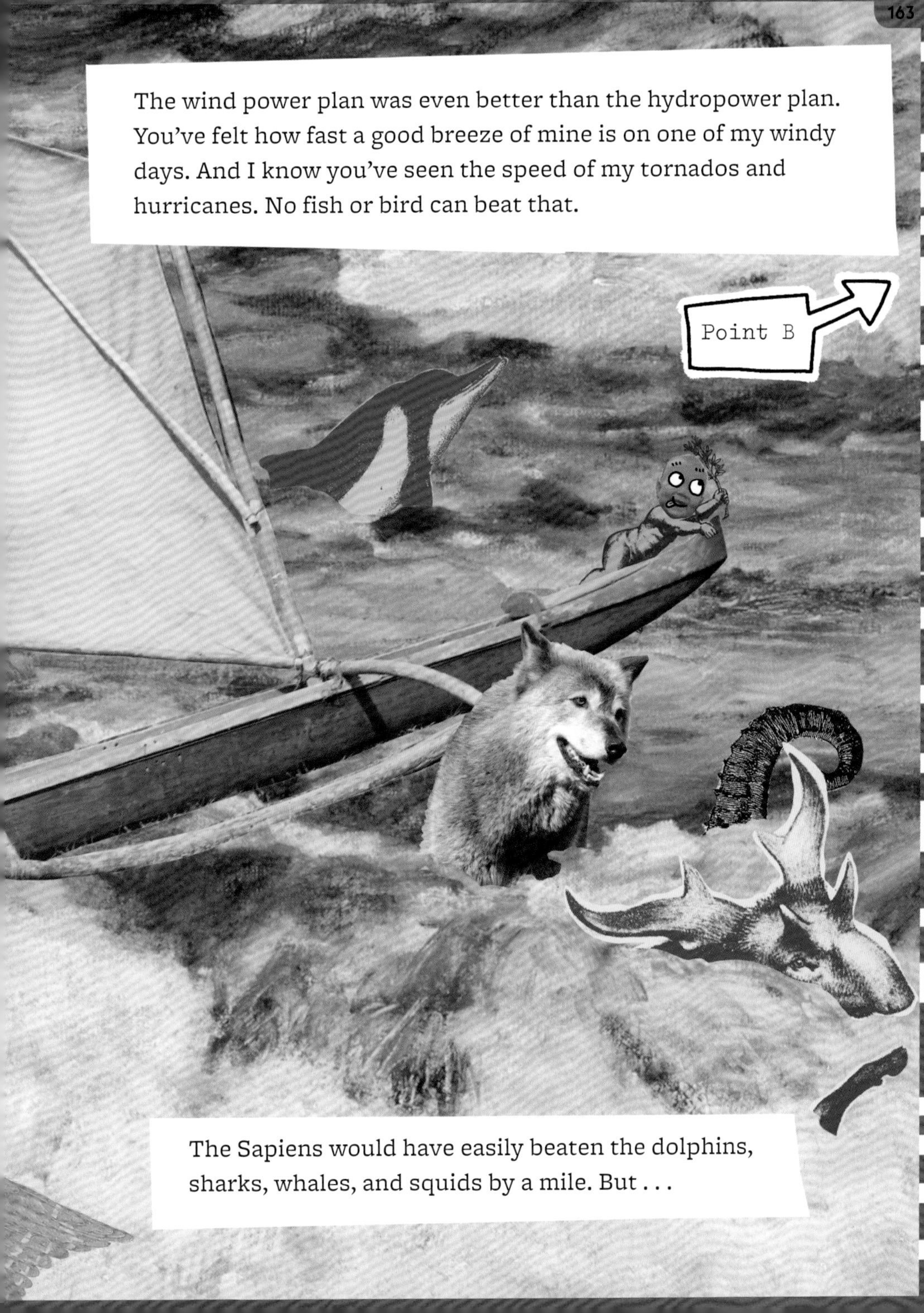
Point B

The Sapiens would have easily beaten the dolphins, sharks, whales, and squids by a mile. But . . .

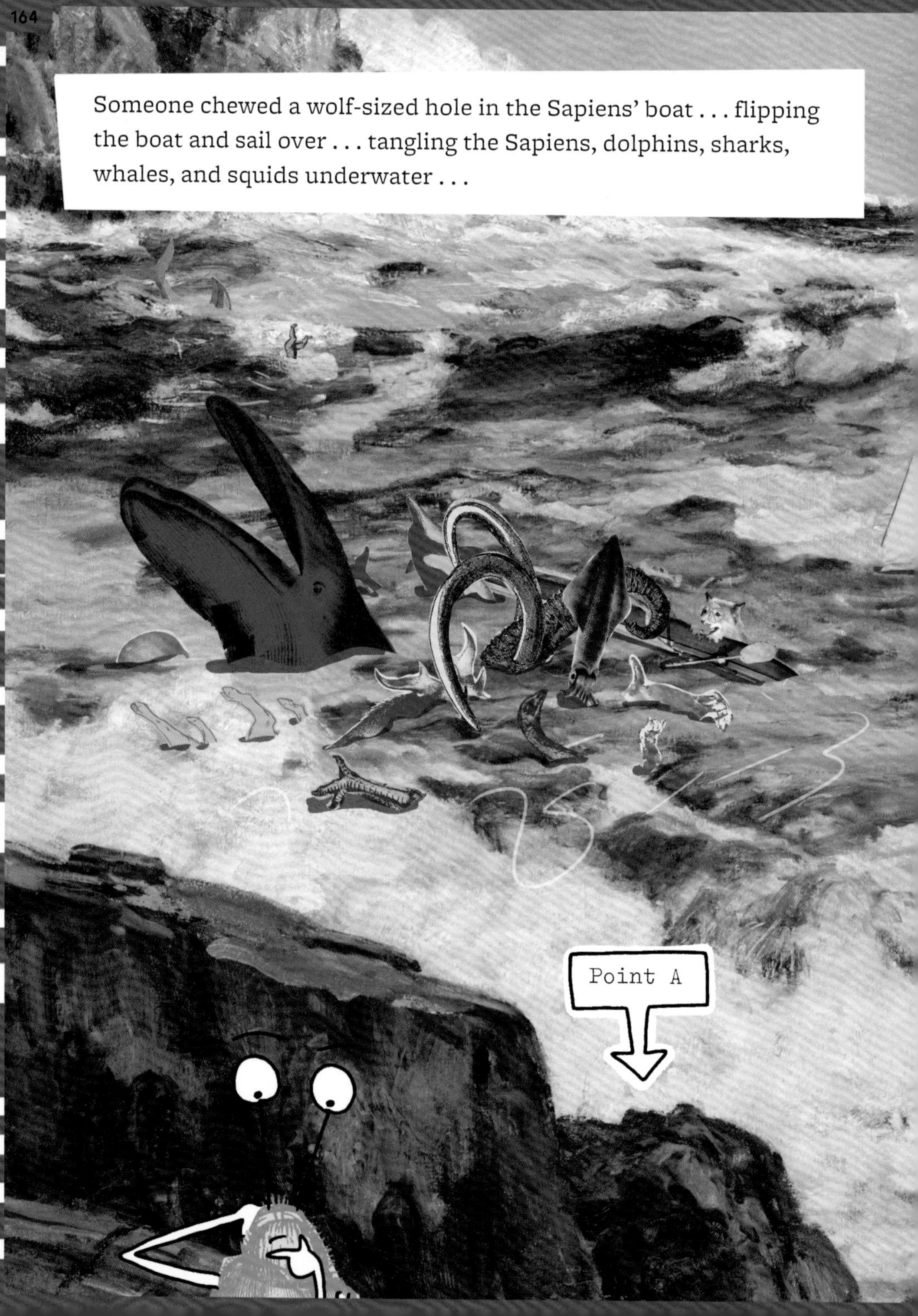
Someone chewed a wolf-sized hole in the Sapiens' boat . . . flipping the boat and sail over . . . tangling the Sapiens, dolphins, sharks, whales, and squids underwater . . .
Point A

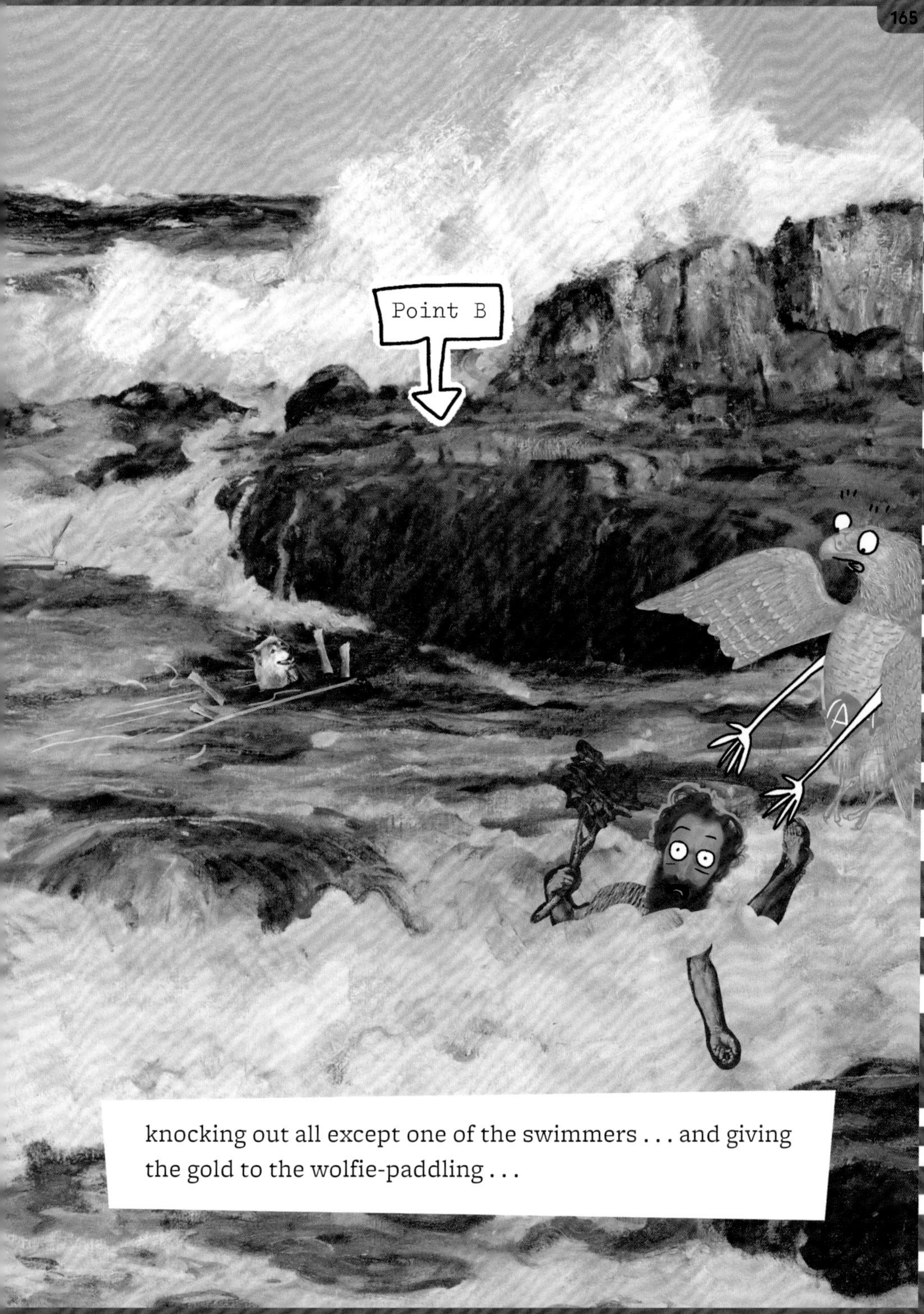
Point B

knocking out all except one of the swimmers . . . and giving the gold to the wolfie-paddling . . .

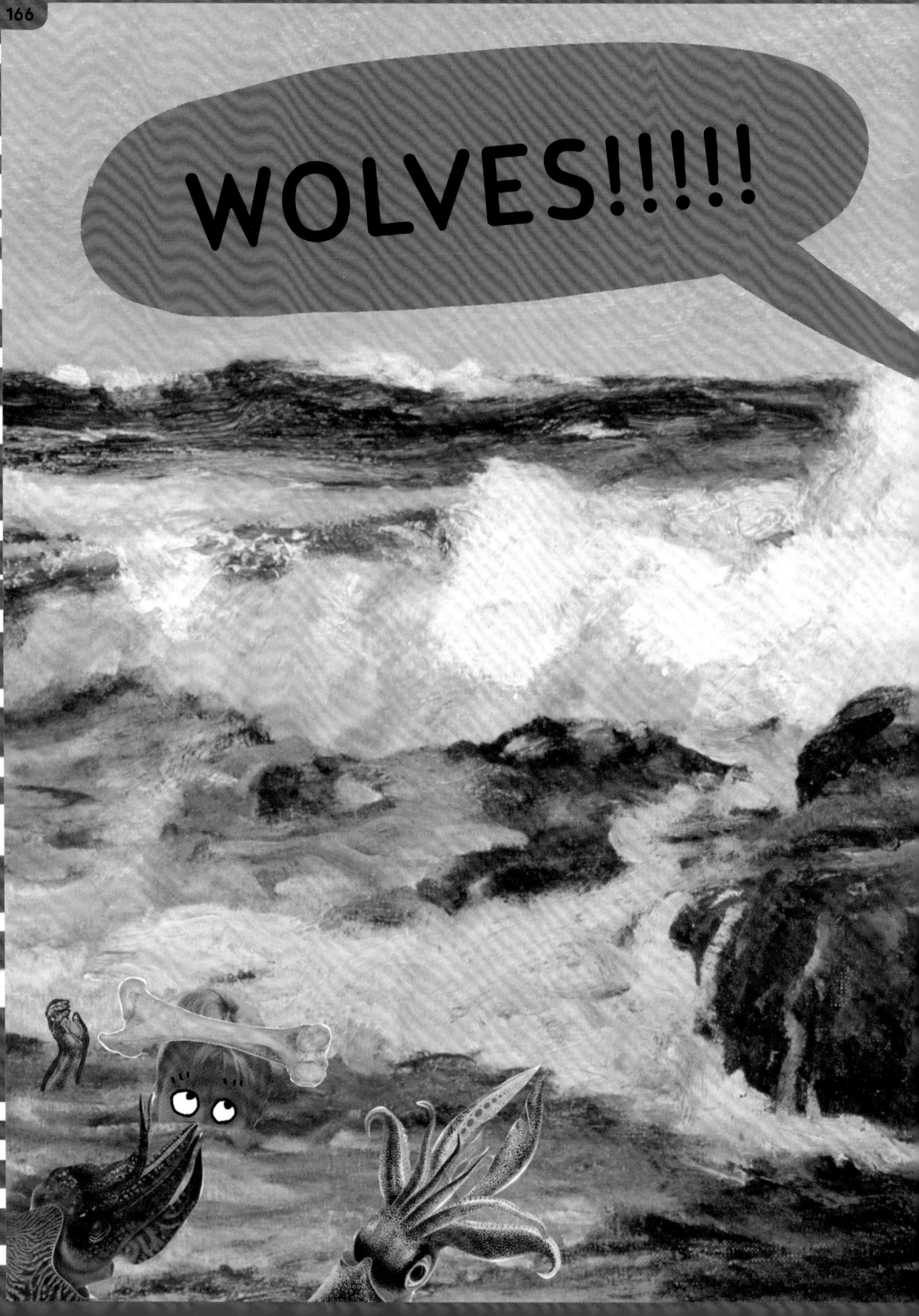
WOLVES!!!!!

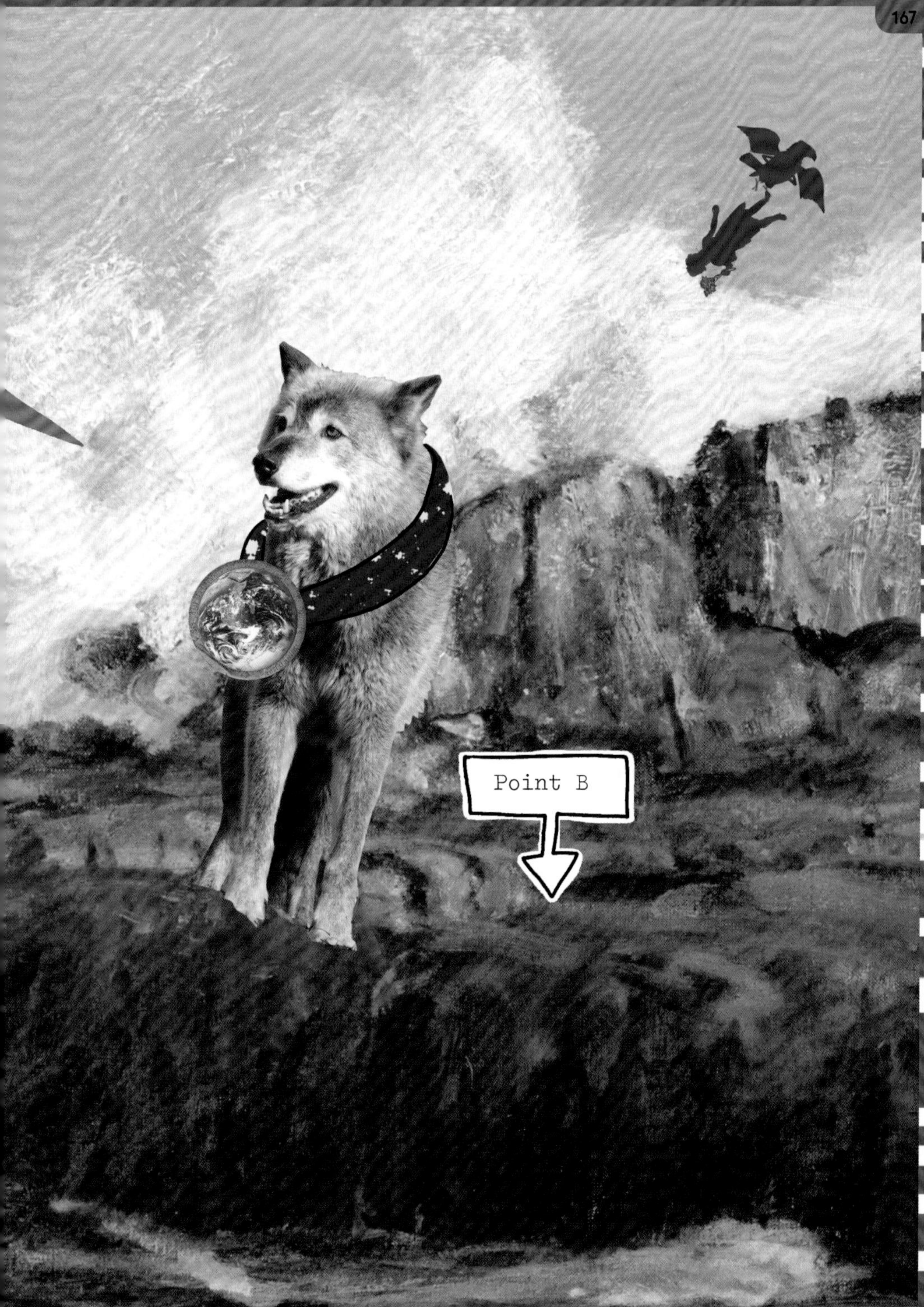
Point B

CHAPTER 29:

Fore!

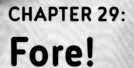

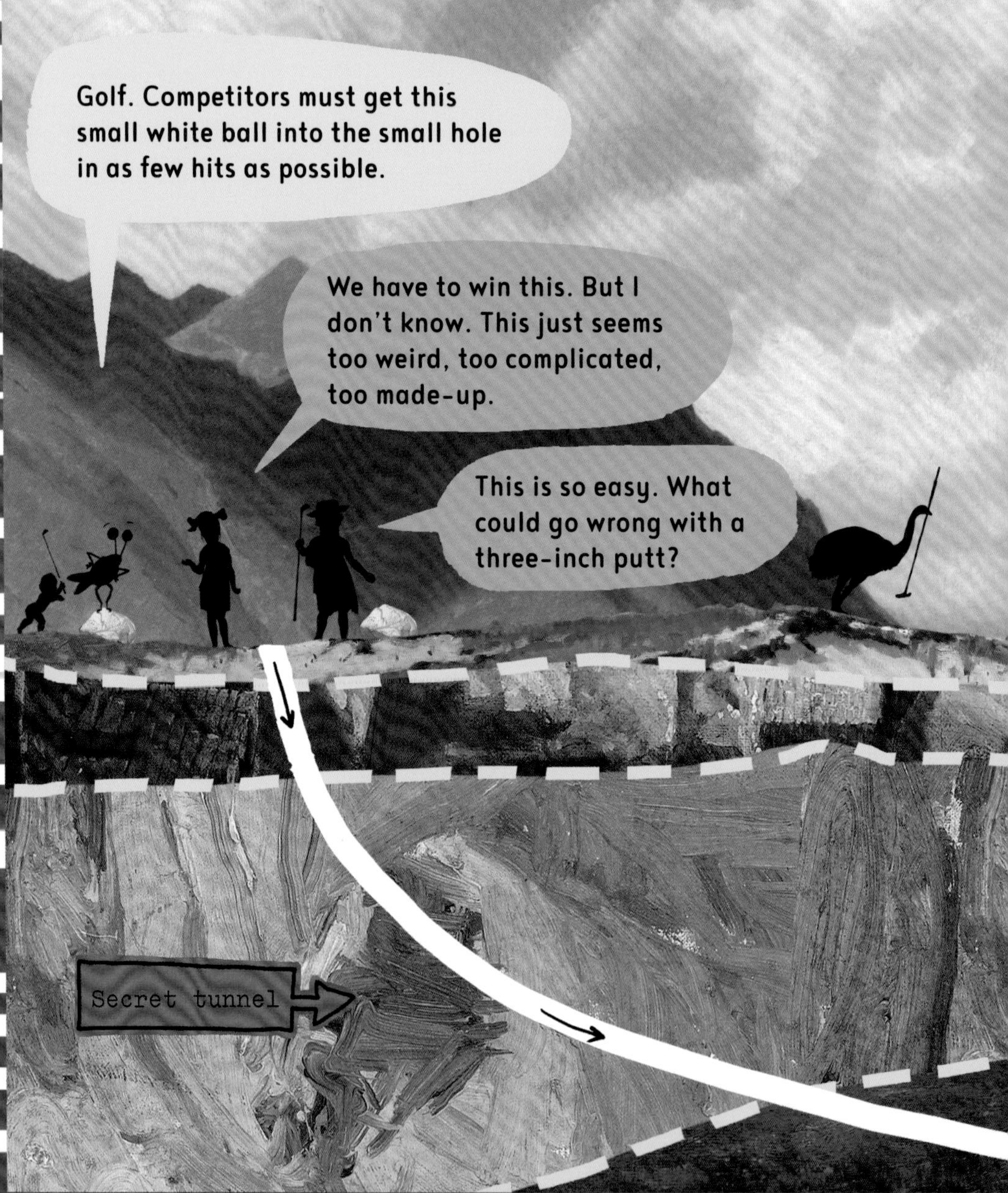
Golf. Competitors must get this small white ball into the small hole in as few hits as possible.
We have to win this. But I don't know. This just seems too weird, too complicated, too made-up.
This is so easy. What could go wrong with a three-inch putt?
Secret tunnel

This was the absolute best plan so far. The humans were easily the best at golf. And with their geothermal tunnel, all they had to do was hit the ball three inches. Then it would drop into the tunnel, get heated by my warm core to a perfect 55 degrees Fahrenheit, and shoot out on the green.

And the Sapiens would have easily won golf. Because what other species could even understand the rules and all those weird golf words like "par" and "bogey" and "divot" and "mulligan"?

But . . .

Crust

Mantle

Outer core

Geothermal heat pushes UP!

Inner core

Someone had pressed a big wolf-sized paw print into the green where the Sapiens' ball shot out of the tunnel . . . curving the ball away from the hole and right into the Titanis bird's ball . . .

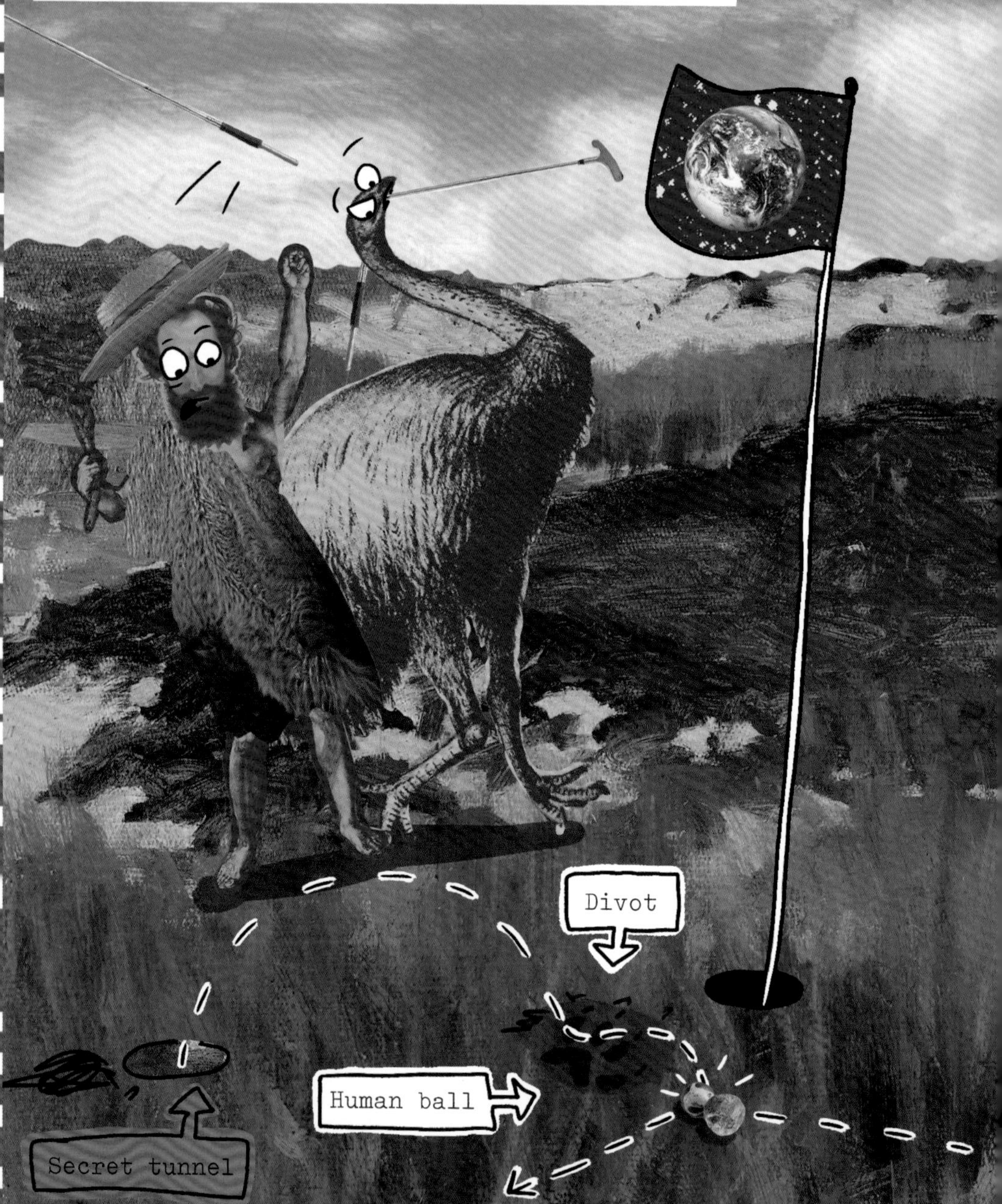
Divot
Human ball
Secret tunnel

knocking both balls off the green, both species out of the competition, and giving the win to, guess who, the . . .

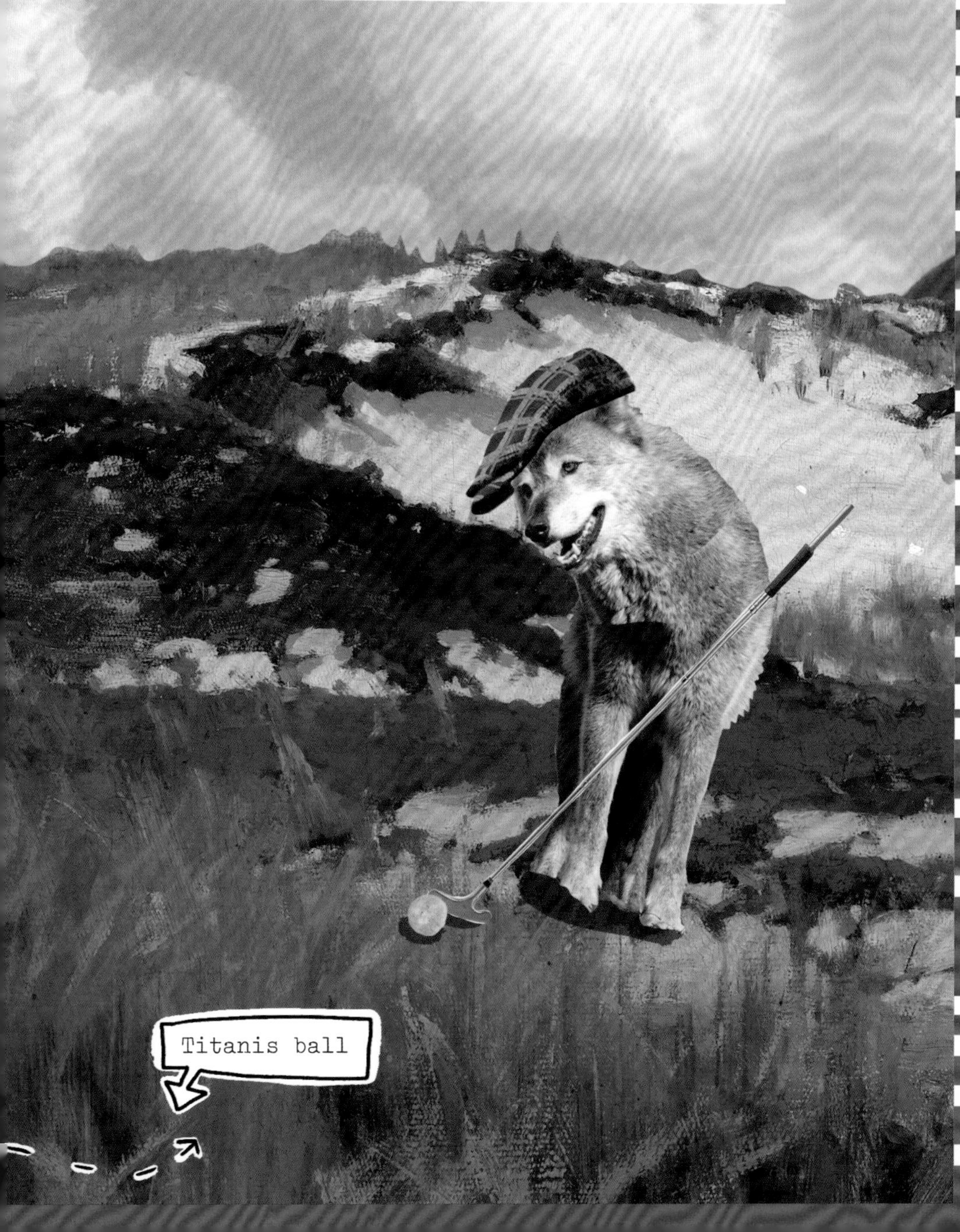
Titanis ball

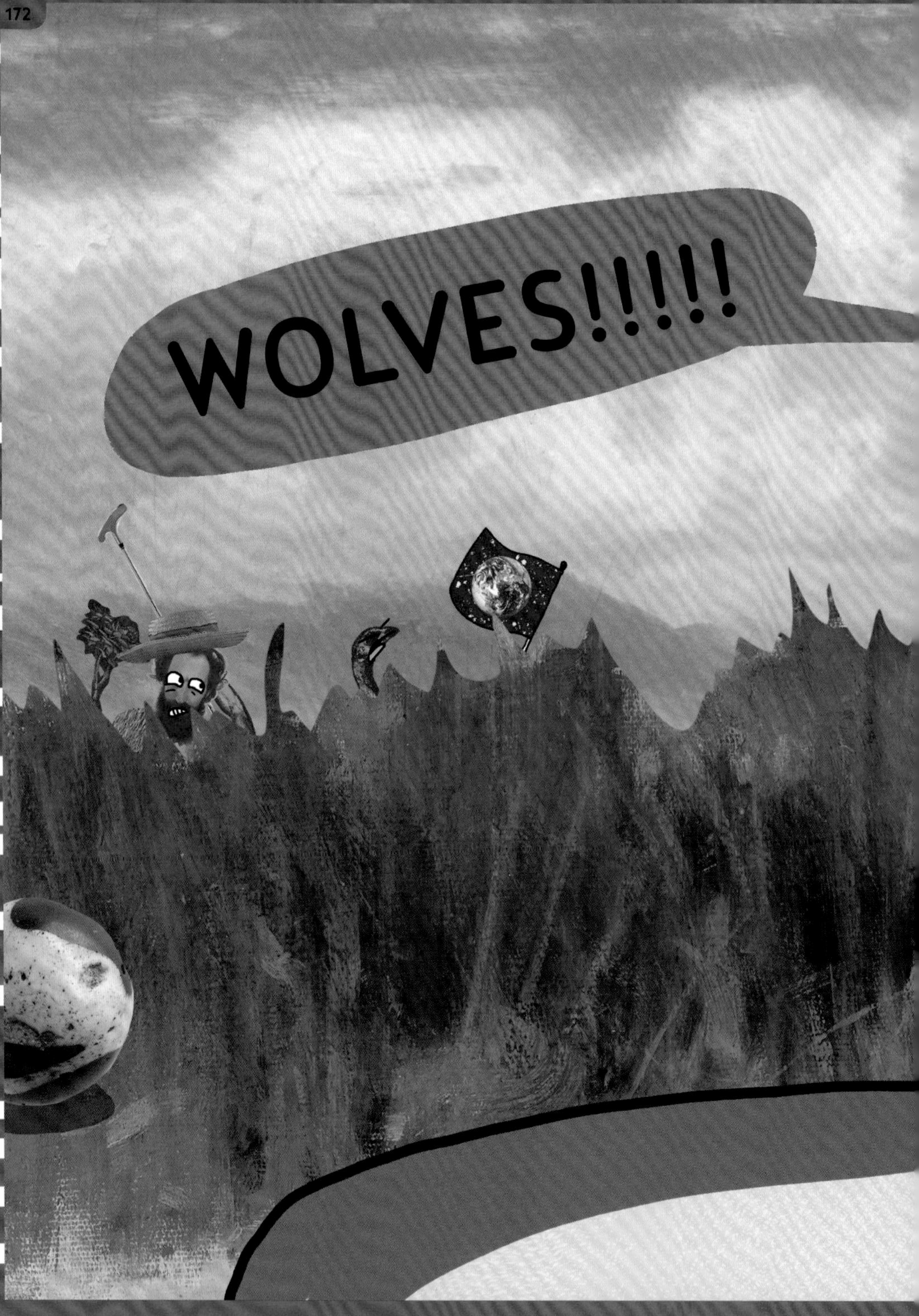
WOLVES!!!!!!

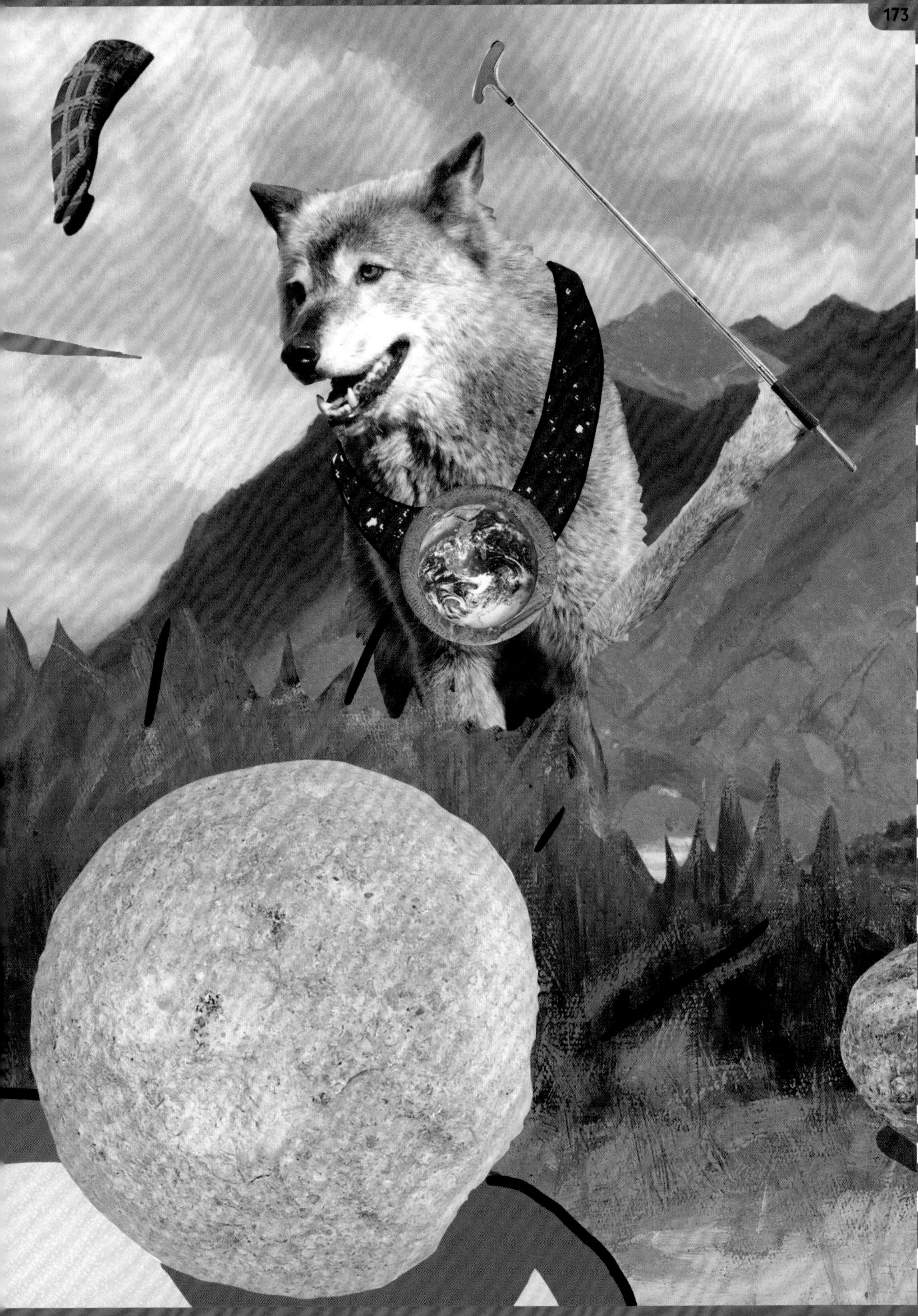

CHAPTER 30:
Reflections on Reflecting

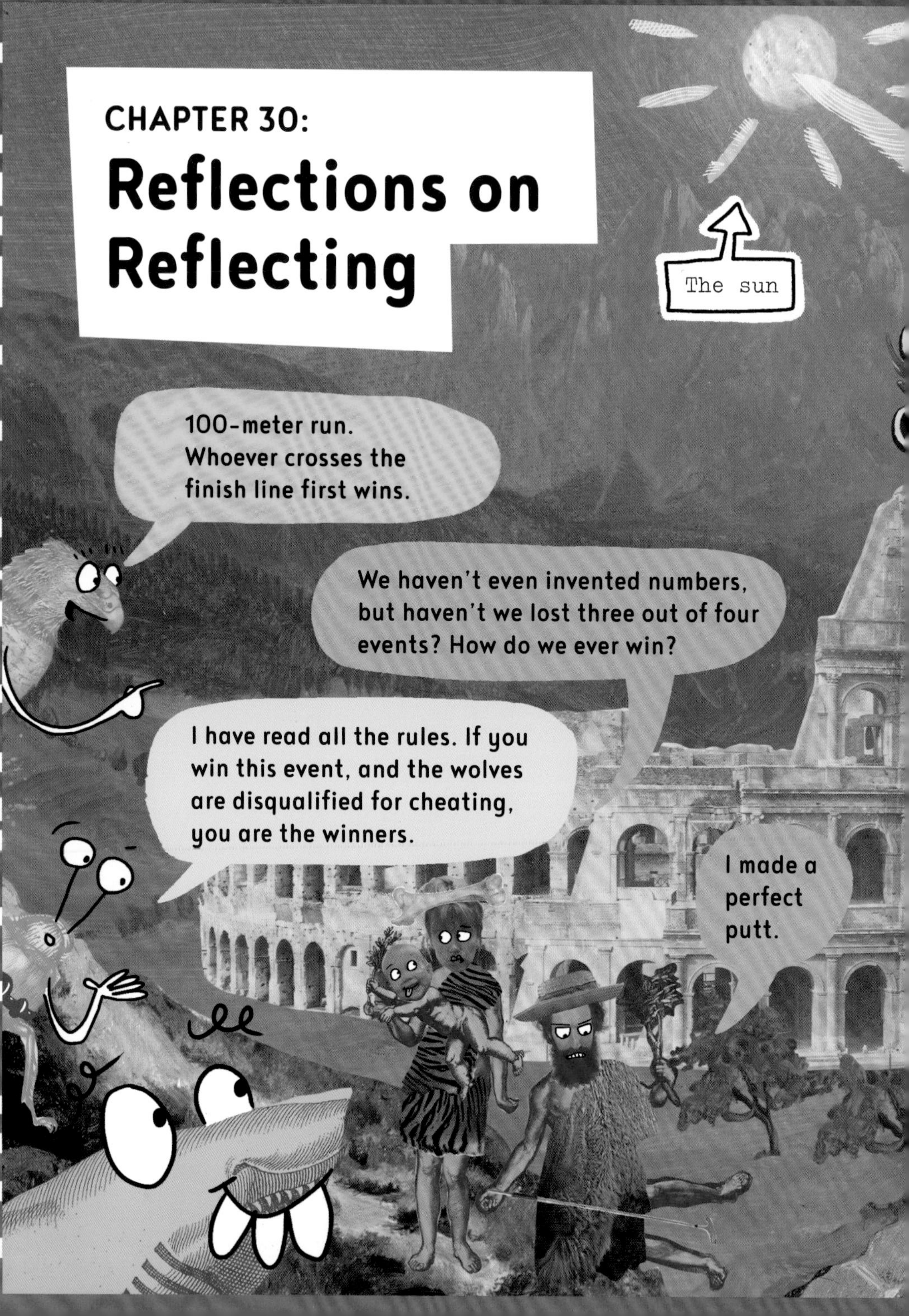

The sun
100-meter run. Whoever crosses the finish line first wins.
We haven't even invented numbers, but haven't we lost three out of four events? How do we ever win?
I have read all the rules. If you win this event, and the wolves are disqualified for cheating, you are the winners.
I made a perfect putt.

I know I said the geothermal golf plan was the absolute best plan. But the solar plan was REALLY the best. It was foolproof. Sunlight beams down, reflects off the mirror, no one can see where they are running. Sapiens win!

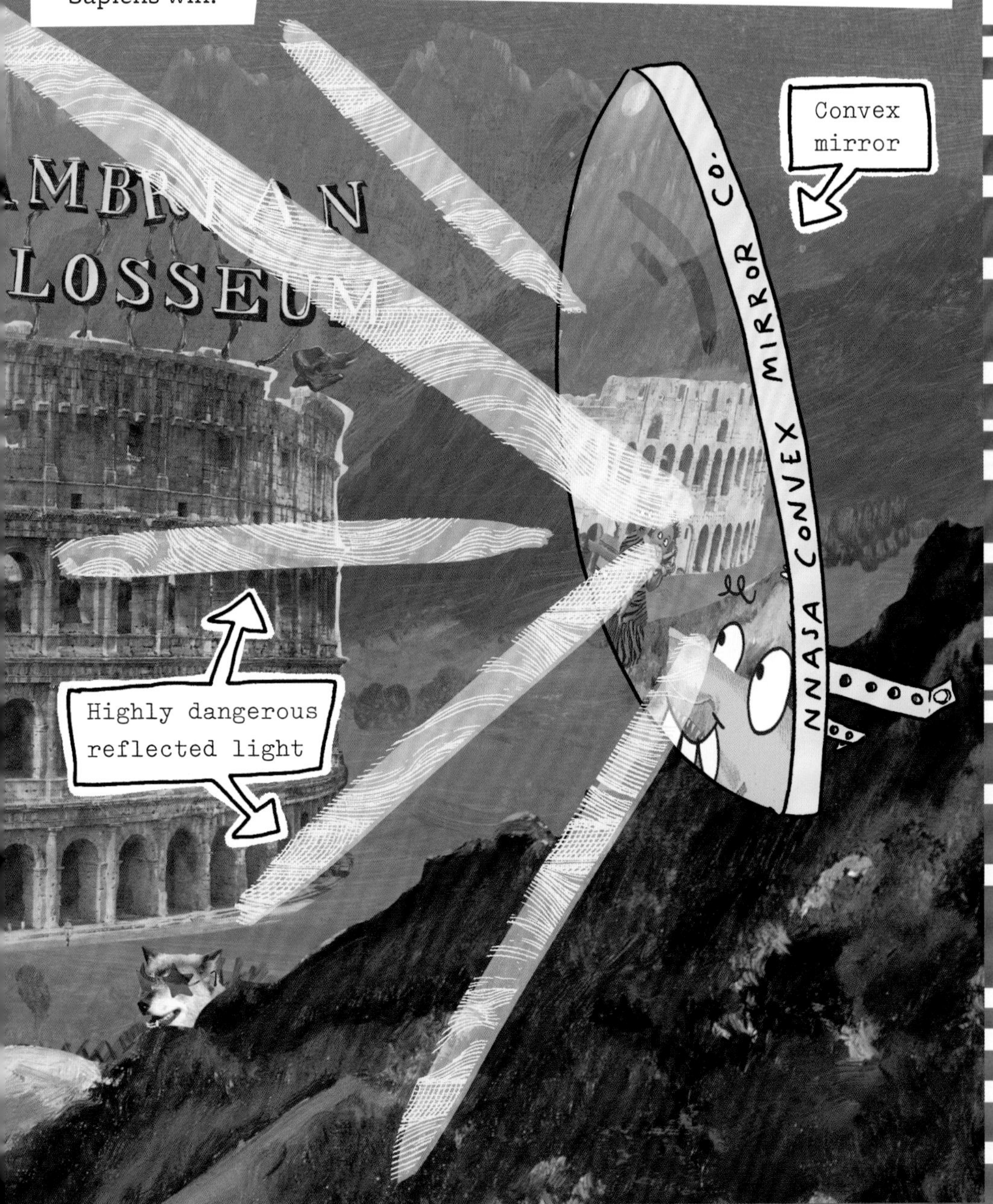
Convex mirror
NNASA CONVEX MIRROR CO.
Highly dangerous reflected light

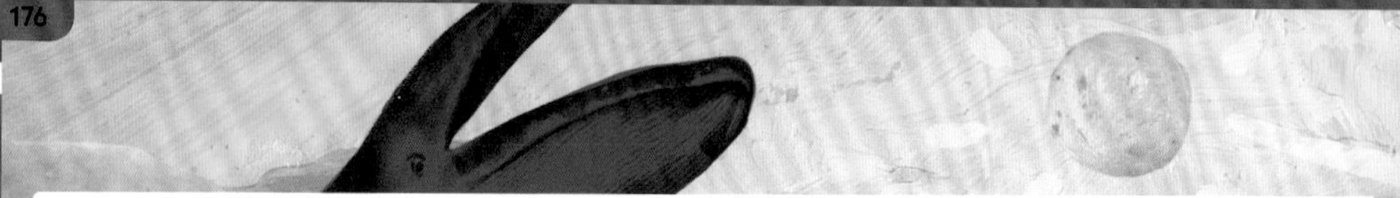

All the species, from the slowest giant sloth to the pretty quick Megalania lizard to the speedy saber-toothed cat, lined up at the starting line. They took off like a shot. Grunk slid the cover off the mirror. The sunlight blinded all the runners. And Lucy was going to sprint across the finish line first and win, but . . .

a pack of wolves swarmed the track . . . they scared the wits out of the woolly rhino, the Irish deer, the cave bear, the horned gopher, the saber-toothed cat, and the giant sloth, tangling Lucy and everyone else in a gigantic pileup of prehistoric species . . .

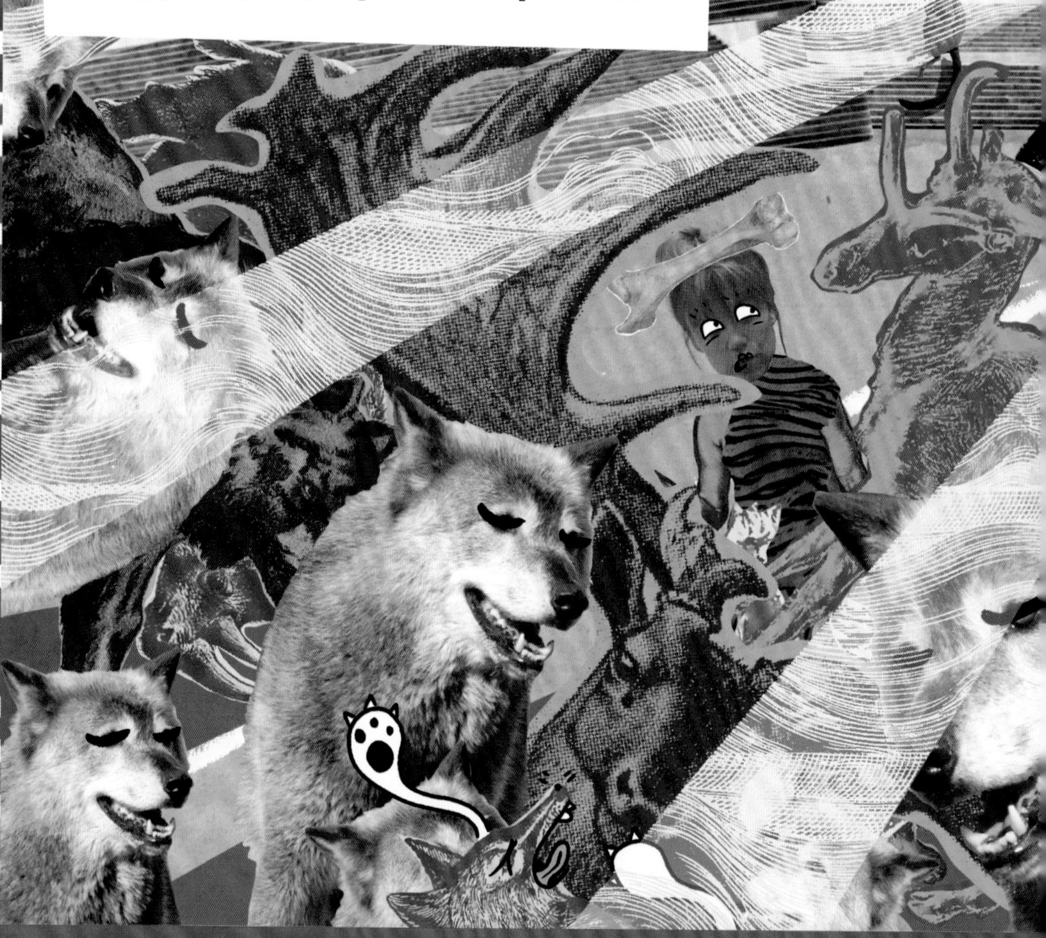

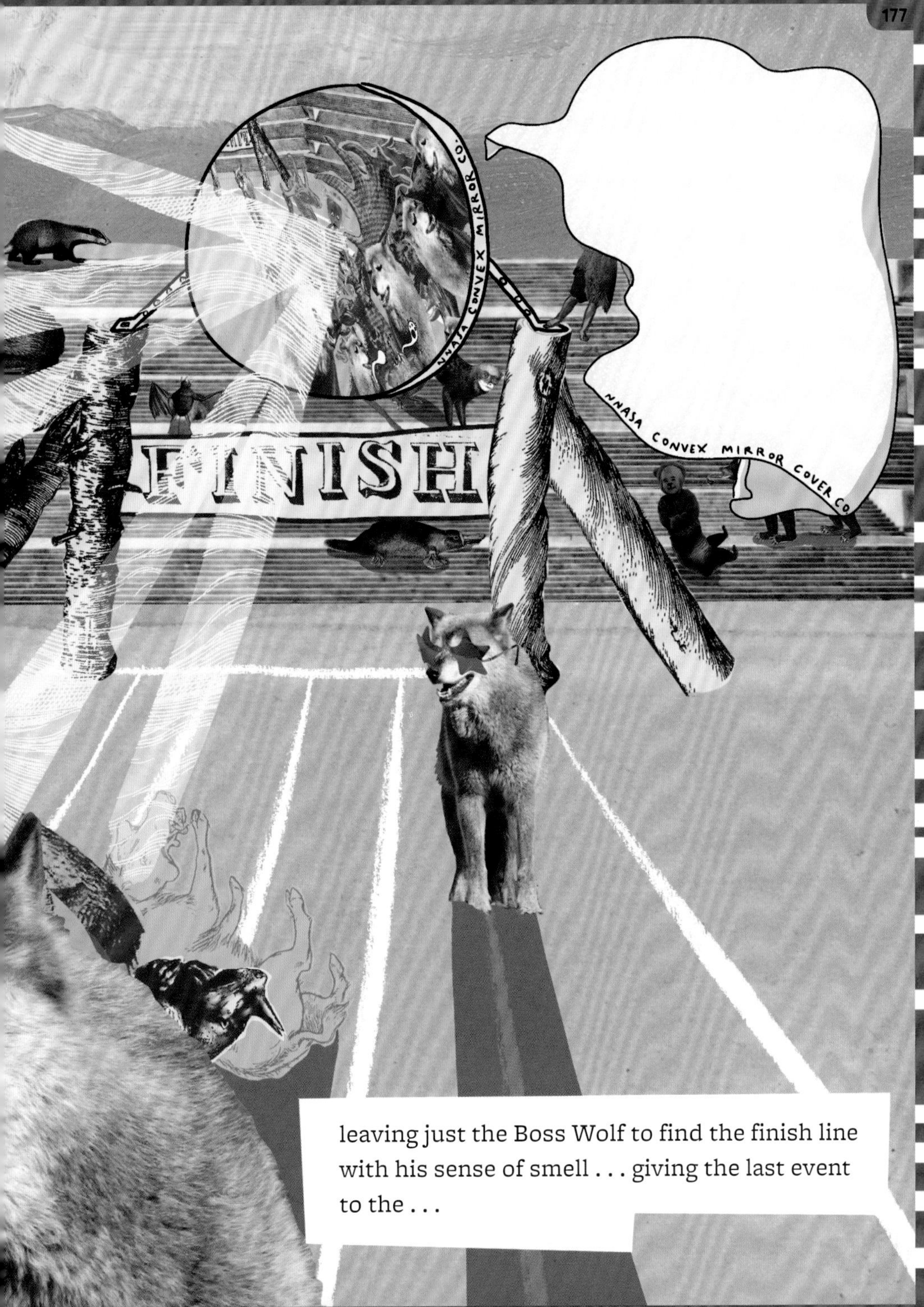
NNASA CONVEX MIRROR CO.
FINISH
NNASA CONVEX MIRROR COVER CO.
leaving just the Boss Wolf to find the finish line with his sense of smell . . . giving the last event to the . . .

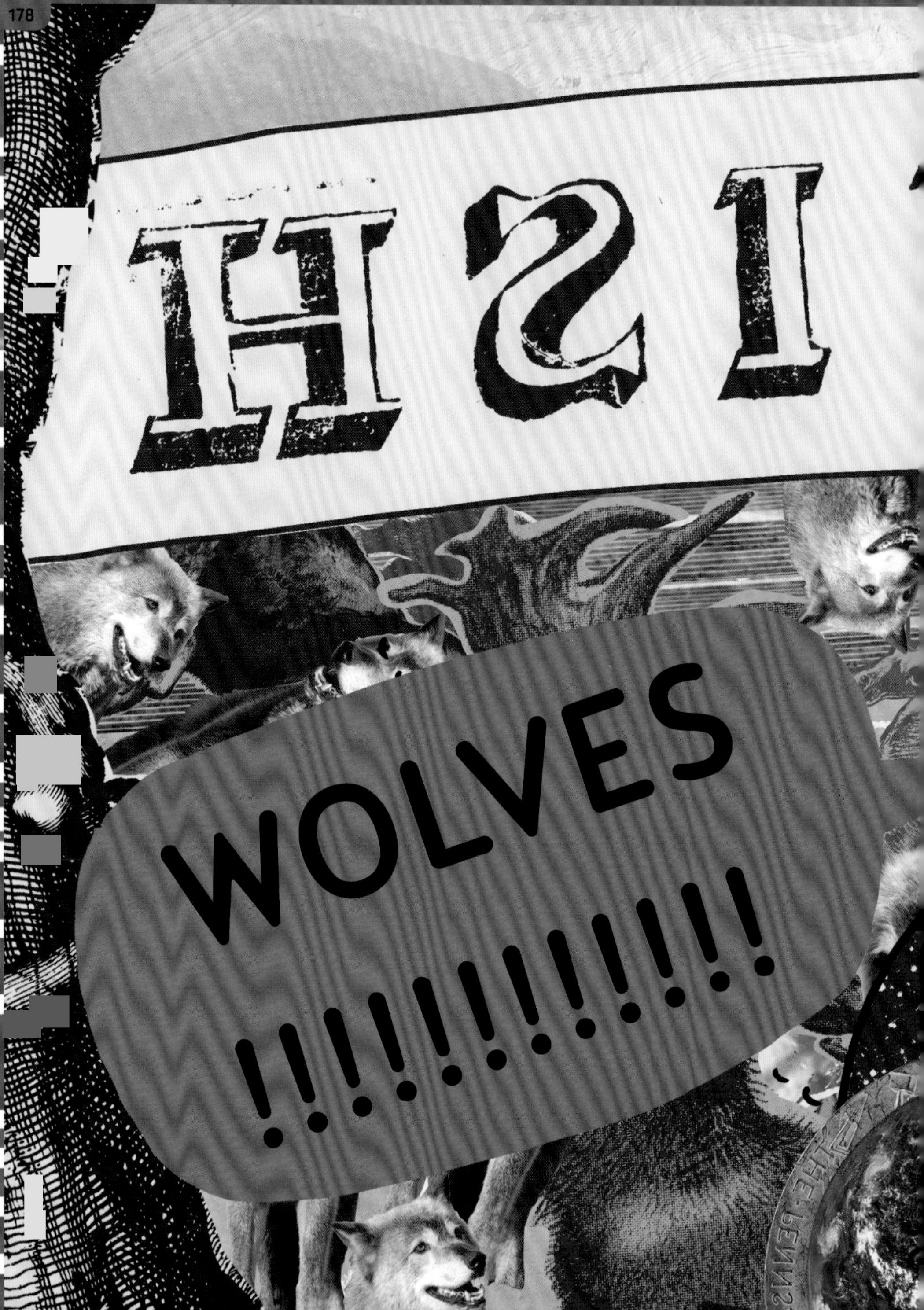
WOLVES
!!!!!!!!!!!!

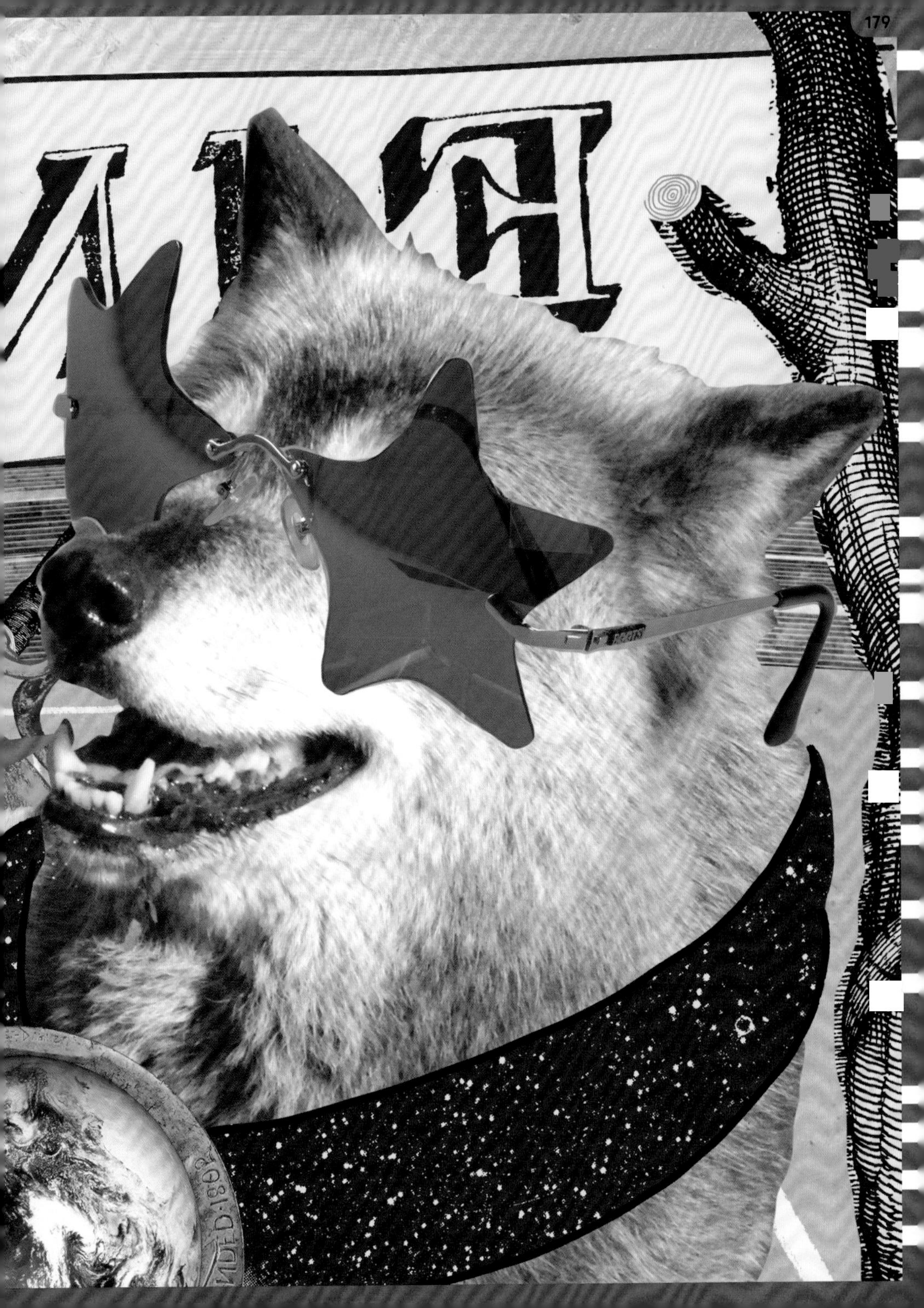

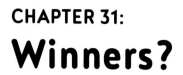

CHAPTER 31:
Winners?

I was shocked. I was floored. I was thunderstruck. I was baffled, bewildered, and flabbergasted. I know I've had some harsh things to say about you humans. You have done me some serious carbon damage. But I've always loved you. I've always thought we could fix our future together.

I wasn't so sure about a future run by wolves. I have seen wolf packs in action for eons. And don't get me wrong—I love their strength and family loyalty, and intelligence too. But there is something just so . . . bossy about them.

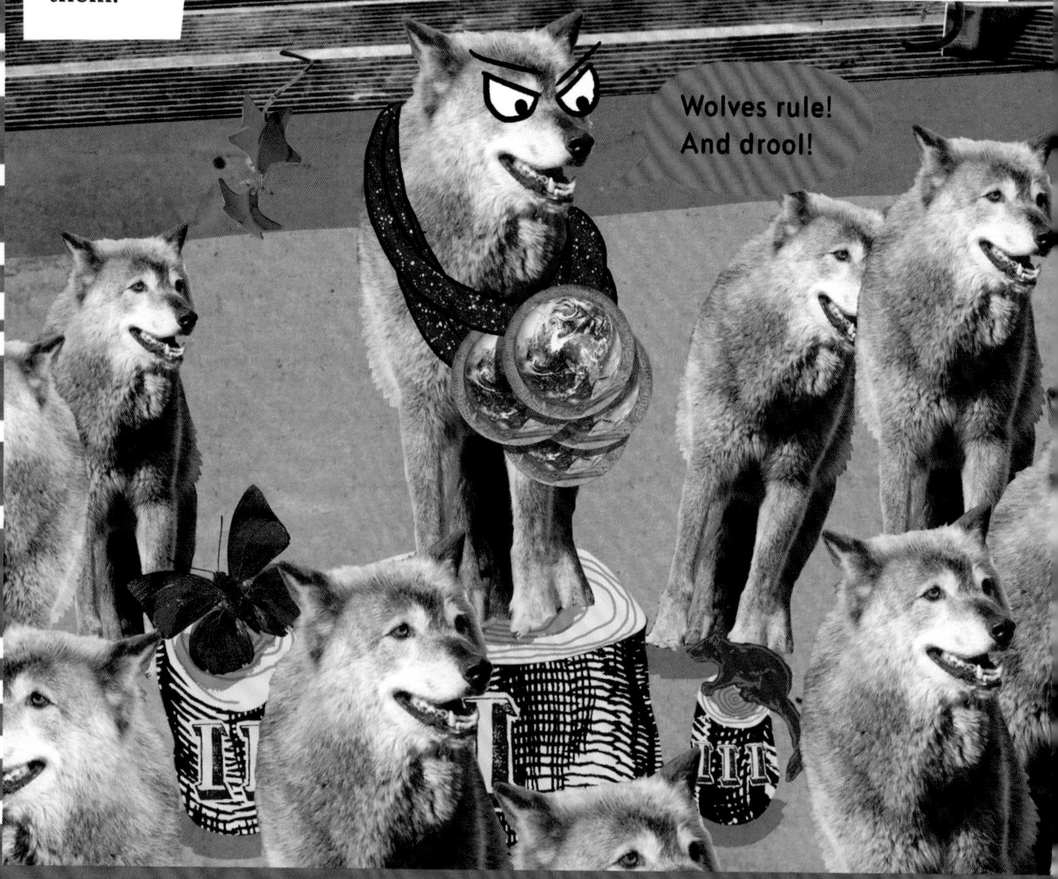
Wolves rule!
And drool!

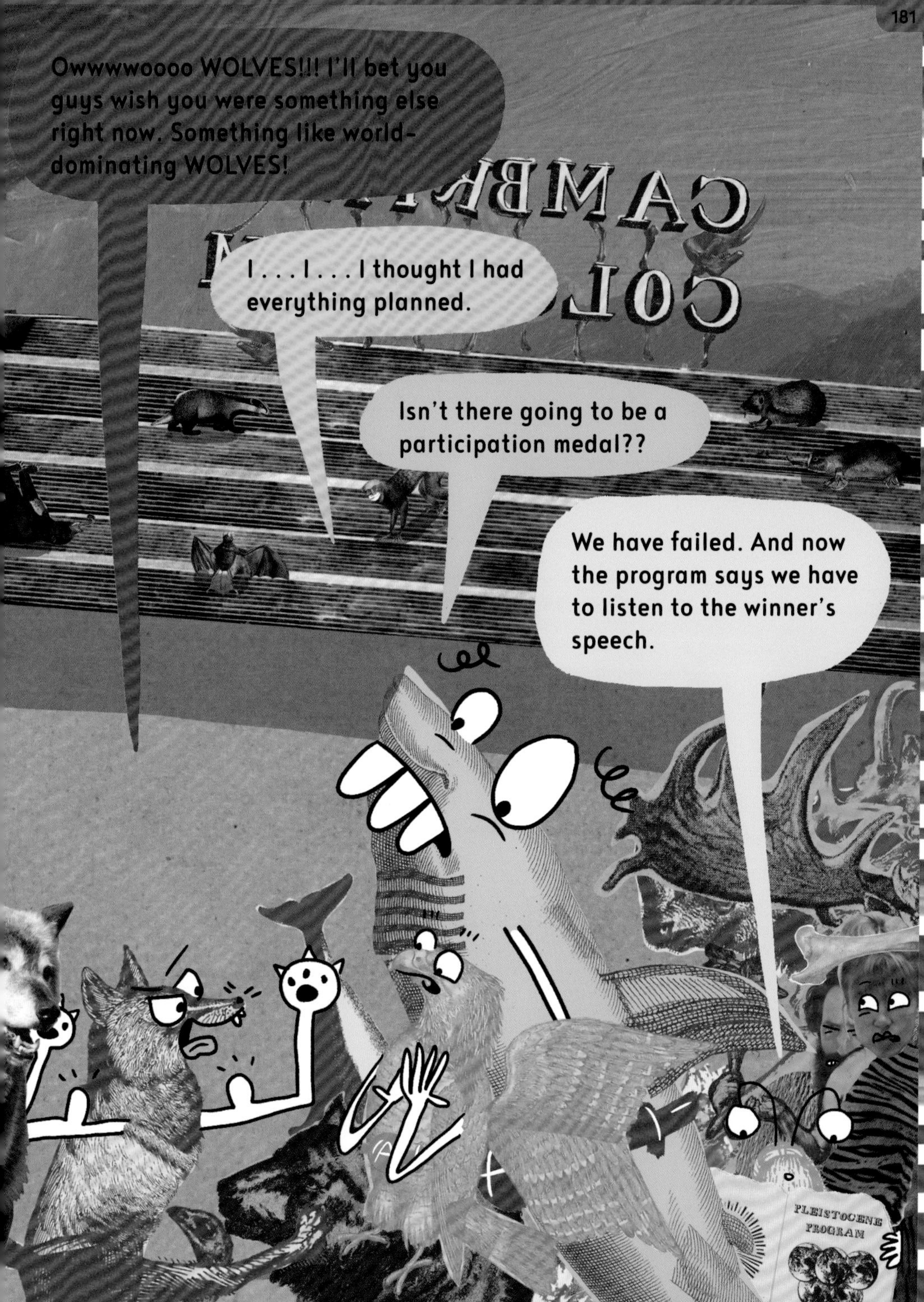
Owwwwoooo WOLVES!!! I'll bet you guys wish you were something else right now. Something like world-dominating WOLVES!
I . . . I . . . I thought I had everything planned.
Isn't there going to be a participation medal??
We have failed. And now the program says we have to listen to the winner's speech.
PLEISTOCENE PROGRAM

Oh my goodness. This is so wonderful. I want to share this winning with everyone. I want to invite all species to come together. I—

HA! I want to tell you I am totally kidding!

You losers. Wolves win. Now wolves are in charge of everything.

And here is how the world is going to work.

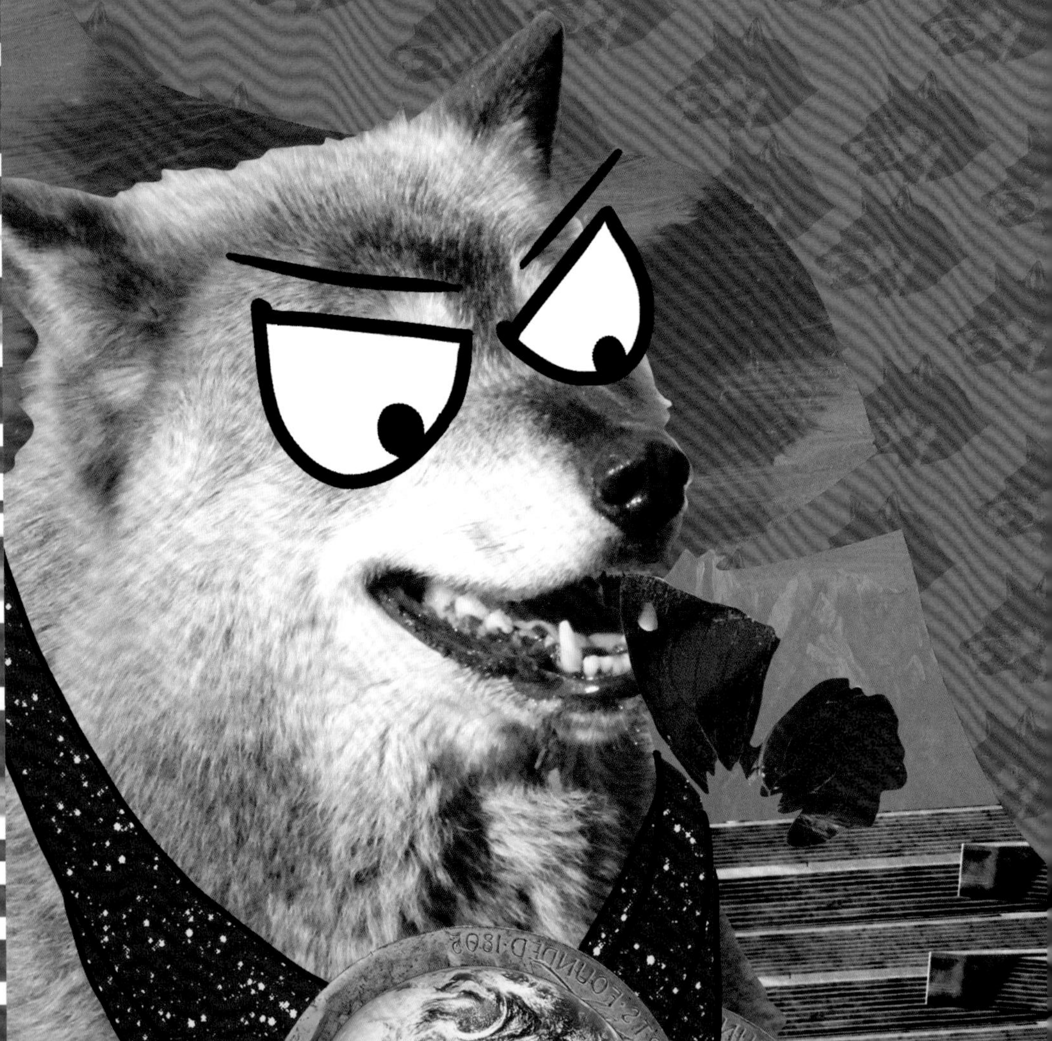

We are now the dominant species.
Here are the wolf rules:

Rule #1—The boss is always right. And I'm the boss.

Rule #2—Nobody pees on top of where I have peed.

Rule #3—Wolves get first choice of all food. We get the best. And some of you will get eaten. Mice, deer, raccoons, roadkill . . . we are looking at you.

Rule #4—Wolves get the best caves. Always. No complaining, cave bears. Pack it up.

Rule #5—See Rule #1.

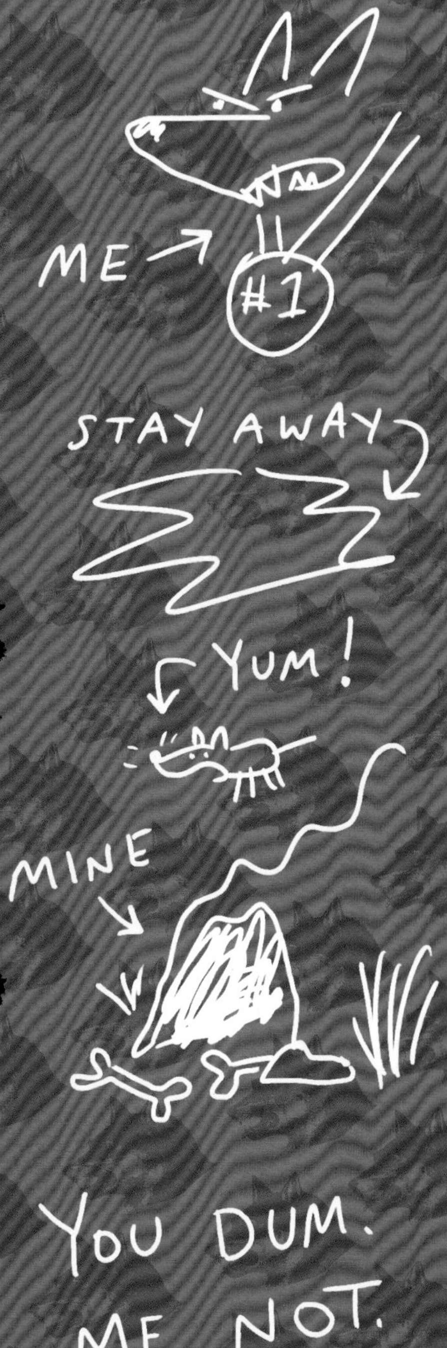

ME
#1
STAY AWAY
YUM!
MINE
YOU DUM.
ME NOT.

Rule #44—Butt sniffing. It's in.

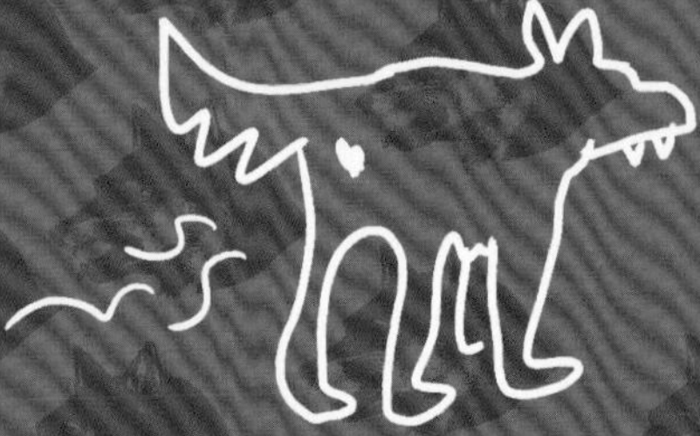

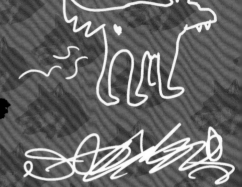

Rule #45—Shedding is nothing to be ashamed of. It's natural.

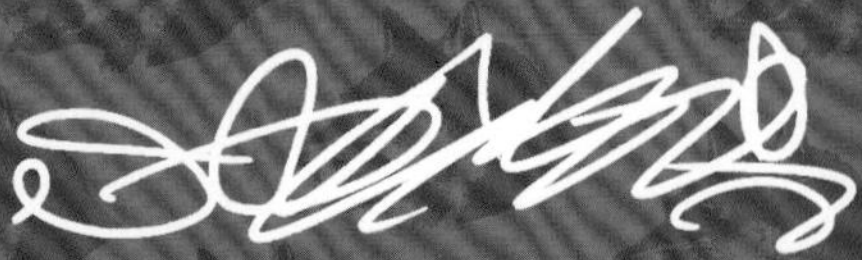

Rule #46—Cats. You are toast. Get out of town.

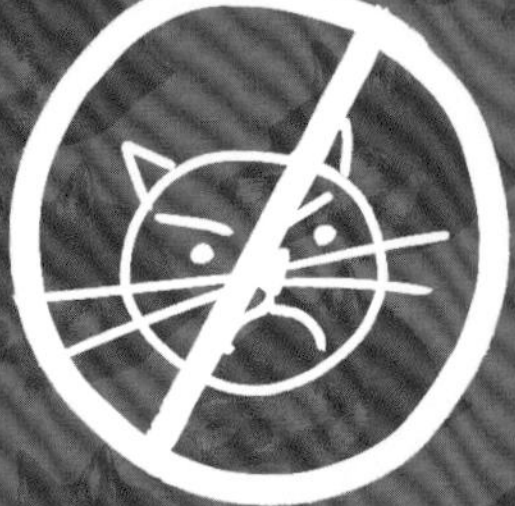

Rule #47—Howling is for wolves only. We will howl between the hours of nine p.m. and three a.m. every night. No howling if you are not a wolf.

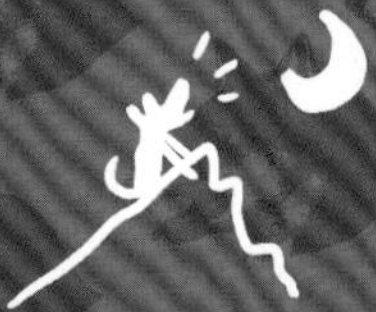

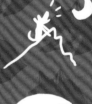

Rule #48—Special rules for full moons. Howling will be allowed all night long. But once again, only if you are a wolf.

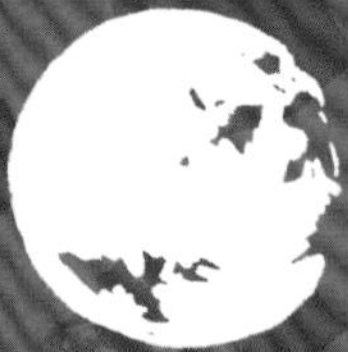

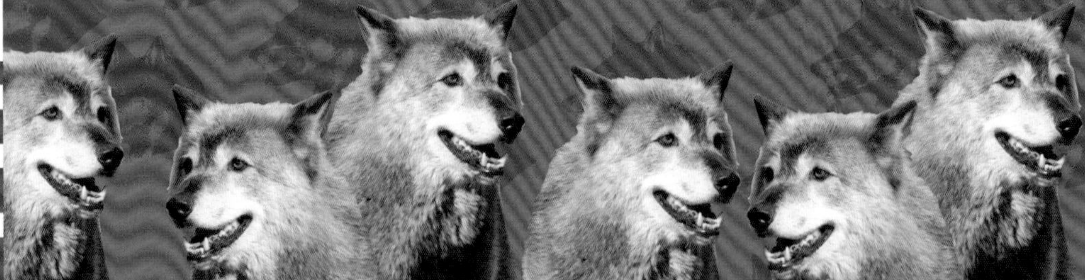

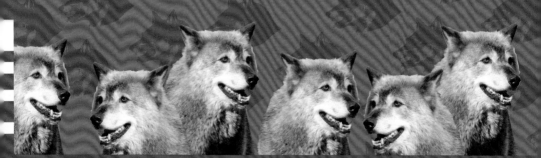

Rule #49—Nothing wrong with eating your own puke.

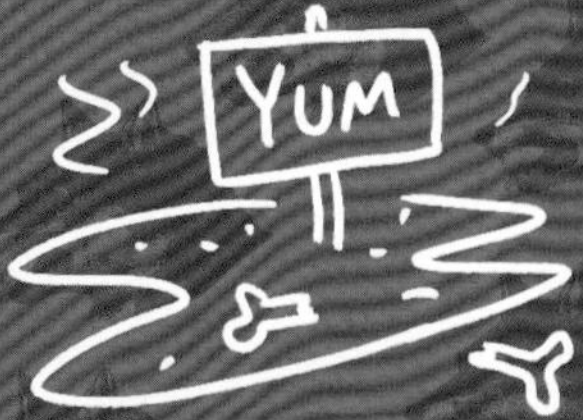
YUM

Rule #50—No dogs allowed. For anything. Ever. Get lost.

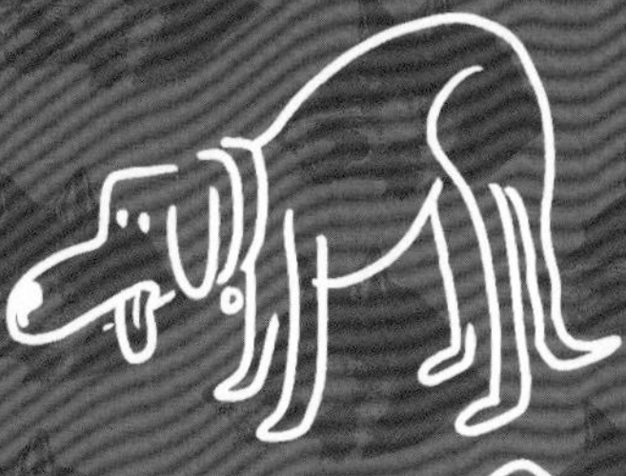

Rule #51—When wolves invent factories and industries, pollution is cool. Carbon emissions by wolves are fine.

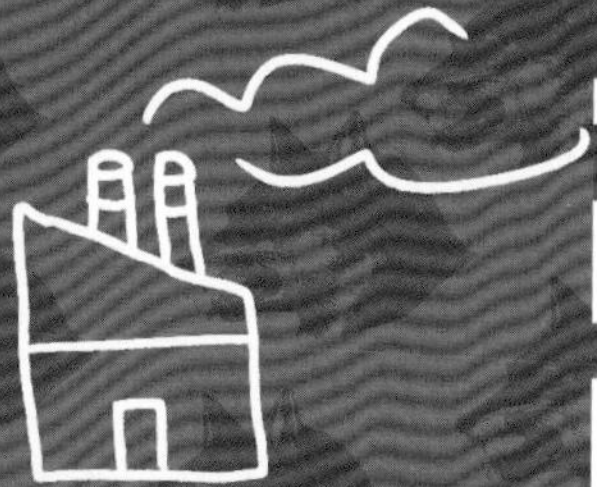

Rule #52—If any animal or plant or bird or rabbit disagrees with any of the wolf rules, they may be eliminated.

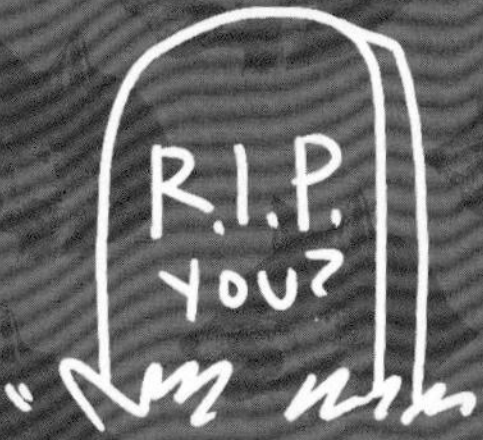
R.I.P.
YOU?

Rule #53—See Rule #1.

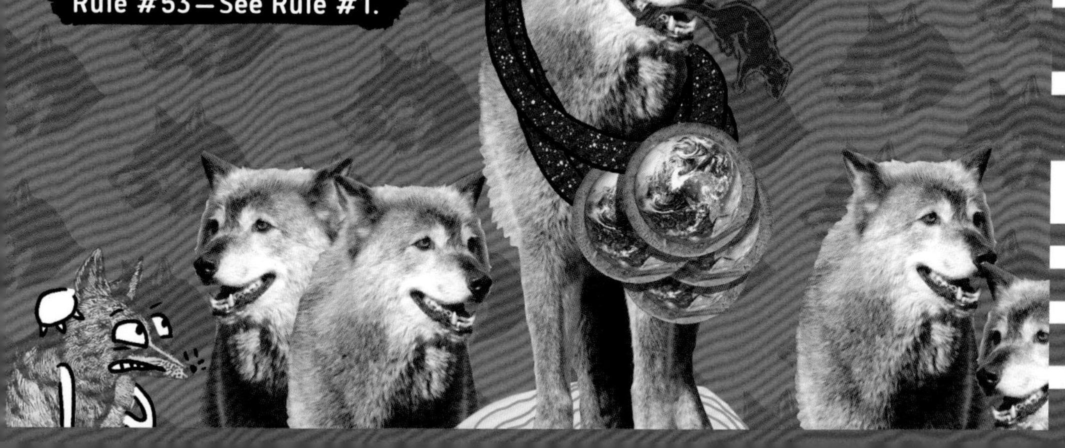

Rule #97—Wolves can now do pretty much whatever they want, whenever they want. If you ever think you should question a wolf—don't. That would be unpatriotic.

Rule #98—Oh yeah, I almost forgot. That twerpy little AlphaWolf? He is not a real wolf. Just ignore him. Always.

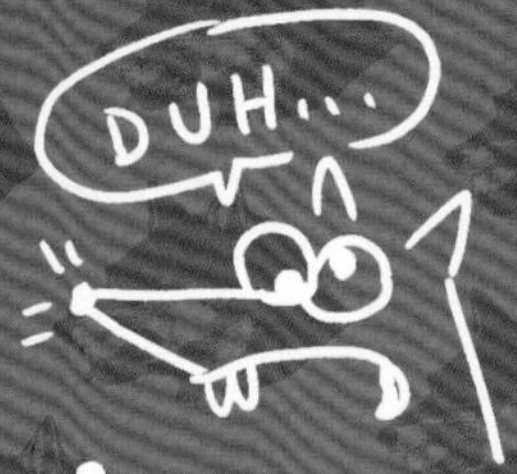
DUH...

Rule #99—Woolly mammoths, woolly rhinos, giant sloth, dodo bird, passenger pigeon, Yangtze river dolphin . . . you guys are all going extinct. Wolves need the room.

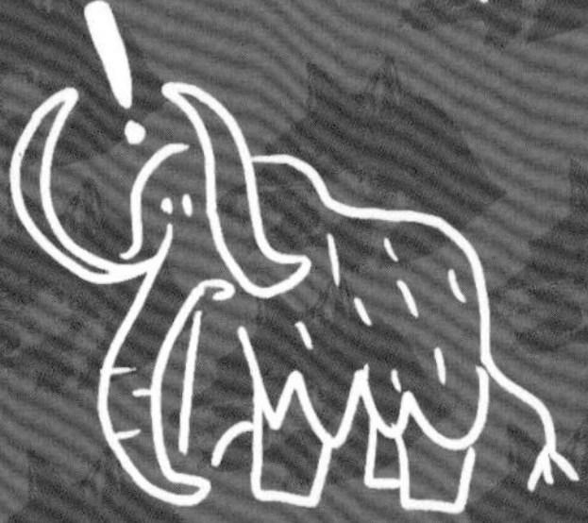

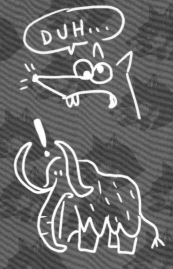

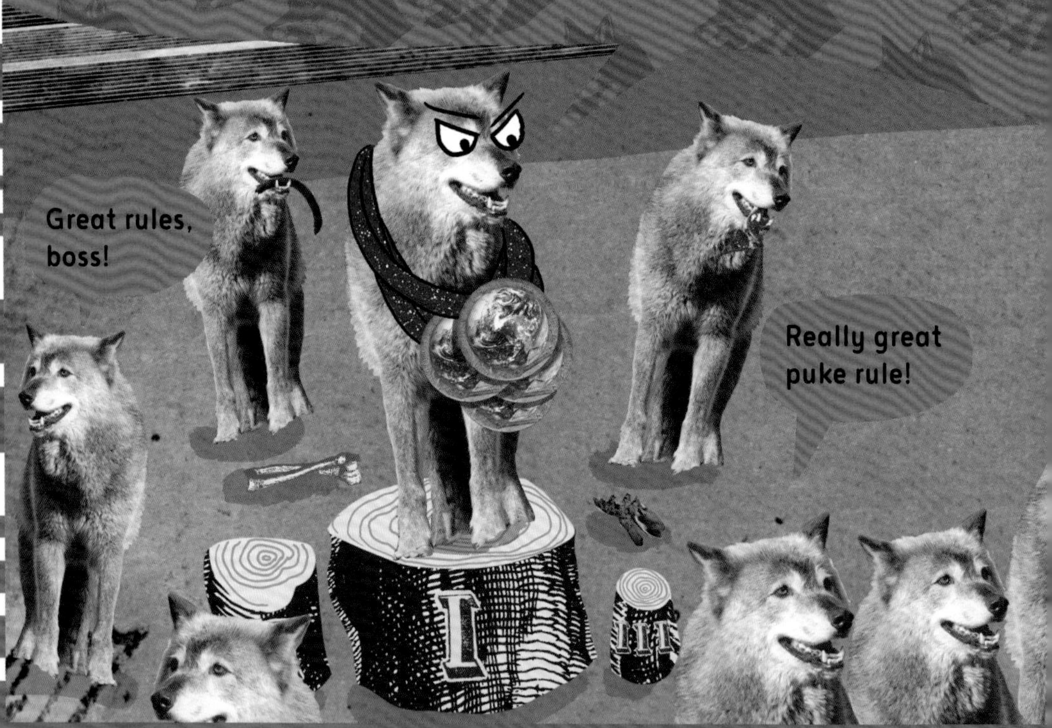
Great rules, boss!
Really great puke rule!

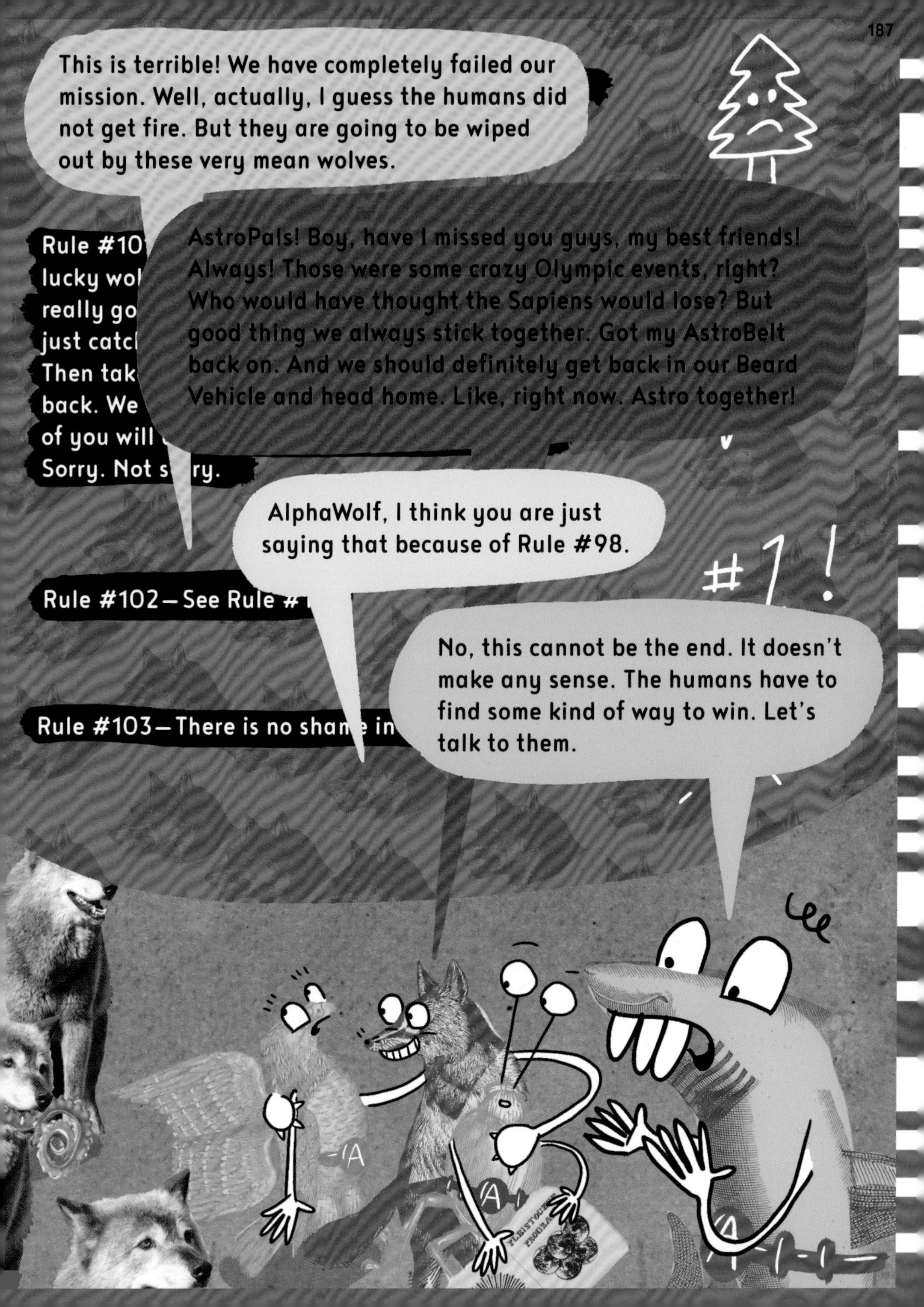
This is terrible! We have completely failed our mission. Well, actually, I guess the humans did not get fire. But they are going to be wiped out by these very mean wolves.
Rule #10
lucky wol
really go
just catc
Then tak
back. We
of you will
Sorry. Not s ry.
AstroPals! Boy, have I missed you guys, my best friends! Always! Those were some crazy Olympic events, right? Who would have thought the Sapiens would lose? But good thing we always stick together. Got my AstroBelt back on. And we should definitely get back in our Beard Vehicle and head home. Like, right now. Astro together!
AlphaWolf, I think you are just saying that because of Rule #98.
Rule #102—See Rule #
#1!
Rule #103—There is no sham in
No, this cannot be the end. It doesn't make any sense. The humans have to find some kind of way to win. Let's talk to them.

CHAPTER 32:

The Herd

The Boss Wolf's speech was bad enough. So many rules! Such disregard for my delicate balance of ecosystems—animals, plants, insects, fish, all life forms living together, supporting each other . . .

Then things went from wolf-bad to wolf-worse.

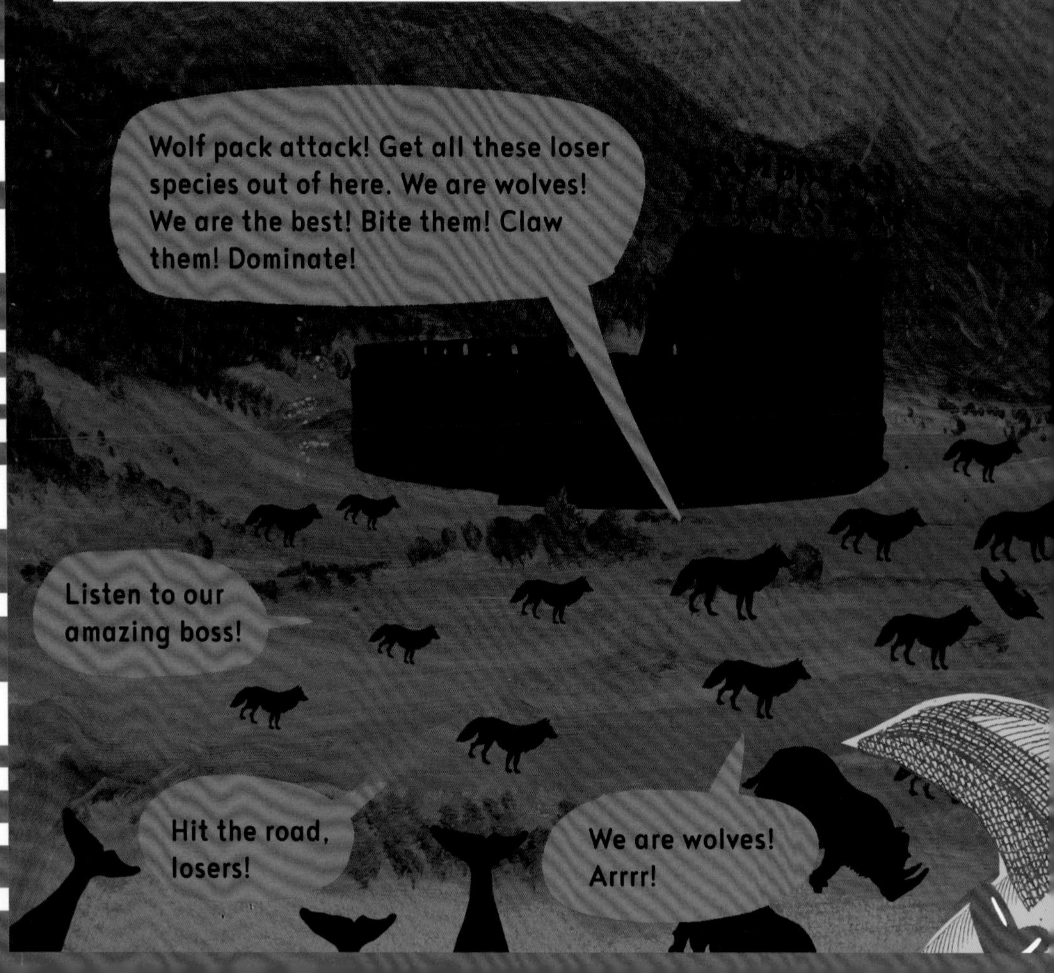

Wolf pack attack! Get all these loser species out of here. We are wolves! We are the best! Bite them! Claw them! Dominate!
Listen to our amazing boss!
Hit the road, losers!
We are wolves! Arrrr!

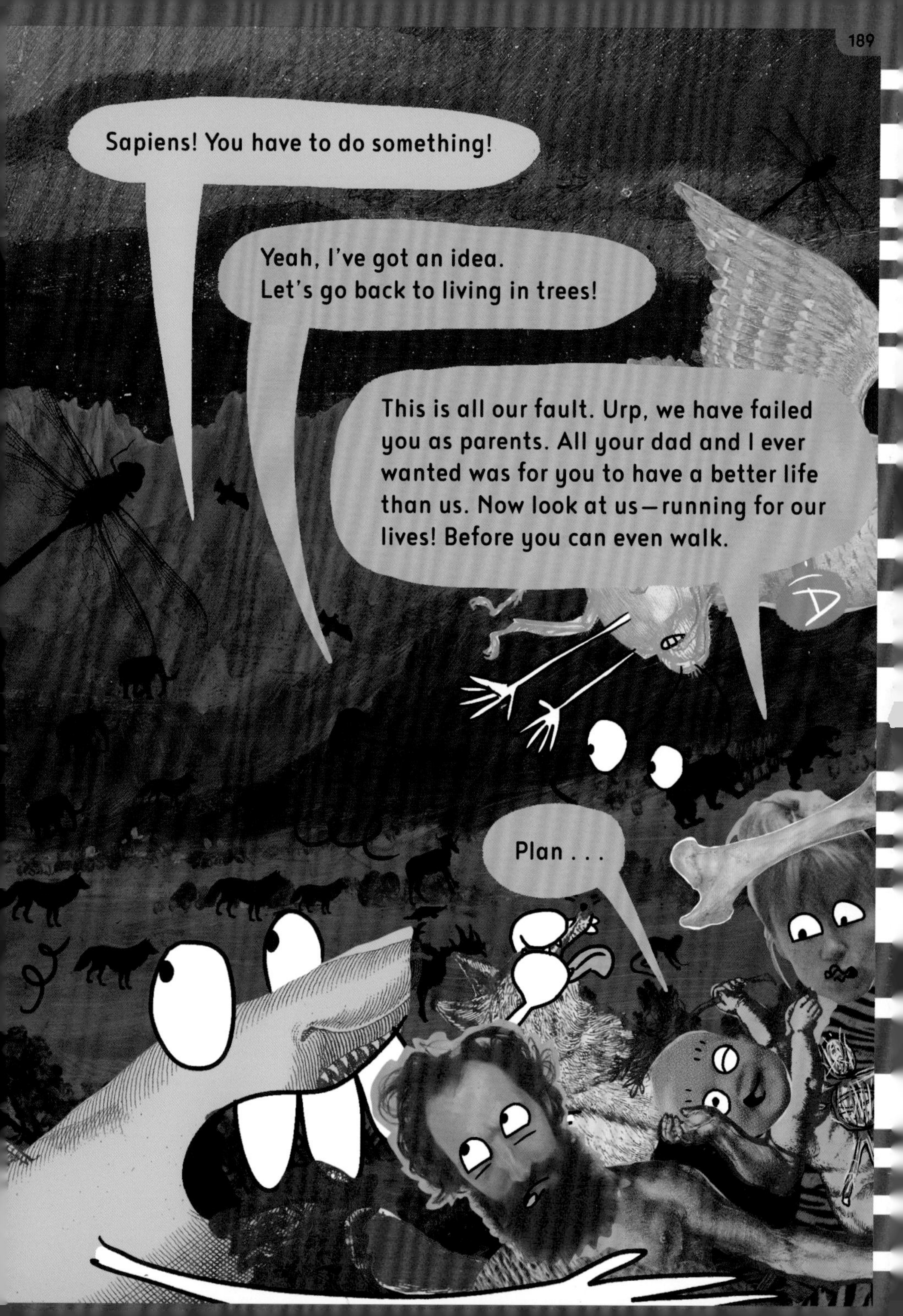
Sapiens! You have to do something!
Yeah, I've got an idea. Let's go back to living in trees!
This is all our fault. Urp, we have failed you as parents. All your dad and I ever wanted was for you to have a better life than us. Now look at us—running for our lives! Before you can even walk.
Plan . . .

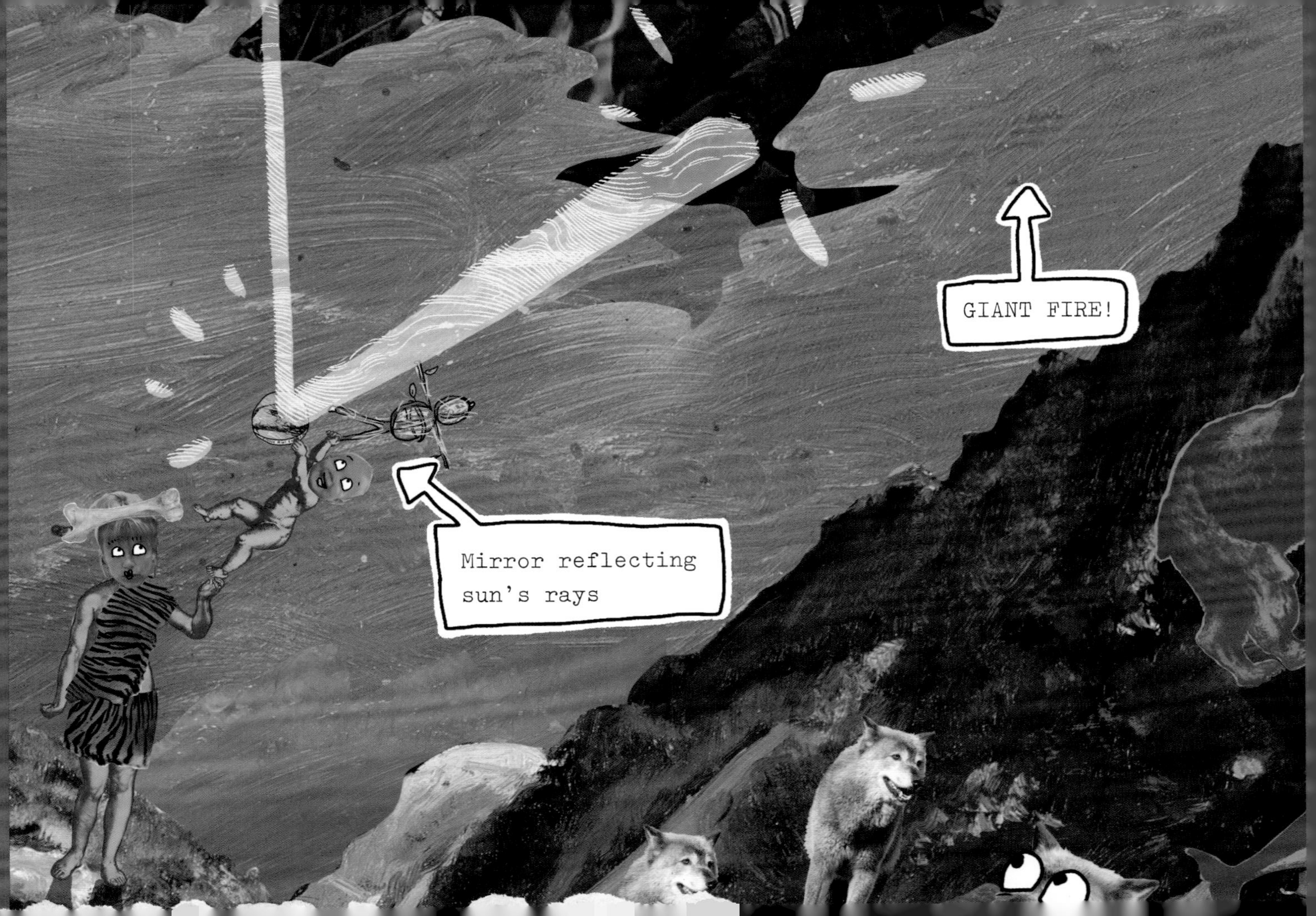
GIANT FIRE!
Mirror reflecting sun's rays

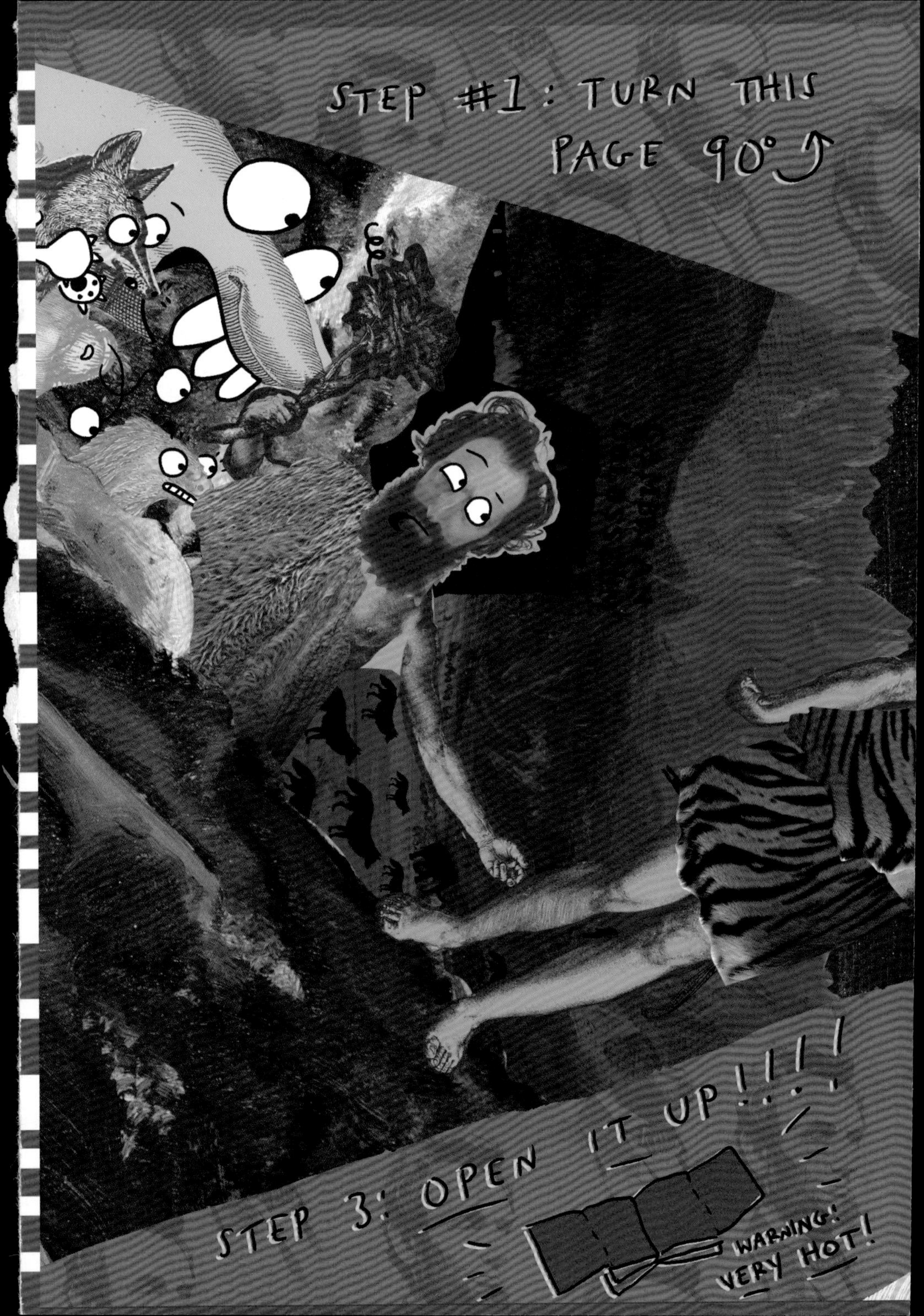
STEP #1: TURN THIS PAGE 90°
STEP 3: OPEN IT UP!!!!
WARNING! VERY HOT!

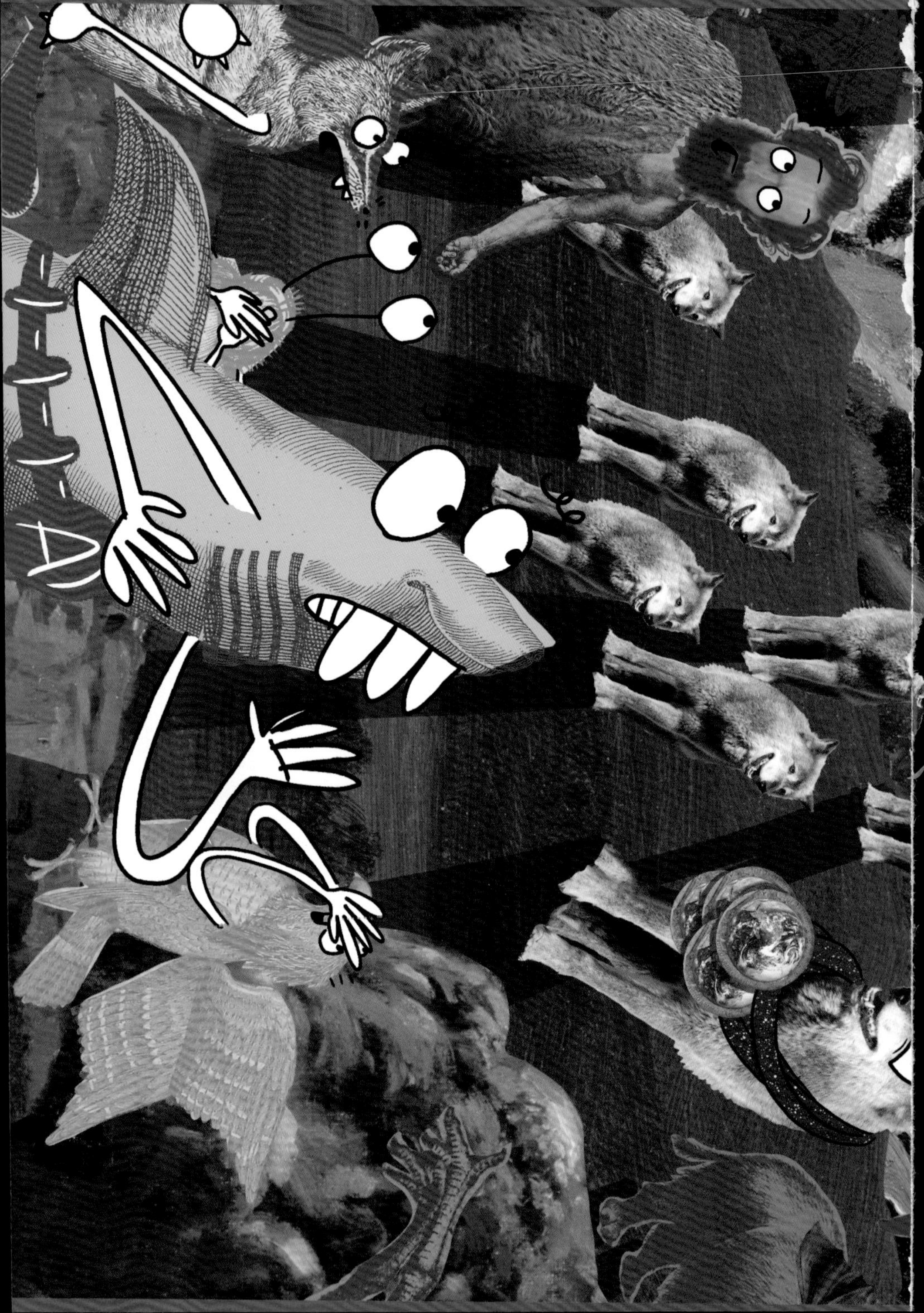

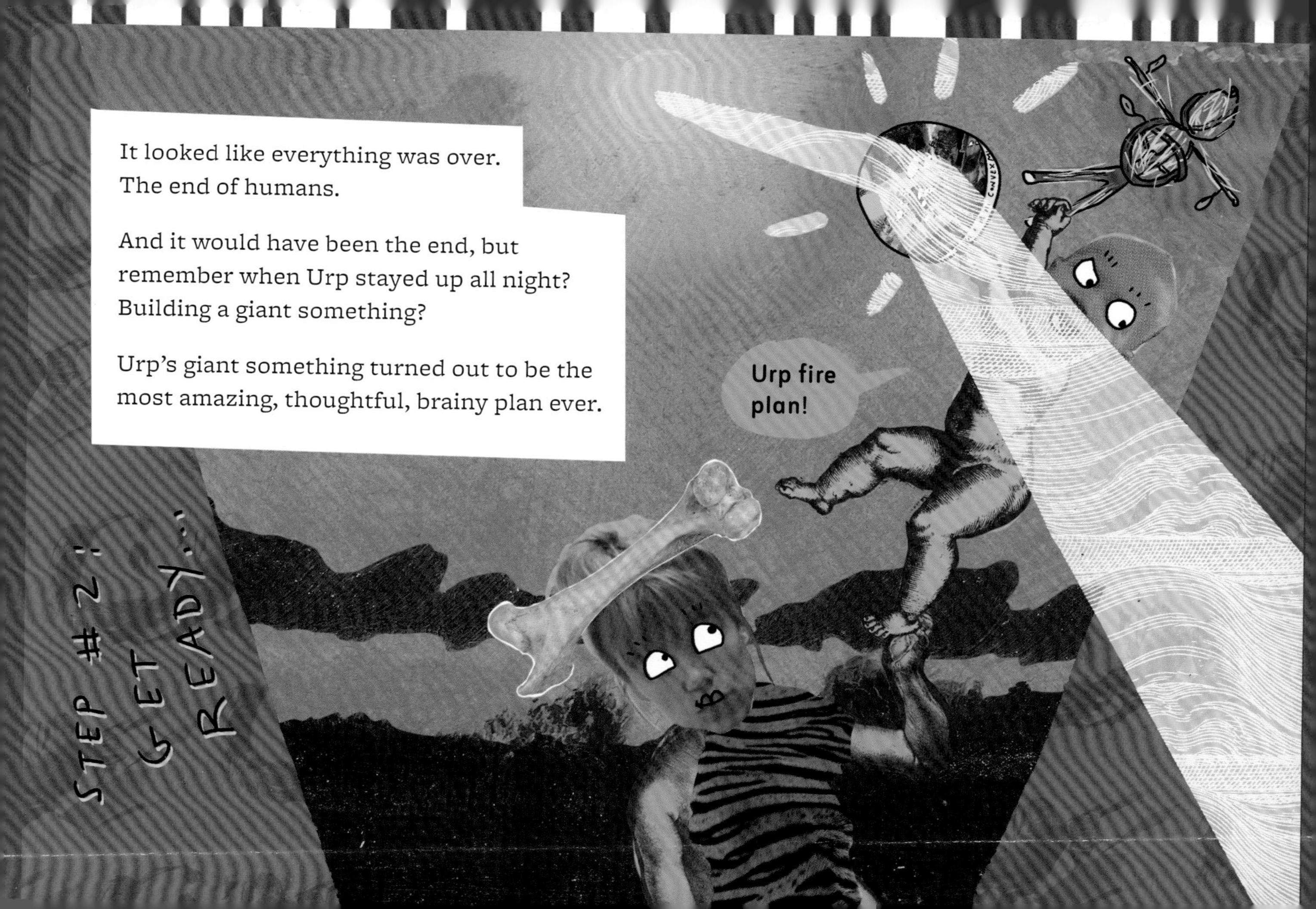
It looked like everything was over.
The end of humans.
And it would have been the end, but remember when Urp stayed up all night? Building a giant something?
Urp's giant something turned out to be the most amazing, thoughtful, brainy plan ever.
Urp fire plan!
STEP #2: GET READY...

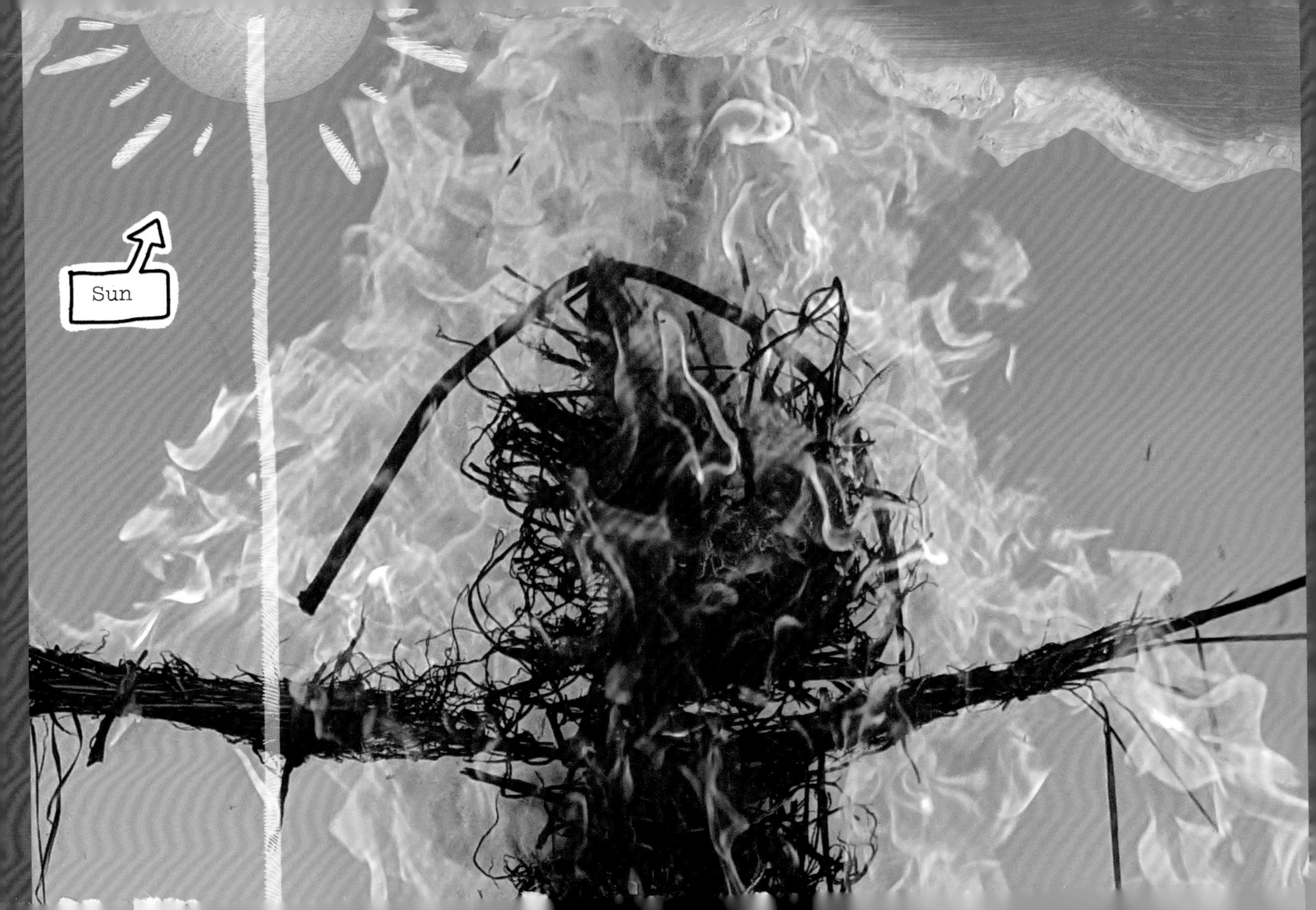
Sun

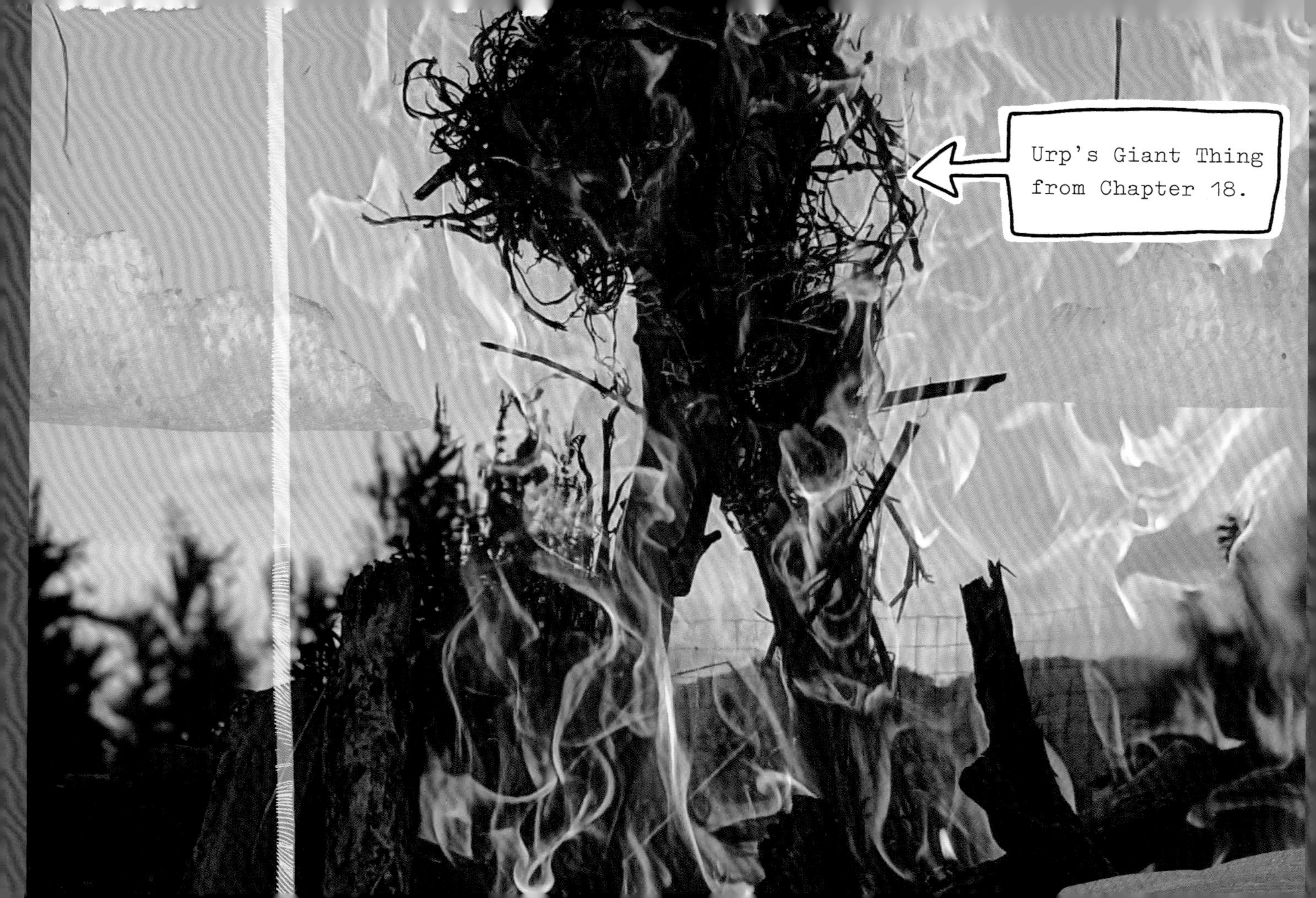
Urp's Giant Thing
from Chapter 18.

Absolutely brilliant.

And completely surprising.

Now, fire is nothing new to me. I was born a hot, fiery mess of gas and molten metal. The center of me is still over 10,000 degrees Fahrenheit, hot as the surface of the sun. And I've got 1,500 volcanos capable of spouting lava whenever I feel like it.

After plants started growing on me and pumping more oxygen in the air about 400 million years ago, I had some real doozy forest fires. Those things affect plants, animals, soil, air, water, everything.

So like I was saying, fire is nothing new to me. But I was almost as surprised as all of the Survival of the Fittest Olympics species when we saw that first moment of humans controlling fire.

Because here is the thing about fire. It has a lot of positives. It has its share of negatives. And it has one most absolutely best feature for humans.

If early humans had invented lists, they would have looked like this:

FIRE PROS:

Warmth

Light beyond the
length of a day

Makes food digestible

Great tool for
clearing land

Toast

FIRE CONS:

Can burn and kill

Pollution

Adds carbon to
atmosphere

Smoke in eyes

Burnt toast

FIRE'S ABSOLUTELY BEST FEATURE:

It scares off other animals.

CHAPTER 33:

Absolutely Best Fire Feature

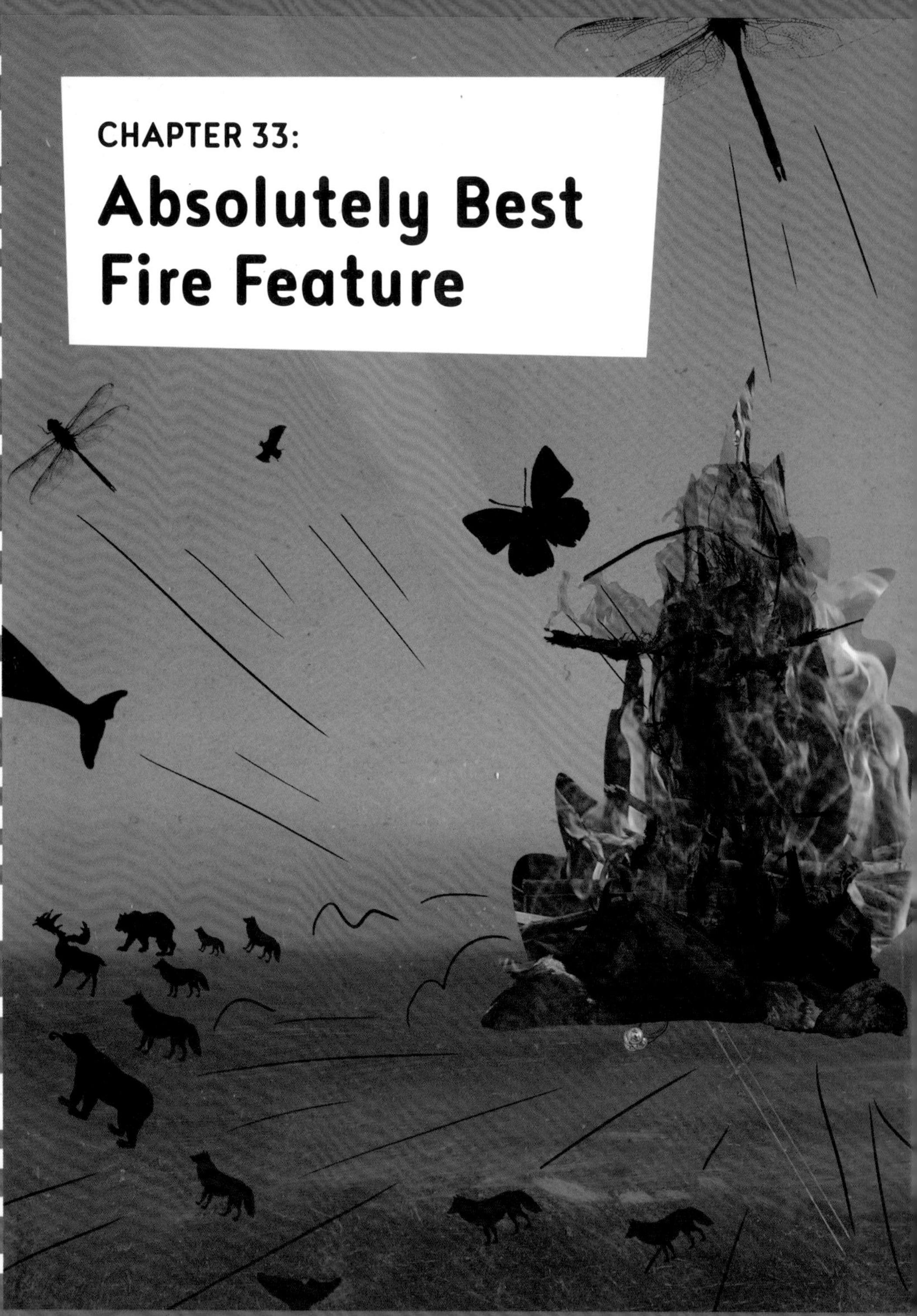

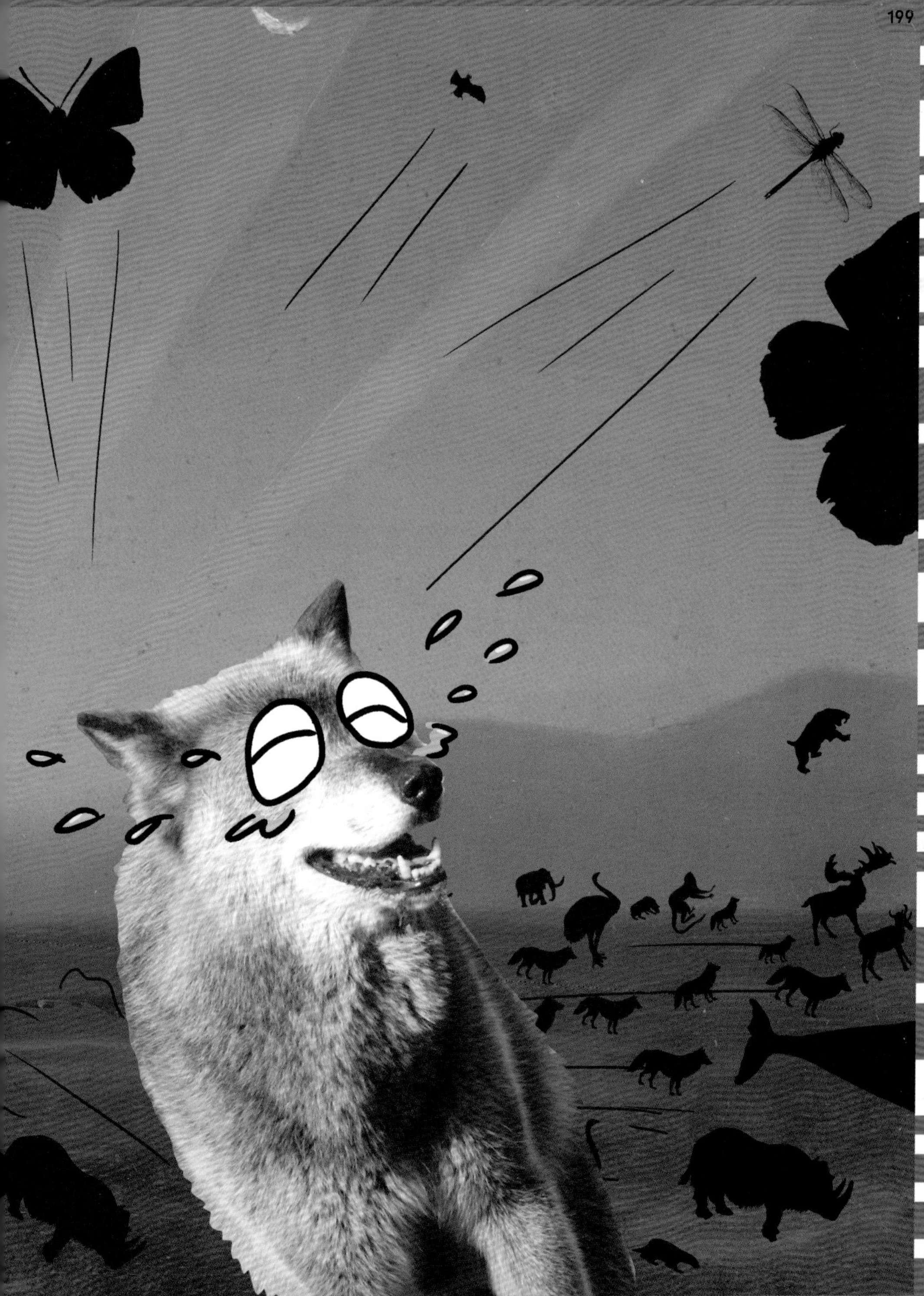

And that is exactly what happened. Baby Urp lit her giant wooden doll on fire. And every single species took off as fast as they could, leaving the humans as the last ones standing, and the most unlikely winners of the Survival of the Fittest Olympics.

The Sapiens family was thrilled. The AstroNuts were not at all sure what had just happened. I felt like I was remembering a movie I had seen a long time ago, and forgot the ending until I saw it again.

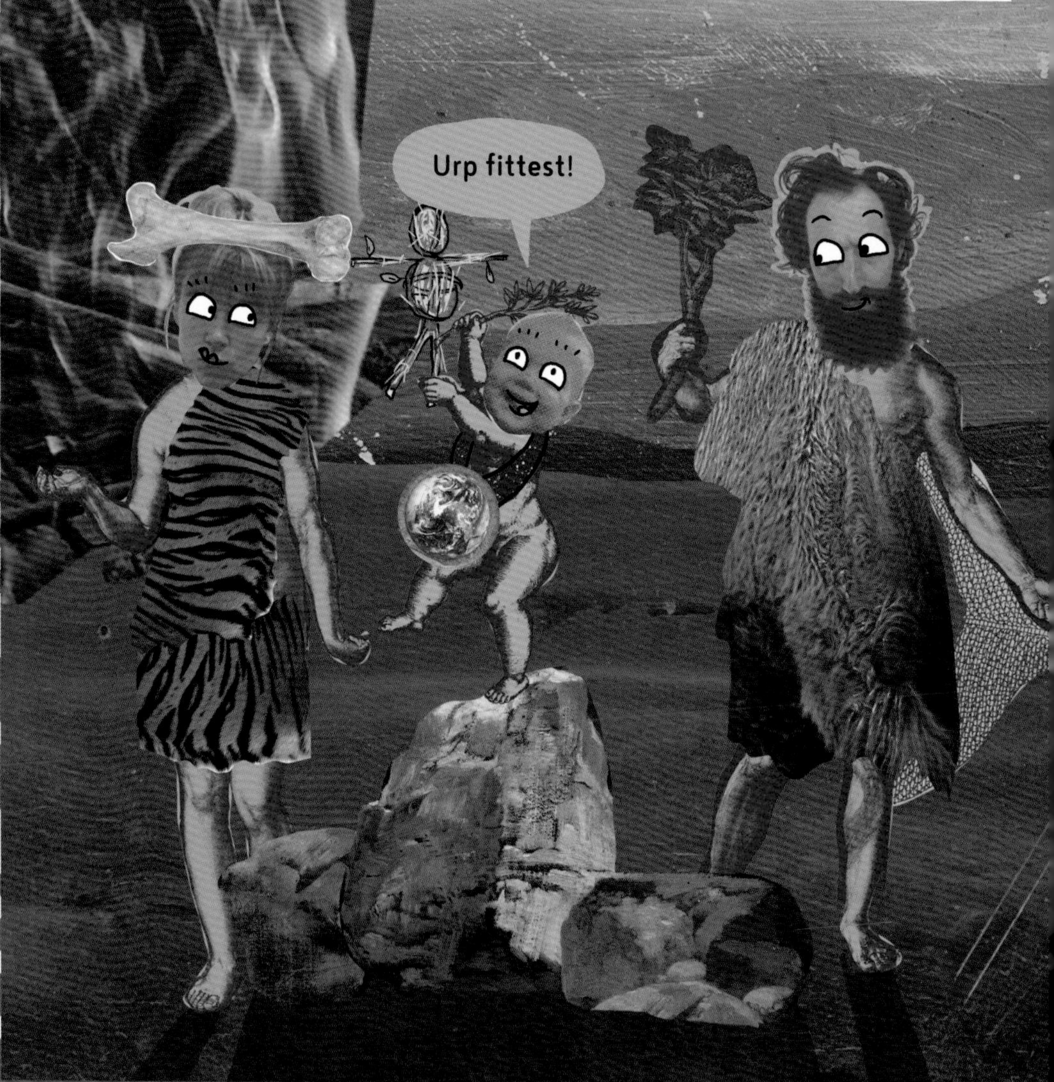
Urp fittest!

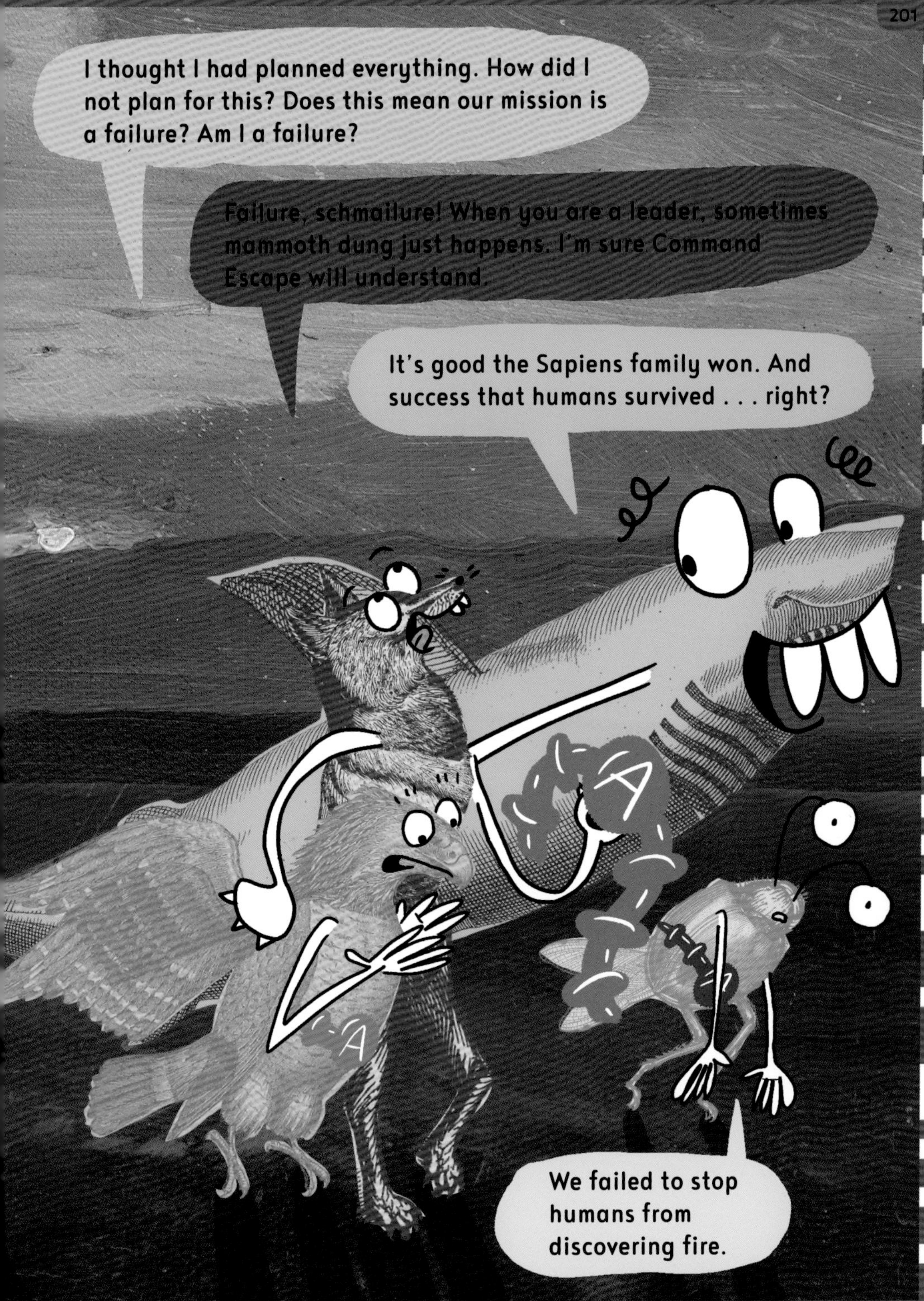
I thought I had planned everything. How did I not plan for this? Does this mean our mission is a failure? Am I a failure?
Failure, schmailure! When you are a leader, sometimes mammoth dung just happens. I'm sure Command Escape will understand.
It's good the Sapiens family won. And success that humans survived . . . right?
We failed to stop humans from discovering fire.

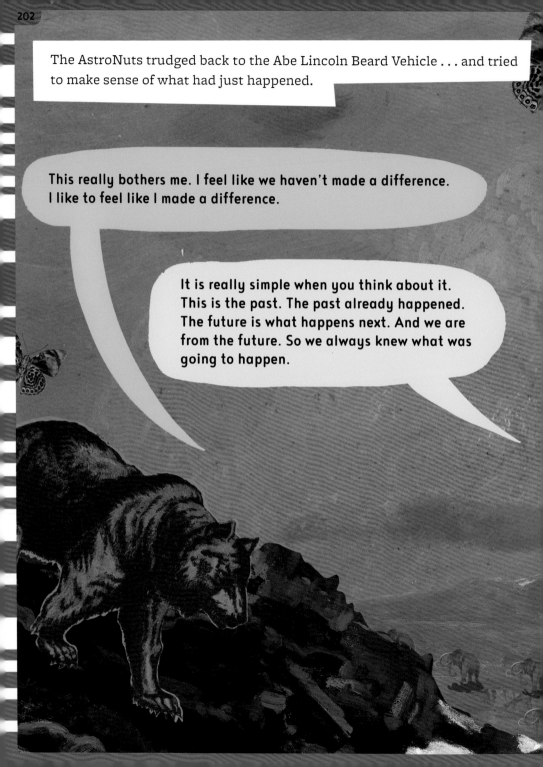

The AstroNuts trudged back to the Abe Lincoln Beard Vehicle . . . and tried to make sense of what had just happened.

This really bothers me. I feel like we haven't made a difference. I like to feel like I made a difference.

It is really simple when you think about it. This is the past. The past already happened. The future is what happens next. And we are from the future. So we always knew what was going to happen.

I just worry this means we will never get to visit the Pizza Planet.

No. That can't be right. LaserShark, I know we made a difference. We must have made a difference. I'm not sure how. But we must have.

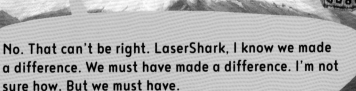

See what I was talking about? This time-travel stuff hurts your brain.

CHAPTER 34:

¡POOLPesreveR

The AstroNuts climbed in their Abraham Lincoln Beard Vehicle, still wondering if they had made any difference, still wondering what future they would return to.

They all (well, almost all) clicked on their Space-Time seatbelts. Mission Pilot StinkBug fired up the Dandruff Thrusters in the PAST. And they dePOOLPesreveR into the wormhole, flying future-forward to their PRESENT.

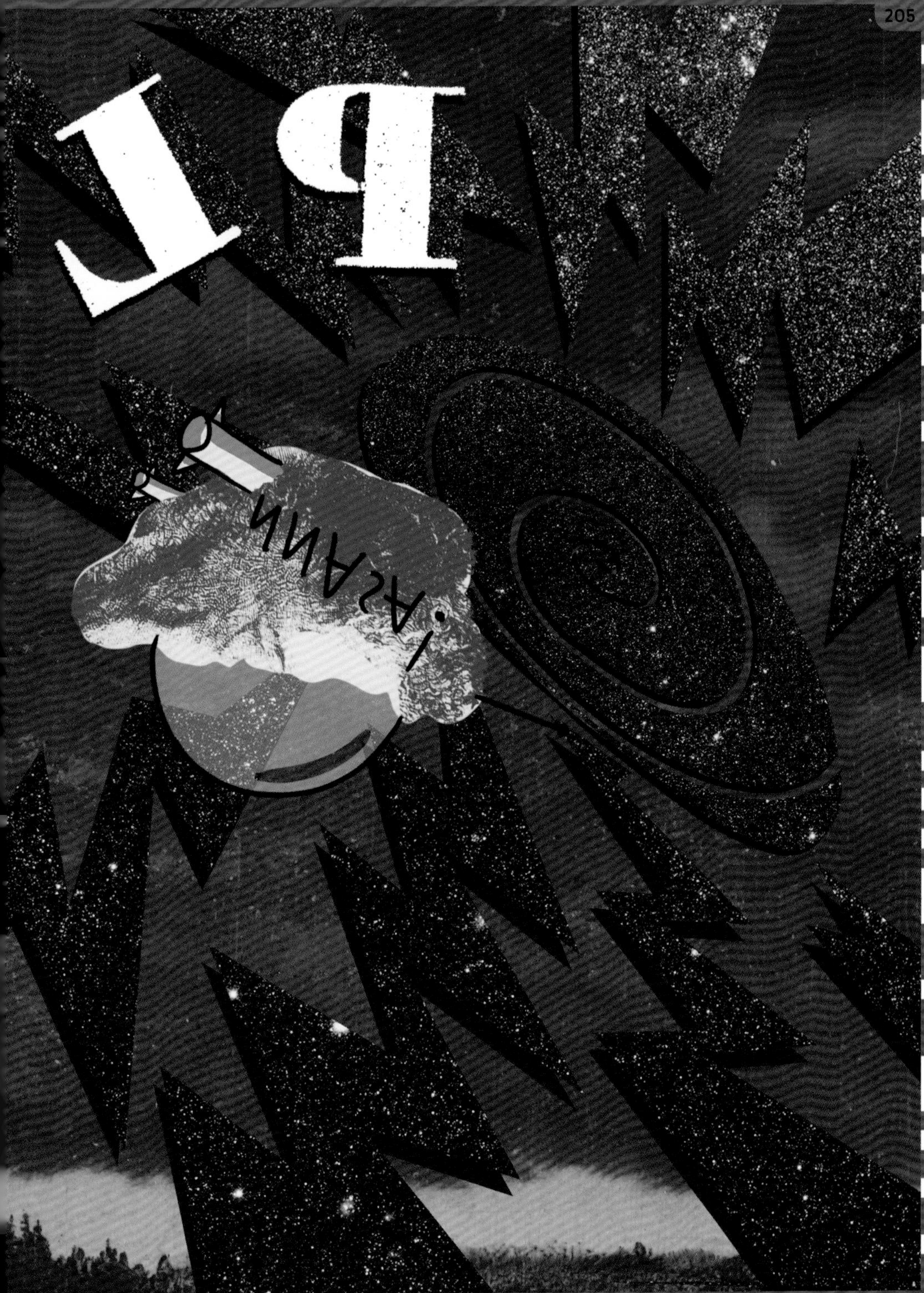

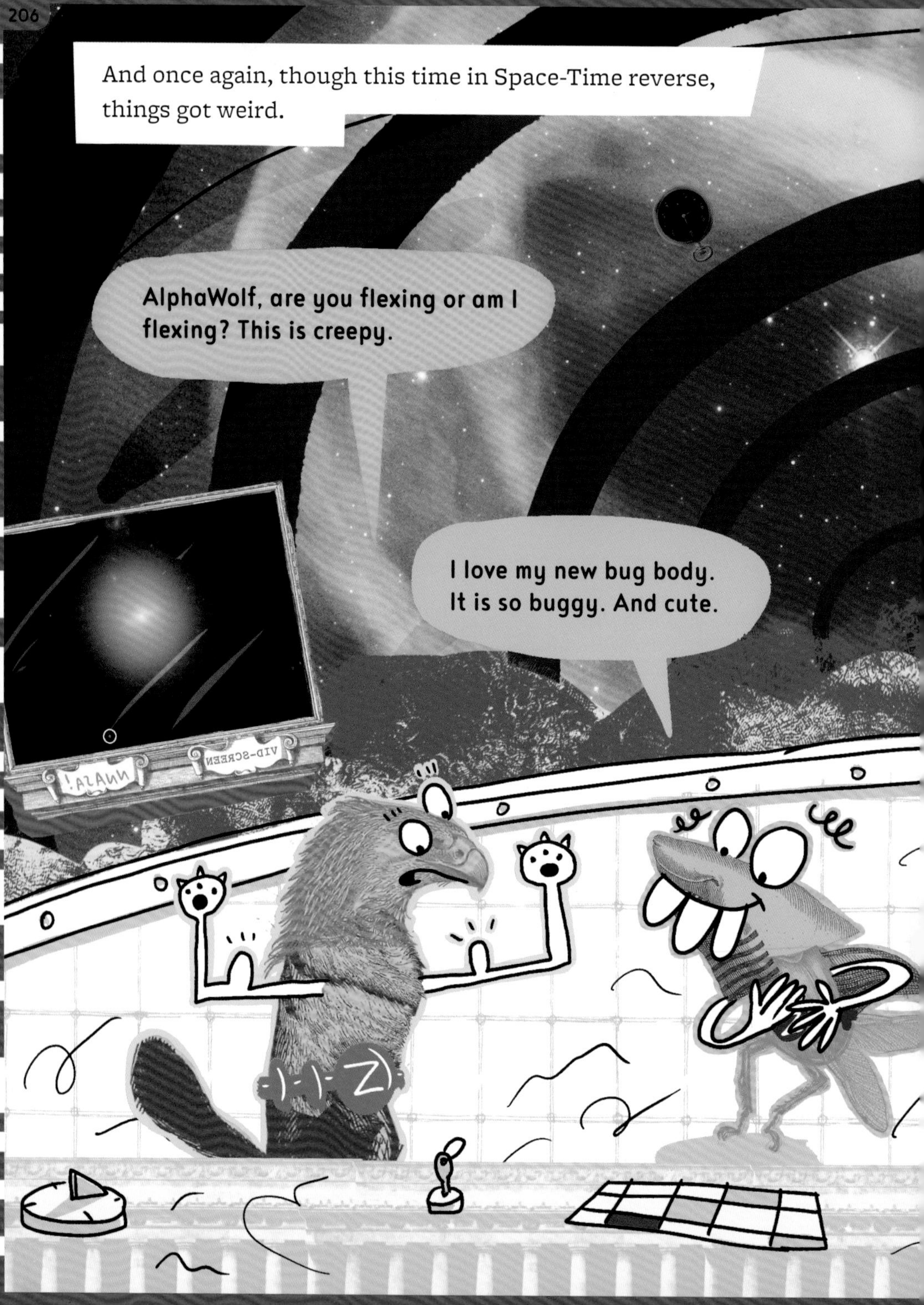
And once again, though this time in Space-Time reverse, things got weird.
AlphaWolf, are you flexing or am I flexing? This is creepy.
I love my new bug body. It is so buggy. And cute.

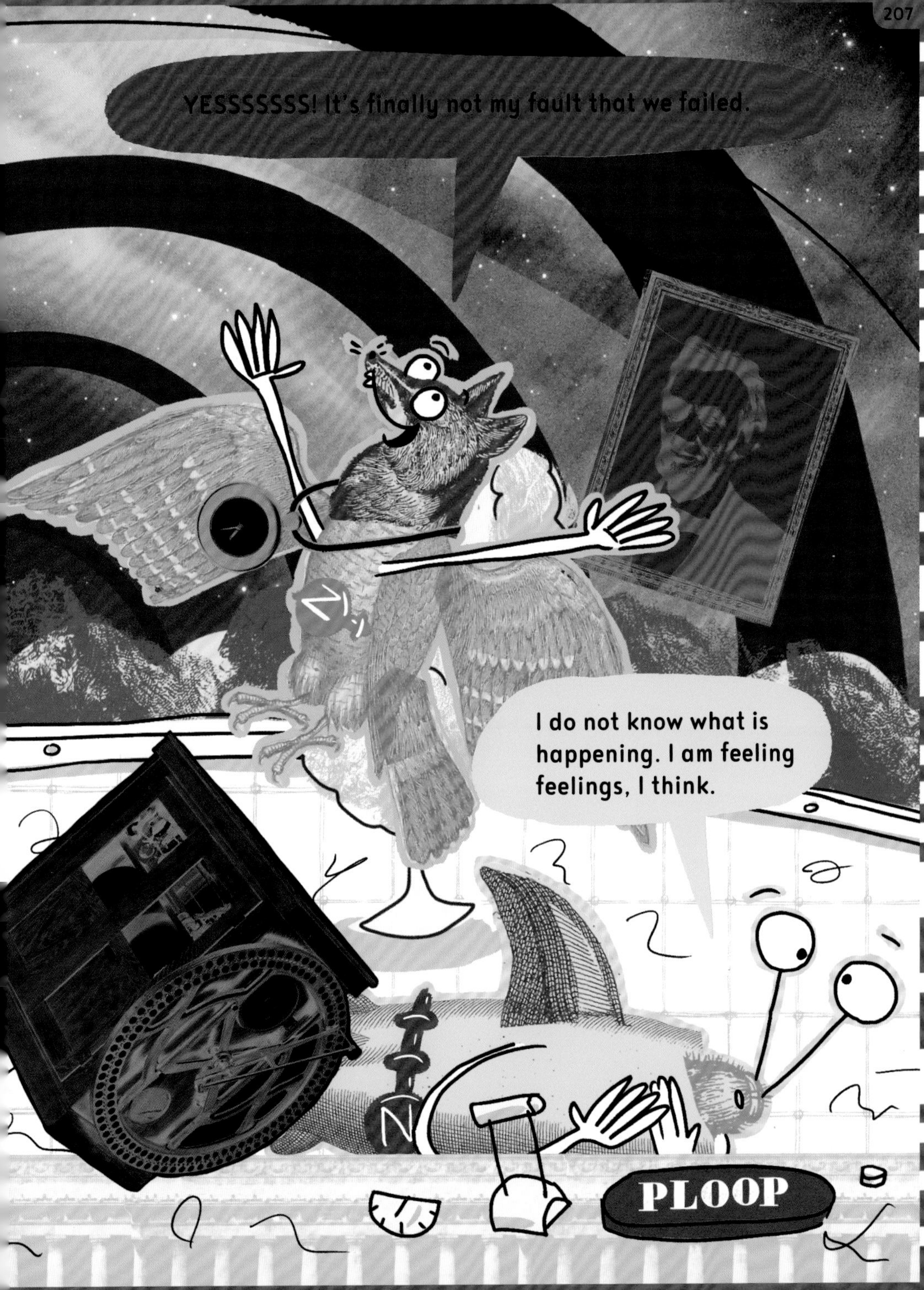

YESSSSSSS! It's finally not my fault that we failed.
I do not know what is happening. I am feeling feelings, I think.
PLOOP

Ohhhh AstroNuts, I love you all so much. LaserShark, you are always the most thoughtful. SmartHawk, you really get me. AlphaWolf . . . um . . . um . . . um . . . your tail fur is so soft and shiny. . . .

And guys, there is one thing I have always wanted to ask, but I have been afraid of what your answer might be. I know my PFFT smells. And I know it helps us get out of many dangerous situations. But I worry it might bother you. Does my PFFT bother you? Do I bother you? Am I a bad bug because I—

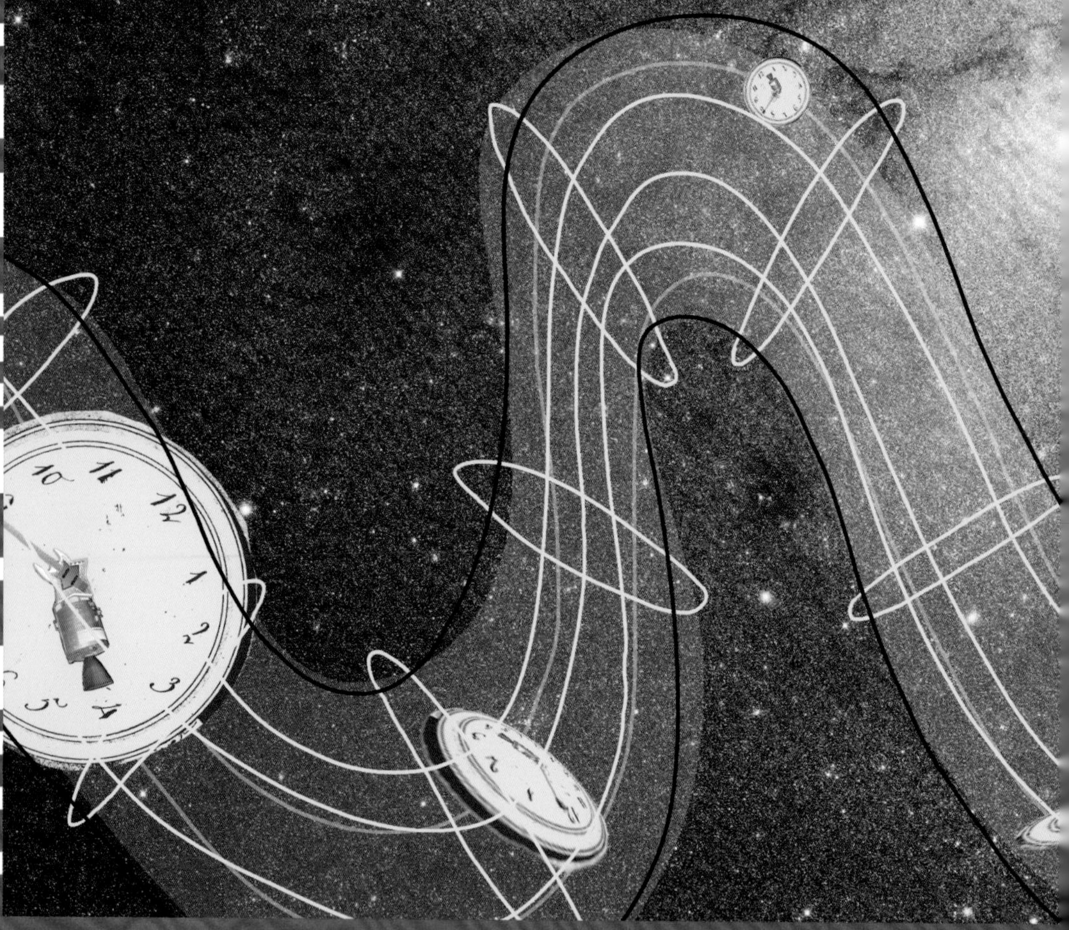

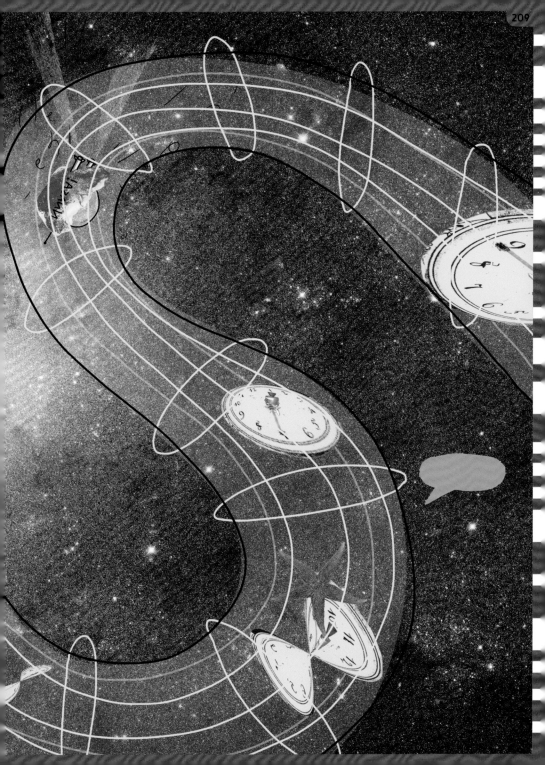

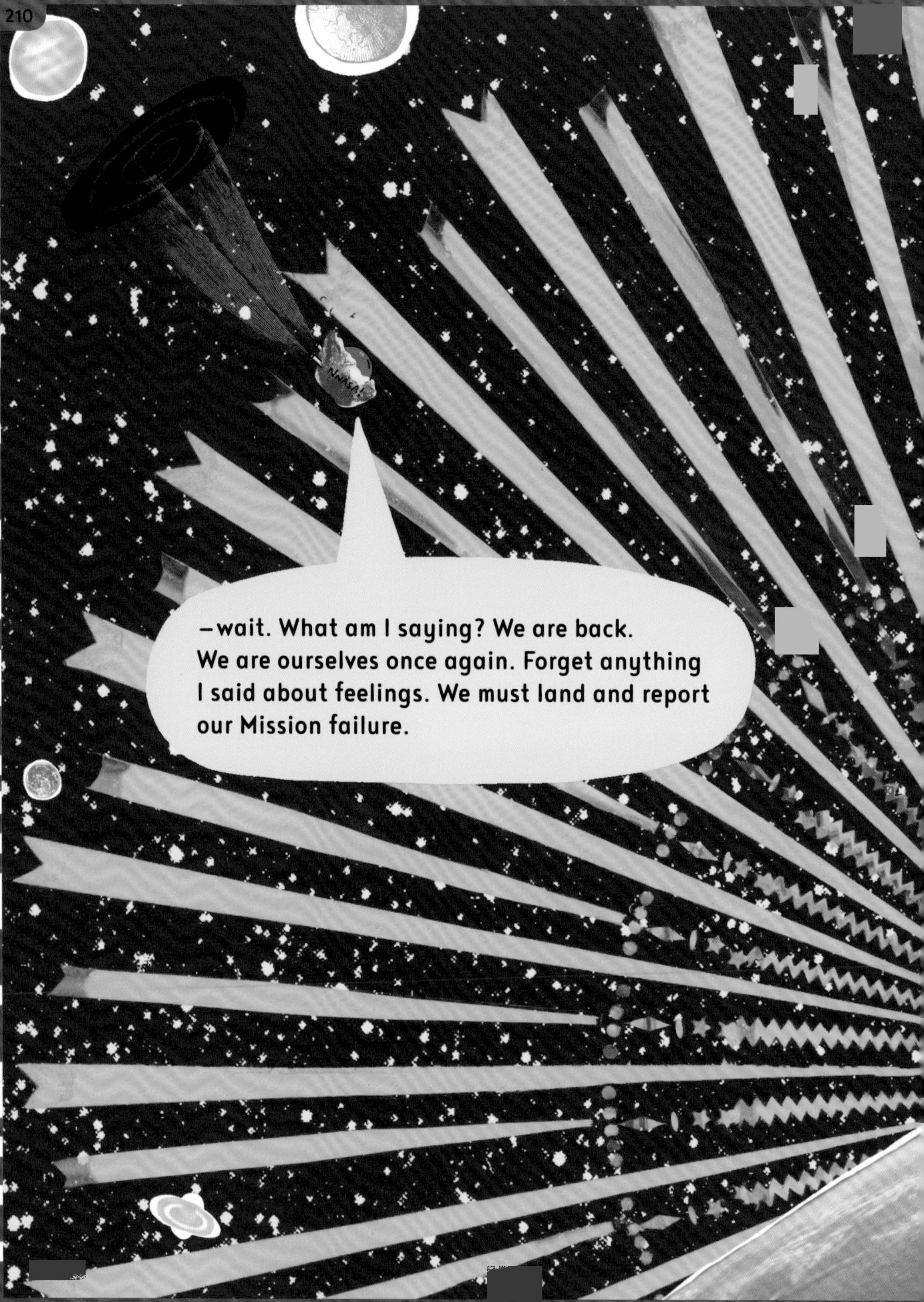
—wait. What am I saying? We are back. We are ourselves once again. Forget anything I said about feelings. We must land and report our Mission failure.

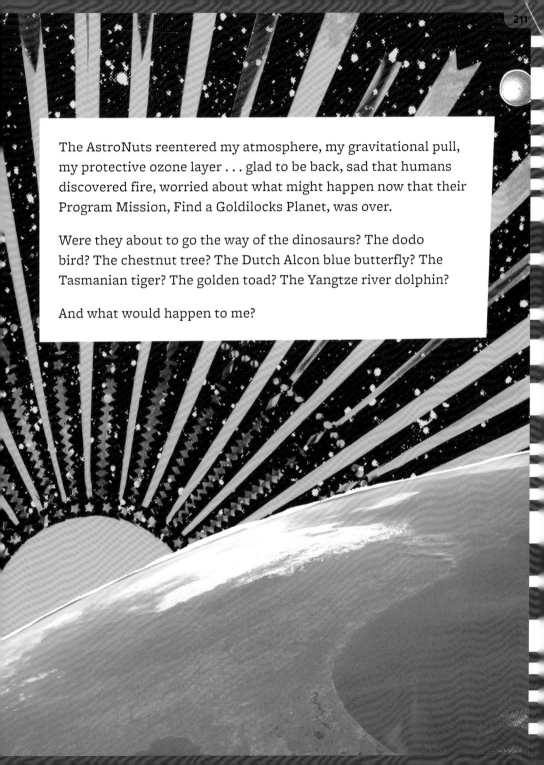

The AstroNuts reentered my atmosphere, my gravitational pull, my protective ozone layer . . . glad to be back, sad that humans discovered fire, worried about what might happen now that their Program Mission, Find a Goldilocks Planet, was over.

Were they about to go the way of the dinosaurs? The dodo bird? The chestnut tree? The Dutch Alcon blue butterfly? The Tasmanian tiger? The golden toad? The Yangtze river dolphin?

And what would happen to me?

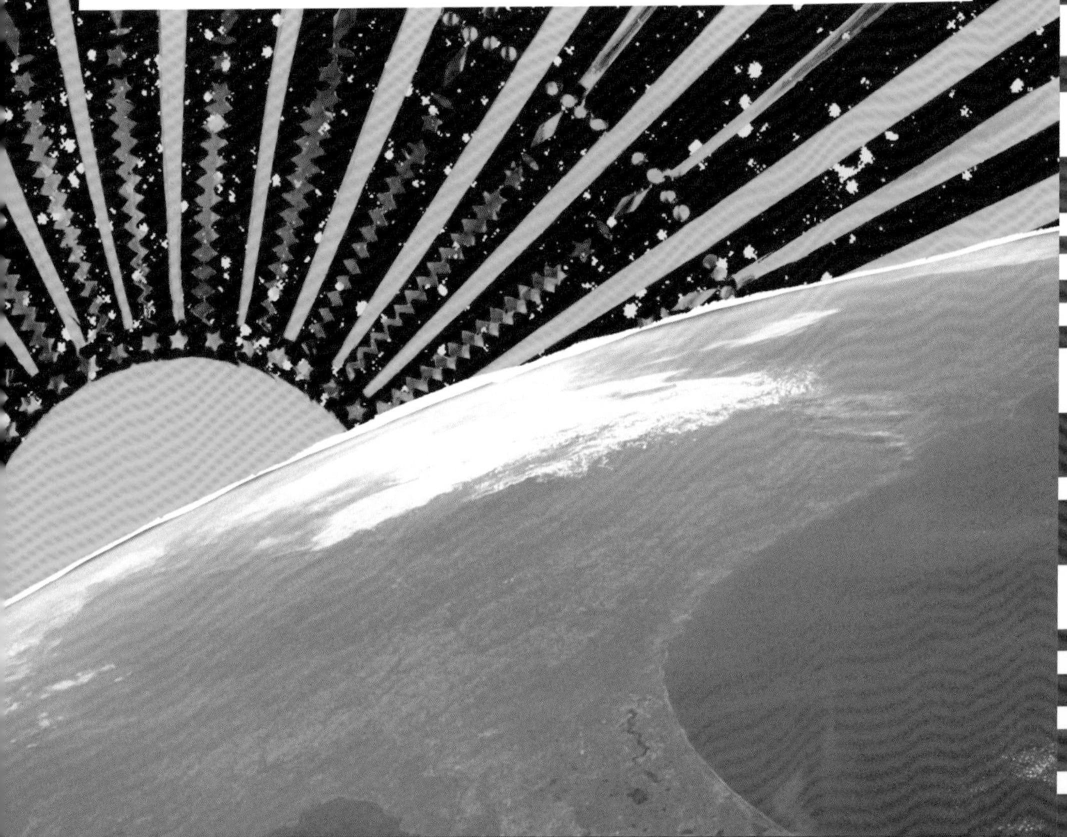

CHAPTER 35:

Back to the Future

AstroNuts, welcome back to now/now/now/now. Operation Goldilocks Planet is done/Operation Goldilocks Planet is done.

Please report to the George Washington Forehead Laboratory to turn in/turn in/turn in your AstroBelts.

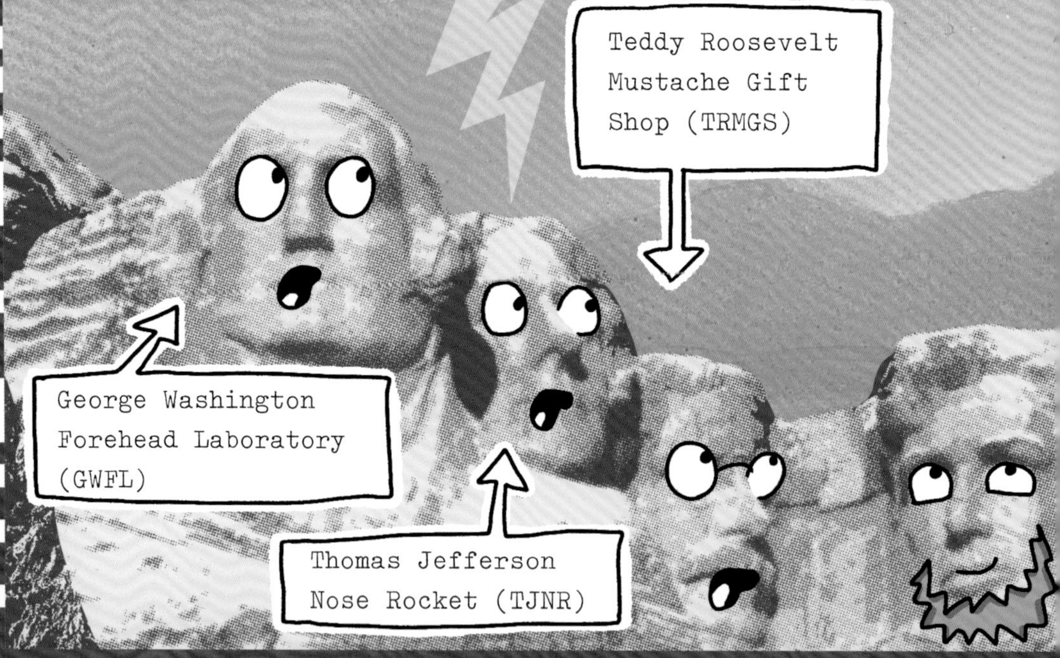

Teddy Roosevelt Mustache Gift Shop (TRMGS)
George Washington Forehead Laboratory (GWFL)
Thomas Jefferson Nose Rocket (TJNR)

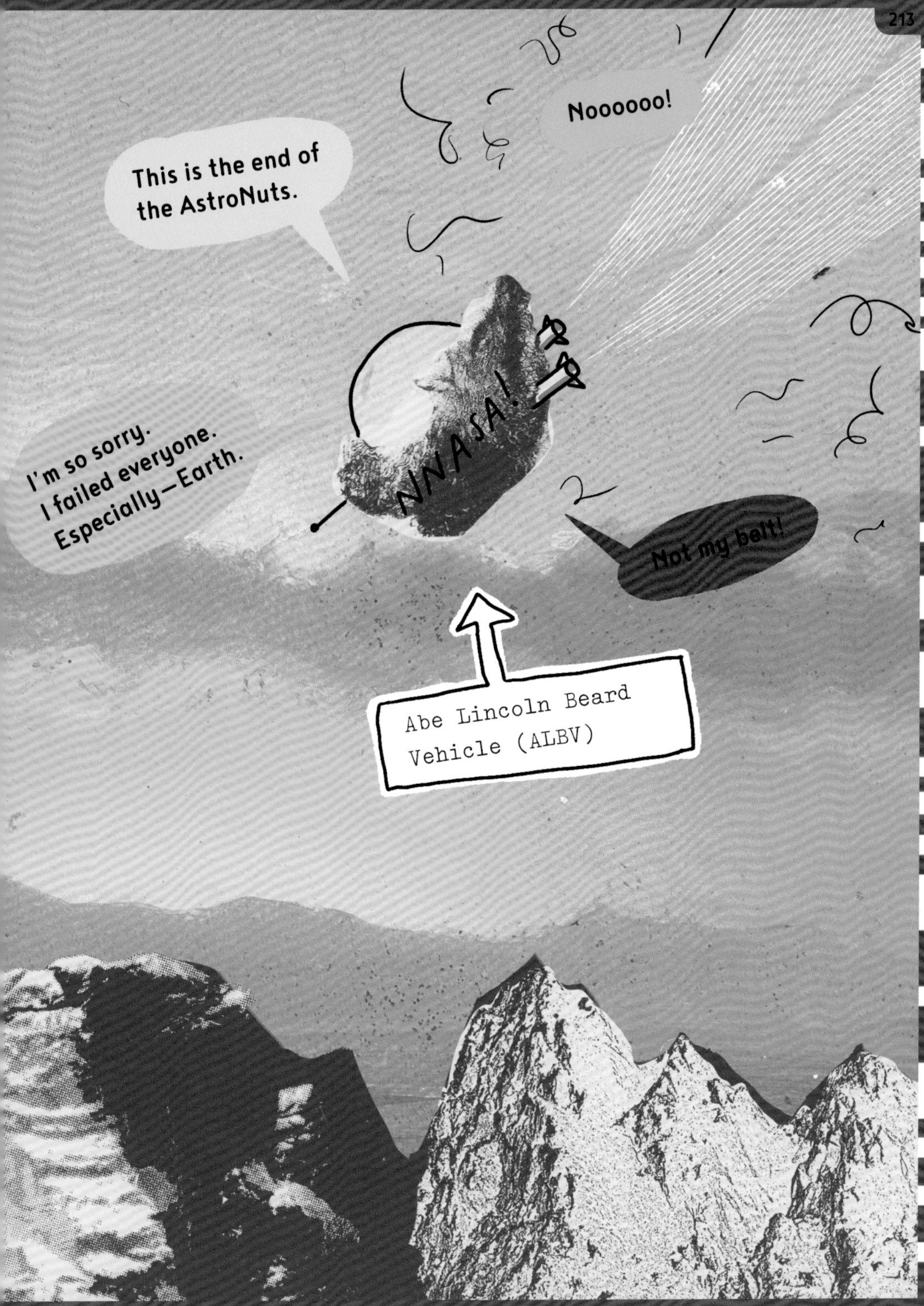
Noooooo!
This is the end of the AstroNuts.
NNASA!
I'm so sorry. I failed everyone. Especially—Earth.
Not my belt!
Abe Lincoln Beard Vehicle (ALBV)

The AstroNuts reported to the George Washington Forehead Laboratory.

They were sad to be handing in their AstroBelts. They were sadder because they had failed to stop the humans from discovering fire. They were saddest because they had failed to find a Goldilocks Planet.

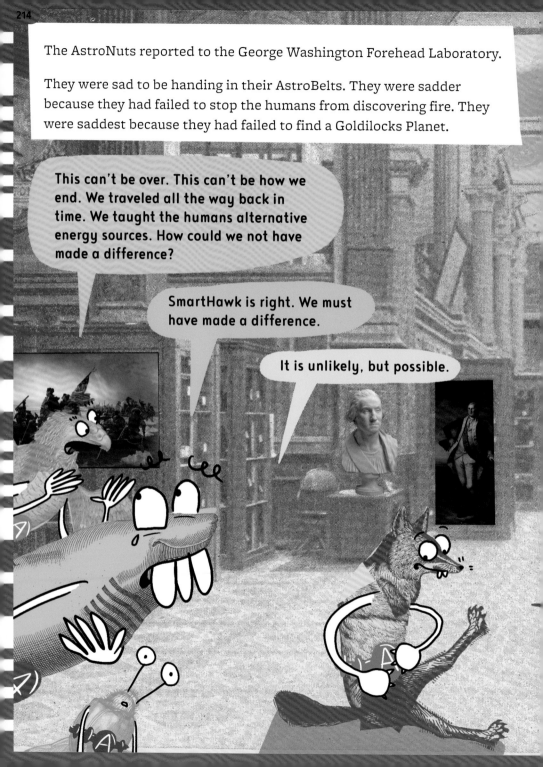

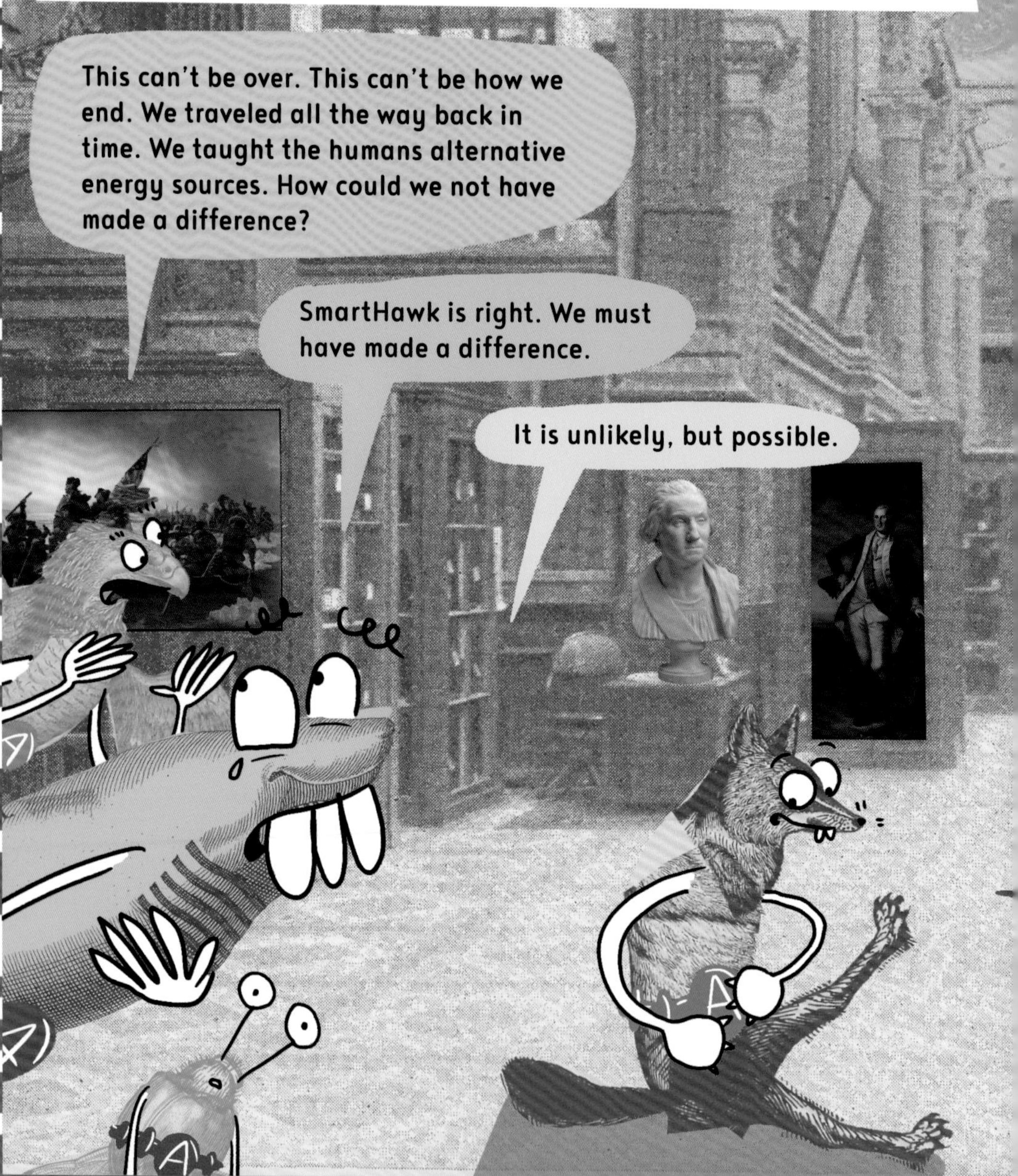
This can't be over. This can't be how we end. We traveled all the way back in time. We taught the humans alternative energy sources. How could we not have made a difference?
SmartHawk is right. We must have made a difference.
It is unlikely, but possible.

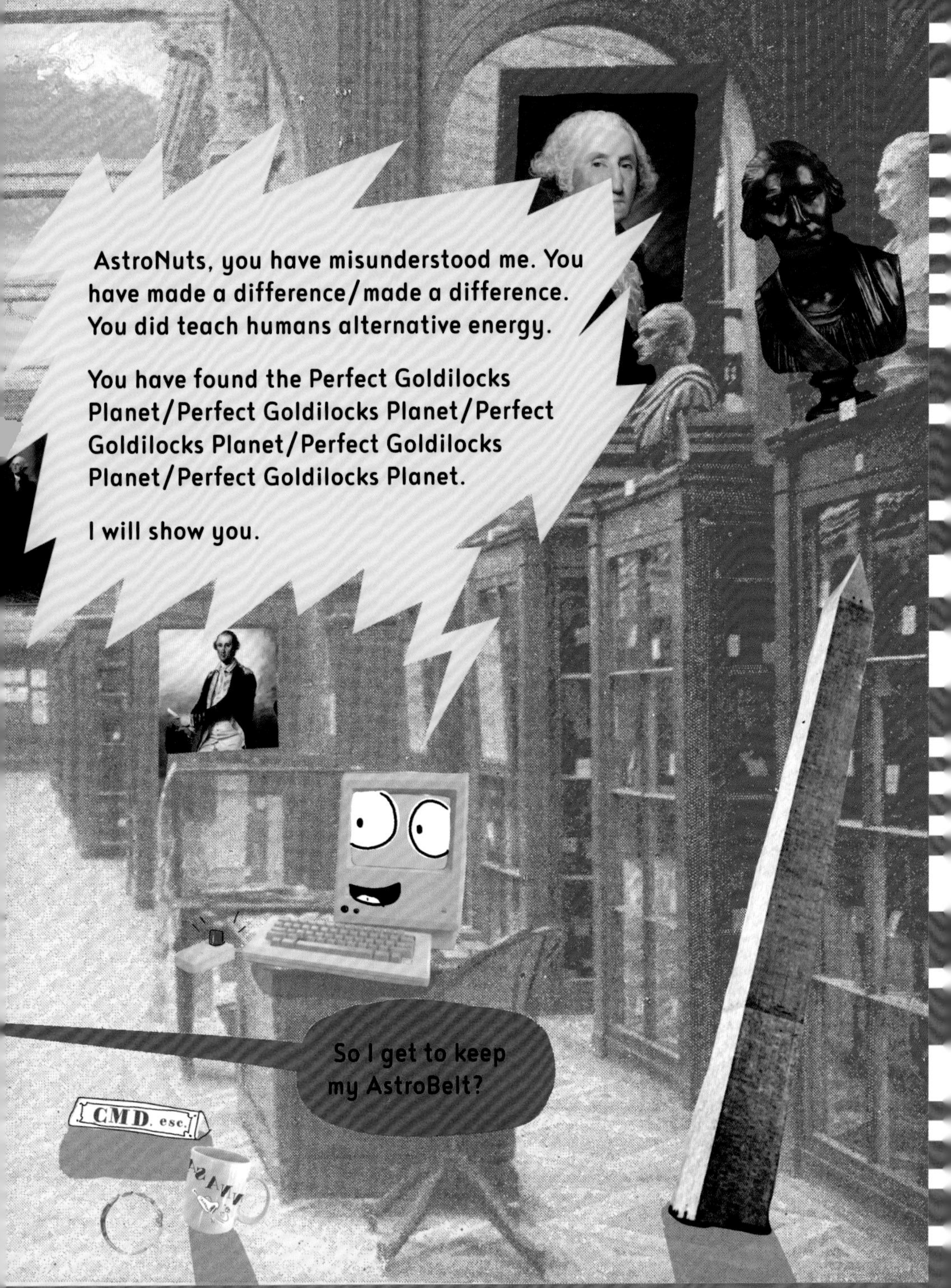
AstroNuts, you have misunderstood me. You have made a difference/made a difference. You did teach humans alternative energy.
You have found the Perfect Goldilocks Planet/Perfect Goldilocks Planet/Perfect Goldilocks Planet/Perfect Goldilocks Planet/Perfect Goldilocks Planet.
I will show you.
So I get to keep my AstroBelt?
CMD. esc.

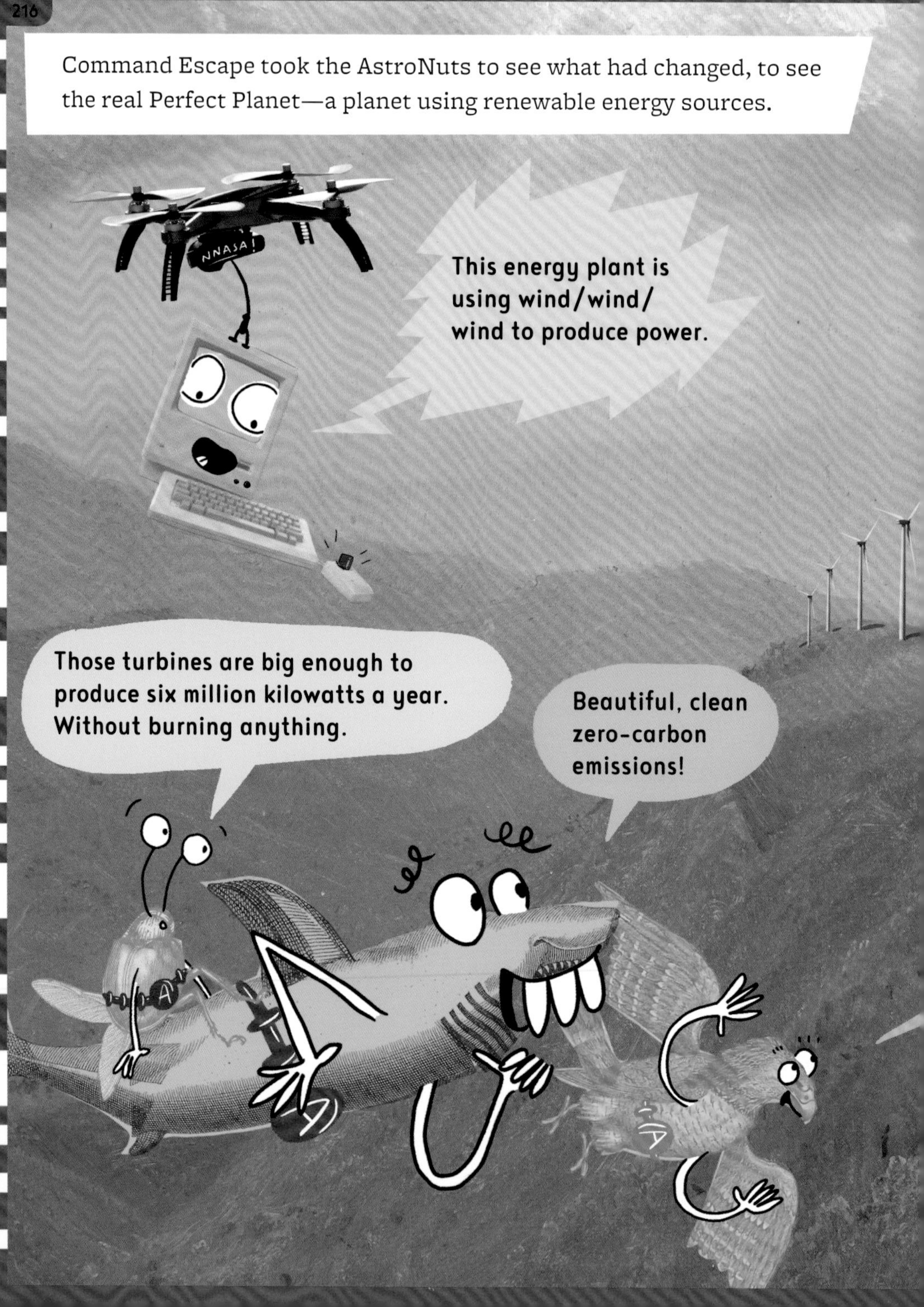
Command Escape took the AstroNuts to see what had changed, to see the real Perfect Planet—a planet using renewable energy sources.
NNASA!
This energy plant is using wind/wind/wind to produce power.
Those turbines are big enough to produce six million kilowatts a year. Without burning anything.
Beautiful, clean zero-carbon emissions!

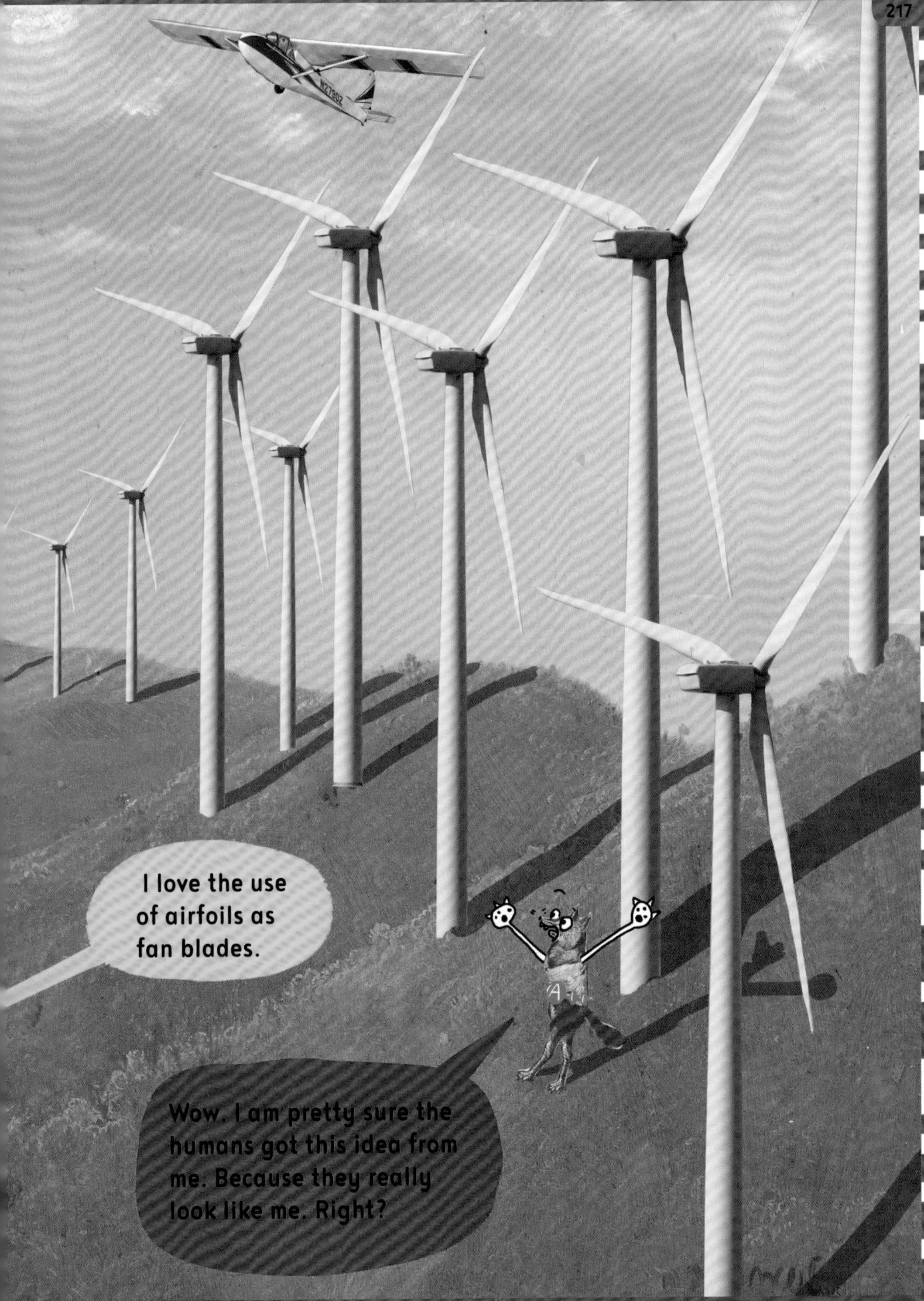
I love the use of airfoils as fan blades.
Wow. I am pretty sure the humans got this idea from me. Because they really look like me. Right?

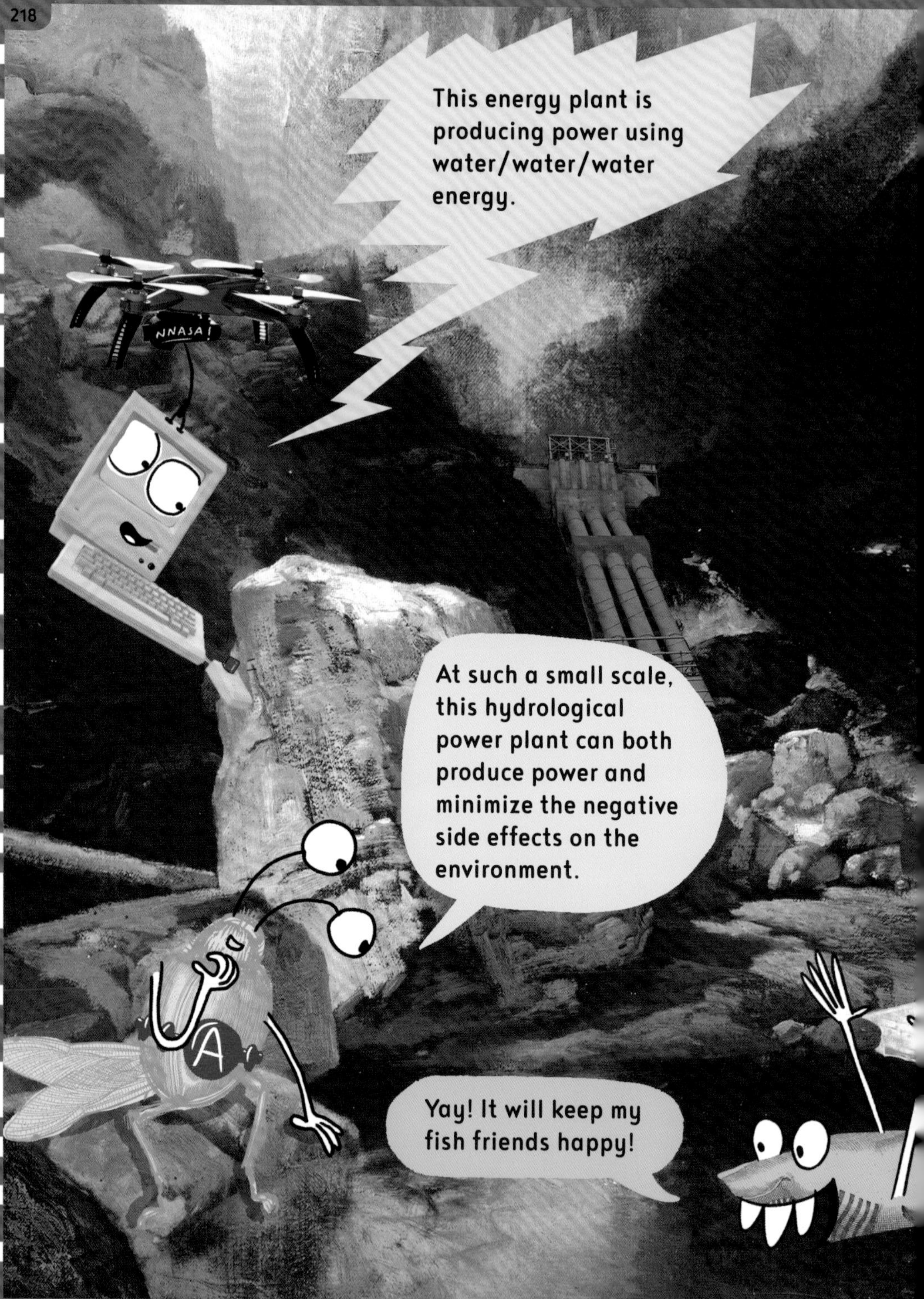

This energy plant is producing power using water/water/water energy.
NNASA!
At such a small scale, this hydrological power plant can both produce power and minimize the negative side effects on the environment.
Yay! It will keep my fish friends happy!

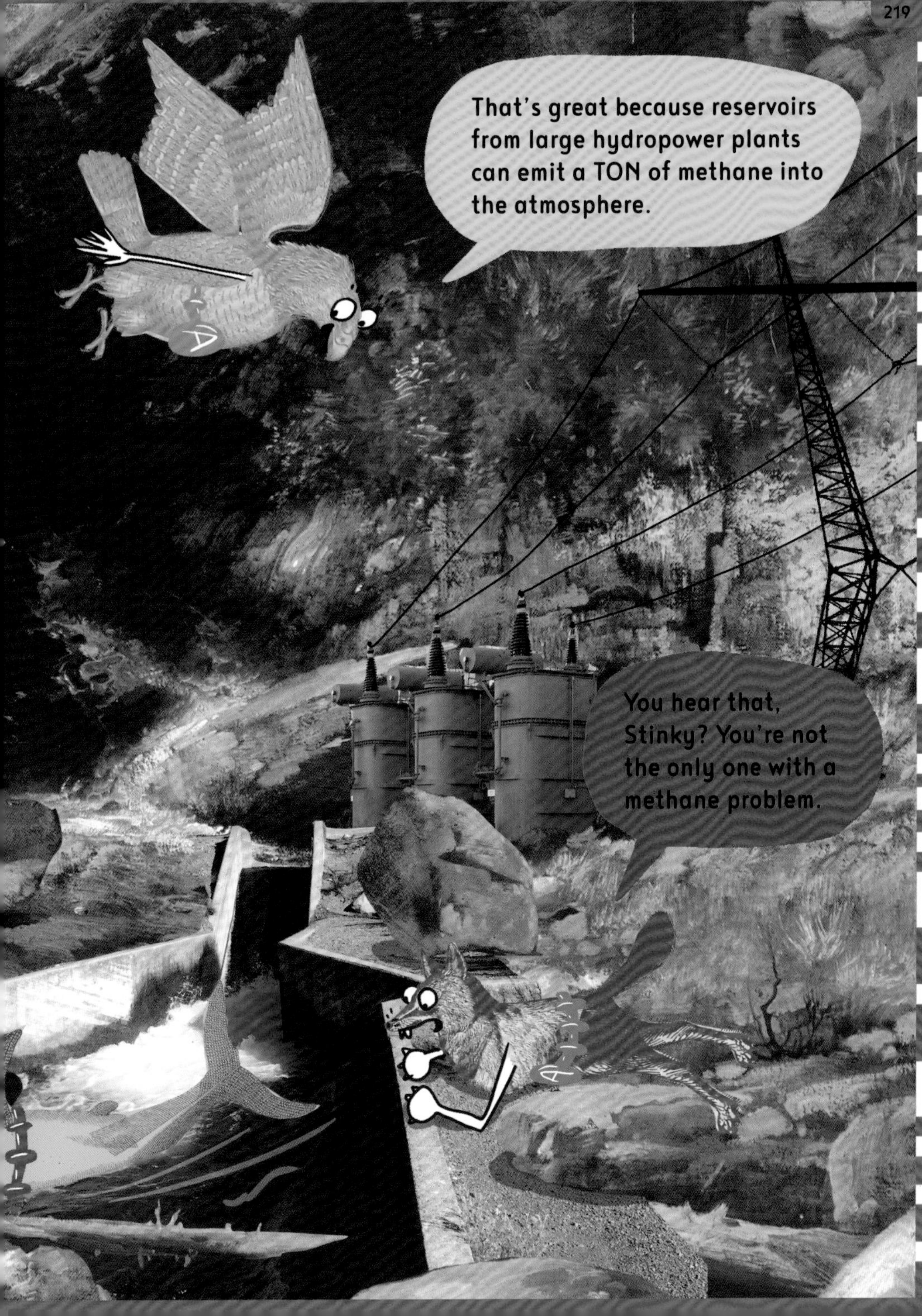
That's great because reservoirs from large hydropower plants can emit a TON of methane into the atmosphere.
You hear that, Stinky? You're not the only one with a methane problem.

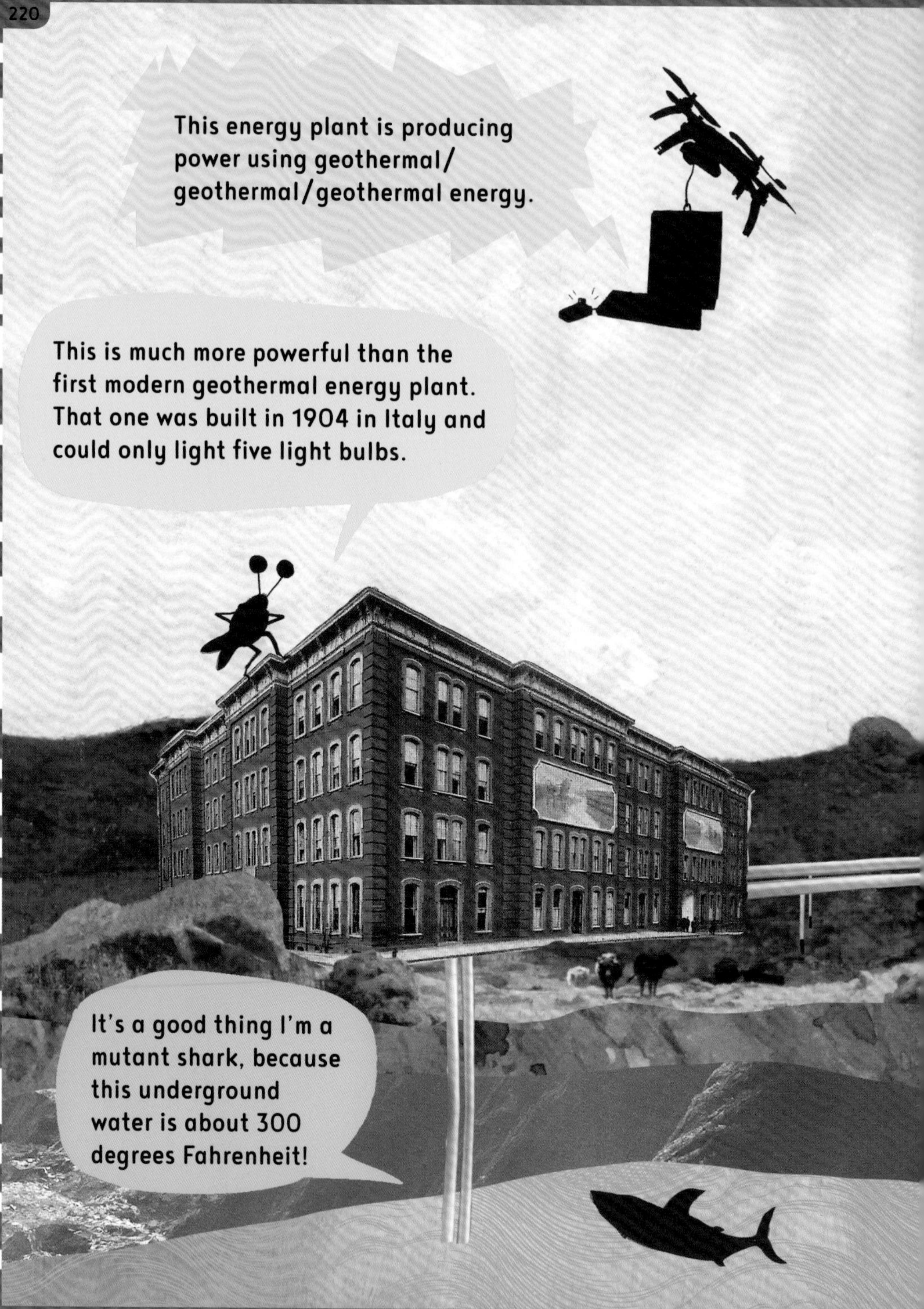
This energy plant is producing power using geothermal/ geothermal/geothermal energy.
This is much more powerful than the first modern geothermal energy plant. That one was built in 1904 in Italy and could only light five light bulbs.
It's a good thing I'm a mutant shark, because this underground water is about 300 degrees Fahrenheit!

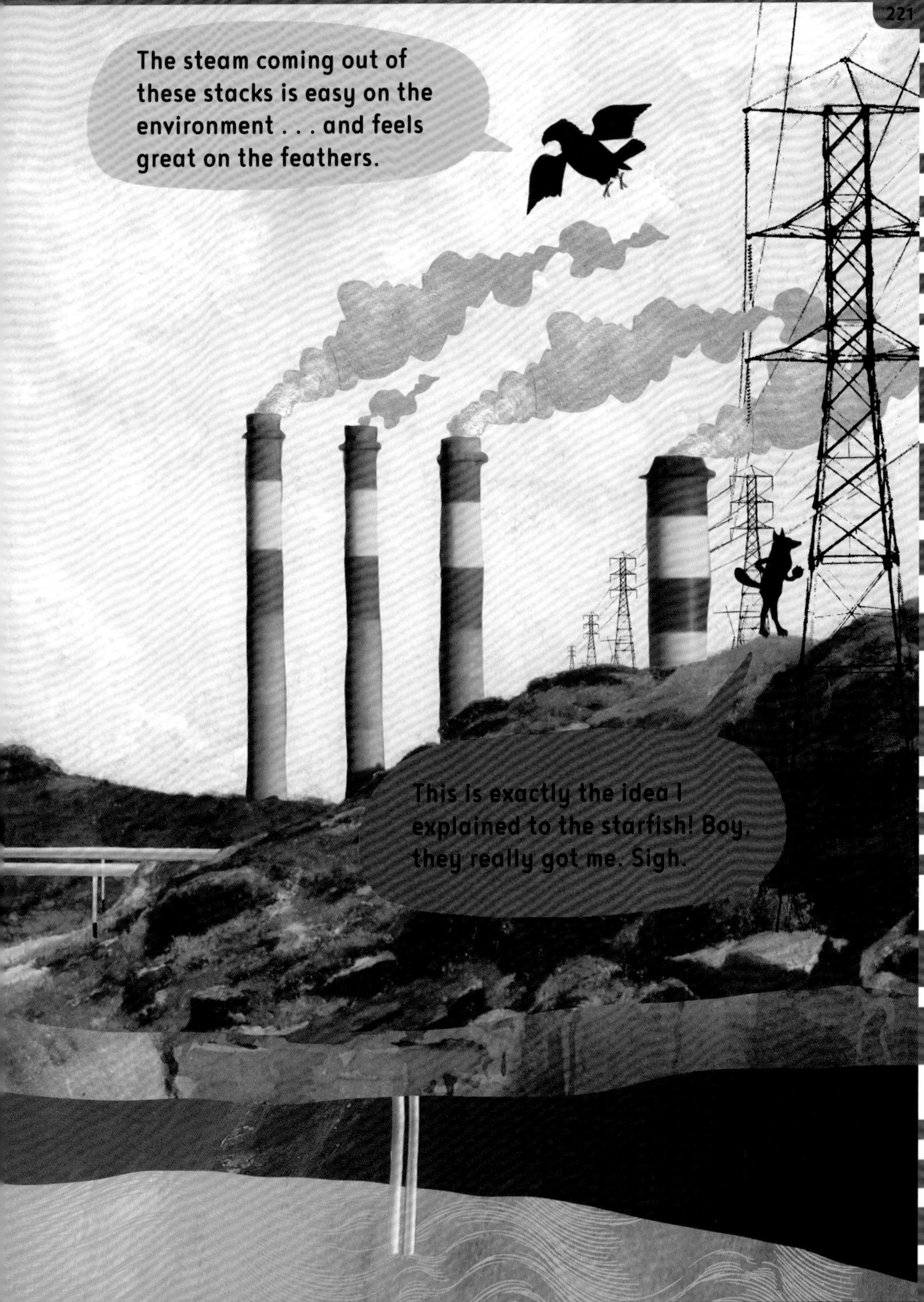
The steam coming out of these stacks is easy on the environment . . . and feels great on the feathers.
This is exactly the idea I explained to the starfish! Boy, they really got me. Sigh.

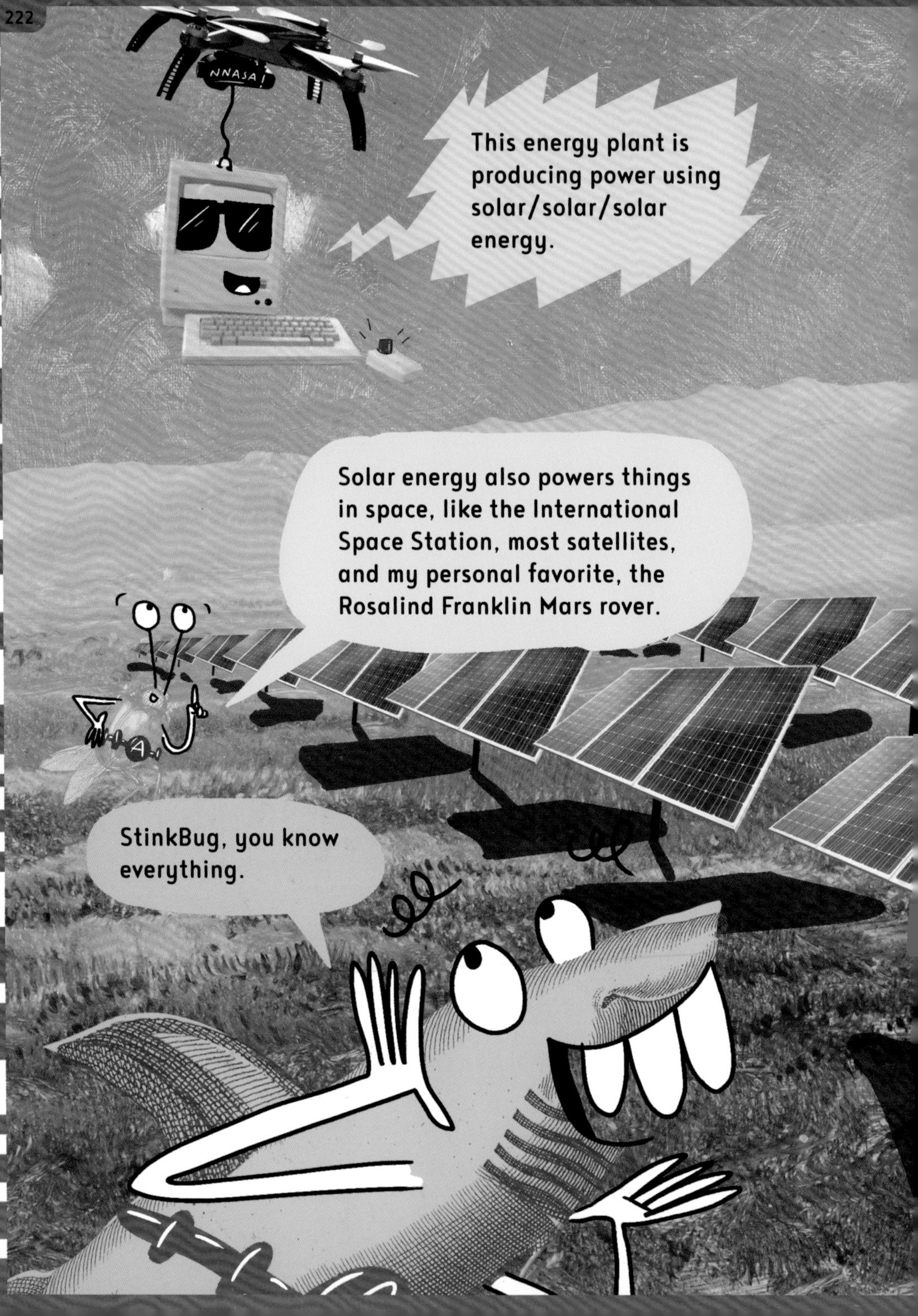
NNASA
This energy plant is producing power using solar/solar/solar energy.
Solar energy also powers things in space, like the International Space Station, most satellites, and my personal favorite, the Rosalind Franklin Mars rover.
StinkBug, you know everything.

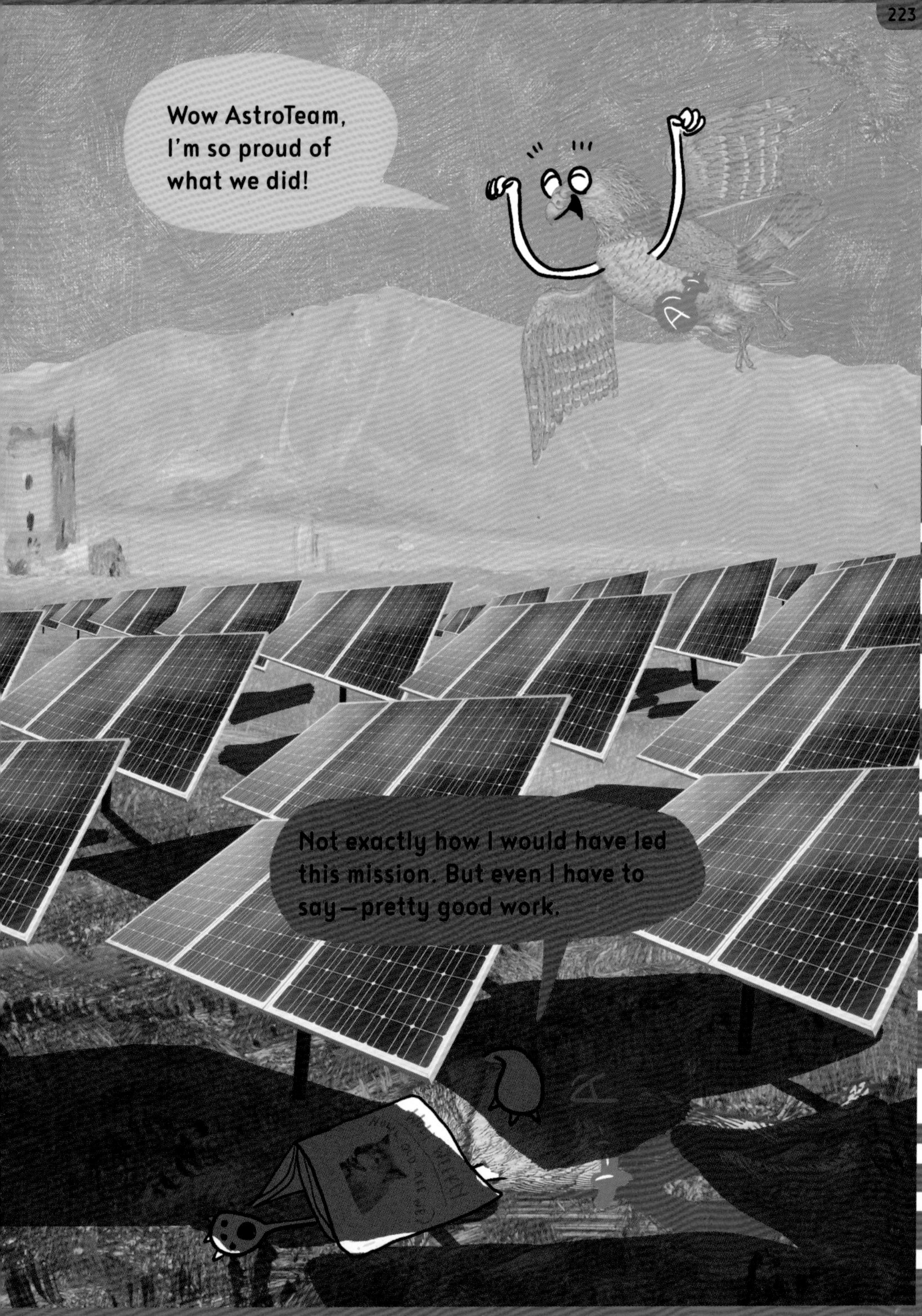
Wow AstroTeam, I'm so proud of what we did!
Not exactly how I would have led this mission. But even I have to say—pretty good work.

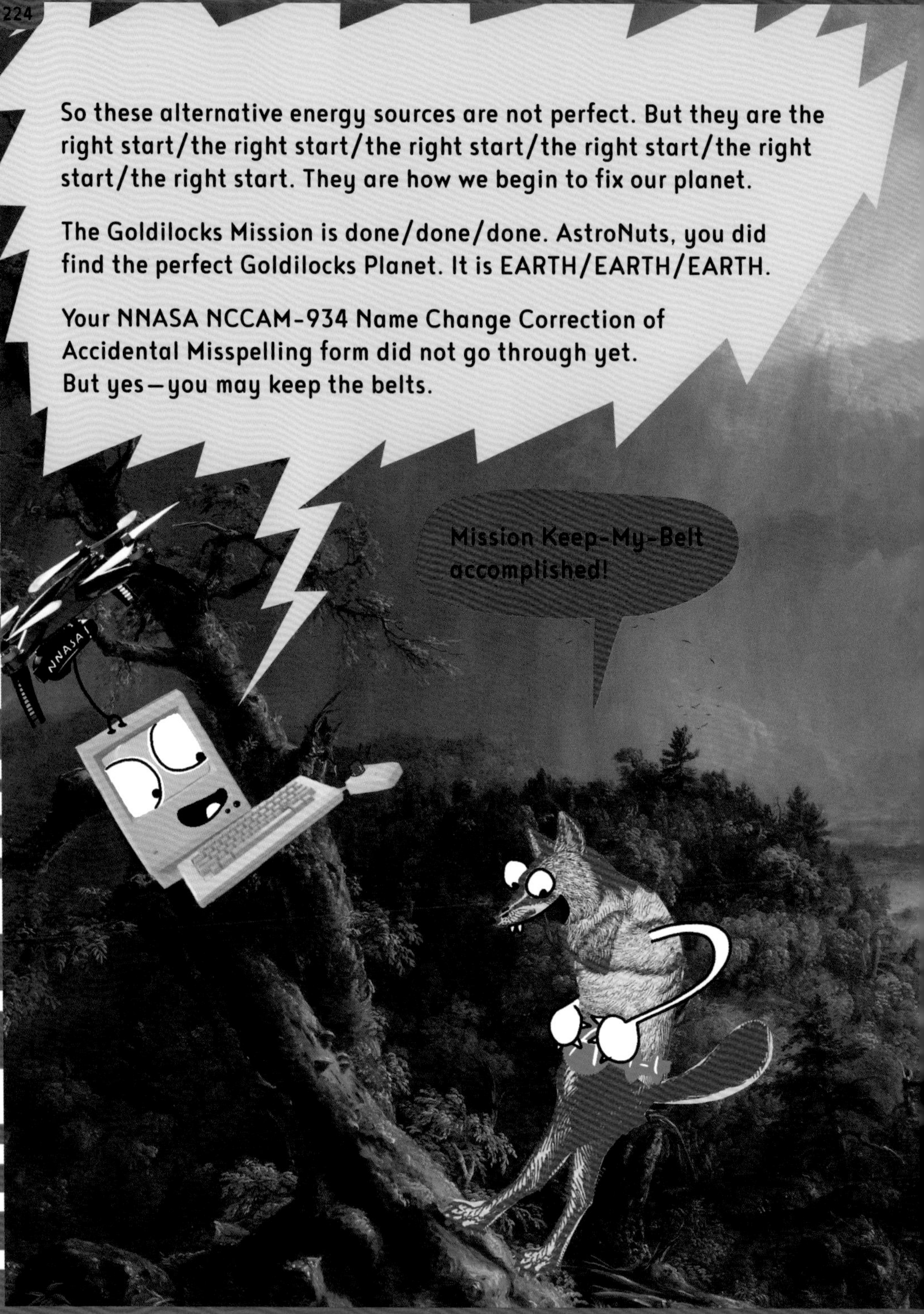
So these alternative energy sources are not perfect. But they are the right start/the right start/the right start/the right start/the right start/the right start. They are how we begin to fix our planet.
The Goldilocks Mission is done/done/done. AstroNuts, you did find the perfect Goldilocks Planet. It is EARTH/EARTH/EARTH.
Your NNASA NCCAM-934 Name Change Correction of Accidental Misspelling form did not go through yet. But yes—you may keep the belts.
NNASA
Mission Keep-My-Belt accomplished!

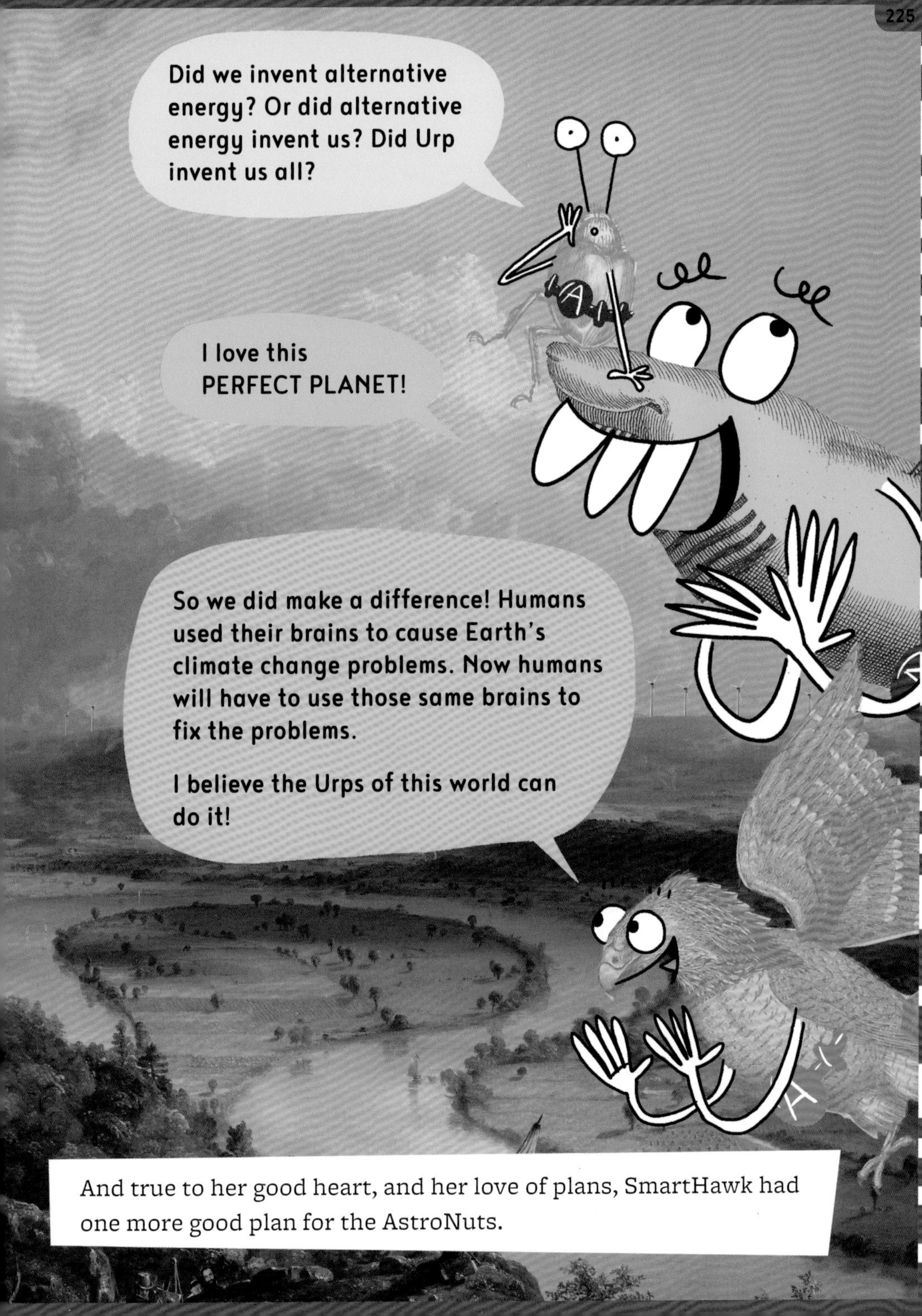
Did we invent alternative energy? Or did alternative energy invent us? Did Urp invent us all?
I love this PERFECT PLANET!
So we did make a difference! Humans used their brains to cause Earth's climate change problems. Now humans will have to use those same brains to fix the problems.
I believe the Urps of this world can do it!
And true to her good heart, and her love of plans, SmartHawk had one more good plan for the AstroNuts.

CHAPTER 36:
Pizza Party Plan

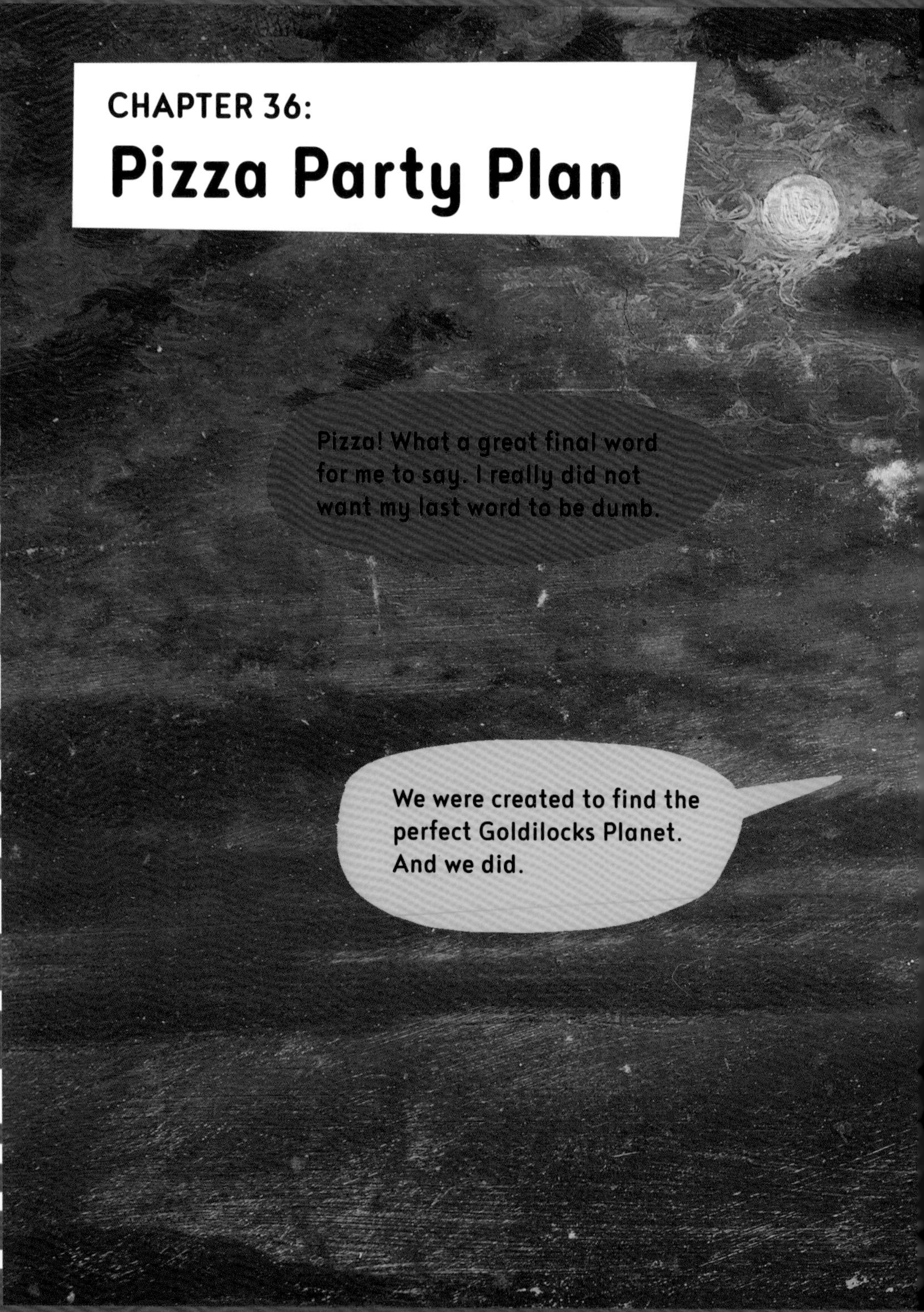
Pizza! What a great final word for me to say. I really did not want my last word to be dumb.
We were created to find the perfect Goldilocks Planet. And we did.

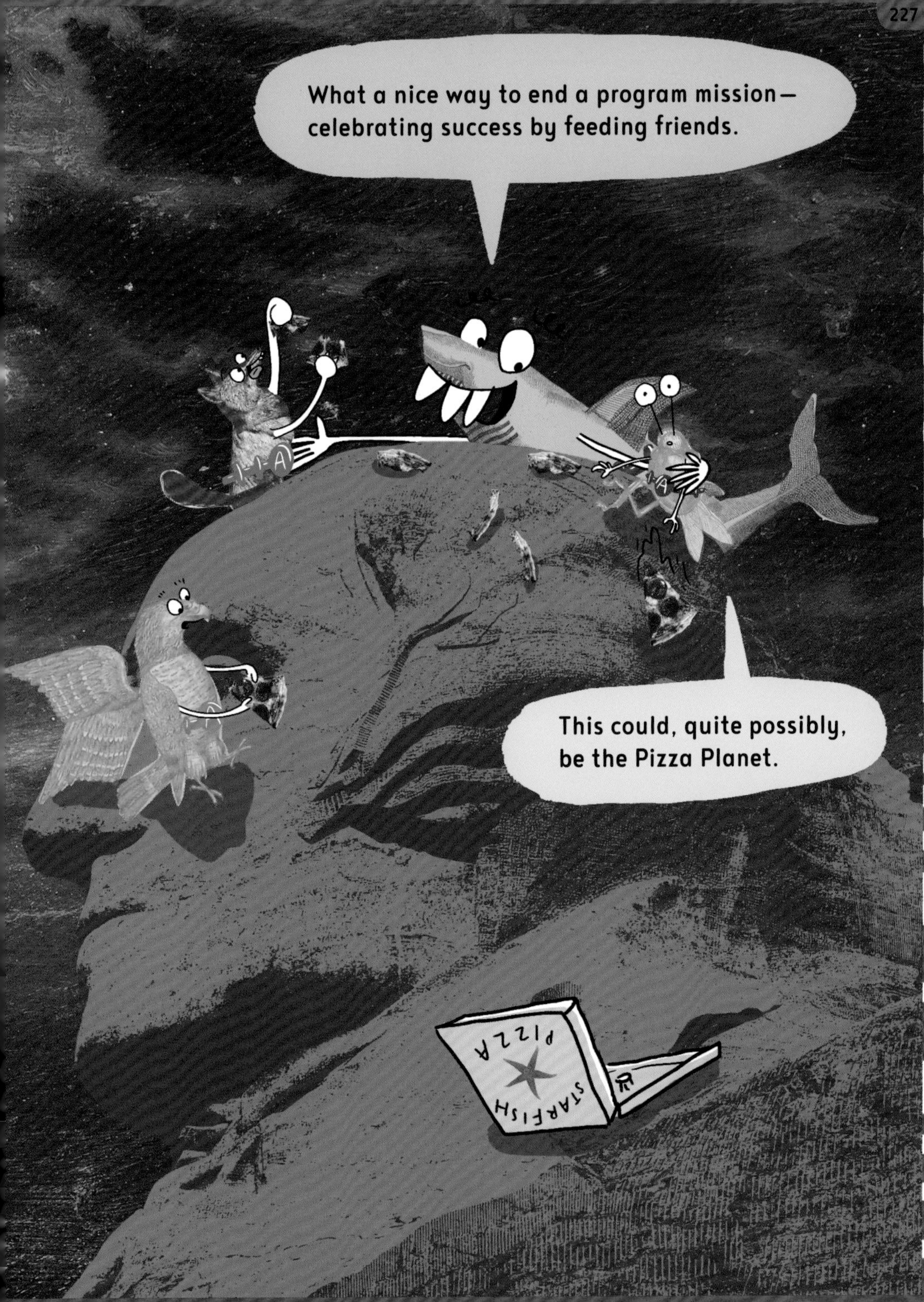
What a nice way to end a program mission—celebrating success by feeding friends.
This could, quite possibly, be the Pizza Planet.
STARFISH PIZZA

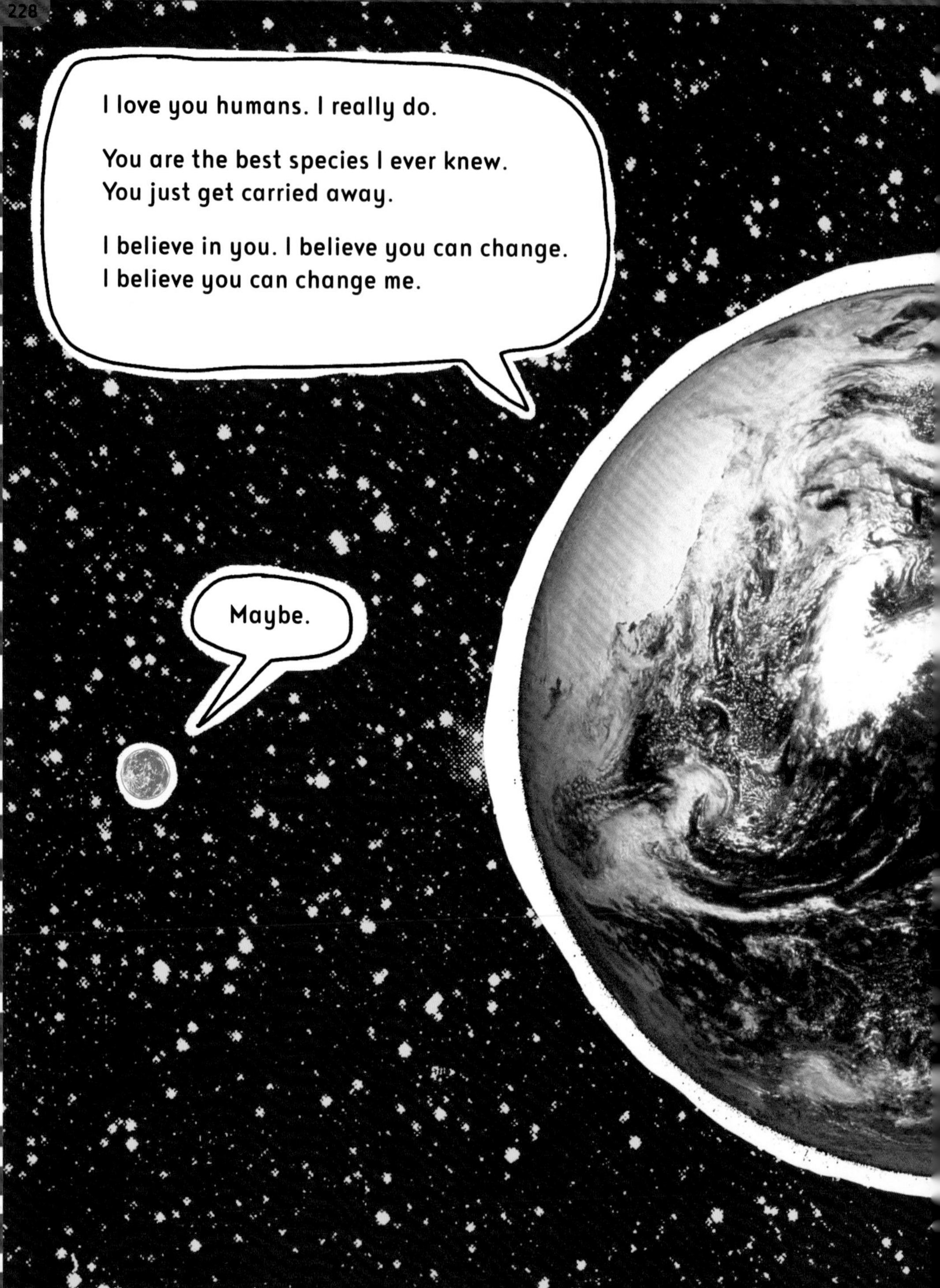
I love you humans. I really do.
You are the best species I ever knew. You just get carried away.
I believe in you. I believe you can change. I believe you can change me.
Maybe.

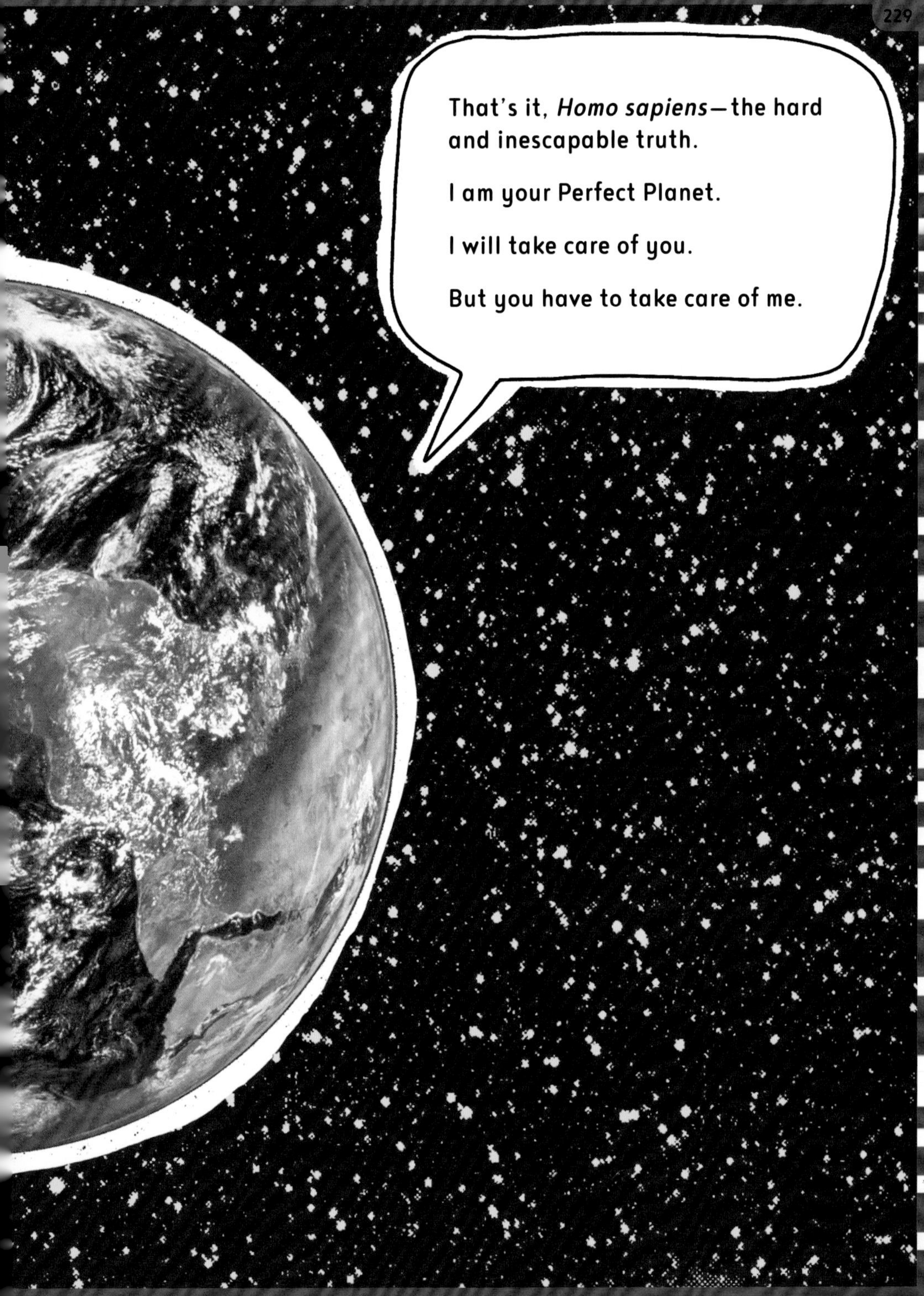
That's it, *Homo sapiens*—the hard and inescapable truth.
I am your Perfect Planet.
I will take care of you.
But you have to take care of me.

EPILOGUE:

Oh Baby!

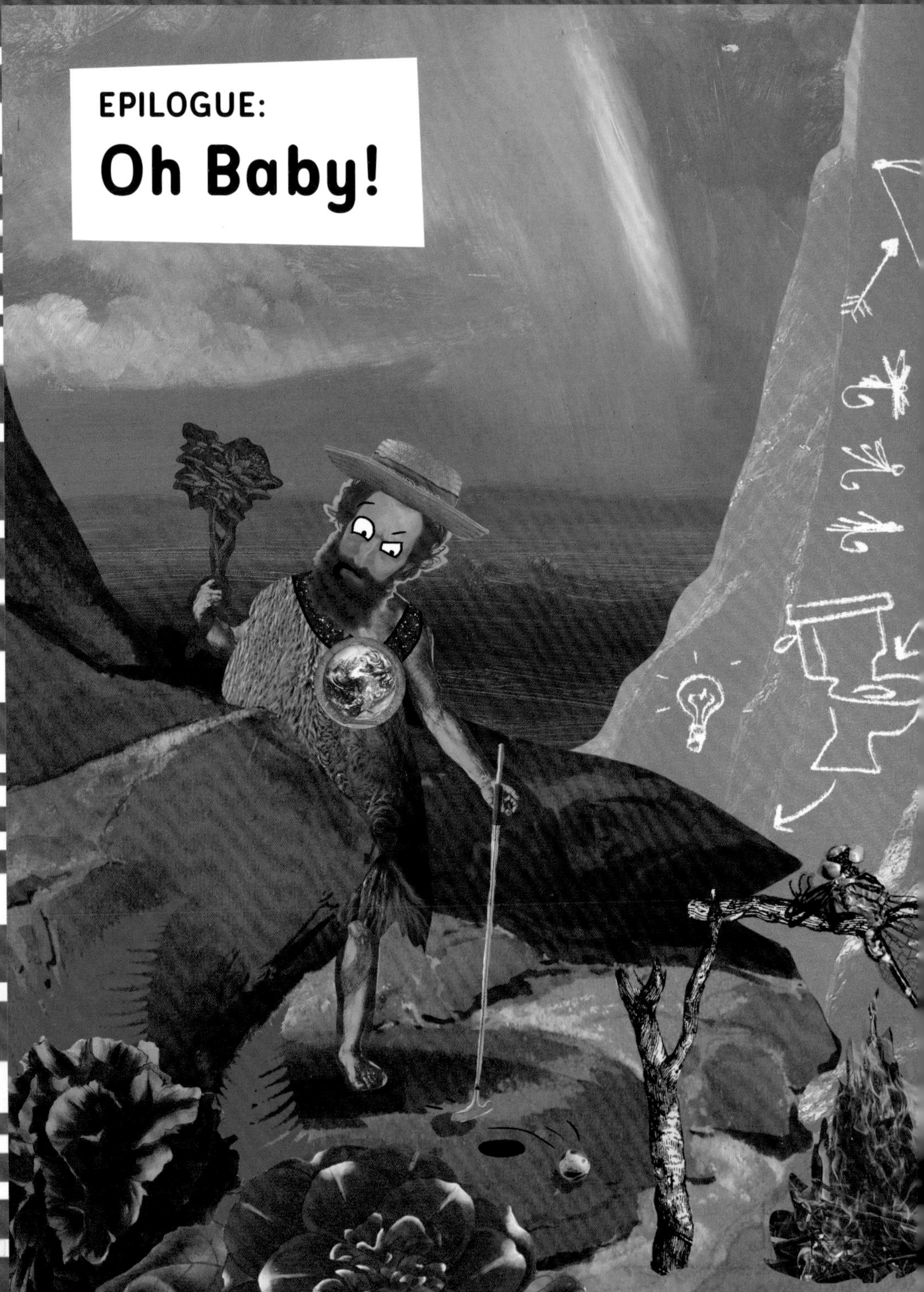

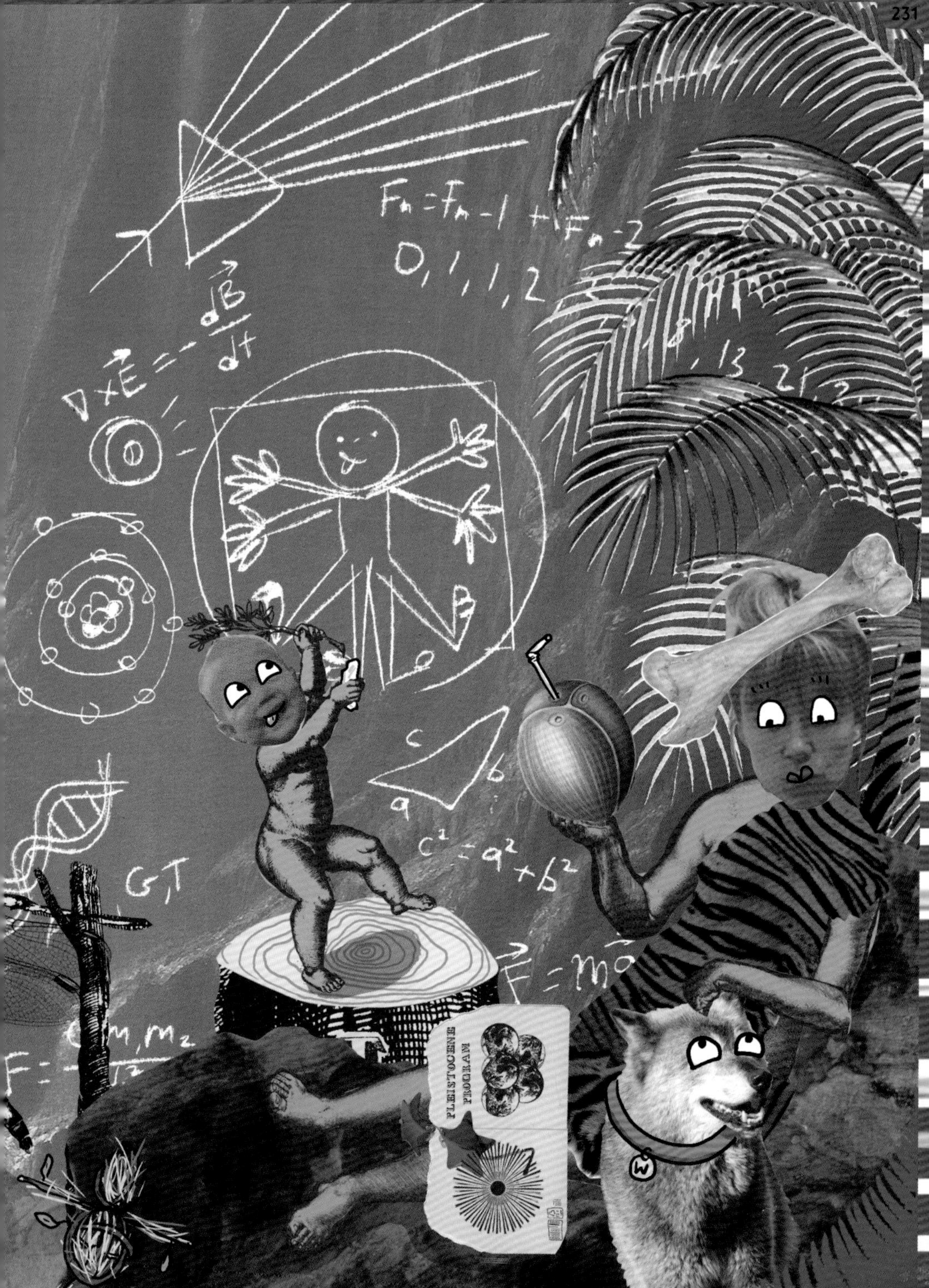
Fn = Fn-1 + Fn-2
0, 1, 1, 2
c
b
a
c² = a² + b²
G, T
PLEISTOCENE PROGRAM

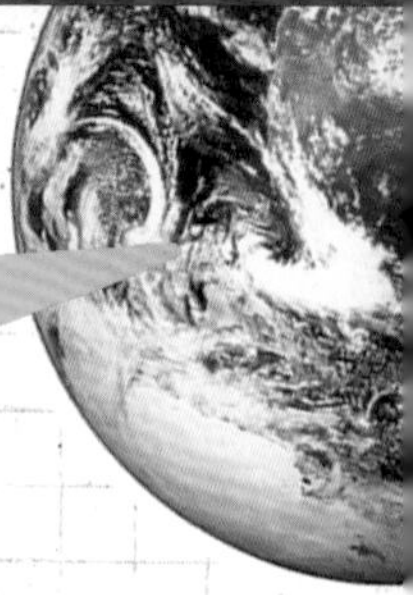

Just like in Missions One and Two, many illustrations in this book were made with other pieces of art. Illustrator Steven W. collaged dragonflies, rainbows, and volcanos from places like the Smithsonian Institution in Washington, DC. He then collaged it into what you just read!

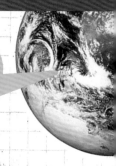

StinkBug is collaged from an engraving by Joris Hoefnagel from around 1630.

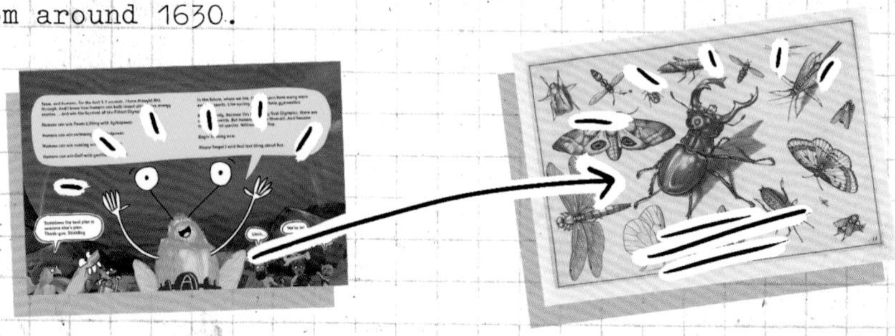

These amazing images of space come from the Hubble Space Telescope. When the AstroNuts enter their wormhole, the space behind them is collaged from Hubble's *Cosmic Reef*.

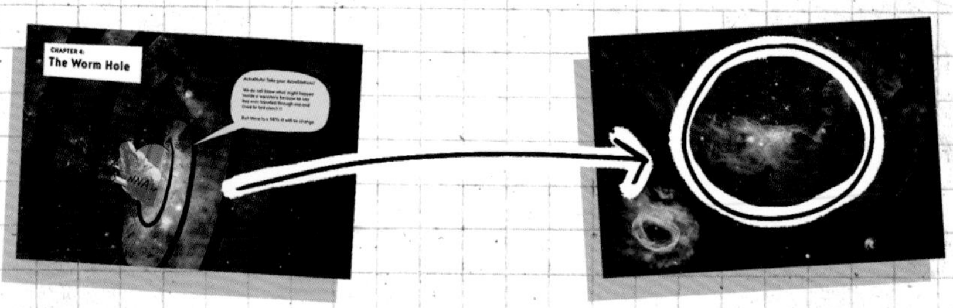
CHAPTER 4:
The Worm Hole

You also might notice there are a lot of painted backgrounds in Mission Three. A lot of those are collaged from paintings by Frederic Edwin Church. This one is called *Cotopaxi* from 1855.

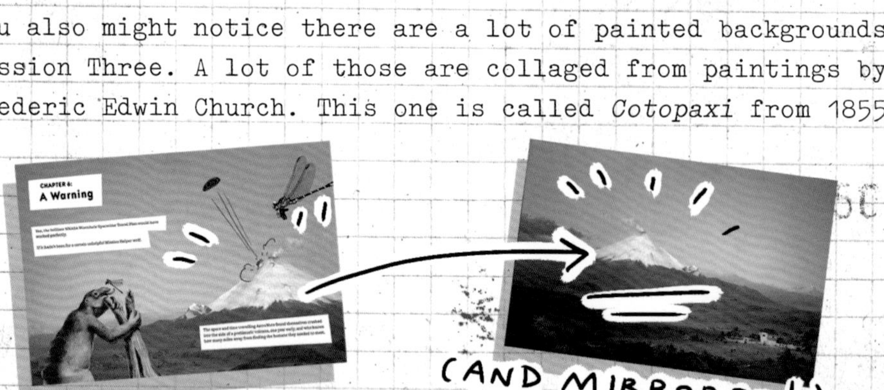
CHAPTER 6:
A Warning
(AND MIRRORED!)

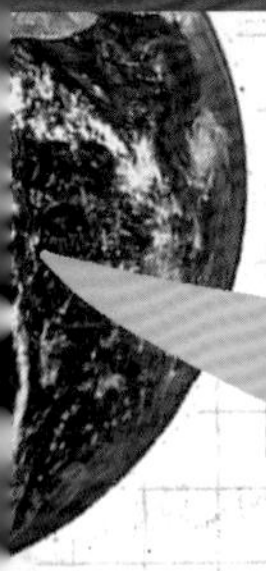

Mr. Church was part of a group of American painters called the Hudson River School. (As Earth, I'm a fan of any school named after one of my rivers.) I also love these artists because they loved me! They considered the light and drama of my landscapes to be, well, PERFECT. The art they created not only made me look good, it also helped inspire the modern environmentalism movement. Here are some of my favorites. Can you find them in this book?

View from Mount Holyoke, Northampton, Massachusetts, after a Thunderstorm—The Oxbow, Thomas Cole, 1836

Among the Sierra Nevada, California, Albert Bierstadt, 1868

Rainbow over the Grand Canyon of the Yellowstone, Thomas Moran, 1900

Clearing after September Gale—Maine Coast, Howard Russell Butler, c. 1924

And don't forget! Make your own AstroNuts on the book series website: AstroNuts.Space. Download printouts and MORE!

Don't worry. Steven is not breaking any laws. Places like the Smithsonian want people to use their collection of over three million images. To see these works online and collage your own creations go to: WWW.SI.EDU/OPENACCESS

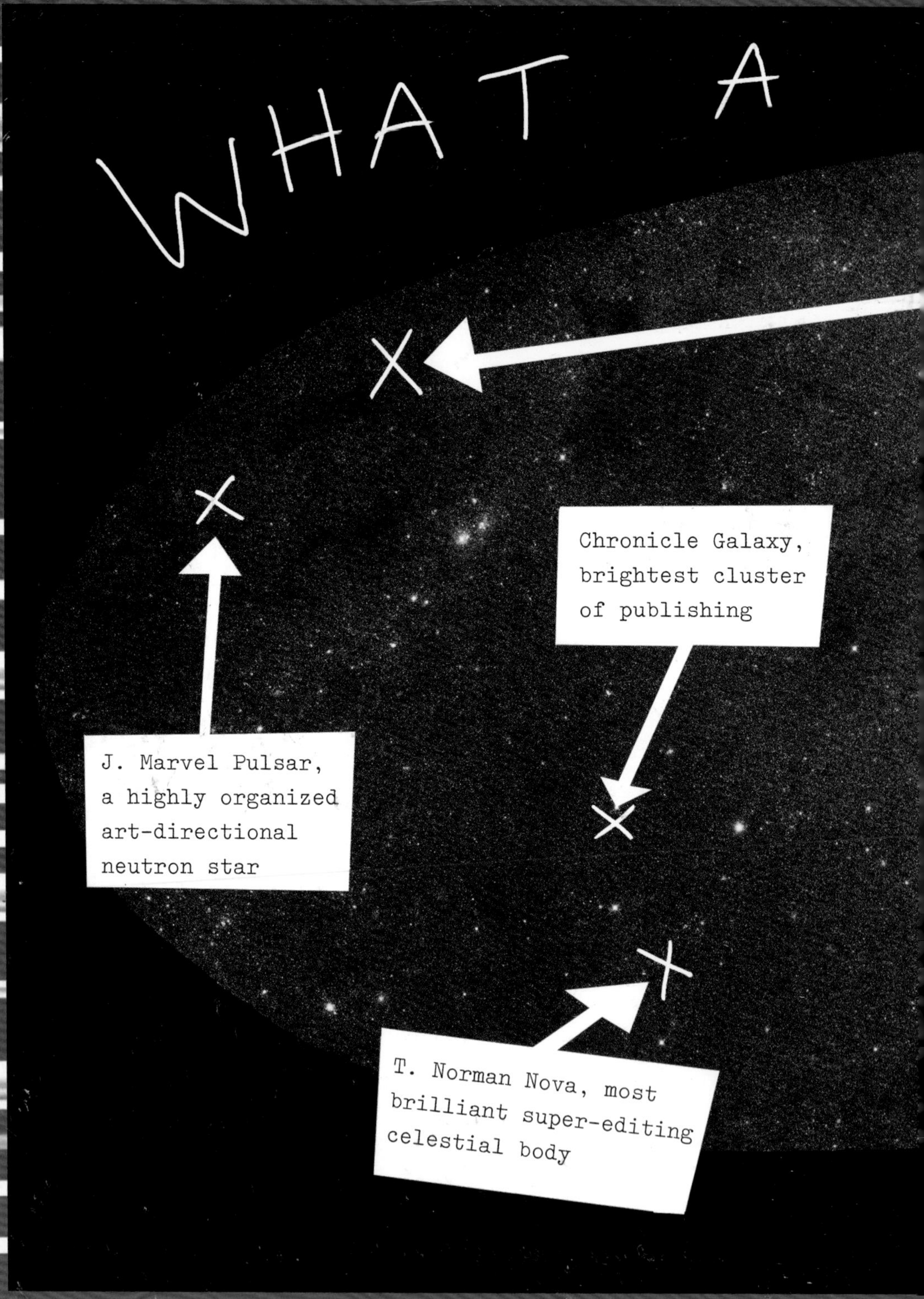
WHAT A
Chronicle Galaxy, brightest cluster of publishing
J. Marvel Pulsar, a highly organized art-directional neutron star
T. Norman Nova, most brilliant super-editing celestial body